"What am I going to do about you?"

Angeline asked aloud as she stepped forward again, right into the vee of his legs. Her chocolate-brown eyes were on a level with his mouth, and their focus seemed to be fixated there.

"You're going to bandage me up," he said, but his voice was gruff. Damn near hoarse.

"In a minute," Angeline whispered. She leaned into him, tilting her head, and light as a whisper, she rubbed her lips over his.

She'd started out feeling tenderness.

That was all, Angeline reassured herself. Just tenderness for this man whose unexpected acts of kindness touched her just as much as his more "creative" stunts shocked her.

But tenderness was abruptly eaten up in the incendiary flames that rose far too rapidly for her to fight.

Instead, she stood there, caught, as wildfire seemed to lick through them both.

WYOMING
★ COUNTRY LEGACY ★

THE RANCHER'S SECRETS

New York Times Bestselling Author
Allison Leigh

Lynnette Kent

Previously published as *Wed in Wyoming* and
A Husband in Wyoming

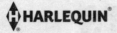

ISBN-13: 978-1-335-46772-0

Wyoming Country Legacy:
The Rancher's Secrets
Copyright © 2020 by Harlequin Books S.A.

Wed in Wyoming
First published in 2007. This edition published in 2020.
Copyright © 2007 by Allison Lee Johnson

A Husband in Wyoming
First published in 2015. This edition published in 2020.
Copyright © 2015 by Cheryl B. Bacon

Recycling programs
for this product may
not exist in your area.

This edition published by arrangement with Harlequin Books S.A.

For questions and comments about the quality of this book, please contact us at CustomerService@Harlequin.com.

Harlequin Enterprises ULC
22 Adelaide St. West, 40th Floor
Toronto, Ontario M5H 4E3, Canada
www.Harlequin.com

Printed in U.S.A.

CONTENTS

Though her name is frequently on bestseller lists, **Allison Leigh**'s high point as a writer is hearing from readers that they laughed, cried or lost sleep while reading her books. She credits her family with great patience for the time she's parked at her computer, and for blessing her with the kind of love she wants her readers to share with the characters living in the pages of her books. Contact her at allisonleigh.com.

WED IN WYOMING

Allison Leigh

For my editor, Ann Leslie. Thank you for your patience, flexibility and general excellence. I think we've come a long way together!

Prologue

November

"Are you insane? What if someone sees you here?" Angeline Clay looked away from the tall man standing in the shadows of the big house to the wedding reception guests milling around behind her, barely twenty yards away.

"They won't." The man's deep voice was amused. "You forget, sweet cheeks, what I *do* for a living."

She rolled her eyes. They stood outside the circle of pretty lights that had been strung around the enormous awning protecting the tables and the dance floor from the chilly Wyoming weather. Her cousin Leandra and her brand-new husband, Evan Taggart, were in the center of the floor dancing away, surrounded by nearly every other member of Angeline's extensive family. "I'm not likely to forget, Brody," she assured drily.

Since then, her brief encounters with the man had been few and far between, but they'd nevertheless been memorable.

Annoying, really, considering that Angeline prided herself on keeping her focus squarely where it belonged. Which was most assuredly *not* the impossible appeal of the elusive Brody Paine.

She flexed her bare fingers around the empty platter that she had been on her way to the kitchen to refill when Brody had stepped into her path. "How'd you even know I was here, anyway?"

The corner of his lips lifted. "It's a small world, babe. You know that."

Sweet cheeks. Babe.

She stifled a sigh. She couldn't recall Brody *ever* using her actual name. Which was probably one of the reasons why she'd never tried very hard to take the man seriously when it came to anything of a personal nature.

When it came to the work he did, however, she took him quite seriously because Brody Paine was well and truly one of the good guys. Since she'd learned at a particularly early age that the world was definitely on the shy side when it came to such people, she tried to give credit where it was due.

"I'm just visiting Weaver," she reminded him. "For the Thanksgiving holiday and Leandra's wedding. I'm going back to Atlanta soon."

He blandly reeled off her flight number, telling

her not very subtly that he was perfectly aware of her schedule. "The agency likes to keep track of its assets."

She looked behind her again, but there was nobody within earshot. Of course. Brody wouldn't be likely to mention the agency if there had been. "I'm hardly an asset," she reminded him needlessly. She was a courier of sorts, true. But in the five years she'd worked for the agency, all she conveyed were pieces of information from one source to another. Even then, she was called on to do so only once or twice a year. It was a schedule that seemed to suit everyone.

"Believe me, hon. You've got more than any woman's fair share of assets," he assured drily. His gaze—she'd never been certain if it was naturally blue or brown because she'd seen his eye color differ over the years—traveled down her body. "Of course for some stubborn reason you keep refusing to share them with *me*."

She'd seen appreciation in men's eyes when they looked at her since she'd hit puberty. She was used to it. But she still felt absurdly grateful for the folds of the cashmere cape that flowed around her taupe-colored dress beneath it. "That's right," she said dismissively. "I assume this *isn't* a social call?"

His lips twitched again. "Only because you're a stubborn case, sweet cheeks."

Her lips tightened. "Brody—"

"Don't get your panties in a twist." He lifted one long-fingered hand. "I'm actually in the middle of another gig." He looked amused again. "But I was asked to give you this."

She realized that a small piece of paper was tucked

between his index and middle finger. She plucked it free, careful not to touch him, only to nearly jump out of her skin when his fingers suddenly closed around her wrist.

She gave him a startled look.

The amusement from his face had been wiped away. "This is important."

Nerves tightened her throat. She wasn't used to seeing Brody looking so serious. "Isn't it always?" He'd told her, chapter and verse, from the very beginning just how important and sensitive her work with Hollins-Winword was.

"Like everything else in life, importance can be relative."

Behind them, the deejay was calling for everyone's attention since the bride and groom were preparing to cut their wedding cake. "I need to get back there. Before someone comes looking for me."

He slowly released her wrist. She stopped herself from rubbing the tingling that remained there just in time.

The man was entirely too observant. Which was, undoubtedly, one of the qualities that made him such an excellent agent. But the last thing she wanted him to know was that he had *any* kind of affect on her.

They were occasionally connected business associates and that was all. If the guy knew she'd been infatuated with him for years—well, she simply didn't want him knowing. Period. Maybe the knowledge would make a difference to him, and maybe it wouldn't. But she didn't intend to find out.

Playing immune to him was already hard enough.

She couldn't imagine how hard it would be if she spent any real time with the man.

He gave that small smile of his that had her wondering if mind reading was among his bag of tricks. "See you next time, babe." He lifted his chin in the direction of the partygoers. "Drink some champagne for me."

She glanced back, too. Leandra and Evan were standing in front of the enormous, tiered wedding cake. "I can probably get you a glass without anyone noticing. Cake, too."

She looked back when he didn't answer.

The only thing she saw was the dark, tall form of him disappearing into the cold night.

Chapter 1

May

"I still think you're insane."

Since Angeline had last seen Brody Paine almost six months ago, he'd grown a scruffy brown beard that didn't quite mask the smile he gave at her pronouncement.

His sandy-brown hair hung thick and long around his ears, clearly in desperate need of a cut, and along with that beard, he looked vaguely piratical.

"Seems like you're always telling me that, babe."

Angeline lifted her eyebrows pointedly. They were sitting in a Jeep that was currently stuck lug nut deep in Venezuelan mud. "Take a clue from the theme," she suggested, raising her voice to be heard above the pounding rain.

As usual, he seemed to pay no heed of her opinion. Instead, he peered through the rain-washed windshield, drumming his thumb on the steering wheel. The vehicle itself looked as if it had been around about a half century.

It no longer possessed such luxuries as doors, and the wind that had been carrying sheets of rain for each of the three days since Angeline had arrived in Venezuela kept up its momentum, throwing a stinging spray across her and Brody.

The enormous weather system that was supposed to have veered away from land and calmly die out over the middle of the ocean hadn't behaved that way at all. Instead, it had squatted over them like some tormenting toad, bringing with it this incessant rain and wind. May might be too early for a hurricane, but Mother Nature didn't seem to care much for the official calendar.

She huddled deeper in the seat. The hood of her khaki-colored rain poncho hid most of her head, but she still felt soaked from head to toe.

That's what she got for racing away from the camp in Puerto Grande the way she had. If she'd stopped to think longer, she might have at least brought along some warmer clothes to wear beneath the rain poncho.

Instead, she'd given All-Med's team leader, Dr. Miguel Chavez, a hasty excuse that a friend in Caracas had an emergency, and off she'd gone with Brody in this miserable excuse of a vehicle. She knew they wouldn't expect her back anytime soon. In *good* weather, Caracas was a day away.

"The convent where the kids were left is up this road," he said, still drumming. If he was as uncomfortable with the conditions as she, he hid it well. "There's no other access to St. Agnes's. Unless a person was airlifted in. And *that* ain't gonna happen in this weather." His head bounced a few times, as if he were mentally agreeing with whatever other insane thoughts were bouncing around inside.

She angled her legs in the hard, ripped seat, turning her back against the driving rain. "If we walked, we could make it back to the camp at Puerto Grande before dark." Though dark was a subjective term, considering the oppressive clouds that hung over their heads.

Since she'd turned twenty, she'd visited Venezuela with All-Med five times, but this was the worst weather she'd ever encountered.

"Only way we're going is forward, sweetie." He sighed loud enough to be heard above the rain that was pounding on the roof of the vehicle. His jeans and rain poncho were caked with mud from his repeated attempts to dislodge the Jeep.

"But the convent is still *miles* away." They were much closer to the camp where she'd been stationed. "We could get some help from the team tomorrow. Work the Jeep free of the mud. They wouldn't have to know that we were trying to get up to St. Agnes instead of to Caracas."

"Can't afford to waste that much time."

She huffed out a breath and stared at the man. He truly gave new meaning to the word stubborn.

She angled her back even farther against the blowing wind. Her knees brushed against the gearshift, and when she tried to avoid that, they brushed against his thigh.

If that fact was even noticeable to him, he gave no indication whatsoever. So she left her knee right where it was, since the contact provided a nice little bit of warmth to her otherwise shivering body.

Shivers caused by cold *and* an uncomfortable suspicion she'd had since he unexpectedly appeared in Puerto Grande.

"What's the rush?" she asked. "You told me we were merely picking up the Stanley kids from the convent for their parents."

"We are."

Her lips tightened. "Brody—"

"I told you to call me Hewitt, remember?"

There was nothing particularly wrong with the name, but he definitely didn't seem a "Hewitt" type to her. Brody was energy itself all contained within long legs, long hands and a hard body. If she had to be stuck in the mud at the base of a mountain in a foreign country, she supposed Brody was about the best companion she could have. She wouldn't go so far as to call the man *safe,* but she did believe he was capably creative when the situation called for it.

"Fine, *Hewitt,*" she returned, "so what's the rush? The children have been at the convent for nearly two months. What's one more night?" He'd already filled her in on the details of how Hewitt Stanley—the real Hewitt Stanley—and his wife, Sophia, had tucked their two children in the small, exceedingly reclusive convent while they trekked deep into the most unreachable portions of Venezuela to further their latest pharmaceutical quest.

Brody had, supposedly, enlisted Angeline's help because he claimed he couldn't manage retrieving both kids on his own.

"The Santina Group kidnapped Hewitt and Sophia two days ago."

"Excuse me?"

Despite the rough beard, his profile as he peered through the deluged windshield could have been chiseled from the mountains around them. "Do you ever wonder about the messages you're asked to dispatch?"

"No."

"Never." He gave her another one of those mind reader looks.

Sometimes, honesty was a darned nuisance.

"Yes. Of course I am curious sometimes," she admitted. "But I don't make any attempt to satisfy that curiosity. That's not my role. I'm just the messenger. And what does that have to do with the Stanleys?"

He raised one eyebrow. "When I gave you that intel back in November, you didn't wonder about it?" He didn't quite sound disbelieving, but the implication was there.

"There are lots of things I wonder about, but I don't have the kind of clearance to know more. Maybe I prefer it that way." The tidbits of information that she dispatched were not enough to give her real knowledge of the issues that Hollins-Winword handled. It was a tried-and-true safety measure, not only for her personal safety, but for those around her, the agency's work and the agency itself.

She knew that. Understood that. Welcomed it, even.

She believed in her involvement with Hollins-Winword. But that didn't mean she was anxious to risk her neck over four sentences, which was generally the size of the puzzle pieces of information with which she was entrusted. Brody's message for her that night at Leandra and Evan's wedding reception had been even briefer.

Stanley experimenting. Sandoval MIA.

She'd memorized the information—hardly difficult in this case—and shortly after she'd returned to Atlanta, she'd relayed the brief missive to the impossibly young-looking boy who'd spilled his backpack on the floor next to her table at a local coffee shop.

She'd knelt down beside him and helped as he'd packed up his textbooks, papers and pens, and three minutes later, he was heading out the door with his cappuccino and the message, and she was sitting back down at her table with her paperback book and her latte.

"You didn't look twice at the name Sandoval."

Somehow, cold water had snuck beneath the neck of her poncho and was dripping down the back of her spine. She tugged the hood of her poncho farther over her forehead but it was about as effective as closing the barn door after the horse was already out, considering the fact that she was already soaked. "Does it matter? Sandoval's not that unusual of a name."

His lips twisted. "How old were you when you left Santo Marguerite?"

The kernel inside her suddenly exploded, turning tense curiosity into a sickening fear that she didn't want to acknowledge. "Four." Old enough to remember that the name of the man who'd destroyed the Central American village where she'd been born, along with nearly everyone else who'd lived there, had been Sandoval.

She reached out and closed her hand over his slick, wet forearm. "I'm no good at guessing games, Brody. Just tell me what you want me to know. Is Sandoval involved with the kidnapping?"

His gaze flicked downward, as if surprised by the contact, and she hastily drew back, curling her cold hands together.

"We haven't been able to prove it, but we believe that he is the money behind the Santina Group. On the other hand, we *know* Santina funds at least two different black market organizations running everything from drugs and weapons to human trafficking. According to the pharmaceutical company Hewitt works for, he was on to something huge. Has to do with some little red frog about the size of my fingernail."

He shook his head, as if the entire matter was unfathomable to him. "Anyway, the pharmacy folks will try to replicate synthetically the properties of this frog spit, or whatever the *hell* it is." His voice went terse. "And in the right hands, that's fine. But those properties are *also* the kind of properties that in the wrong hands, could bring a whole new meaning to what profit is in the drug trade."

"They've got the parents and now they're after the kids, too. Sandoval or Santina or whoever," she surmised, feeling even more appalled.

"We're working on that theory. One of Santina's top men—Rico Fuentes—was spotted in Caracas yesterday morning. Sophia Stanley's parents were Venezuelan, and she inherited a small apartment there when they died. The place was tossed yesterday afternoon."

"How can you be sure the kids are even at the convent?"

"Because *I* tossed the apartment yesterday *morning* and found Sophia's notes she'd made about getting there, and packing clothes and stuff for the kids. I didn't leave anything for ol' Rico to find but who knows who Hewitt and Sophia may have told about their kids' whereabouts. I've got my people talking to everyone at the pharmaceutical place, and so far none of them seems to know anything about the convent, but…" He shrugged and looked back at the road.

"Hewitt obviously knew they were on to something that would be just as significant to the bad guys as to the good," he told her. "Otherwise, why squirrel away their kids the way they did? They could have just hired a nanny to mind them while they went exploring in the tepuis." He referred to the unearthly, flattop mountains located in the remote southeast portion of the country. She knew the region was inhabited by some extremely unusual life-forms.

"Instead," he went on, "they used the convent where Sophia's mother once spent time as a girl."

"If this Rico person gets to the children, Santina could use them as leverage to make sure Hewitt cooperates."

"Bingo."

"What about Hewitt and Sophia, though? How will they even know their kids are still safe? Couldn't these Santina group people lie?"

"Hell yeah, they could lie. They *will* lie. But there's

another team working on their rescue. Right now, we need to make certain that whatever threats made concerning those kids *are* a lie."

She blew out a long breath. "Why not go to the authorities? Surely they'd be of more help."

"Which local authorities do you think we can implicitly trust?"

She frowned. Miguel had often complained about the thriving black market and its rumored connection to the local police. "Brody, this kind of thing is way beyond me. I'm not a field agent. You know that better than anyone." Her involvement with Hollins-Winword had only ever involved the transmittal of information!

A deep crevice formed down his cheek as the corner of his lips lifted. "You are now, sweet cheeks."

"I do have a name," she reminded.

"Yeah. And until we get the kids outta this country, it's Sophia Stanley."

"I beg your pardon?"

"Beg all you want. There's a packet in the glove box."

She fumbled with the rusting button and managed to open the box. It was stuffed with maps and an assortment of hand tools. The packet, she assumed, was the dingy envelope wedged between a long screwdriver and a bundle of nylon rope. She pulled it out and lifted the flap. Inside was a narrow gold ring with a distinctive pattern engraved on it and several snapshots.

He took the envelope and turned the contents out into his hand. "Here." He handed her the ring. "Put this on."

She gingerly took the ring from him and started to slide it on her right hand.

He shook his head. "Left hand. It's a wedding ring, baby cakes."

Feeling slightly sick to her stomach, she pushed the gold band over her cold wedding-ring finger. It was a little loose. She curled her fingers into her palm, holding it in place.

She'd never put a ring on that particular finger before, and it felt distinctly odd.

"This," he held up a picture, "is Sophia."

A laughing woman with long dark hair smiled at the camera. She looked older than Angeline, but overall, their coloring was nearly identical, from their olive-toned skin to their dark brown eyes.

"Not a perfect match," Brody said. "You're prettier. But you'll have to do."

She frowned, not sure if that was a compliment or not, but he took no notice.

"These are the kids. Eva's nine. Davey's four." He handed her a few more pictures, barely giving her time to examine one before handing her the next. "And this is papa bear."

If the situation hadn't been as serious as she knew it was, she would have laughed right out loud. The real Hewitt Stanley definitely matched the mental image his name conjured.

Medium height. Gangly and spectacled. Even from the snapshot, slightly blurred though it was, the man's *un*-Brody-ness shined through. Other than the fact that they were both male, there was nothing remotely similar between the two men. "*This* is who you're pretending to be."

"You'd be surprised at the identities I've assumed," he said, taking back the photographs when she handed them to him. He tucked them back in the envelope, which then disappeared beneath his rain poncho.

"Why do we even need to pretend to be the Stanleys, anyway? The nuns at the convent will surely know we're *not* the people who left their children in their safekeeping."

"Generally, the Mother Superior deals with outsiders. She's definitely the only one who would have met with Hewitt and Sophia when they took in the children. And she's currently stuck in Puerto Grande thanks to the weather that *we* are not going to let stop us."

"Maybe we can fool a few nuns," she hesitated for a moment, rather expecting a bolt of lightning to strike at the very idea of it, "but the kids will know we're not their parents. They will certainly have something to say about going off with two complete strangers."

"The Stanleys had a code word for their kids. Falling waters. When we get that to them, they'll know we're there on behalf of their parents."

The situation could not possibly become anymore surreal. "How do you know *that?*"

"Because I do. Believe me, if I thought we could just walk into that convent up there and tell the nuns we were taking the kids away for their own safety, I would. But there's a reason Hewitt and Sophia chose the place. It's hellacious to reach, even on a good day. It's cloistered. It's small; barely even a dot on the satellite imaging."

Again she felt that panicky feeling starting to crawl up her throat. "W-what if we fail?" The last time she'd failed had been in Atlanta, and it hadn't had anything to do with Hollins-Winword. But it had certainly involved a child.

He gave her a sidelong look. "We won't."

"Why didn't you tell me all this when you showed up at the aid camp?" If he had, she would have found some reason to convince him to find someone else.

"Too many ears." He reached beneath his seat and pulled out a handgun. So great was her surprise, she barely recognized it as a weapon.

In a rapid movement he checked the clip and tucked the gun out of sight where he'd put the envelope of photographs beneath his rain poncho.

She'd grown up on a ranch, so she wasn't unfamiliar with firearms. But the presence of rifles and shotguns hanging in the gun case in her father's den was a far cry from the thing that Brody had just hidden away. "We won't need that though, right?"

"Let's hope not." He gave her a look, as if he knew perfectly well how she felt about getting into a situation where they might. "I don't want to draw down on a nun anymore than the next guy. If we can convince them we're Hewitt and Sophia Stanley, we won't have to. But believe me, sweet cheeks, they're better off if I resort to threats than if Santina's guy does. They don't draw the line over hurting innocent people. And if we're not as far ahead of the guy as I hope, you're going to be pretty happy that I've got—" he patted his side "—good old Delilah with us, sweet cheeks."

He named his gun Delilah?

She shook her head, discomfited by more than just the gun.

Sandoval certainly hadn't drawn the line over hurting people, she knew. Not when she'd been four and the man had destroyed her family's village in a power struggle for control of the verdant land. When he'd been in danger of losing the battle, he'd destroyed the land, too, rather than let someone beat him.

"It's not sweet cheeks," she said, and blamed her shaking voice on the cold water still sneaking beneath her poncho. "It's Sophia."

Brody slowly smiled. "That's my girl."

She shivered again and knew, that time, that it wasn't caused entirely by cold or nerves.

It was caused by *him*.

Chapter 2

They abandoned the Jeep where it was mired in the mud and proceeded on foot.

It seemed to take hours before they managed to climb their way up the steep, slick mountainside.

The wind swirled around them, carrying the rain in sheets that were nearly horizontal. Angeline felt grateful for Brody's big body standing so closely to hers, blocking a fair measure of the storm.

She lost all sense of time as they trudged along. Every step she took was an exercise in pain—her thighs, her calves, her shins. No part of her seemed excused until finally—when her brain had simply shut down except for the mental order to keep moving, keep moving, keep moving—Brody stopped.

He lifted his hand, and beat it hard on the wide black plank that barred their path.

A door, her numb mind realized. "They won't hear," she said, but couldn't even hear the words herself over the screaming wind.

His fingers were an iron ring around her wrist as the door creaked open—giving lie to her words—and he pulled her inside. Then he put his shoulder against the door and muscled it closed again, yanking down the old-fashioned wooden beam that served as a lock.

The sudden cessation of battering wind was nearly dizzying.

It was also oddly quiet, she realized. So much so that she could hear the water dripping off her onto the stone floor.

"Señora." A diminutive woman dressed in a full nun's habit held out a white towel.

"Thank you." Angeline took the towel and pressed it to her face. The weave was rough and thin but it was dry and felt positively wonderful. She lowered it to smile at the nun. *"Gracias."*

The woman was speaking rapidly to Brody in Spanish. And though Angeline hadn't spoken the language of her birth in years, she followed along easily enough. The nun was telling Brody that the Mother Superior was not there to welcome the strangers.

"We're not strangers," Brody told her. His accent was nearly flawless, Angeline realized with some vague surprise. "We've come to collect our children."

If Angeline had held any vague notions of other children being at the convent, they were dissolved when the nun nodded. *"Sí. Sí."* The nun turned and began moving away from the door, heading down the middle of the three corridors that led off the vestibule.

Brody gave Angeline a sharp look when she didn't immediately follow along.

She knew she could collapse later, *after* they knew the children were safe. But just then she wanted nothing more than to just sink down on the dark stone floor and rest her head back against the rough, whitewashed wall.

As if he could read her thoughts, Brody wrapped his hand around her wrist again and drew her along the corridor with him in the nun's wake.

Like the vestibule, the hallway had whitewashed walls. Though the wash looked pristine, it didn't mask the rough texture of the wall beneath it. There were no windows, but a multitude of iron sconces situated high up the wall held fat white candles that kept the way well lit. The few electrical sconces spread out less liberally were dark.

Angeline figured they'd walked a good fifty feet before the corridor turned sharply left and opened after another twenty or so feet into a wide, square room occupied by a half-dozen long wooden tables and benches.

The dining hall, the nun informed them briskly. Her feet didn't hesitate, however, as she kept right on walking.

"You catching all that?" Brody asked Angeline in English.

She nodded. She'd come to English only when Daniel and Maggie Clay had adopted her after her family's village was destroyed. And though Angeline had deliberately turned her back on the language of her natural parents, she'd never forgotten it, though she'd once made a valiant effort to do so.

She'd already been different enough from the other people in that small Wyoming town where she'd gone to live with Daniel and Maggie. Even before she'd been old enough to understand her actions, she'd deliberately rid the accent from her diction, and copied the vague drawl that the adults around her had possessed. She'd wanted so badly to belong. Not because any one of her adopted family made her feel different, but because inside, Angeline had known she *was* different.

She'd lived when the rest of her natural family had perished. She'd been rescued from a poor Central American orphanage and been taken to the U.S., where she'd been raised by loving people.

But she'd never forgotten the sight of fire racing through the fields her cousins had tended, licking up the walls and across the roofs of their simple houses. And whatever hadn't been burned had been hacked down with axes, torn apart with knives, shot down with guns.

Nothing had escaped. Not the people. Not the livestock. Not the land.

Only *her*.

It was twenty-five years ago, and she still didn't understand why she'd been spared.

"Sophia." Brody's voice was sharp, cutting through the dark memories. Angeline focused on his deep blue eyes and just that abruptly she was back in the present.

Where two children needed them.

"I'm sorry." How easily she fell back into thinking

in Spanish, speaking in Spanish. "The children," she looked at the nun. "Please, where are they?"

The nun looked distressed. "They are well and safe, *señora.* But until the Mother Superior returns and authorizes your access to them, I must continue to keep them secure."

"From me?" Angeline didn't have to work hard at conjuring tears in her eyes. She was cold, exhausted and entirely undone by the plot that Brody had drawn her into. "I am their mother." The lie came more easily than she'd thought it would.

The nun's ageless face looked pitying, yet resolute. "You were the ones who made the arrangement with Mother. But now, you are weary," she said. "You and your husband need food and rest. We will naturally provide you with both until Mother returns. The storm will pass and soon she will be here to show you to your children."

"But—"

Brody's hand closed around hers. "*Gracias,* Sister. My wife and I thank you for your hospitality, of course. If we could find dry clothes—"

"*Sí. Sí.*" The nun looked relieved. "Please wait here. I will send Sister Frances to assist you in a moment if that will be satisfactory?"

Brody's fingers squeezed Angeline's in warning "*Sí.*"

She nodded and turned on her heel, gliding back along the corridor. Her long robes swished over the stone floor.

The moment she was out of sight, Brody let go of Angeline's wrist and she sank down onto one of the long wooden benches situated alongside the tables. She rubbed her wrist, flushing a little when she realized he was watching the action. She stopped, telling herself inwardly that her skin wasn't *really* tingling.

What was one more lie there inside that sacred convent, considering the whoppers they were already telling?

Brody sat down beside her and she wanted to put some distance between them given the way he was crowding into her personal space, but another nun—presumably Sister Frances—silently entered the dining area. She gestured for Brody and Angeline to follow, and Brody tucked his hand beneath Angeline's arm as he helped her solicitously to her feet.

They followed the silent nun down another corridor and up several narrow flights of stairs, all lit with those same iron wall sconces. Finally she stopped and opened a heavy wooden door, extending her hand in a welcoming gesture. Clearly they were meant to go inside.

Angeline passed the nun, thanking her quietly as she entered the room. Brody ducked his head to keep from knocking it against the low sill and followed her inside. The dim room contained a single woefully narrow bed, a single straight-backed wooden chair and a dresser with an old-fashioned ceramic pitcher and basin atop it.

The nun reached up to the sconce on the wall outside the door and pulled down the lit candle, handing it to Brody. She waved her hand toward the two sconces inside the bedroom, and Brody reached up, setting the flame to the candles they contained.

Warm light slowly filled the tiny room as the flames caught. Brody handed the feeder candle back to the nun, who nodded and backed two steps out of the room, pulling the wooden door shut as she went.

Which left Angeline alone with Brody.

The room had no windows, and though Angeline was definitely no fan of small, enclosed spaces, the room simply felt cozy. Cozy and surprisingly safe, considering the surreal situation.

"Well," he said in a low tone, "that was easier than I expected."

She gaped. "Easy? They won't even let us *see* the children."

"Shh." He lifted one of the candles from its sconce and began prowling around the room's small confines.

She lowered her voice. "What are you looking for?"

He ignored her. He nudged the bed away from the wall. Looked behind it. Under it. Pushed it back. He did the same with the dresser. He turned the washbasin and the pitcher upside down, before replacing them atop the dresser. He even pulled the unlit bare lightbulb out of the metal fixture hanging from the low ceiling. Then, evidently with nothing else to examine, he returned the fat candle to the sconce.

"Don't think we're being bugged."

Her lips parted. "Seriously?"

"I'm a big believer in paranoia." He looked up at the steady candle flames. "Walls in this place must be about a foot deep," he said. "Can hardly hear the storm out there."

And she was closed within them with *him* in a room roughly the size of the balcony of her Atlanta apartment. "Sorry if I'm not quick on the uptake here. Is that supposed to be good or bad?"

He shrugged, and began pulling off his rain poncho, doing a decent job of not flinging mud onto the white blanket covering the bed. "It ain't bad," he said when his head reappeared. "At least we probably don't have to worry about that hurricane blowing this place to bits." He dropped the poncho in the corner behind the door. The Rolling Stones T-shirt he wore beneath it was as lamentably wet as her own, and he lifted the hem, pulling the gun and its holster off his waistband.

He tucked them both beneath the mattress.

"Probably," she repeated faintly. "Bro— Hewitt, what about the children?"

"We'll get to them," he said.

She wished she felt even a portion of the confidence he seemed to feel. "What happened to that all-fire rush you were feeling earlier?"

"Believe me, it's still burning. But first things first." His long arm came up, his hand brushing her poncho and she nearly jumped out of her skin. "Relax. I was just gonna help you take off your poncho."

She felt her cheeks heat and was grateful for the soft candlelight that would hide her flush. "I knew that."

He snorted softly.

Fortunately, she was saved from further embarrassment when there was a soft knock on the door.

It only took Brody two steps to reach it, and when it swung open, yet another nun stood on the threshold carrying a wooden tray. She smiled faintly and tilted her head, her black veil swishing softly. But like the sister who'd shown them to the room, she remained silent as she set the tray on the dresser top and began unloading it.

A simple woven basket of bread. A hunk of cheese. A cluster of green grapes. Two thick white plates, a knife, two sparkling clear glasses and a fat round pitcher. All of it she left on the dresser top. She didn't look at Brody and Angeline as she bowed her head over the repast.

She was obviously giving a blessing. Then she lifted her head, smiled peacefully again and returned to the door. She knelt down, picked up a bundle she'd left outside, and brought it in, setting it on the bed. Then she let herself out of the room. Like Sister Frances, she pulled the door shut as she went.

"Grub and fresh duds," Brody said, looking happy as a pig in clover. He lifted the off-white bundle from the bed and the items separated as he gave it a little shake. "Pants and top for you. Pants and top for me." He deftly sorted, and tossed the smaller set toward the two thin pillows that sat at the head of the modest bed.

She didn't reach for them, though.

He angled her a look. "Don't worry, beautiful. I'll turn my back while you change." His lips twitched. "There's not even a mirror in here for me to take a surreptitious peek. Now if you feel so compelled, *you're* welcome to look all you want. After all," his amused voice was dry, "we are married."

Her cheeks heated even more. "Stop. Please. My sides are splitting because you are sooo funny."

His lips twitched again and he pulled his T-shirt over his head.

Angeline swallowed, not looking away quickly

enough to miss the ripped abdomen and wealth of satin-smooth golden skin stretched tightly across a chest that hadn't looked nearly so wide in the shirt he'd worn. When his hands dropped to the waist of his jeans, she snatched up the clean, dry clothing and turned her back on him.

Then just when she wished the ground would swallow her whole, she heard his soft, rumbling chuckle.

She told herself to get a grip. She was a paramedic for pity's sake. She'd seen nude men, women and children in all manner of situations.

There's a difference between nude and naked, a tiny voice inside her head taunted, and Brody's bare chest was *all* about being naked.

She silenced the voice and snatched her shirt off over her head, dropping it in a sopping heap on the floor. Leaving on her wet bra would only make the dry top damp, so she snapped it off, too, imaging herself anywhere but in that confining room with Brody Paine. She pulled the dry top over her head.

She tried imagining that she was a quick-change artist as she yanked the tunic firmly over her hips—grateful that it reached her thighs—then ditched her own wet jeans and panties for the dry pants.

She immediately felt warmer.

She knelt down and bundled her filthy clothes together, tucking away the scraps of lace and satin lingerie inside.

"Trying to hide the evidence that you like racy undies?"

Her head whipped around and the towel tumbled off her head.

Brody was facing her, hip propped against the dresser, arms crossed over the front of the tunic that strained slightly in the shoulders. He had an unholy look in his eyes that ought to have had the storm centering all of her fury on them considering their surroundings.

"You promised not to look."

His mobile lips stretched, revealing the edge of his very straight, very white teeth. "Babe, you sound prim enough to be one of the sisters cloistered here."

Her cheeks couldn't possibly get any hotter. "Which doesn't change the fact that you promised."

He lifted one shoulder. "Promises are made to be broken."

"You don't really believe that."

"How do you know?"

It couldn't possibly be anymore obvious. "It doesn't matter how many lines you give me, because the truth is, you couldn't do the work you do if you didn't believe in keeping your word," she said simply.

Chapter 3

Brody looked at Angeline's face. She looked so... earnest, he thought. Earnest and sexy as hell in a way that had *nothing* to do with those hanks of black lace he'd gotten a glimpse of.

She'd always been a deadly combination, even in the small doses of time they'd ever spent together.

Was it any wonder that he'd been just as interested in consuming a larger dose as he'd been in avoiding just that?

Complications on the job were one thing.

Complications off the job were nonexistent because that's the way he kept it.

Always.

But there she was, watching him with those huge, wide-set brown eyes that had gotten to him even on their first, ridiculously brief encounter five years earlier.

He deliberately lifted one eyebrow. "It's a job, sweet cheeks. A pretty well-paying one."

"Assembling widgets is a job," she countered. "Protecting the innocent? Righting wrongs? That's not just a job and somehow I doubt you do it only for the money."

"You're not just prim, you're a romantic, too," he drawled.

She frowned a little, possibly realizing the topic had gone somewhat awry. "So what's the next step?"

He held up a cluster of grapes. "We eat."

Right on cue, her stomach growled loud enough for him to hear. "Shouldn't we try to find the children?"

"You wanna pull off our own kidnapping?" He wasn't teasing.

"That's essentially what your plan *was*."

"I'd consider it more a case of protective custody."

She pushed her fingers through her hair, holding it back from her face. She didn't have on a lick of makeup, and she was still more beautiful than ninety-nine percent of the world's female population.

"Fine. Call it whatever," she dismissed. "Shouldn't we be doing something to that end?"

"I told you. First things first. How far do you think we'll get if we set out right this second? You're so exhausted I can see the circles under your eyes even in *this* light and I'm not sure who's stomach is growling louder. Yours or mine." He popped a few grapes into his mouth and held up the cluster again. "Come on, darlin'. Eat up."

"I think we should at least try to see the children. What if that password thing doesn't work?" But she plucked a few grapes off the cluster and slid one between her full bow-shaped lips. She chewed and swallowed, and avoiding his eyes, quickly reached for more.

"It will." He tore off a chunk of the bread and handed it to her, and cut the wedge of cheese in half. "Here."

She sat on the foot of the bed and looked as if she was trying not to wolf down the food. He tipped the pitcher over one of the glasses, filling it with pale golden liquid. He took a sniff. "Wine." He took a drink. "Pretty decent wine at that." He poured the second glass and held it out to her.

She took it from him, evidently too thirsty to spend a lot of effort avoiding brushing his fingers the way she usually did. "Wine always goes straight to my head."

"Goody goody." He tossed one of the cloth napkins that had been tucked beneath the bread basket onto her lap. "Drink faster."

She let out an impatient laugh. "Do you *ever* stop with the come-ons?"

"Do you *ever* take me up on one?"

She made a face at him. "Why would I want to be just another notch?"

"Who says that's what you'd be?"

She took another sip of wine. "I'm sure that's the only thing women are to you."

"I'm wounded, babe. You're different than all the others."

She let out a half laugh. "You are so full of it."

"And you are way too serious." He bit into a hunk of bread. He was thirty-eight years old—damn near a decade her senior—but he might as well have been sixteen given the way he kept getting preoccupied with that narrow bed where she was gingerly perched.

"I'm a serious person," she said around a not-entirely delicate mouthful of bread. "In a serious business."

"The paramedic business or the spy business?"

"I'm not a spy."

He couldn't help smiling again. "Sugar, you're a courier for one of the biggies in the business." He tipped more wine into his glass. "And your family just keeps getting pulled in, one way or the other."

"You ought to know. You're the one who approached me in the first place to be a courier."

He couldn't dispute that. "Still. Don't you think it's a little…unusual?"

She didn't even blink. "You mean how many of us are involved with Hollins-Winword?"

At least she wasn't as in the dark as her cousin Sarah had been. Sarah'd had no clue that she wasn't the only one in her family hooked up with Hollins-Winword; probably wouldn't know even now if her brand-spanking-new husband, Max Scalise, hadn't tramped one of his own investigations right through Brody's assignment to protect a little girl named Megan. They'd been staying in a safe house in Weaver, set up by Sarah, who mostly made her living as a school teacher when she wasn't making an occasional "arrangement" for Hollins-Winword. But she'd only learned that her uncles were involved. She hadn't learned about Angeline.

Or the others in that extensive family tree.

And now, he'd heard that Sarah and Max were in the process of adopting Megan.

The child's parents had been brutally murdered, but she'd at least have some chance at regaining a decent life with decent people raising her.

She'd have a family.

The thought was darker than it should have been and he reached for the wine pitcher again, only to find it empty. Thirty-eight years old, horny, thirsty and feeling envious of some innocent, eight-year-old kid.

What the hell was wrong with him? He'd been several years older than Megan had been when his real family had been blown to bits. As for the "family" he'd had after that, he'd hardly term a hard-assed workaholic like Cole as real.

Sitting across from him on the foot of the bed, Angeline had spread out the napkin over her lap, and as he watched, she delicately brushed her fingertips over the cloth.

She had the kind of hourglass figure that men fantasized over, a Madonna's face and fingers that looked like they should have nothing more strenuous to do than hold up beautifully jeweled rings. Yet twice now, he'd found her toiling away in the ass-backwards village of Puerto Grande.

That first time, five years ago, his usual courier had missed the meet and Brody had been encouraged to develop a new asset. And oh, by the way, isn't it convenient that there's a pretty American in Puerto Grande whose family is already involved with Hollins-Winword.

The situation had always struck Brody as too convenient for words. But he'd gone ahead and done his job. He'd talked her into the gig, passed off the intel that she was to relay later when she was back in the States and voilà, her career as a courier was born.

The second time he'd found her working like a dog in Puerto Grande had been, of course, just that morning. He'd called in to his handler at Hollins-Winword to find out who he could pull in fast to assist him on getting the kids, only to learn that, lo and behold, once again the lovely Señorita Clay was right there in Puerto Grande. She would be the closest, quickest—albeit unlikely—assistant. And one he'd had to think hard and fast whether he wanted joining him or not. Desperate measures, though, had him going for it.

Not that it had been easy to convince her to join him. As she'd said, she wasn't a field agent. Not even close. Her experience in such matters was nil. *And* she had her commitment to All-Med to honor. The small medical team was administering vaccinations and treating various ailments of the villagers around Puerto Grande.

He'd had to promise that another volunteer would arrive shortly to replace her before she'd made one single move toward his Jeep.

She was definitely a woman of contrasts.

When she wasn't pulling some humanitarian aid stint, she worked the streets of Atlanta as a paramedic, yet usually talked longingly of the place she'd grown up in: Wyoming.

And there wasn't a single ring—jeweled or otherwise—on those long, elegant fingers, except the wedding band that had been his mother's.

Usually, he kept it tucked in his wallet. As a reminder never to get too complacent with life. Too comfortable. Too settled.

Considering how settled he'd been becoming lately, maybe it was a timely reminder.

"Do you remember much of Santo Marguerite?"

Her lashes lifted as she gave him a startled look. Just as quickly, those lush lashes lowered again. She lifted one shoulder and the crisp fabric of the tunic slipped a few inches, giving him a better view of the hollow at the base of that long, lovely throat.

"I remember it a little." She pleated the edge of the napkin on her lap then leaned forward to retrieve the wineglass that she'd set on the floor. "What do you even know about the place? It no longer exists."

She had a point. What he knew he'd learned from *her* file at Hollins-Winword. The dwellings of the village that had been destroyed were never rebuilt, though Sandoval had been in control of the land for the last few decades, guarding it with the violent zealousness he was known for.

She evidently took his silence as his answer. "Where did *you* grow up?" she asked.

"Here and there." He straightened from his perch and stretched. Talking about her past was one thing. His was off-limits. Even he tried not to think about it. "You figure that bed's strong enough to hold us both?"

Her eyes widened a fraction before she looked away again. "I… I'm used to roughing it in camps and such. I can sleep on the floor."

"Hardly sounds like a wifely thing to do."

She scrunched up the napkin and slid off the bed. "I'm not a wife."

"Shh." There was something wrong with the way he took such pleasure in seeing the dusky color climb into that satin-smooth complexion of hers.

Her lips firmed. "You've already established that these walls don't have ears."

"So I did. Kind of a pity, really. I was looking forward to seeing how well we played mister and missus for the night."

Giving him a frozen look, she polished off the rest of her wine. Then she just stood there, staring at the blank wall ahead of her.

In the candlelight, her hair looked dark as ink against the pale cloth of her tunic, though he knew in the sunlight, those long gleaming locks were not really black at all, but a deep, lustrous brown.

"Whatcha thinking?"

She didn't look back at him. She folded her arms over her chest. Her fingertips curled around her upper arms and he saw the wink of candlelight catching in the gold wedding band. "I wonder why they don't have windows here."

"Considering the way the weather was blowing out there, that's probably a blessing about now." He watched her back for a moment. The tunic reached well below her hips, and though he'd always had the impression of her being very tall, he knew that it was merely the way she carried herself. Not that she was short, but he had her by a good seven or eight inches.

And there, in that tunic and pants, her feet bare, she seemed much less Wonder Woman than usual.

Vulnerable. That was the word.

She looked vulnerable.

It wasn't necessarily a comfortable realization.

"You claustrophobic?"

She stiffened and shot him a suspicious look. "Why?"

"Just curious." Though the walls in the room were probably going to feel mighty closed in the longer they were confined together with that single, narrow bed.

Her hands rubbed up and down her arms. "The electricity here would be from a generator, wouldn't it?"

"I'd think so, though that doesn't explain why it's not running. Maybe they've got concerns with the gas it would take. Why? You cold?"

"Some. You, um, you suppose there's plumbing here?"

He hid a smile. The convent was cloistered, and located in a highly remote location. But it wasn't entirely out of the middle ages. "This is built like a dorm," he said. "I saw the bathroom a floor down."

She dropped her arms, casting him a relieved look. "You did?"

"Probably better facilities here than you had in that hut at Puerto Grande." He reached for the door. "After you, my darling wife."

When they got to the bathroom door, Brody stopped. "Place is built for women," he reminded her. "You'd better go first. Make sure I don't send some poor nun into heart failure."

"I won't be long." She ducked inside.

In his experience, women were forever finding reasons to spend extra time in the bathroom. Lord only knew what they did in there.

But she did open the door again, almost immediately. "All clear." She slipped past him back into the corridor and he went inside.

The halls were still silent when they made their way back up the narrow staircase and to the room. They passed a half-dozen other doors as they went. All closed.

"Where do you suppose the children are?"

He wished that he had a good answer. "We'll find out soon enough."

"I don't understand why you're still feeling so awfully patient, considering your hurry to get up here."

"Honey, I'm not patient. But I am practical."

She stopped. "What's so practical about getting all the way here, with no means of getting back *out* of here?"

"Oh, ye of little faith." He caught a glimpse of swishing black fabric from the corner of his eye.

"Bro—"

He pulled Angeline to him and planted his mouth over hers, cutting off his name.

She gave out a shocked squeak and went ramrod stiff. Her hands found their way to his chest, pushing, and he closed his hands around hers, squeezing them in warning.

She went suddenly soft, and instead of fighting him, she kissed him back.

It took more than a little effort for him to remember the kiss was only for the benefit of the nun, and damned if he didn't feel a few bubbles off center when he managed to drag his mouth from those delectably soft lips and give the sister—Sister Frances, in fact—an embarrassed, Hewitt-type apology.

She tilted her head slightly. "The sacrament of marriage is a blessing, *señor*. There is no need for apology." Her smile took in them both. "You will be comfortable for the night? Is there anything else we can provide for you?"

He kept his hands around Angeline's. "A visit with our children would be nice."

"I'm sorry. The Reverend Mother must return first."

Angeline tugged her hands out of his. "We understand, Sister. But won't you tell them that we're here for them? That we'll be going home just as soon as we can?"

"Of course, *señora*. They will be delighted." She gave them a kind look. "Rest well. The storm will hopefully have passed by morning and Mother will be able to return." She headed down the hall toward the staircase.

Brody tugged Angeline back into their room and closed the door.

The second he did, she turned on him. "You didn't need to do that."

"Do what?"

Her lips parted. She practically sputtered before any actual words came out. "Kiss me."

He slid his hand over her shoulder and lowered his head. "Whatever you say, honey."

She shoved at him, and he stepped back, chuckling. "Relax, Sophia. We have the nun's blessing, re-member?"

"Very funny." She put as much distance between them as the small room afforded. "I'm not going to have to remind you that no means *no,* am I?"

He started to laugh, but realized that she was seri-ous. "Lighten up. If I ever get serious about getting you in the sack, you'll know."

"You're impossible."

"Usually," he agreed. He yanked back the cover on the bed, and saw the way she tensed. "And you're act-ing like some vestal virgin. Relax. You might be the stuff of countless dreams, but I do have *some* control."

Her cheeks weren't just dusky rose now. They were positively red. And her snapping gaze wouldn't meet his as she leaned past him and snatched one of the thin pillows off the mattress. "If you were a gentleman, *you'd* take the floor."

"Babe, I'll be the first one to tell you that I am *not* a gentleman."

"Fine." She tossed the pillow on the floor, and gath-ered up the top cover from the bed. She flipped it out on the slate by the pillow, and sat down on one edge, drawing the other side over her as she lay down, back toward him.

"You're really going to sleep on the floor."

She twitched the cover up over her shoulder. "Looks that way, doesn't it?"

He didn't know whether to laugh or applaud. "If I needed a shower despite the one that Mother Nature gave us that badly, you could have just told me."

She didn't respond.

He looked at the bed. A thin beige blanket covered the mattress. The remaining pillow looked even thinner and more Spartan now that its mate was tucked between Angeline's dark head and the cold hard floor.

Brody muttered a mild oath—they *were* in a convent, after all, and even he didn't believe in taunting fate quite that much—and grabbed the pillow and blanket from the bed and tossed them down on the ground.

She twisted her head around. "What are you doing now?"

"Evidently being shamed into sleeping on this godforsa— blessed floor." He flipped out the blanket and lowered himself onto it. Sad to say, but nearly every muscle inside him protested the motion. He was in pretty decent shape, but climbing the mountain hadn't exactly been a picnic.

"You don't *have* any shame," she countered.

He made a point of turning his back on her as he lay down, scrunching the pillow beneath his head. The area of floor was significantly narrow, but not so narrow that he couldn't have kept his back from touching hers if he'd so chosen.

He didn't choose.

So much for trying to convince the higher powers that he was entirely decent.

She shifted ever so subtly away from him, until he couldn't feel the warmth of her lithe form against him. He rolled onto his back, closing the gap again.

She huffed a little, then sat up and pushed at him to move over. When he didn't, she scrambled to her feet and stepped over him, reaching back for her bedding.

"Where are you going?" He rolled back onto his side and propped his head on his hand, watching her interestedly.

"Away from *you*," she assured. She flung the cover around her shoulders like an oversized shawl and climbed onto the bed. "When lightning strikes you down, I don't want to be anywhere near."

Brody smiled faintly. "That's good, because I was beginning to think you were afraid of sleeping with little ol' me."

She huffed. "Please. There is *nothing* little about you."

"Babe. I'm flattered."

She gave him a baleful look that made him want to smile even more. "You know they say the larger the ego, the smaller the, um—"

"Id?" he supplied innocently.

She huffed again and threw herself down on the pillow. "Blow out the candles."

"I thought you'd never ask." He got up and did so, turning the small, cozily lit room into one that was dark as pitch.

She was silent. So silent he couldn't even hear her breathe.

"You all right?"

"It's *really* dark."

He wondered how hard it had been for Angeline to admit that. She damn sure wouldn't appreciate him noticing the hint of vulnerability in her smooth, cool voice.

Two steps to his right and he reached the dresser. The small tin of matches was next to the pitcher and

bowl and he found that easily, too. A scrape of the
match against the wall, a spit of a spark, the flare of
sulfur, and the tiny flame seemed to light up the place
again. "I can leave one of the candles lit."

"You said you weren't a gentleman."

He set the flame to one of the candles and shook
out the match. "I'm not," he assured.

"Then stop acting like one, because now I *have*
to give you room on this bed, too." She moved on
the mattress, and the iron frame squeaked softly. She
groaned and covered her face with her hand.

He laughed softly. "It's just a few squeaky springs.
I doubt any of the good sisters are holding glasses
against these thick walls hoping for a listen. You act
like you've never shared a bed with a guy before."

She didn't move. Not just that she was still, but that
she *really* didn't move.

And for a guy who'd generally considered himself quick on the uptake, he realized that this time
he'd been mighty damn slow. "Ah. I…see." Though
he didn't. Not really. She was twenty-nine years old.
How did a woman—a woman who looked like her, yet,
with her intelligence, her caring, her…everything—
how the hell did she get to be that age and never sleep
with a guy?

"Why are you still—why haven't you ever—oh,
hell." Disgruntled more at himself than at her, he
scraped his hand down his face. "Forget it. It's none
of my business."

"No," she agreed. "It's not. Now, are you going to
sleep on the bed or not?"

He snatched up the pillow from the floor and tossed it beside her.

She's a virgin. The thought—more like a taunt—kept circling inside his head. Probably what he got for catching a glimpse of that sexy underwear of hers when he'd promised not to look.

He lay down next to her, and the iron bed gave a raucous groan.

"Not one word," she whispered fiercely.

That worked just fine for him.

Chapter 4

Angeline didn't expect to sleep well.

She knew she'd *sleep,* simply because she'd learned long ago to sleep when the opportunity presented itself. And even though Brody's long body was lying next to hers, his weight indenting the mattress just enough that the only way she could keep from rolling toward him was to hang on to the opposite edge of the mattress, she figured she would still manage to catch some z's.

What she didn't expect, however, was to sleep soundly enough, deeply enough, to miss Brody *leaving* the bed.

Or to find that someone had filled the pitcher on the dresser and laid out a freshly folded hand towel on the dresser top.

Okay. So she'd *really* slept soundly.

Not so unusual, she reasoned, as she dashed chilly water over her face and pressed the towel to her cheeks. Making that climb in the storm had been exhausting.

Or maybe you're more comfortable with Brody than you'd like to admit.

She turned and went out of the room, leaving that annoying voice behind.

As before, the corridor was empty, still lit by candles in the sconces. She went down the stairs, visited the long, vaguely industrial-like restroom and then went searching.

But when she reached the ground floor without encountering the impossible-to-miss dining hall, she knew she'd taken a wrong turn somewhere along the way.

Annoyed with herself, she turned on her heel, intending to head back and make another pass at it, but a muffled sound stopped her in her tracks.

Footsteps?

Nervousness charged through her veins and she tried to shake it off. She was in a convent, for pity's sake. What harm could come to them there?

Even if the nuns realized the identity fraud they were perpetrating, what would they be likely to do about it, other than call the authorities, or kick them out into the storm? It wasn't as if they'd put them in chains in a dungeon.

Nevertheless, Angeline still looked around warily, trying to get her bearings. She went over to the nearest window, but it was too far above her head. She couldn't see out even when she tried to jump up and catch the narrow sill with her fingers. So she stood still, pressing a hand to her thumping heart, willing it to quiet as she listened for another sound, another brush of feet, a swish of long black robes.

But all she heard now was silence. She was listening so hard that when melodious bells began chiming, she very nearly jumped out of her skin.

She leaned back against the roughly textured wall and waited for the chiming to end.

"If you're praying, there's a chapel within spitting distance."

Her heart seemed to seize up for the eternal moment it took to recognize the deep, male voice.

She opened her eyes and looked at Brody. She came from a family of tall, generally oversized men, much like Brody. And she was used to the odd quietness with which most of them moved. But Brody seemed to take that particular skill to an entirely new level. "It's a good thing my heart is healthy," she told him tartly, "because you could give a person a heart attack the way you sneak ar<u>ou</u>nd!"

"Who needs to sneak?"

"Evidently *you* do," she returned in the same quiet whisper he was using.

Despite the wrinkles in his gender-neutral tunic and pants, he looked revoltingly fresh, particularly compared to the rode-hard-and-put-up-wet way that she felt.

"Did you know you pretty much sleep like the dead?"

She wasn't going to argue the point with him when ordinarily, as a result of her paramedic training, she was quite a light sleeper. "What are you doing sneaking around? Do you know what time it is?"

"It's almost 3:00 a.m. And what are *you* doing

sneaking around? I've been trying to find you for ten minutes."

"I needed the restroom," she whispered. A portion of the truth at least.

He cocked his head. "You got your boots on. Good." He closed his long fingers around her wrist and started walking along the hallway, sticking his head through doorways as he went. "While you were dreaming of handsome princes, I was scoping out this place. Hard to believe, but the fine sisters have an interesting collection of vehicles."

Her stomach clenched. "You'll ask to borrow one?"

Despite the dim lighting, she could tell that his expression didn't change one iota.

She swallowed a groan. "We can't steal one of their cars," she said under her breath.

"Babe." He sounded wounded. "Steal is a harsh word." He stopped short and she nearly bumped into him. "I like *borrow* better."

"That only works when you intend to ask permission to do so," she pointed out the obvious.

"Details. You're always getting hung up on details." He reached up and plucked a candle out of one of the sconces, then pulled open the door beside him and nudged her through. "I wanna move fast, but we've gotta stay quiet. Think you can manage that?"

Her lips parted. "Yes, I can be quiet," she assured, a little more loudly than she ought.

He raised his eyebrows and she pressed her lips together, miming the turning of a key next to them.

His lips quirked. "Good girl."

The spurt of nervousness she'd felt before was nothing compared to the way she felt now as Brody drew her through the doorway. He stopped long enough to hold the door as it closed without a sound.

After tramping down a warren of alarmingly narrow halls, the tile floor gave way to hard-packed dirt.

She swallowed again, feeling like they were heading down into the bowels of the mountain. "Did you sleep at *all?* How long did it take you to discover this rat maze? Do you even know where we're going?"

He paused again, letting her catch up and the candle flame stopped the wild dance of light it cast on the walls. "Yeah, I slept enough. And yeah, I know where we're going. Don't you trust me? We're going to get the kids and get the hell outta Dodge while the going's good."

"But what about your big first-things-first speech?"

"You slept some, didn't you?" His voice was light. "And ate."

She pressed her lips together, determined not to argue. "Your sudden rush just surprised me," she finally managed stiffly.

"Well, along with their various vehicles," he said in such a reasonable tone that she felt like smacking him, "the fine sisters here have a satellite phone system. Hardly the kind of thing one would expect, but hey. Maybe one of the local politicians figures he's buying his way into heaven or something. Anyway, I checked with my handler. The Stanleys have been moved again. And despite the weather, the Mother Superior has found a guide to get her back to her flock. She's supposed to be here shortly after sunup."

"A guide," Angeline echoed. Her irritation dissolved. "What kind of guide?"

"The kind who won't let a washed-out road get in his way."

"You don't think it's that Rico person who searched Sophia and Hewitt's place?"

His gaze didn't waver.

Dismay congealed inside her stomach. "This is a nightmare."

"Nah. Could be worse. Way worse," he assured.

She looked over her shoulder in the direction from which they'd come. What was worse? Going forward or going back? Either way, she really, *really* wanted to get out of this narrow, closed-in tunnel. She looked back at him only to encounter the look he was giving her—sharp eyed *despite* the gloom. *"What?"*

"You tell me. What's bothering you?"

Aside from the entire situation? She moistened her lips. "I, um, I just don't much care for tunnels."

He held the candle above his head, looking up. Then he moved the candle to one side. And the other.

She knew what he was looking at. The ceiling overhead was stucco. The walls on either side of them were stuccoed, as well. And though the floor was dirt, it wasn't as if it were the kind of dirt that had been on the road where the Jeep had gotten stuck. Her boots had encountered no ruts. It seemed perfectly smooth, perfectly compacted.

Not *exactly* a tunnel.

She knew that's what Brody was thinking.

But "We're almost there," was all he said. "Think you can stand it for another couple minutes?"

Pride lifted her chin if nothing else would. This

was part of St. Agnes, not a culvert running beneath the city of Atlanta. "Of course."

He didn't smile. Just gave a single nod and turned forward again.

His simple acceptance of her assurance went considerably further than if he'd taken her hand and drawn her along with him like some frightened child. She focused on watching *him,* rather than the confining space, as they continued their brisk pace.

As he'd promised, it was only a few minutes—if that—before she followed Brody around another corner, up several iron stairs and out into the dark, wet air. A vine-twined trellis overhead kept the drizzling rain from hitting them, though Angeline shivered as the air penetrated her clothes.

Thunder was a steady roll, punctuated by the brilliant flicker of lightning.

She got a quick impression of hedges and rows of plants. The convent's garden? Surely there would have been an easier route to take.

It was then that Brody took her hand in his, lacing his fingers through hers.

She looked up at him, surprise shooting through her.

"Remember, Sophia," he murmured softly, and squeezed her hand. "Falling waters."

She nodded, and right before her very eyes, Brody's expression changed. His shoulders seemed to shrink, and it was as if he no longer towered over her. He even pulled a pair of wire-rimmed glasses from somewhere and stuck them on his face.

Clearly, he wanted to be prepared in case they were discovered.

She wondered suddenly if he had his gun tucked beneath the wrinkled tunic.

Then he drew her from beneath the awning and they dashed across the thick, wet grass toward the building wing on the far side of the garden. They went in through a narrow door, up a flight of stairs and then Brody stopped next to a door. He pushed it open quietly, and pulled her inside.

The room was nearly identical to the one she and Brody had been given, only here, two narrow beds had been pushed against the walls. Small forms were visible beneath the white blankets.

"Let's get her first." Brody nodded toward the bed with the slightly larger hump beneath the covers. He tucked the candle against the basin and pitcher on the dresser and headed to the bed on the right. He touched the covered mound. "Eva—" his voice was soft "—come on, kiddo, rise and shine."

The girl mumbled and shifted, dragging the blanket nearly over her head.

Brody tried again.

This time, the dark head lifted. But at the sight of the strangers, she sucked in a hard breath and opened her mouth.

"Shh." Brody covered her mouth with his hand. "It's okay. Don't scream."

The girl tried scrambling away from Brody, but he held her fast.

"We're here for your parents," Angeline whispered, aching for the child. "Falling waters, right?" She knew from the pictures that Brody had showed her that the girl was pretty with the petite, refined features of her father and the coloring of her mother. But now, in the dark room above the hand Brody still held over her mouth, her eyes were nothing but wide pools of fear.

At the code the Stanleys had instituted, however, the girl's resistance began to ebb.

Angeline knelt beside the bed, closing her hands gently over the fists Eva had made around the edge of the blanket, and willed the girl to trust them.

"Everything is fine," she promised. "Just fine. We're going to take you to your parents just as soon as we can." She prayed that would come to pass. That the team sent to rescue them would be successful.

Eva slowly blinked.

"You need to stay quiet," Brody told her. "Can you do that?"

Again, she blinked. Finally, she gave a faint nod, and Brody gingerly pulled back his hand.

"Who are you?" Eva's whisper shook.

"He's Brody. I'm Angeline. We're...friends of your parents."

"But Sister Frances told us that our parents were already *here*." She knuckled her eyes. "But she wouldn't let us see them. Davey cried."

"*They* aren't actually here," Angeline explained awkwardly. "We, um, we used your parents' names."

Eva drew her eyebrows together. "But—"

"I need you to wake your brother up," Brody interrupted. He'd moved away from the bed and began silently pulling open dresser drawers. "So he's not so frightened." He pulled out several items of clothing and tossed them onto the bed beside the girl. "Do you two have hiking boots or anything? What about a suitcase?"

She nodded warily. "Under the bed."

Brody dropped down and retrieved the boots. He took one look at the unwieldy suitcase and pushed it back beneath the bed. "Thank God for pillowcases," he muttered, and plucked one of the pillows from behind Eva. He yanked the case off and shoved the clothing inside.

"My parents were working in the tepuis. Why didn't they come themselves? And why did you lie to the sisters?" Eva might only be nine, but she certainly knew how to speak her mind.

"They're still working," Angeline assured, lying right through her teeth and hating every moment of it. She squeezed Eva's fists. "Come on now. Let's get Davey awake."

Eva pushed back the blankets and slid off the bed. The hem of her long nightgown settled around her bare feet as she crossed to the other bed and sat down beside her brother. "Davey." She jiggled him. "Wake up." Her attention hardly left Brody, though, as he moved back to the dresser and found some more items to add to the pillowcase.

Davey sat up, looking bleary-eyed. However, at the sight of two strangers—who definitely weren't the nuns he was used to—he practically buried his head against his sister's side.

Even though he was more than half her size, Eva pulled him onto her lap, circling her arms around him protectively. "Mom and Daddy aren't here, after all," she told him. "But they want us to go home."

Angeline could have applauded. The child was showing much more adaptability than Angeline felt.

"In the dark?" Davey asked. He was as blond as his sister was dark, though from the pictures, Angeline knew his eyes were the same deep brown. "How come?"

Angeline sent a beseeching look toward Brody. He ignored it as he pushed his latest handful of clothing into the pillowcase and crouched next to the bed.

She stifled a sigh and tried to find an explanation that wouldn't scare the children anymore than they already were. "You know that we're here for your parents, but Reverend Mother doesn't know that. She only knows that your folks left you in her care, and she's not to release you to anyone *but* your parents. And that's why we told them we were them."

"So, just tell the truth," Eva said.

Davey weighed in. "Mama says to always tell the truth."

"Mama is right," Angeline said. She looked at Brody. "They need to know."

"No. They really don't. But we've gotta move now."

Angeline crouched in front of Eva. "I know this is probably scary for you and your brother. But it's very important that we leave quickly."

Eva's arms tightened around her brother. "My mom and dad are in trouble, aren't they. That's why you're here."

"They're going to be fine," Brody said with enough calm assurance that even Angeline felt inclined to believe him. "But they need us to get you to a safer place than here."

Eva's eyes widened. "But—"

"We'll talk more on the way," Angeline promised. She ran her hand down the girl's arm. "For now, though, we need to listen to Brody."

"We're not s'posed to talk to strangers," Davey whispered loudly.

"Right," Angeline said quickly. "And you remember that. But we're not quite strangers, are we? Your—your mom and dad, they told us what to tell you so you'd know that."

"Falling waters," Davey said. "'Cause they al-ays wanna take us to see Angel Falls." He named the world's tallest waterfall.

"I think we should stay here," Eva said warily. "With the sisters. Then—"

"We need to get off the mountain before morning," Brody said quietly. "Which means we have to go now. Right now."

A very large tear slowly rolled down Eva's cheek. "They're dead, aren't they. They fell off the mountain they were climbing or something."

"Oh, honey. No." Angeline shook her head. "Of course not."

Brody muffled an oath and suddenly plucked Davey off Eva's lap. The boy went even wider-eyed. "Think of this as an adventure," he told the child. "You can be Peter Pan. He was always my favorite. Had his sword. Could even fly."

Angeline knew that Brody's cases usually involved children, but she was nevertheless surprised with the competent way he began stuffing the boy's feet into socks and boots as he began extolling the exciting virtues of Pan as if he really had been his favorite.

And Davey was soaking it all up like a sponge.

"They're not dead?" Eva's voice was choked.

Angeline couldn't help herself. She pulled the girl close, hugging her. "Of course not."

Another set of bells began ringing, and they both jerked, startled at the sound. "That's the four o'clock bell," Eva said. "The sisters will get up for prayers before they fix breakfast."

Brody's eyes met Angeline's. He dropped a piece of paper on Eva's vacated bed. "Just get her boots on," he muttered. "And hurry up about it."

Angeline quickly helped Eva pull on the boots. Then she tugged the sweatshirt Brody tossed her over the girl's head, right on top of the long flannel nightie.

"She's a funny looking Tinkerbell," Davey said, giggling.

Angeline figured that was much better than crying.

Brody tossed the bulging pillowcase to Angeline, blew out the candle and opened the door, cautiously looking out. A moment later, they were hurrying down the hall.

The bells fell silent and almost simultaneously, a dozen doors along the corridor opened.

Angeline held her breath and Brody muttered an oath.

No *wonder* he'd taken such a circuitous route to the children's room.

It was smack in the middle of nun central.

"You said a bad word," Davey piped out clearly.

And Brody said quite a few more as he grabbed Eva off her feet, too. Angeline ran after him as they disappeared down the narrow back staircase and out into the drizzle before any of the nuns spotted them.

Chapter 5

The "interesting collection" of vehicles evidently included a Hummer.

Stalwart and sturdy looking where it sat parked on
the other side of the garden.

And though Angeline kept expecting someone to
come racing after them across the wet grass, taking
them to task for not waiting for the Mother Superior's
all clear, no one did.

She supposed that Brody didn't waste time on such
concerns. He certainly didn't waste time on manners
when they reached the vehicle. He dumped the kids
inside through the rear door leaving Angeline to manage for herself, and he had the engine running by the
time she made it around to the passenger's side.

"Buckle up." He didn't wait to make sure they

obeyed before he put the vehicle in gear and slid around in an uneven circle.

"Hold on," he warned, heading straight for a stand of bushes. "This ain't gonna be a smooth ride."

"That's an understatement," Angeline gasped moments later as the vehicle began rocking violently downward. Her head banged the window beside her, and she couldn't tell if they were on the road or not.

Another sharp drop and both Davey and Eva cried out. "We're flying," Davey hooted. "And we don't got no pixie dust even!"

"Seems like it," Brody agreed.

Angeline closed her eyes.

"What're you praying?" Brody's voice was almost as exhilarated as Davey's, and he didn't have the excuse of being four years old and innocent.

"I'm asking forgiveness for *borrowing* this vehicle and…and…oh—!" her head knocked the side window again "—and taking the kids the way we did."

"I left the sisters a note. I said someone from All-Med would return the vehicle."

Angeline gaped at him. Now he was pulling the volunteer crew in on this? "But, but that means we'll have to stop in Puerto Grande."

"Just long enough for you to fill in Dr. Chavez about getting the truck back to the convent. Believe me, we won't be staying long, and we won't be doing any rounds of visiting. There's no guarantee that our pal Rico won't have ears around."

"What if Miguel doesn't *want* to help? You know, he and the team are plenty busy without—"

"He will."

If only *she* felt as much certainty as Brody exhibited oh so easily. A tree branch slapped against the windshield and she winced. The windshield wipers were slapping away as much flying mud as rain as they hurtled down the mountain.

He'd said he wanted to get the children out of Venezuela. That wasn't going to happen on foot. "If, um, we leave the Hummer in Puerto Grande, what are we going to use as transportation then?"

"Miguel's got an SUV, doesn't he?"

She frowned. "*All-Med* has an SUV."

"And Miguel Chavez—" he broke off, cursing under his breath as they began sliding sideways. He spun the wheel, the vehicle jerked, smacked another bush straight on and continued downward again. "Like I was saying, Miguel Chavez is the head of All-Med's team. Same difference."

Not exactly. All-Med had a dozen teams that were assigned a dozen different locations.

"You're making my head hurt," she muttered.

He just grinned, and they continued bucking their way over the treacherous terrain.

The sky had begun to lighten when she finally saw from a distance their Jeep. The river of mud had climbed even higher since they'd abandoned it, and the empty vehicle listed to one side.

She swallowed a wave of nausea. If they had tried to walk back to Puerto Grande as she'd wanted, they'd have been on the road that was now fully flooded.

"Guess we won't be going that way," Brody said, clearly seeing the same thing she was.

"And neither will the Reverend Mother," Angeline

pointed out. "There's no way she and her *guide* could get up the road again."

"I imagine a creative person would find a means," he countered.

Goodness knows Brody had.

Nothing like the creativity of *stealing* a Hummer from a bunch of nuns.

She pressed her fingertips to her eyes.

What she wouldn't give to be sitting in a coffee shop about now, doing her *regular* kind of work for Hollins-Winword.

But no, she'd had to spend her two weeks of vacation pulling another stint with All-Med.

"How'd you even find me in Puerto Grande?"

Brody had turned away from the teeming mud flow and, if her sense of direction hadn't gone completely out the window, was heading west, away from the river where the village was located.

"I told you, babe. The agency keeps track of its assets."

Right. He had. She pinched the bridge of her nose, willing away the pain that was centered there.

"You were the closest one they could find for me in a pinch," he added. His lips twitched. "Bet it makes you want to sing for joy, doesn't it?"

She wondered what he'd have done if the nearest Hollins-Winword agent had been a grizzly-looking man. Probably have come up with some other impossible plan.

"You didn't tell us why we have to go somewhere safer," Eva reminded.

The pain in Angeline's head just got worse. She

lifted her brows when Brody gave her a look, as if she ought to answer. "You're the expert in these situations."

He looked about as thrilled as she felt.

But he pulled the vehicle to a stop and slung his arm over the seat, looking back at the children. "Because there's a guy—not a nice one—who wants something from your parents and *they* wanted to make sure he didn't come bothering you two at the convent before they could get back. So they asked for us to help them."

Eva swallowed. "What does he want?"

"Some of your dad's research. But that's not going to happen. So all you two need to do is stick with us. We're going to go back to the United States, and then your parents will come to meet you there. But until then, that whole talking to strangers thing? That still goes. Got it?"

Looking scared out of her wits, the girl nodded.

Davey tugged at Eva's arm, whispering something in her ear. "He has to go to the bathroom," she relayed.

Brody raked his fingers through his hair. "Anyone else?"

Eva shook her head.

Angeline felt her face flush a little as Brody looked to her. "No."

"All right, then." Leaving the vehicle running, he climbed out and opened the back door for Davey. "Us men, we got it easy," he said to the boy, who looked pretty amazed at being referred to as a man.

Eva didn't speak until after Brody closed the door and headed away with Davey. "Are you guys married?"

"What?" Angeline looked back at Eva, surprised.

The wedding ring on her finger seemed to grow warm. "Oh. No. No, no. We just…work together."

Eva plucked at the nightgown hanging down below her sweatshirt. "The rain got me all wet."

"We'll get you both dried and changed when we stop in Puerto Grande." She hoped that wasn't another promise she might not be able to back up. "It looked like Brody grabbed plenty of your clothing."

"I think he's nice."

Angeline pressed her lips together and she watched Brody lead young Davey off to the side out of their eyesight. "Yes," she said after a moment. "I think you might be right."

Getting to Puerto Grande proved almost as harrowing as getting off the convent's mountain. Particularly when the rain picked up again, gaining almost as much force as it had shown the previous day.

Washed out as it was, they couldn't take the main road. So Brody put the Hummer through some severe paces, carving out their own road, until finally, what seemed hours later, they came upon the small village.

It was comprised mostly of thatched huts, some stilted, clustered along a riverside that was lush with vegetation.

Right now, the trees and bushes were swaying madly in the wind, while the river pushed well beyond its banks.

Angeline felt numb surveying the damage as Brody plowed the vehicle through the mud, keeping to higher ground as much as he could in order to reach the shack that All-Med was using.

When they finally made it, Brody pulled to a stop beside an SUV parked behind the shack. The vehicle was covered in mud and was considerably smaller than the one they'd appropriated from the nuns. "If it weren't pouring, I'd have had you leave me with the kids back by the river while you finagled Chavez out of his SUV. Now we're going to have to chance someone seeing the kids."

Angeline still didn't know how she was going to explain the situation to Miguel. She held none of Brody's confidence that the doctor who headed the team would simply hand over his keys to her. He'd been unhappy enough when she'd abandoned the camp the day before.

"You'd better get moving," Brody suggested blandly. "Just tell the guy you've still got an emergency in Caracas, but you need to borrow his truck to get you there."

"Sure. Make it sound easy." She pushed open the door and ducking her head against the rain, jogged across the rutted ground toward the shack.

She untied the flap of heavy canvas that served as a door and dashed her long sleeve over her forehead before slipping inside, refastening the flap after her.

The shack had three rooms, shotgun style, that not only served as All-Med's temporary clinic, but their sleeping quarters, as well, and she headed through to the very rear section.

"Hey there," she greeted, striving for nonchalance and surely failing miserably. "Look what the wind blew in."

Obviously startled by her appearance, Robert

Smythe dropped the cards he was dealing at an ancient folding table. Maria Chavez hopped up from the folding chair on the other side of the table. "Angel! Good heavens, girl, you look like you've been swimming in the river. You and your friend surely haven't made it to Caracas and back, already?"

Along with her doctor husband, Miguel, Maria was in charge of the team. She was lithe and dark haired with skin the color of cream and caramel and with a decade on Angeline in years, she could have been an even closer "double" for Sophia Stanley.

"No. The storm stopped us." She smiled faintly at the thin blond girl who made up the third at the table. The replacement Brody had promised?

"Did you at least have some shelter last night?" Maria asked.

"Yeah." Hoping that her lies weren't too transparent, she busied herself with the pile of linens that were stacked on one of the upturned milk crates and picked a towel from the stack. "A local family—I didn't know them—took us in for the night. We, um, we borrowed their truck to get back here."

Maria looked past Angeline, as if she expected to see the man who Angeline had left with the day before.

"Brody's waiting for me in the truck," Angeline said quickly, only to wish that she'd come up with some other name for him.

Evidently, his paranoia was rubbing off on her.

She wrapped the towel around her shoulders and flipped her hair over the top of it. "It's pretty wet out there. Wet enough to keep the visitors away, I see."

They'd seen at least a hundred villages despite the weather before Angeline had gone off with Brody.

"A lot of them are heading inland for higher ground." Robert deftly gathered together the cards again. "Should probably introduce you to Persia." He nodded toward the blonde. "She arrived yesterday evening."

Definitely the replacement that Brody had promised. Was this slip of a girl another Hollins-Winword asset? The newcomer looked as if she weren't even out of her teens.

She crossed the room, her hand out. "Angeline Clay. Nice to meet you."

The girl's handshake was firm. "Persia Newman. I was sorry to hear about your friend's accident. I assume you came back to pick up your stuff?" Persia's gaze stayed steady on Angeline's face.

"Uh, yes. Right. My stuff."

The girl nodded. "I thought so. I hope you don't mind, but since I was using your cot, anyway, I took the liberty of packing up your duffel. You know. Just in case you had to grab it and run."

"Miguel thought we'd maybe have to try running it up to you in Caracas," Maria added. "You'll certainly need your passport along the way."

They were so helpful that Angeline wanted to crawl through the wood floor. "Thanks." She watched Persia move into the center room that housed the cots that made up their sleeping quarters. "So, Maria, what's the plan for the team? Are you still going to head for Los Llanos when you're finished here?"

Maria shook her head. "The plains are flooding

too badly. We hear most of the roads are already underwater. Instead, we'll work our way along the coast until we end up in Puerto La Cruz." She named the popular tourist hub. "After that, we'll wait for All-Med to determine where we're best needed. This storm is going to cause some major damage, I fear." She lifted her hand. "But you don't worry about that. You just get yourself to Caracas and tend to your friend there."

Angeline moistened her lips and swallowed. Maria and Miguel and the rest were *used* to rolling with the punches and she had to think about the safety of the Stanley family. But that didn't make lying to this woman whom she considered a friend any easier. "Yes, well. About that."

Persia returned with Angeline's battered blue duffel bag. "You're good to go. Passport is in the zippered pocket inside."

"Thanks."

"How are you even getting there?"

Young she might be, but Persia Newman was definitely better at subterfuge than Angeline was. "Actually, that's another reason we came back. The, um, vehicle we borrowed belongs to the convent at St. Agnes."

Maria's eyebrows shot up. "How on earth did you get it?"

"The family we stayed with last night. Anyway, we—Brody and I—" she almost winced at saying his name yet again "—said we'd try to see that it gets returned for them to the convent, so they wouldn't have to do it themselves."

"Robert and I could drive it there," Persia offered,

looking impossibly enthusiastic. "Once the weather clears a little, that is." She looked toward Maria. "You and the doctor could spare us for a few hours, right?"

"Of course." Maria readily agreed. "But that still doesn't solve Angeline's problem of getting to Caracas."

"She will take the Rover, of course." Miguel, himself, walked into the room, dashing his hand over his wet, black hair. "I was out visiting the Zamoras. They even sold their Jeep, evidently, to add to Brisa's college fund." He didn't skip a beat, jumping back to his original topic. "The keys are already in it, as usual. The Rover, that is. Why didn't you tell me that your emergency was so serious?"

"I—"

"I saw your friend, Brody, waiting outside. He told me your college friend in Caracas may not survive." Miguel dropped his hand on Angeline's shoulder. "We will all pray for her, *niña*."

Miguel had seen Brody, obviously.

But what about the children? It didn't seem as if he'd seen *them*.

"Here." Persia pushed the duffel into Angeline's hands, as well as a canvas bag of food. "You'll need something to eat along the way."

Angeline eyed the loaves of bread, fresh fruit and the tall steel thermos that filled the bag. It just reminded her that it had been quite some time since she'd supped with Brody the night before. "But what will you guys do without the Rover?"

Manuel smiled easily. "You just leave the Rover at

the All-Med office in Caracas. They'll arrange to get it back to us."

"I—I don't know what to say. Thank you."

"Angeline."

She whirled. Brody stood just inside the canvas flap. "Yes?"

"We should hurry."

"Yes." Maria began pushing Angeline toward the front of the shack where Brody waited. "We will work together again, my friend. For now, you take care of what you need."

She returned Maria's fast hug, handed back the towel and once again found herself dashing through the rain, Brody by her side.

It was beginning to feel oddly comfortable.

Chapter 6

The kids, it turned out, had been stowed by Brody out of sight inside the Rover before he'd approached the shack. Now, Eva and Davey stayed huddled down beneath a blanket as Brody took the wheel and headed away, and they didn't come out until they'd left the village of Puerto Grande entirely behind.

Brody didn't worry about finding an out-of-the-way route to Caracas. The weather was so awful that there was hardly any other traffic for them to encounter anyway, so he kept to one of the main—marginally safer—roads as they headed north.

In the backseat, Eva and Davey managed to change into some of the dry clothes that Brody had brought. Then Angeline divvied out the food, and they all took turns drinking the hot soup that filled the thermos.

And showing the resilience of youth, it was only a

few hours before Eva and Davey were hunched against each other in the backseat, sound asleep.

"You should sleep, too," Brody told her when he handed her back the empty thermos lid that they'd used as a cup. She'd already tipped the last of the soup into it, assuring him that he should finish it off.

"You had even less sleep last night than I did." She was tired, but her nerves were still in such high gear that she couldn't have slept if her life depended on it. "I'm used to short nights, anyway."

"Work the late shift in Atlanta a lot?"

She tilted her head back against the headrest. "I'm surprised you don't already know."

He slanted her a look. "Turns out there are a *few* things I didn't know about you."

Her cheeks warmed. Naturally he wasn't going to let her forget his discovery the night before.

That would hardly be Brody's style.

Of course, she hadn't thought it would be his style to play the Peter Pan card in order to keep a little boy from becoming too frightened, either.

"So, talk to me." Brody's attention was square on the road ahead of them once again. "Keep me awake, because that soup is trying to do a number on me."

"Talk about what?" she asked warily.

"Anything. What took you to Georgia in the first place."

She folded her hands together in her lap, surprised even more by his unexpected retreat from a topic that could have given him plenty of entertainment.

She wasn't ashamed of her virginity, but at her age it wasn't necessarily something she felt the need to explain, and she definitely didn't like it being the subject of amusement for someone.

"J.D. moved there first, actually," she said, not bothering to explain that J.D. was her sister when he undoubtedly already knew.

"She's the horsey one. And your brother, Casey, is the bookworm."

Despite herself, she felt a smile tug at her lips at the aptly brief descriptions. Neither sibling was hers by blood, but that hadn't kept her and J.D. from being thick as thieves. The two of them were as different as night and day, and she wasn't only Angeline's sister, she was her best friend. "Casey's finishing his graduate degree in literature—and women," she added wryly. "And J.D. is a trainer on a horse farm in Georgia."

"But she trains Thoroughbreds for racing. Kind of a departure from the whole cattle-herding thing your family does in Wyoming, isn't it?"

"She could train cutting horses just as happily. Doesn't matter to J.D., as long as she's got her beloved equines. Anyway, I followed her to Atlanta about a year after she went there."

"You were already an EMT."

She nodded. "In Casper. I got my paramedic license in Atlanta, though." She worked long hours, and when she wasn't, she was studying, taking other classes, and generally trying to decide just what she ought to be doing with her life.

"I imagine Atlanta is a whole different ball game in the medical emergency biz."

"Busier, maybe," Angeline said smoothly. She didn't really want to talk about her work. One of the reasons she'd chosen to spend her vacation time with All-Med was to get entirely away from it.

"So what are you *not* saying?"

"I don't know what you mean," she lied. Since he'd found her in Puerto Grande, she'd been doing a lot of that.

She pushed back her hair, only to have her fingers get caught in the tangles. Nothing like a reminder that she probably looked like the Wicked Witch of the West. And she couldn't easily reach her duffel at the moment where, presumably, Persia had packed her meager toiletries, because Brody had stowed it in the very rear of the vehicle.

"Yeah, right," he drawled. "Fine. Keep it to yourself. For now."

Her fingers were useless with her hair. "What are we going to do once we get to Caracas?" Focusing on the situation at hand was infinitely more appealing than thinking about Atlanta.

"We're going to get out of the country as unnoticeably as we can."

"By flying? Aside from the storm, which I would think would make that sort of difficult, we don't even have the kids' passports." She certainly hadn't noticed him adding the items when he'd filled the pillowcase with the kids' clothing.

"Yes, we do," he corrected smoothly. "I…appropriated them when I found that satellite phone. They were stored in the desk there."

She had an instant image of him rifling through the Mother Superior's desk and wondered what sort of karmic punishment *that* would deserve.

Endless rain upon an entire country?

"But it doesn't matter," he went on, oblivious to her thoughts. "Can't use them through customs anyway, because our movements could be traced. At this point we can only hope the sisters at St. Agnes bought our charade. Otherwise they could report us for taking the kids just as much as they could for us borrowing the Hummer. And even if *they* don't send up a hue and cry, it's damn sure that Rico will be watching for any sight of them when he realizes they're *not* at the convent. Which means using the international airport is not even a consideration."

"So we're going to leave the country illegally."

"Creatively," he countered. "Don't let it shock that good-girl head of yours too badly. We're not doing anything immoral. It's not as if we're running drugs or something."

She knew that. But still…. "It just seems like Hollins-Winword should be able to find more official means to get us back to the States."

The corner of his lips lifted and she realized with a start that she was actually beginning to get used to his beard and mustache. "I thought it was only your cousin Sarah who was naive about Hollins-Winword."

"Sarah's not naive," she defended. Her cousin had one of the kindest hearts she knew and was, first and foremost, an elementary school teacher. Learning last November that she'd also been pulling a stint with Hollins-Winword had come as a big surprise. Angeline had been hard pressed not to let slip what *her* work with them involved.

Her family already worried enough about her and

J.D. off in Atlanta and away from the bosom of Wyoming. Add into that her cousin Ryan who was in the Navy and had been missing now for the better part of a year, and the Clays had way more than enough concerns. She wanted to add to that with the truth about her courier sideline about as much as she wanted to beat herself with a stick.

As it was, she was hoping that this current insanity with Brody would be resolved before her vacation was up.

Nobody back home would ever be the wiser.

Brody was snorting softly. "Sarah might set up safe houses now and then, but she definitely puts a kinder face on the powers that be than I would."

Angeline pulled the last apple out of the canvas bag. "Considering that it was those same 'powers that be' who have helped to arrange her and Max adopting Megan—the girl *you* were protecting in Weaver last November—I'd have to say that my cousin seems more on the mark than you."

He'd pulled out a pocket knife earlier so she could use it to cut the apples for the kids, and she flipped the wicked blade open again, deftly slicing the fruit in quarters.

"Yeah, well, said powers don't make a habit of it." His voice went flat.

She leaned across the narrow console separating their seats and held a piece of apple up for him.

Instead of taking it from her fingers, though, he just leaned forward and grabbed it with his strong white teeth, biting off half.

She swallowed and sat back in her seat, the remaining wedge of apple still in her fingers. "We, uh, we're just going to have to agree to disagree. If it weren't for Hollins-Winword and Coleman Black, in particular—" she named the man who'd been at the helm of the underground agency for as long as she'd been alive "—I would have grown up in a Costa Rican orphanage. Instead, I ended up with Dan and Maggie. They were able to adopt me, and I even received citizenship without having to go through the usual channels."

He had an odd expression as he finished the apple piece. One she couldn't possibly hope to read. She fed him the second half, all the while trying to pretend that doing so wasn't sending odd frissons down her nerve endings.

"He was there when Santo Marguerite fell," Brody said abruptly when he'd polished off the second bite.

He referred to her father, Daniel Clay. "I know." He'd been assigned there by none other than Coleman Black. She knew there wasn't a day that passed that he hadn't felt the weight of responsibility for being unable to prevent Sandoval's destruction there. "He's my father. Of course he told me."

"Just don't expect every situation to come up blooming the same kind of daisies."

She swallowed, instinctively looking back at the sleeping children. "Hollins-Winword operations are usually successful," she said.

"You telling me or asking me?" He shot her one of those disturbingly perceptive looks of his.

She looked away from it, focusing on the apple again. She cut another smaller wedge and leaned over, feeding it to him.

Even *that* was easier than feeling like he'd just taken a tiptoe through every fear she possessed.

When there was nothing left but the apple core, she opened the window just enough to toss it out.

"Littering." Brody shook his head, tsking and sounding more like his normal self again. "You're turning into a regular rebel."

She flicked the rainwater that had blown in at him and told herself that she really did *not* find her insides jigging around a little at the sight of the dimple that showed, despite his disreputable whiskers.

After wiping the knife blade, she folded it again and set it back in one of the cup holders molded into the center console.

She was well aware of the periodic looks that Brody gave to the rearview and side view mirrors.

As if he expected someone to be following them.

But every time she looked back, she saw only empty road.

"Why keep pulling EMT hours when you could make more with a helluva lot less effort by focusing just on Hollins?"

"Being a courier works only because I'm able to fit it *into* my regular life. I don't want it to *become* my regular life." She lifted her hand, trying to encompass everything—the muddy vehicle, the treacherous weather, the children. "Who wants this kind of thing to be their entire life?" She shook her head, dropping her hand back to her lap. "Not me."

"I'll let the dig you just gave me pass," he said drily.

"I didn't mean—"

"Forget it." He reached up and adjusted the rearview mirror. "The truth is, my life isn't too many people's cup of java. And me, hell, I'd be bored stiff if I had to stay in any one place for too long a stretch. But I didn't mean that you should try to be in the field all the time. Just that you could be kept a lot busier as a courier than you are, if you wanted."

She shook her head. "I don't."

"Smart girl," he murmured almost as if to himself. Then he shot her a look. "As a source of excitement, your job probably gives plenty, right?"

Her fingers strayed to the tangles in her hair again. "I suppose." She'd dealt with everything from delivering babies to people who'd died peacefully in their sleep. And most everything in between.

She knew what it felt like to lose a battle that she couldn't have won no matter what, and that was fine. She still slept at night.

It was the battle that she hadn't *had* to lose that plagued her. The one where she'd hesitated, where she'd made the wrong choice, taken the wrong action. That was the thing she wasn't able to accept. The thing that made her question pretty much everything she'd thought she wanted to do with her life.

Supposedly, knowing any problem—identifying it, putting a name to it—was supposed to be the first step in dealing with it.

So far, the theory hadn't helped her one iota.

She'd still let a fourteen-year-old kid down, in the most final of ways because she'd thought she could get to him without having to climb through a culvert.

Brody flicked the windshield wipers to a higher setting. They swished back and forth so rapidly, they were almost nothing but a blur of motion. He checked the rearview again.

Angeline looked back through the window. All she could see was the misty swirl of water kicked up by the tires as it warred with the rain. "You don't think we're being followed, do you?" The notion tasted acrid.

"No."

She turned forward once more and chewed on her lower lip for a moment. "Are you lying?"

"I've always thought that one of those useless no-win questions." His voice was considering.

She folded her arms. "Well, pardon me."

"Seriously, think about it." His thumb lifted off the steering wheel. "If a person *is* lying, they're hardly going to want to admit it. If they say they're not, why is that anymore believable than the original lie? And no matter whether they ever admit that they are lying, the person who asked the question in the first place is going to be no happier knowing it. Because they either want to believe what the person did say or they don't."

She squinted at him. "I'm sorry. Was that supposed to make *any* sense?"

He shrugged.

She propped her elbow on the door and covered her eyes with her hands. "Davey's the one who had it right, anyway. It's just better to tell the truth."

"Maybe in a perfect world." He gave her a look. "This ain't a perfect world, Angeline. The sooner you face that, the better off you'll be."

Angeline.

So he *could* manage her name when he felt like it.

Unfortunately, she now knew—too late of course— that hearing her name roll off his lips was far more disturbing to her peace of mind.

* * *

Once they reached Caracas, even with the aid of the city map Angeline found in the glove box, it took two efforts before she was able to direct Brody through the confusing streets to the All-Med office. Naturally, when they got there, the small storefront was locked up tight for the night.

When Brody strolled past, speculatively studying the assortment of vehicles parked on the street, Angeline was too tired to muster any surprise. "Nobody's going to be at the office until tomorrow morning to do anything about returning this thing to Miguel. Don't you think we might as well keep driving it until then? The kids need to eat, Brody. You and I need to eat. And a shower and some fresh clothes wouldn't necessarily hurt any of us, either."

"How much cash do you have?"

"Not much. Just what I had back at the camp in Puerto Grande. I don't carry a lot cash when I come here; it's easier to use my credit card."

"Can't use that."

She wasn't surprised. Electronic means were too easily traced.

In the rear, Davey was pushing at Eva, complaining that she was hogging too much of the seat. Angeline reached her hand back, automatically trying to separate them. "You two have been great all day today, and I know you're tired. But just have patience for a little while longer," she urged.

Brody raked his hand down his face. "We've already stayed with this SUV too long."

Angeline swallowed. The reality of their situation

had hovered beneath the surface throughout the long day of driving. Now it gurgled again to the surface like some dank, oily monster. But throwing up her hands in panic wasn't going to solve anything.

The children still needed food and some chance to stretch their legs before they got some sleep in a proper bed.

Brody turned on the interior light and pulled the map across the steering wheel. "Do you know this area?" he asked pointing to a spot.

Angeline shook her head. "I don't know much of Caracas at all, except the airport and how to get from there to the All-Med office."

Eva sat forward, poking her head between the seats. "Tell Davey to stop kicking me or I'm gonna *punch* him."

"Nobody is going to kick or punch *anyone*," Angeline said, giving them both a firm look.

Brody pushed the map back toward Angeline, turned off the overhead light and began driving up the narrow street. "We'll find a place to hole up for the night, and get you settled with the kids. Once that's done, I'll ditch the SUV back at All-Med."

Somehow she doubted that he'd be catching a taxi back to the hotel after he'd done so. But she didn't want to delve too deeply into what alternative means he'd likely use.

This time, when it seemed as if they were driving around the city in circles, it wasn't because she'd told him to turn the wrong direction toward All-Med. It was because he was doing it deliberately.

Just in case. The realization was sobering.

Then finally, *finally,* he pulled up to a nondescript hotel that seemed as if it was located about as far from All-Med's office as it could be.

"Amazing," he murmured. "This place is still here." He shot her a quick look. "Stay here. Keep the doors locked. This place is no St. Agnes."

She pressed her lips together. She was perfectly aware that many of the cheap hotels were more in the business of renting by the hour than playing home base for vacationing families. Judging by the few people she saw milling around, she suspected that the hourly rate probably wasn't all that high, either.

"I don't like this place," Eva said once Brody disappeared into the building.

"Neither do I," Angeline murmured. "But it might be the best we can do in a pinch. And Brody will make sure we're safe."

"Are you sure?"

Was she?

She swallowed, ready to offer the lie that would keep the girl from worrying any more than she already was.

But then she saw Brody heading back toward them, his stride long and purposeful. The lamppost nearby cast a circle of light over him, highlighting the sparkle of raindrops catching in his disheveled hair.

A curious calm centered inside her.

"Yes, Eva, I'm sure."

There wasn't an ounce of untruth in her words.

Chapter 7

"Here." Brody tossed the oversized room key into Angeline's lap as he climbed behind the wheel once more. He was becoming heartily sick of the rain. "It's a room in the very back. Supposed to be more...quiet than some."

She held the key between her long fingers. "You seem familiar with the place. Have you stayed here before?"

"No."

She lifted her eyebrows, clearly expecting more of an explanation.

He was more interested in getting rid of the All-Med vehicle as quickly and thoroughly as possible than he was in satisfying Angeline's curiosity over his sometimes misspent years.

He drove the truck around to the far back side of the

building. Habit had him cataloging not only the people loitering about but also the vehicles parked there, as well.

He parked, and took the key back from Angeline. "Let me check the room."

"More paranoia?"

"Paranoia keeps me sane, baby cakes." He opened the door, hit the door locks to lock them in again, and crossed the laughable excuse of a sidewalk to room number twenty-nine.

The interior wasn't going to win any awards, but it looked cleaner than he'd expected. The two beds appeared marginally adequate. Unfortunately, both had mirrors mounted on the ceilings above them, but they weren't in a position to be finicky. There was also a television, a couple of chairs and a bathroom.

He stepped into the doorway, gesturing for Angeline and the kids.

Neither Davey nor Eva wasted any time. They raced into the room, jockeying for first dibs on the bathroom.

Eva won.

Brody chucked Davey under the chin as he morosely stomped away from the door that his sister had shut in his face. "Get used to it, son. Girls *always* get dibs on the loo."

Angeline dropped the kids' pillowcase on the table. "Sounds like you speak the voice of experience."

"What's a loo?"

"A bathroom," Angeline told Davey when Brody didn't answer.

Dragging his thoughts away from the experience he *had* once had was difficult. Too difficult.

He must be more tired than he thought. Why the hell else would he keep thinking about Penny? About things that had occurred decades before?

His sister was dead.

Just like the rest of his family.

He didn't let himself think at all about the man who'd taken him in after that. Not when he blamed him for all of it in the first place.

Angeline was walking back and forth in front of him and the boy, evidently well into female mode as she clucked over the ceiling mirrors that Davey had just discovered and seemed fascinated by.

Wondering what kind of thoughts filled Angeline's head about the presence of the mirrors was enough, at least, to help Brody close the door on the past again.

When she noticed him watching her, dusky color filled her cheeks and she quite obviously turned her attention to the thin spreads on the bed, the pillows, the metal hangers hanging in the cupboard. Not even the surface of the dresser missed her examination.

"Sorry I don't have a white glove handy," he drawled.

Angeline pursed her lips together, and she'd probably have been appalled that the look didn't really have the intended effect on him. He didn't exactly feel taken to task when he was more interested in exploring the faint dimple that appeared, just below the corner of those smooth, full, pressed-together lips.

Flirting with Angeline was one thing. She was eminently flirtworthy. The perfect mark: a combination of smarts and wit and innocence—hell, he'd never be able to forget just *how* innocent after he'd stepped onto that particular buried mine—that combined together in one impossibly appealing package.

Fortunately, Eva opened the bathroom door then, ensuring that Brody—plagued with unwanted memories and inconvenient desires—didn't do something really stupid.

The young girl barely had time to get out of the way as Davey bolted inside.

The clothes that Eva had changed into in the SUV all those hours ago were mismatched and wrinkled, and he wasn't all that surprised when she hugged her arms around her thin body, giving wary looks to both him and Angeline, who was now busy trying to make some order out of the pillowcase contents. Eva sidled around the room to sit in one of the chairs near the small window next to the door.

The long ride after their precipitous exit from St. Agnes and then Puerto Grande had lulled her into a quiet acceptance of the situation. But now, her Stanley mind was probably ticking furiously away over everything that had occurred.

Angeline sighed, and pushed nearly all of the newly folded clothing neatly back into the pillowcase. It looked to him like what she'd left out was for the following day. Then she turned and folded her arms over her chest.

She, like he, hadn't had the advantage of changing out of the tunic and pants the nuns had provided and he wondered if she was as aware as he just how thin the linen really was as it closely draped her magnificent curves.

"You didn't manage to grab any pajamas," she told Brody.

He shrugged. That was the least of their worries. "That's what T-shirts are for," he dismissed.

She accepted it without argument.

Which only made his stupid brain drift on down the dangerous avenue of wondering just what Angeline usually wore to bed.

T-shirts?

Little silky nightgowns?

Nothing at all?

He scrubbed his hand down his face. He'd be better off envisioning her in thick flannel from head to toe, but suspected that even that wouldn't derail him. "Food," he said abruptly. "I'm gonna go scavenge up some food for everyone."

Eva couldn't hide the relief on her young face at that idea and Brody felt a pang inside. He'd pushed hard all that day and the kids had been troopers. Angeline, too, for that matter.

But they weren't used to being on the run.

He went to the door, opened it enough to look through the crack, then stepped out. "Angeline."

She joined him.

He pulled her farther out the door, closing it slightly so that Eva couldn't see. Being at the end of the building, he didn't worry much about being seen by any of the guys who were hanging around the hotel.

Angeline eyed him. "What is it?"

He deliberately reached out and grabbed her slender waist, pulling her until she stood less than a foot from him.

Her lips parted, startled. "Brody—"

When he lifted the hem of her tunic, her expression went frosty and she slammed her palms hard against his inner elbows.

"Relax," he muttered, even as he was sort of impressed with the strength behind the movement that had knocked his unprepared hands clean away from her all-too-lovely body.

He lowered his head toward hers, enjoying way too much how she stiffened. Whether it was pride or not that kept her from sliding a step back from him as he invaded her personal space even more, he couldn't tell.

He lifted the hem of her tunic again, drawing it right up over those curving hips. High enough to see the drawstring that held the pants—not very effectively he noticed—around her very narrow waist.

His fingers brushed against the satin-smooth plane of her belly.

She inhaled on a hiss. "What—"

"Shh," he hushed, and because he was running on no sleep, no food and clearly no smarts, he grazed his lips over hers.

Whether that shocked her more than the Glock he tucked into the front and center waist of her pants or not as he kissed her, he couldn't tell.

Fortunately though, some cells in his brain were still in functioning order, and he brusquely tugged her tunic back down in place, and stepped away. "Take care of Delilah for me."

Her hand slapped against her belly, obviously holding the weapon in place. "I don't want her. *This.*"

"I don't care." He knew she was capable of shooting it, because he knew what kind of training Hollins-Winword had put her through.

Even couriers needed to know how to fire a weapon whether or not it was ever likely to be necessary.

Besides, she'd grown up on a ranch. She'd probably known way more about firearms at an early age than *he* had.

Kids born to a British barrister and a surgeon didn't have much need to be around weapons.

Or they shouldn't have had a need if Cole would have just kept his distance from Brody's mother.

"Do you really think Rico would show up here?" Angeline lifted one hand, cutting off the pointless speculation going on inside his head. He'd given up years before wondering what would have happened if anything had been different.

"You drove around in so many circles, I don't even have a clue where in the city we are," she went on. "Nobody could possibly have followed us without us noticing."

"What I hope for versus what I know is possible are two very different things. There's an extra clip in your duffel bag. The cash I've got is in there, too."

"When did you put it in there— oh, never mind." She looked resigned. "You *are* just going out to get us some food, right?"

"Now, I am. Consider this a run through for when I take the SUV back to All-Med."

"When will that be?"

"Later. The point is, you have to be prepared for anything, Angeline."

She moistened her lips. He saw the swallow she

made work its way down her long, lovely throat. "O-okay."

"If I'm not back by dawn—that's *if,*" he emphasized when she looked startled, "I want you to go back to the office here, talk to Paloma. She said she'll still be working even in the morning. She used to be sort of trustworthy—"

"*Used* to be?" Her fingers closed over his wrists, only to let go again, to press against her waistband. "I'm really not liking the sound of this."

"Yeah, well, beggars can't be choosers. Necessity is the mother of invent— Hell." He dropped the light tone. "Just listen. She'll get you to a guy who can get you all to Puerto Rico."

"But what about the storm? There aren't even any flights going right now."

"*Now* is not tomorrow morning. Try not to agree to a price that'll use up all the cash—but do it if you have to. Once you get to Puerto Rico, look up a hotel called Hacienda Paradise. Owner's name is Roger. Think you can remember that?"

She looked insulted. "Of course. Roger. Hacienda Paradise. Hardly complicated."

"Tell him Simon sent you."

Her eyebrows rose. "Simon?"

"Just tell him. He'll get you back into the States."

"Just on the say-so of Simon. What is that? Another one of your aliases?"

He exhaled. "Can you do that?"

"Yes, I can do that. But it's not going to be necessary. Because *you're* going to be back." Her voice lost a little tartness. "Aren't you?"

"I'm going to try like hell," he said evenly. "But even the best situations can fall apart. And, sorry to say, babe, this isn't the best of situations. If I'd had a little more time to prep the op, it would have been kind of helpful. As it is, we're sort of flying by the seat of my pants."

"Well." She tugged at her disheveled hair. "Better your pants, than flying by someone else's."

"Babe." He pressed his hand to his heart. "I'm touched."

She exhaled suddenly, rolling her eyes, and reached for the door again to go back inside. "Just hurry up and get us some food, would you please? My stomach is about ready to eat through itself to the other side." She slipped into the room and closed the door.

He waited until he heard her slide the lock into place.

Good girl.

She's not a girl, you twit.

He ignored the voice, perfectly well aware that Angeline was entirely *all* woman.

Then he went in search of the only kind of sustenance he was going to be sharing with his beautiful, virginal partner.

By the time Brody made it back *with* food, Angeline had run the kids through baths and into their improvised pajamas—a pale green scrub top of Angeline's for Eva, and a T-shirt of Eva's for Davey. She supposed that he was just too worn-out to protest the T-shirt with the glittery princess printed on the front.

In any case, they were clean and barely keeping

their eyes open as they watched the grainy television channel showing a Spanish-dubbed version of an old American sitcom, when Brody knocked on the door.

Angeline's hand went to Delilah—she couldn't believe she was thinking of the Glock like another woman—that was tucked into her pants. It had been hidden there ever since he'd tucked it in her waistband, well over an hour earlier. She peeked through the dingy orange drape hanging at the window and relief made her feel positively weak-kneed at the sight of him standing on the other side of the door.

She quickly undid the lock and opened it for him.

He pushed the large brown bag into her hands and headed for the bathroom.

"Come on, my dears. Supper time," she said cheerfully.

Davey's tiredness almost miraculously abated at the idea of food. Eva, however, just shuffled silently to the table, slipping into one of the two chairs closest to the wall.

The feast Brody had returned with turned out to be a filling one. There were red beans and rice, and some sort of pork and chicken, tortillas and several bottles of water, as well as a few cans of soda with the easily recognizable kind of logos that transcended translation and a handful of wax-paper-wrapped sweet pastries. Soon Brody joined them.

Like Angeline, he sat on one side of the bed facing the table. And he ignored the paper plate she'd left for him, instead using the foil container that had held the beans and rice as his plate.

He didn't say much of anything as he ate, and when

he thanked her for the opened bottle of water she handed him, she knew something was up.

Not from the tone of his voice. Goodness, no. She could hardly ever tell anything from his voice—or not very accurately, anyway. Nor was it his expression, which was as inscrutable as it ever was. His blue eyes—she was almost positive now that they must be his natural color, because she hadn't once seen him take out or put in contact lenses since they'd stared up the mountain to St. Agnes—were unreadable.

And it certainly wasn't anything he expressed in words, which at the moment—around mouthfuls of food—tended to center on answering Davey's questions about how high did Brody think he could jump when using a mattress as a springboard.

Brody gave Angeline a quick look. "Wants to jump on the bed, does he?"

She nodded. "He wants to see his handprints on the mirror up there." It was better than if the boy had expressed too much curiosity over *why* there were mirrors on the ceiling. She hadn't let him jump on the bed, of course, but she'd still considered it a good sign that he wasn't becoming too distressed over their activities. She wished she could believe the same was true about Eva.

The girl was becoming increasingly withdrawn.

She didn't even bat an eye when Davey slid the onions he'd carefully picked out of his chicken concoction onto her paper plate or when he plucked her pastry out of its wrapper and broke a gargantuan piece from it.

"Davey," Brody said, his tone warning.

The boy's shoulders drooped. He handed the pastry back to his sister.

She just shook her head. She'd only eaten half her meal. "You can have it. I'm full, anyway." She began to push herself back from the tiny table. "Oh. May I be excused?"

"Of course." Angeline caught the thin paper napkin that had been on Eva's lap before it fell to the floor as the girl slipped out from between the table and the wall and went over to the far bed.

She climbed onto one side, and lay facedown, burying her head in the pillow.

"She just sleepy?" Brody's voice was low.

Angeline watched the prone girl for a long moment. She couldn't decide what was more worrisome— wondering what was bothering Brody that he wasn't telling her, or Eva's exhaustion. "I hope so."

"Well, sleep is what you all need," he said. He grabbed the other uneaten half of Eva's fruit-filled pastry, and polished it off in just two bites.

She began wrapping up the trash, setting aside the water and sodas they hadn't yet opened. They wouldn't go to waste because they'd definitely need them sooner or later. Brody stuffed the trash back into the sack. "I'll pitch it in the bin outside," he said.

Which only had disquiet curling through her all over again, because Brody's remaining task for the night had yet to begin.

She told Davey to wipe his hands and face and get into the unoccupied bed. "Brody, wait." She joined him at the door.

"Planning a little segregation of the sexes tonight?

Girls in one bed? Guys in the other?" His lips twitched as he lowered his head closer to hers. "They'd be good chaperones, babe, just in case you're worried that two nights in a row with me in the same bed might be more temptation than you can handle."

She felt her face heat. "Get over yourself, would you?"

He chuckled softly, but when he straightened again, his expression was serious. "Don't forget now. Palo—"

"Paloma. Roger, Hacienda Paradise. Simon. I know. I know."

He nodded and turned to go, but she put her hand on his arm, stopping him. "Something's bothering you," she said quietly. "What?"

His expression didn't change. "Nothing new."

"Right. Too bad I don't believe that." She looked over her shoulder at the children. Davey's attention was focused once more on the television set, and all she could see of Eva was the back of her head. "What happened when you went out for the food?"

"Nothing."

"And I believe that like I believe in Santa Claus."

"Well, you are as untouched as an eight-year-old," he drawled, "so it wouldn't surprise me at all to find you sitting in front of the fireplace every Christmas Eve ready to greet the jolly old dude with milk and cookies warm from your oven."

Her lips tightened. "Don't patronize me."

He sighed roughly. "There's nothing you can do about it anyway, so forget about it."

Her fingers tightened on his uncompromisingly hard arm. "Do...about...*what?*"

"I couldn't reach my handler."

She frowned a little. "So?"

He looked upward. "So. So, that's a problem."

"Because someone didn't answer a phone just once when you expected them to? Maybe he was busy."

"She."

"Fine. Maybe *she* was busy."

"Handlers don't do *busy*. They're available 24/7. Period."

She rubbed her neck. "Well, you'll just have to try again," she stated the obvious, and received a wry "you think?" look right back from him as a result.

"Getting us all back to the States is going to be a helluva lot easier with some help than without," he told her. "I'm not saying it's impossible without it. What I am saying is that it's…unusual…not to be able to reach her. Plus, no contact means no updates on the Stanleys' situation."

It was a sobering thought. "Who is your handler, anyway?" The world that Hollins-Winword operated in was often murky and ill defined. They didn't operate counter to the federal government, of course, who often found it helpful that the agency was able to move where official means were impossible. Nor did it matter if the problem was small and domestic, or invasive and international. The people involved with the agency were sometimes far-flung, and they certainly didn't operate out of any typical office building.

"You know I'm not gonna tell you," Brody was looking amused again. "No offense, babe, but that's strictly need to know."

"But what if I did need to know?" She hugged her

arms to herself. "Theoretically speaking, I mean. Would you ever break *those* rules?" She was acutely aware of his propensity for breaking others.

"It's pretty obvious there are plenty of rules I'm willing to break." His gaze drifted downward, seeming to hesitate around her mouth. "But there are a few—probably too few to make much of a saint out of me—that I won't." Then he closed the door.

She swallowed, her mouth suddenly dry. She wasn't sure just exactly what they were talking about, but she feared it had nothing to do with her question about his handler.

Chapter 8

Angeline was awake and sitting in the chair, facing the door, when the fingers of dawn light crept eerily around the edges of the ill-fitted orange window drape.

In one bed, Eva slept soundly. She hadn't stirred once all night long.

In the other bed, Davey slept, too, though he'd tossed and turned enough for both himself and his sister.

Climbing into bed, herself, was just not something she could make herself do. Not with Brody's "in case of emergency" instructions circling in her head.

Brody hadn't returned.

Which meant that, if she were a good Hollins-Winword agent, she'd get the children up and dressed and race down to the office and this Paloma whom Brody *thought* might be trustworthy.

She rubbed her eyes and the dim light just grew stronger.

Problem was, she *wasn't* a particularly good Hollins-Winword agent. She wasn't cut out for this cloak-and-dagger stuff. She was just a courier of information for them. That's all she'd *ever* been!

And he expected her to get the kids, ultimately, back to the United States and just leave him behind?

How on earth was she supposed to make herself do that?

Not even during her worst shifts in Atlanta had she felt so tired. So rattled. So unsure of herself.

It was even worse than—

The doorknob jiggled and she sat up like a shot, dragging her feet off the second chair so quickly that it tipped onto its back, bouncing softly on the threadbare carpet.

She tossed aside the bright blue towel she'd draped over her lap and Delilah after she'd raced through her own shower, and scrambled over the chair, nearly tripping on the legs as she made for the door.

She threw open the lock and yanked open the door.

Brody stood there, looking furious. "What the *hell* are you still doing here?"

"Be quiet," she muttered, "just be quiet." And she wasn't sure who she shocked more when she reached up and wrapped her arms around his neck. "Don't *ever* scare me like that again."

His arms had come around her back. "Angel—"

"You were gone *hours!*" She squeezed his neck again. For some reason she couldn't seem to stop herself from clinging.

"Okay. Ohhh-kay." He sounded a little strangled, and his hands went from her back to unhook the ones she'd locked around his neck like some manic noose. He worked the Glock she still held out of her clenched fingers, and tucked it in the small of his back, then closed his hands around her fists and pulled them between them. "Breathe, would you?"

She drew in a huge breath, hardly aware that she'd been holding it in the first place.

"Better." He reached over her shoulder and pushed the door wider. "At least you were armed," he said gruffly. "Get inside."

She backed up as he headed forward enough that he could close the door once more. "Wake them up."

He was still furious, she realized.

And though she felt some compunction for not having followed his exact instructions, she didn't feel overly apologetic, either.

After all, he'd arrived, hadn't he?

He'd arrived, she realized belatedly, wearing a completely different set of clothing than the disheveled tunic and pants that he'd left wearing.

"You've got different clothes."

He was righting the chair that she'd tipped over. *"Now."* He was clearly not referring to her observation.

She sidled past him, heading for Eva. The girl, when she finally sat up, looked glassy-eyed and pale.

Angeline frowned a little, pressing her palm against Eva's forehead. It didn't feel overly warm, though. "Come on, sweetie, it's time for us to get moving again." She pulled over the clothing that she'd set out the night before. "Can you get yourself changed?"

Eva nodded and without argument began exchanging the scrub top for her own jeans and sweatshirt.

Brody had disappeared into the bathroom. She heard the shower come on, and made a face at the closed door. Obviously he wasn't in such a hurry that he couldn't manage a few minutes for that particular necessity.

She turned her attention to Davey. Like the previous day, he didn't wake quite as easily as his sister. But when he did, he began dressing himself, assuring Angeline quite indignantly that he did not need help.

She hadn't even finished tucking the kids' improvised nightwear back into the pillowcase when Brody came out, dressed again in the unexpected blue jeans and dark blue T-shirt. His hair was wet and slicked back from his face, and without looking at her, he picked up her small toiletry bag sitting on the edge of the chipped white sink and began rummaging through it.

"Can I help you find something?"

His gaze met hers briefly in the mirror above the sink as he pulled out her toothpaste and her toothbrush and began brushing his teeth.

She didn't know what disturbed her more.

The fact that he was using her toothbrush, or the fact that she wasn't absolutely appalled that he was using her toothbrush.

He was still watching her through the reflection of the mirror.

She swallowed and bundled up the towel she'd been using as a lap blanket and stuck it back inside her duffel. She pulled on her sturdy boots again, and when she looked toward Brody again, he'd finished brushing his teeth and had soaped up his face with bar soap and was stroking her narrow pink razor over his jaw, muttering an oath with every pass.

Her eyes drifted down from the way the T-shirt stretched tight over his shoulders to the way it was nearly loose at his narrow waist where it—along with the grip of the weapon—was tucked into his jeans.

She quickly looked away again before he could catch her ogling his undeniably *fine* backside, and helped Davey tie his tennis shoes.

When she was finished, Brody was wiping the last bit of soap suds from his newly revealed jawline.

She turned her eyes from the bead of blood on his angular chin and told the kids to be sure to use the restroom before they left.

Once again, Eva—finally showing some energy—darted in first.

Davey's shoulders hunched forward and his head tilted back. "Gaaawwwwwl."

Angeline handed him the pastry that she hadn't eaten from the night before. "Maybe this'll help." She caught Brody's look. "What?" she said defensively. "It's basically a fruit Danish."

"Did I say something?"

She narrowed her eyes. "You didn't have to."

He moved toward her and dropped the toiletry bag in her hand. "Yet when I really *do* say something, you ignore it completely."

Her lips parted. "That is not fair."

His eyebrows rose. His jaw was still shiny and

damp and his raked back hair looked nearly black with
water. He looked like some archangel, fallen to earth.

And was mighty peeved about the entire process.

"Just how is it *not* fair, love? Did you head out at
dawn, like I told you to? Did you speak with Paloma?
Did you buy your way across the water to Puerto Rico?
Did you do any…single…thing… I told you to do?"
His voice dropped with every word, only succeeding
in making his anger even more evident. "Dammit,
Angeline, I trusted you to—"

"To what?" She refused to back away, but keeping
her chin up in the face of that dark, blue-eyed glower
was no small feat. She was also aware of Davey's avid
attention, but couldn't seem to stop her tongue. "To
leave you behind?" She propped her hands on her hips.
"How could you really think I could leave you behind?"

He exhaled, sounding aggravated beyond measure.
"Believe me, I think I could have managed to keep my
head above water, even without your help."

She sniffed imperiously, though the sarcastic words
stung. Deeply. "Well, next time, I won't make the same
mistake, I assure you."

"You'd better not."

She turned away and since both Eva and Davey
had taken their turns with the bathroom, she stomped
across the room and shut herself behind the door.

Only there did she let her shoulders relax.

She pressed her hand to her heart, willing its thun-
derous pounding to still, for the shudders working
down her spine to cease.

But she nearly jumped out of her skin a moment

later when he wrapped his knuckles on the other side of the wood panel. "Hurry it up," he told her brusquely. "We're rolling in five minutes."

She stared at the door. Stuck her tongue out at it and felt both foolish and better.

But before five minutes had passed, she'd finished the most necessary of her morning ablutions, and the four of them left the cheap hotel room behind, toting their ragtag belongings with them.

The air outside was chilly and damp; the sky above a heavy, dull gray that was turning to silver with every centimeter of sunlight that rose.

But it wasn't raining. At least not at the moment. It was one bright spot, she thought, as she took Davey's hand in hers and followed after Brody.

He did not, as she had expected, head for the office to consult with the still-unseen Paloma. Brody crossed the street, heading for the corner where he stopped beside a mustard-yellow taxicab. Despite the lack of a driver sitting behind the wheel, he pulled open the back door, tossed in Angeline's duffel that he'd evidently decided she was too inept to carry herself, and nudged Eva in after. Davey ran ahead to join his sister, and Angeline quickly broke into a jog herself.

Brody shut the door after Davey and flung open the passenger's door, then rounded to the driver's side.

She ought to have known not to be surprised by anything, but she couldn't help herself when she sat down in the front seat next to Brody. "Where's the driver?"

He shrugged. "Hopefully sleeping for another few

hours so we can ditch this someplace before he even realizes it's gone."

Another stolen car.

She sank her teeth into her tongue, determined to remain silent on the matter. He *was* supposed to be the expert, here.

It was strictly her problem that she immediately had visions of the two of them being forever incarcerated in some horrible jail cell on multiple counts of grand theft auto, and kidnapping. And the children—

She couldn't think that way. As long as Brody was around, the children would be safe.

The man in question was weaving through the streets that seemed congested even at such an early hour and Angeline faced the irony in her cogitations.

She was riddled with anxiety over his disregard for legalities, yet she still trusted that he'd see them all safely through this.

But then that's the way it had always been with Brody.

Equal measures of wary fascination and instinctive trust. Both of which she'd been wise to refrain from examining too closely.

Up until now, that had been fairly easy to do, considering how rare and brief their encounters had always been.

He slammed on the brakes suddenly, throwing his arm up to keep her from falling forward.

She pressed her lips together, painfully aware of his palm pressed hard against her sternum as the car shuddered to a stop.

She imagined she could feel each centimeter of those long fingers burning a tattoo into her skin.

So much for easy.

"You okay?"

She nodded even though she was aware that it was the children he'd addressed. Assured that they were, his gaze slid over Angeline and he pulled his palm away from her chest, wrapping it once more around the steering wheel.

Ahead of them, she spotted a three-car pileup. Judging by the trio of men standing around yelling and gesturing, she was fairly certain that nobody had been hurt. At least she couldn't see anybody still inside the vehicles.

Nevertheless, she threw open her door and ran forward, hardly aware of Brody's oath behind her.

She went first to the car that had been hit on both sides, looking through the windows. A woman was lying on her side across the backseat, her hands pressed to her distended abdomen.

Angeline scrambled with the door, but it was too badly crunched to open. She knocked on the window drawing the woman's attention. "Are you hurt?" She repeated it in Spanish when the woman gave her a confused look.

"My baby is coming too fast," she replied.

Naturally. Life wasn't giving any easy outs these days. Angeline smiled encouragingly and promised to return in a moment. She ran to the other cars that were thankfully empty now and headed back to the pregnant woman, trying the opposite door this time with no better results.

Brody was storming toward the cars and she ignored him as she managed to wriggle her arm through the window of the door that seemed to have less damage, and twisted her arm around enough to roll the window down farther. She was amazed it moved at all, given the sharp dent in the door. When it was down, she ducked through, running her hands cautiously along the woman's legs which were bared by the bright red dress she wore. *"Mi nombre es Angeline,"* she told the woman calmly.

"Soledad," the woman replied around panting breaths. "The other car, it came from nowhere. My husband—"

"He's out calling for help," Angeline blithely lied the assurance. As far as she could tell, the three men weren't doing a single productive thing but yelling obscenities at each other. "How far apart are your pains?"

"Minutes."

No easy outs and hellacious innings to boot, she thought. "I'll be right back," she promised the woman, and pulled her torso back out of the window. She turned, nearly bumping into Brody, who was standing behind her, looking thoroughly maddened.

"What the bloody hell do you think you're doing?" His voice was calm. Pleasant even.

She actually felt herself start to quail. But a cry from the woman trapped in the car stiffened her resolve. "She's in labor," she told him hurriedly. "Both doors are jammed. You need to see if any one of those guys—" she threw out her arm "—has called for help."

"In case you've forgotten, we are sort of in the middle of our *own* emergency."

She lifted her hands at her sides. "Is Ri— our friend on our tail right this minute? Have you seen him?" She didn't wait for an answer. "What would you really have me do, Brody? Ignore that poor woman? Good heavens, at least *this* sort of thing I'm trained to handle!"

"Deliver a lot of babies on the side of roads do you?"

"This will be my tenth, if you must know! Now make yourself useful and find some way to get one of those doors open." She pushed past him and hurried back to the taxi.

Eva and Davey were sitting with their arms crossed over the back of the front seat as they watched the action unfold in front of them. Angeline managed a quick look into Eva's face and felt a little better about the girl—she'd worried when she'd woken her that she might be coming down with something. But now, she looked more like her regular self again.

Angeline dragged open her duffel, rooting past the clothes and the small toiletry bag. She dragged out the blue towel again and her bottle of waterless antibacterial soap. Then, at the very bottom of the bag, she found her first-aid kit. She tucked the webbed strap of its holder over her shoulder. "Eva, can you hand me one of the water bottles?"

Eva pulled one out of her pillowcase-luggage and handed it over. "What're you doing?"

"There's a woman about to have a baby in that blue car," she said. "I'm going to help her. You two wait here in the taxi, okay?"

"Brody looks mad," Eva said.

"He's just concerned that we get you two back to the States as quickly as possible." The last part was truthful, at least. "Hopefully, this won't take too long and we'll be doing just that before you can say Jack Sprat."

"Huh?"

She smiled and shook her head before hurrying back to the vehicle. Brody had evidently convinced the arguing parties to pool their efforts in more productive ways since two of them were leaning their weight against a crowbar, trying to work the least mangled door free.

"Wait." Angeline waved off their work for a moment. She tossed her collection of supplies through the window onto the front seat. "Help me climb inside first," she told Brody in English. "I'm worried that she's too far along to wait until you get the door jimmied."

The distinctive wail of sirens suddenly filled the air.

"Great," Brody muttered. "You're playing Nurse Nightingale and the freaking police are getting ready to join the party."

"You're the one used to adapting to the situation. Adapt." She tucked her head and torso through the window as far as she could. "You'll have to push me the rest of the way." She'd do it herself, but she simply couldn't gain enough leverage to either pull or push herself through.

His hands circled her waist and he nudged her inches forward. She wasn't exactly a wide load, but her hips had always been more curvaceous than she'd have liked, and the window was hardly generous. She shimmied and sucked in a hard breath when Brody's hands moved from her waist to plant square against her derriere.

"Desperate situations necessitate desperate measures," he said, sounding amused as her rear cleared the window's confines and she pretty much landed on her face on the front seat.

She dragged her feet in after her. "Keep working on the door," she said, not looking at him as she maneuvered her way awkwardly into the backseat.

The woman was drenched in sweat and amniotic fluid.

Angeline smiled again as she started to draw the woman's soaked skirt upward.

"Are you a doctor?"

"Sort of." Angeline didn't hesitate. "Have you had other babies?"

The woman nodded. *"Tres."*

"Ah. Then you're an old hand at this," Angeline said brightly. She kept up a running conversation in Spanish with the woman—as much as her panting would allow at any rate—to keep her distracted from the pain. She doused her hands liberally with the antibiotic soap, and reminded herself as she checked the woman for dilation that Miguel and Maria Chavez had delivered children with even fewer sanitary conveniences.

Soledad was not just fully dilated, the baby was already crowning.

With the sirens drawing ever nearer, Angeline reached over the seat to drag open her meager medical kit. She had a few packages of sterile gloves but didn't bother at this late stage. She did, however, rip open an alcohol pad to drag it over her sharp little scissors, which were all she had in the kit to cut the umbilical cord with.

"Madre de dios," she heard one of the men breathe outside the windows.

Ignoring them all, Angeline kept encouraging Soledad not to push just quite yet. "Pant, one, two, three, that's right. Good, good." She grabbed a paper-wrapped spool of sterile gauze from the kit, as well as the small blue aspirator bulb, and dropped both on the crumpled dress covering Soledad's belly. "Okay, now, push. That's it. *Push,* Soledad." The baby's head emerged and Angeline caught her breath at the awe-someness of the moment.

No matter how many babies she'd helped delivered it always seemed a miracle to her.

"Keep panting, Soledad. Hold off on pushing for just a moment." She grabbed the bulb and gently, quickly suctioned the infant's nose and mouth. "All right, now. Let's finish the job now. Come on, you can do it. Push!"

The woman gave a mighty yell, hunching forward, and the rest of the baby seemed to nearly squirt right into Angeline's hands.

Soledad's head fell back against the door behind her, exhausted. Angeline joggled the slippery infant in her hands, clearing the mucus again. Already the tiny girl's skin was pinkening and she let out a mewl-ing, very healthy howl.

Soledad cried, pressing her hands against her chest.

"Congratulations, Mama. You have a beautiful daughter," Angeline told the woman, and wrapped the baby in the blue towel that had so recently, she realized surreally, hidden a Glock in her lap. She settled the baby on the woman's belly and ripped open the gauze, cutting off a length to tie around the umbilical cord.

Behind her, the door to the car suddenly sprang open and the men began yelling again as if they'd never stopped. If it weren't for the hands Brody held out for her, Angeline would have tumbled out onto her backside.

"Easy does it," he said, holding her in place. His chin hooked over her shoulder, his chest pressed against her back. "Amazing," he murmured, looking at the tiny baby swathed in terry cloth.

Angeline finished making the knot. She could see the ambulance that had finally pulled up, so she didn't bother tying off the cord a second time in order to cut it. She'd leave that, as well as the afterbirth and washing up the baby to the emergency crew.

As it was, Angeline's wonderfully clean clothing that she'd donned after her shower were—once again—somewhat less than pristine.

With her adrenaline finally slowing, Angeline leaned closer to the baby again. "God speed to you both," she told Soledad.

"*Gracias,* Angeline." The new mother caught Angeline's hand with her own. *"Gracias."*

"We'd better move out of the way," Brody told her softly. The ambulance crew had wheeled a stretcher alongside the wreck.

She ducked her head inside the car just long enough to retrieve her kit, and then they were heading toward the taxi.

It was Soledad's husband who provided the distraction they needed. When he spotted the officer, he ran forward, his hands gesturing wildly as he continued sharing the tale that, Angeline suspected, would just grow in scope with each telling.

They climbed into the cab and showing great decorum, Brody backed up and turned around, pulling into the first side street he came to. Only then did he allow himself to put on some speed.

"Was it gross?" Davey was bouncing in the backseat where there was a lamentable lack of seat belts. "You sure *look* kinda gross, Angeline."

Angeline laughed a little, though her nerves were beginning to set in, making her feel shaky.

"I don't think she looks gross at all," Brody countered.

She gave him a surprised look only to have her gaze captured for a long moment by his.

"In fact, I think she looks pretty amazing."

She swallowed. Hard.

Then he turned that disturbing intensity back onto the road in front of him and it was as if that tight, breathless connection had never occurred. "But you should ditch the T-shirt right now for something less noticeable." His voice was brusque. "God only knows whose attention we've earned *now*."

Chapter 9

Whether or not their detour drew attention, Brody managed to drive through the city without further delay or mishap. Angeline, calling on every pragmatic cell she possessed, exchanged her soiled top right there in the front seat next to Brody for a fresh T-shirt that Eva pulled out of the duffel for her. And the shirt was left, crumpled on the floorboard right along with the taxi that he parked in a teeming lot near the airport. The lot was already congested with cars—what was one more, even if it was big, bright and yellow?

Before they caught one of the city buses that carried them to yet another corner of Caracas, Brody instructed the kids to address him and Angeline as Mom and Dad from here on out. It seemed to bother them much less than it did Angeline, who sat there twisting the mock wedding ring around and around her finger.

Once more, they were showing more resilience than she felt. And if they were feeling paralyzed with worry over their *real* parents, they weren't showing it.

The first bus was followed by three others until finally, they walked into a small, dusty building that sat at the end of an airstrip.

The International Airport it most certainly was *not*.

Fortunately, Angeline had had her share of experiences with small planes back in Wyoming, so she wasn't completely thrown when in short order they were taking off in a minuscule six-seater piloted by a smiling young man who talked a mile a minute.

He didn't seem to notice or care that Brody's responses to his nonstop dialogue were few and far between. Calling them curt would have been charitable.

As for Angeline, she was kept plenty busy keeping Davey from squirming out of his safety belt because he was insatiably curious about everything. Keeping Davey contained was better than looking out the window, though, at the expanse of water beneath them.

When they landed, without incident, in Puerto Rico, Angeline had a strong, *strong* desire to drop to her knees and kiss the dusty unpaved runway on which they'd landed. Instead, she kept the children's attention diverted from the exchange of money between Brody and the pilot.

Then it was a hair-raising cab ride—this time with the proper driver—and more money exchanged hands before they landed on the doorstep of Hacienda Paradise.

It was considerably smaller than even the hotel in

Caracas had been, yet *this* one looked as if it had been designed as a vacation home away from home.

Pristine stucco looked particularly white with the vivid ochre arches over the doors and windows and the wealth of flowering bushes planted against the walls. Situated on a hillside, she could see the ocean beyond and despite the pervasively gray, cloudy sky, it was still a beautiful sight.

They went in through the colorful main door where the interior was as lovely and welcoming as the exterior. There was an expanse of gleaming terra-cotta tile, dozens of potted plants and warm rattan furnishings—all covered with cushions in varying patterns and colors that combined as a whole in pleasing results.

"Wait here," Brody said, gesturing at the collection of tropical-print-upholstered sofas in the lobby. "I haven't seen Roger in a long time and let's just say that we didn't part on the best of terms."

Angeline was too tired to let that little revelation rock her, and she was happy enough to sit and wait for whatever reception they received. The truth was, the run of sleepless nights was beginning to catch up with her. And the rattan sofas were *so* comfortable. She let out a long, soft sigh.

Beside her, Eva made a similar sound. Davey, however, was beyond overtired. He was in constant motion.

Brody crossed the tile heading toward the shining wood reception desk, but before he made it halfway, an exceedingly handsome black man, dressed completely in white, headed for him, a smile wreathing his face.

"Simon," he greeted, his English tinged with an islander's lilt. Without a moment's hesitation, he grabbed Brody in a massive bear hug, slapping him on the back.

Angeline tucked her tongue in the roof of her mouth.

Looked to her like the men were on pretty good terms.

And obviously, she'd been right about "Simon" being another one of Brody's aliases. She watched him turn toward her, extending his long arm. "Darling," he called, using the most perfect British accent she'd ever heard, "come and meet my old friend, Roger."

"Why'd he call him *Simon*," Davey whispered.

Angeline gave Eva a look as she slowly rose.

"That's his name for now," Eva whispered to her brother, pulling him onto her lap. "Don't forget."

"But I thought we was supposed to call him Mr. Dad."

"Just Dad. We are. Shh. We don't want anyone to hear."

Angeline gave them an encouraging smile and continued forward. Her conscience niggled at her for approving of the quick way they adapted to deception. It was disquieting how easily she stomped out that niggling, too.

She reached Brody and Roger and pinned what she hoped was a natural-looking smile on her face. Keeping it firmly in place when Brody slung his arm around her shoulders and pulled her up snug against his side took even more effort.

"Roger Sterling, this is my beautiful wife, Angie. Darling, this old reprobate is an old…friend of mine."

Roger clasped her hand in both of his, bending low to kiss the back of it. "Beautiful Angie. Welcome to my Hacienda. But what your Simon isn't telling you is that we used to work together."

Brody squeezed her shoulder when she gave a little start. "Oh?" She managed to look enquiringly up at her "husband."

"That was aeons ago, Rog." Brody smiled at her. "Back in our ideological youth."

"Youth?" Roger tossed back his head and laughed. "Not even those ten—no, it's twelve years ago now—could you or I claim youthfulness. Now, who are those young ones over there watching us with big brown eyes? Surely not—"

"Angie's kids," Simon-Brody said. "I'm afraid her first husband—"

"—don't bore the man with that old tale, darling," Angeline interrupted. She looked up at Roger who was nearly as tall as Brody. "Simon's a wonderful father," she lied as if she'd been doing it all her life. And it wasn't all a lie, because the fact was, Brody was good with the children. "He even insists on bringing them with us every time we go on vacation."

"So this *is* a holiday?" Roger looked back at Simon. "I'm wounded, old man. You should have given me some notice. As it is, I have only two rooms available."

"We're actually on our way back to the States. If you can let us hole up for one night, we'll be—"

"Sure, sure." Roger lifted his hand, cutting off Simon's words as he went back to the reception desk. He produced an old-fashioned key and came back, dropping it into Brody's palm. "Nothing but the best for my old debating partner. Do you have luggage?"

"Nothing we can't manage," Simon-Brody assured.

He looked at the room key, on which Angeline could see engraved in gold the number ten. "This have a good location?"

"The best," Roger assured. "Perfect view of the pool in one direction and the ocean in the other. I'll have one of my boys show you back."

"No need." Brody slid his hand down Angeline's arm, linking his fingers through hers. "We'll catch up later, after we've had a chance to settle the kids."

Roger's smile was still in place as Brody collected the children in their wake and they all headed back out the front door and around to the side where he'd left her duffel and the children's purloined pillowcase.

"So, *Simon,* you worked with him, did you?"

He ignored her soft comment, and continued striding along the flower-lined sidewalk until they reached the end of the lovely building.

The door Brody stopped at was in the very rear of the courtyard. He unlocked it, quickly set their ragtag belongings inside, and then ushered them in. He pressed his fingers to his lips as he shut the door and fastened the locks.

All four of them.

She frowned a little at the sight of so many locks, and then leaned back against the door as he went into the same hunt-and-seek mode that he'd used at the convent.

Since this room was not a room at all, but a suite, she expected that it might take him some time to appease his paranoia.

Eva pointed to the couch, silently checking with Brody before throwing herself down on it when he nodded. Brody had already turned on the television, and she picked up the remote, slowly flipping through the channels that offered a seemingly dizzying assortment of options.

Angeline unlatched Davey from her hip and picked him up. His head snuggled down into the crook of her neck. "Come on, bud," she whispered. "Let's you and I go have a lie down." She peeked through the open doorways. The first was a bathroom—standard, albeit well-appointed.

She passed it by for the next doorway. A bedroom. Two twin beds, each with its own chair, table and lamp beside it. The last doorway, separated from the other two by a neatly appointed kitchenette, contained only one bed, which looked wide enough to sail home on. Attached to that was another bathroom, this time with a tub large enough for a party.

At least a party of two.

The guilty thought taunted her as she turned tail and headed back to the twin beds.

There, she curled up on the wonderfully soft mattress with Davey tucked against her. She felt reasonably confident that if she kept him still for even five minutes, he'd get the nap he badly needed.

Sleep dragged enticingly at her, and she told herself she'd just grab a nap. A little one.

Then she could face whatever was next on Brody's plan.

While Angeline napped, Brody finished searching every inch of the bedroom right around them.

He added the surveillance bugs he found there to

the small pile of them that was growing on the top of the fancy, satellite-fed television.

On the couch, Eva was sleeping, too. She'd lasted all of ten minutes after Angeline and Davey had hit the mattress.

Catching some shut-eye himself was mighty appealing, but first he'd finish searching out the rest of the suite.

One advantage was that Roger hadn't changed his style over the past decade. When Brody felt reasonably confident that he'd discovered every listening device, he dropped them by handfuls into a glass pitcher that he found conveniently provided in the nicely equipped kitchenette.

Then he filled the pitcher with water and stuck the entire thing inside the refrigerator.

Roger would be pissed, but Brody didn't care.

Then, he went into the main bedroom with its decadent bathroom en suite. He tossed Angeline's duffel on the dresser and rooted shamelessly through it until he found her first-aid kit. He flipped it open, cataloging the contents, and then worked the T-shirt over his head, managing not to dislodge the bandage that he'd taped there what seemed days earlier.

It hadn't been days, though.

It had just been that morning, before dawn.

"Oh, my *God.*"

He whipped his head around, wincing as the adhesive tape he'd slapped copiously around the mound of gauze pads over his ribcage pulled. "I thought you were sleeping," he groused.

Angeline's lips were parted, her gaze trained on the

less-than-professional work he'd made of the bandage. She stopped next to him and prodded her fingers none too gently against his shoulder. "Turn so I can see better. Good Lord, Br—Simon, who taped up this mess?"

"*I* did," he admitted grumpily. He didn't assure her that the suite was safe to speak openly, though.

She huffed, and began picking at the edge of one long strip. "It clearly didn't occur to you to say something about this earlier." Her voice was snippy, a perfect accompaniment to her withering expression. She freed the edge finally and took definite delight in yanking it off his skin.

He winced. "Hells bells, woman. Go a little easy there."

She tore another strip, literally, off his hide. "Why? You're the big macho man who doesn't have to admit to any sort of weakness." She yanked a third off.

He yelped and covered her hand with his. "Dammit! What is this? Nurse Ratchet has replaced the saintly Florence?"

But he realized that her hand beneath his was trembling.

"Dammit," he said again, only this time with far less heat.

He slid his arm around her shoulders as she turned into him, burying her face against his chest, inches above where the gauze had done a reasonable job of keeping the seeping knife wound from staining his shirt.

Her hand swept up his spine. "What happened?" Her voice was muffled, her words warm puffs against his flesh. "*Was* it our, uh, our friend? No wonder you were so furious when I insisted on stopping to help Soledad."

"It wasn't him." He circled her braid with his fingers; it was thick as her wrist and silkier than anything he'd ever felt in his life. So much for thinking that he'd keep her at a distance if she thought they might be listened in on. "Merely a couple blokes who didn't appreciate me interrupting their drug deal."

"Merely." She shuddered against him. "God. You should have said something sooner. Like when you came back to the hotel this morning."

"We were already running late. Too late."

She tilted back her head, her dark eyebrows pulling together. Her hand settled over his bandaging as gently as a whisper.

In its way, that soft touch was more painful than her wrenching off the sticking adhesive strips.

"This is why you weren't back before dawn."

"Yes."

She moistened her lips and ducked her forehead against his chest again. Ground it softly against him.

A whole new set of pain surged; the kind he couldn't—wouldn't—allay.

As if realizing it, she went still for a gut-twisting moment. Then she took a step back. The thick ridges of her braid slid smoothly out of his hand.

She gathered up the first-aid kit. "Come into the bathroom," she said. "There's probably better light in there." She led the way, turning on every light—and there were a good half-dozen of them.

"Sit there." She gestured at the wide plank of earth-toned granite that spanned the distance between the two hammered copper sinks.

He sat.

She ran water until it was hot in one of the sinks, and wet one of the thick washcloths, which she then held over the adhesive, helping to loosen what he now considered an overly effective death grip. Then patiently, she managed to coax the strips loose until she could peel away the gauze that he'd bunched together over the slash.

She sucked in a hard breath when she saw the extent of the wound. She tossed the gauze into the other unused sink. "This should have been sutured."

"I didn't have a lot of free time," he reminded, trying not to wince like a damn baby.

But, *Christ,* it hurt.

Her slender, deft fingers moving on him were causing plenty of their own torment, too.

She made a soft hmming sound, and wet another cloth with warm water, which she used to clean away the dried blood around the perimeter of the gash. "How, exactly, did this happen? There were two of them?"

"Three."

She hmmed again. It reminded him of his mother, actually, whenever she was withholding judgment over his defense of some mischief he and Penny had gotten into.

For once, thinking of his sister didn't make everything inside him want to shut down. Maybe it was just because it seemed to be happening more often, lately.

Maybe it was just the company he was keeping of late.

She cast a look up at him through her lashes. The compress carefully moved over the gash and drizzled warm water over it. "And?"

She was using plenty of water. It slid down his belly, soaking into his jeans. At the rate she was going, he'd be out of dry pants for the rest of the day.

"And nothing. They didn't like me interrupting them."

"But where were you? Where'd this happen? At the All-Med office, or after?"

"After."

She pursed her lips, bringing into evidence that little dimple below her lips—situated there like some pretty birthmark on a long-ago pinup girl. "I don't suppose you went to the police."

"No." His voice was dry.

"How'd you get the supplies to bandage yourself up?"

"You mean the stellar example of proper first aid that you so admire?"

The dimple disappeared as she smiled. "Ah, now there's the wit I know." She dropped the sopping cloth back into the water in the sink, sending a small cascade over the edge where it soaked into his jeans.

"I'm going to need to use Roger's damn laundry service," he muttered.

"Where *did* you get the clothes?"

"In the same drugstore where I pinched the gauze and tape."

"You actually found a drugstore that was open at that hour?"

He gave her a look.

"Oh, dear." She sighed faintly. "Does it not bother you *at all* to avail yourself of…of…things that don't belong to you?"

"Nobody's going out of business as a result of it," he defended drily. "And the trucks have all gone back to their rightful owners, assuming that your peeps at All-Med made it up to St. Agnes already." When things got back to normal, he might just have to satisfy his curiosity over who'd donated that unusual equipment to the convent…and why.

"There's the Jeep we left stuck in the mud."

"Hey. I'll have you know that I purchased that decrepit transport, and paid a few bucks *more* than I ought to have, considering its deplorable condition."

"Really." She stepped back, holding the tube of antiseptic aloft. "Who'd you buy it from then?"

"Some lad in Puerto Grande, if you must know." If he'd heard that defensive tone in anyone else's voice he'd have laughed uproariously. As it was, he was considerably annoyed by it. "His whole family was trying to sell off nearly all their belongings," he finished. "A bicycle missing a wheel, a radio that was a good twenty years old, a swaybacked excuse of a mule. They were trying to get enough together to pay for the kid's sister's first—"

"—first semester of college," she finished, taking the words right out of his mouth.

He frowned. "Yeah."

"Puerto Grande is a small village," she murmured.

"We all knew about the Zamora family. Brisa is the youngest and will be the first member of their family ever to go to college. *You're* the one who bought their Jeep."

"Isn't that what I've been trying to say?"

She smiled softly and stepped forward again, right into the vee of his legs. Her chocolate-brown eyes were on a level with his mouth, and their focus seemed to be fixated there. "What am I going to do about you, Mr. Simon?"

He dug his fingers into the granite on either side of him.

Of course, the stone didn't have a helluva lot of give.

Not like the gilded skin stretched taut over her supple arms would.

He deliberately racked his head against the expanse of mirror behind him.

"You're going to bandage me up," he said, but his voice was gruff. Damn near hoarse.

"In a minute," she whispered. She leaned into him, tilting her head, and light as a whisper, she rubbed her lips over his.

Chapter 10

She'd started out feeling tenderness.

That was all, Angeline assured herself. Just tenderness for this man whose unexpected acts of kindness touched her just as much as his more "creative" stunts shocked her.

But tenderness was abruptly eaten up in the incendiary flames that rose far too rapidly for her to fight.

Instead, she stood there, caught, as a wildfire seemed to lick through both of them.

His arm came around her shoulders, an iron band holding her needlessly in place, his mouth as hungry as hers. A sound, raw and full of want, rose in her throat—or was it his?

She couldn't tell, and didn't much care, as he pulled her tighter against him, tighter until she felt the heat of his bare chest burning through her T-shirt, tighter until she felt that undeniably hard ridge rising and pushing against her, making her want to writhe against him in response.

Her fingers pressed greedily into the sinewy muscles cording his bare shoulders and she dragged in a hoarse breath when his lips burned from hers, down over her cheek. Her jaw. Her neck.

His hand curled around her braid, tugging her head back more, until he touched his tongue to the pulse beating frantically at the base of her throat. Again that needful moan filled the room.

It was definitely coming from her. A thoroughly unfamiliar sound—one that was vaguely shocking in some far distant reach of her mind.

She stared up blindly at the gleaming light fixture above their heads. Pinpoints of light shone in her mind, less from the bulbs than from the dazzling wonder of his touch.

Without conscious direction, her hands slid over those wide, wide shoulders, around his neck, into his brown hair that slipped, smooth and thick, through her sifting fingers.

Her braid bunched in his hand, he cupped the back of her head, pulling her mouth back to his. His other hand swept down her spine, around her hip, between them, urging her closer, closer—

"Ouch, oh, sh—" He yanked his head back, knocking his head against the mirror again, this time far less intentionally. "*Bloody* hell."

Angeline froze, reason returning with one swift, hard kick.

She stared at his chest, at the hideous knife wound

running parallel to his ribs that looked as if it would bleed again at any moment, at his large hand still cupped over her breast.

His thumb moved, rubbing over the tight hard crest that only rose even more greedily for him.

Horrified at herself, she jerked back, snatching up the antiseptic tube from the floor that she'd dropped somewhere along the way.

Like when she'd been dragging her hands all over his body, completely forgetting the basic fact that the poor man was wounded!

"I'm sorry," she said quickly. She fumbled with the threaded top on the tube. She got it off, only to have the tiny top slip through her shaking fingers. "I... I don't know what I was thinking."

"I know what *I* was thinking." His voice was even deeper than usual. Huskier.

And it sent another ribbon of desire bolting through the ribbon parade already working from her heart down to knees that felt as substantial as jelly.

"I shouldn't have done that." She licked her lips, forcing her attention to stay on his wound as she squeezed an uneven glob of antibiotic cream over it.

He sucked in a hard breath, the ridged muscles of his abdomen jerking. "No, *that* you shouldn't have done," he muttered, and caught the hand delivering the cream and dragged it away before she could do more damage.

She sank her teeth into her tongue for a long moment, trying to master the burning behind her eyes before she did something even more embarrassing than throwing herself at him. "I need to d-dress your wound."

His teeth bared slightly. His eyes were slits of blue between his narrowed lashes. "Pardon me if I tell you that I'd rather *you* just simply undress."

Angeline felt as if she'd lost her ability to speak.

So she just stood there.

Staring at him.

Wanting him.

He looked like an oversized jungle cat, lying in wait for his prey to draw near. And *she* was the prey.

"Here."

She blinked, looking stupidly at the packet of gauze pads he'd picked up from the kit beside him.

"Come on, Angie. Finish the job."

Angie. And spoken in that perfectly British accent that she realized, belatedly, he hadn't dropped for even one moment.

She sucked in another hard breath, this one formed of cold, hard mortification.

He suspected they were being listened in on. He'd done his usual search and destroy, but had he found some sort of bug, after all?

Had someone really been *listening* to them?

To her? To that utterly sexual moan that had flowed out of her, more than once?

She racked her brains, trying to think if she'd said his name, as well—God, it had been screaming through her mind, her body—

She snatched the packet from him and tore it open. Tossed the sterile packaging aside to gently fit the gauze over his wound. "It would be better if I had a few butterflies instead of just this gauze to pull it together more tightly." The hoarseness of her voice went a long way toward diffusing her brusque words.

"Keep talking, babe." He'd tilted his head back slightly, watching her from beneath his lashes. "I'm getting hotter by the second."

She flushed and layered on more gauze, creating a cushioned dressing. He pulled the spool of tape from the kit and held it looped over his finger.

Unfortunately, his finger was attached to his hand that was resting on the very firm bulge of thigh covered in somewhat damp denim.

She swallowed on her dry throat again, and slid the tape off his finger, trying to pretend that she wasn't perfectly aware of his erection mere inches away.

She tore off a length of tape and carefully sealed the edges of the dressing. "This is paper tape. It won't hurt when we have to change it," she assured, putting all of her effort into keeping her voice steady and smooth, and failing miserably. "But you'll want to keep it dry, so when you shower, we'll cover it with plastic first."

"Easier to take a bath. You can wash my back."

Her gaze slid guiltily to the enormous built-for-two tub and she knew, if he told her to turn on the taps right that instant, she'd have been hard pressed not to do just that. No matter that the walls might have ears, no matter that Eva was sound asleep in one room on the couch and Davey in another.

No matter that she'd never shared a bath with any man, much less shared her body.

When it came to Brody-Hewitt-Simon Paine, she

feared she was excruciatingly willing to share *everything*.

She pressed her palms together, feeling the wedding ring on her finger. It no longer felt so strange wearing the gold band.

Which was a realization that on its own was enough to make her feel somewhat daunted.

"Do, uh, do you need something for the pain? I've only got over-the-counter stuff, I'm afraid, but you could take a prescription dosage of it."

"Is that the only pain you're willing to take care of?"

She opened her mouth. Closed it again before the assurance came out that she didn't really mean, anyway. Instead, she admitted the raw truth. "No."

His eyes narrowed again. He let out a hiss between his teeth. "You know how to make it hard on a man, don't you." His voice seemed to come up from somewhere deep inside him.

She flushed all over again.

"No pun intended," he added.

The flush grew even hotter.

He sat forward, wincing a little as he pressed his palm against the new dressing, and straightened from the granite countertop. "You know, it's a lot easier to resist you when I think you're going to be strong enough for the both of us. If you're going to look at me with those eyes a man could drown in and be *honest* like that, I don't know what the hell to do with you."

Her eyebrows rose with sudden boldness. "You don't *know?*"

He gave a short laugh. "Angeli—" He bit off the rest of her name.

She pressed her lips together.

"I don't often forget myself," he murmured. He lifted his hand and brushed the back of his finger down her cheek. "But you sure do have a way of getting me right to that point."

Her knees evidently decided jelly was too substantial, and dissolved into water instead.

Then he closed his hand around hers and drew her out of the sinful bathroom, past the bed she couldn't bring herself to look at and back into the main room where he opened the door of the refrigerator and gestured.

Angeline peered at the pitcher of water, which was the only thing inside, except for the gleaming shelves. "Good grief. Are those—?" At least three inches of metallic-looking discs—each no larger than a watch battery—were sunk in the water, filling the bottom of the pitcher.

Brody nodded.

He'd told her that paranoia kept him sane, but she'd sort of taken that as an exaggeration.

Looking at those dozens of discs now, she wasn't so sure it was an exaggeration.

Not when they were dauntingly real.

He pushed the refrigerator door closed again.

Angeline folded her arms tightly over her chest and looked around, as if she'd be able to see if there were any more bugs still hidden around. That, of course, was as likely as her being able to jump over the moon.

If Brody hadn't found them, why on earth would she?

"You think there might be others?" She looked back at him, only to find his gaze fixed on her arms, folded across her breasts.

The ribbon parade inside her jumped right back into action, sliding into an all-out rumba.

"Possibly."

She dropped her arms and deliberately turned her back on him, looking over at Eva, who still slept, sprawled facedown on the sofa. The television remote control sat on the rattan table next to the sofa. The device wouldn't be very useful, unless Brody saw fit to put the parts back together.

"Is this how Roger always greets you? With such, well, such *nice* accommodations?"

"Pretty much."

"But he said you worked together. With—" She didn't know what she could dare to say—whether she ought not to mention Hollins-Winword—but Brody, showing his usual perception, understood, anyway.

He shook his head.

Roger had talked about their association being twelve years past. But Angeline had been quite sure Brody had been with Hollins-Winword since his very early twenties. He'd told her that the very first time they'd met. She'd told him about coming from Wyoming and he'd told her he didn't come from anywhere.

And then he'd given her a gargantuan flirtatious grin and told her that if she needed anyone to show her the ropes, he had plenty that he'd be willing to lasso around her.

"Then what did you and he…" She trailed off when he lifted his hand. The universal *stop* sign.

She sighed. Her curiosity would have to go unappeased, obviously. At least for now. But later, she fully intended to discover more about the things that made Brody tick.

"I'm going to go out and stretch my legs," he said abruptly. "You'll be fine here, though. If you need anything, just ring Roger."

She looked toward the door again, with its four substantial locks. Not even in her apartment in Atlanta did she have that much security on her door. "Are you, uh, going to take the girl?"

He smiled suddenly. "Delilah, you mean? Yes."

Obviously, he didn't worry about someone wondering who Delilah was. "Are you going to try to reach your—" handler "—friend about our travel arrangements?"

"That's the plan."

"Will you be gone long?"

"Why? You going to miss me?" He tilted his head closer to hers, his voice dropping even lower. "Go swim in that big tub while I'm gone," he suggested. "Think of me."

She pursed her lips together, giving him an annoyed look that didn't fool him for a solitary second, if the unholy gleam in his eyes was anything to go by.

He disappeared into the bedroom and came out a minute later, the blue T-shirt back in place. He hadn't tucked it in, though, and she assumed that was all the better to hide Delilah with.

"The children will need to eat when they wake," she told him, wondering if whoever was listening—

if anyone was listening—thought she sounded like a proper wife.

"Then eat," he said simply.

Which made her feel idiotic. As if he thought she couldn't make a simple decision like that. "I *meant,* would you prefer that we wait for you to return, so we can all eat together." That's what families did mostly. At least in her experience.

Her parents had sat down at the dinner table nearly every night with her and J.D. and Casey while they'd been growing up. They'd talk about their day, sometimes they'd argue, but far more often than that, there was laughter.

And always there had been the security of knowing their roots were set in an unshakeable foundation.

It was the kind of home she'd wanted to make someday for *her* children, if she ever had any. These days, that desire had come less and less frequently, though. Not because she still didn't want it someday, but because it had become more difficult to see herself sitting across her own dinner table from the man of her dreams.

"Touching," he said, which made her search his expression for amusement.

But she found none and realized that was even more disturbing.

"I'll probably be back in an hour or so. If I'm not, go on down to the restaurant. Have Roger charge it to the room." At *that,* he did look amused.

Which made her wonder if he intended to finagle his way out of paying for their lodgings altogether.

She'd have asked, but assumed that was probably not one of those things he'd want to be possibly overheard.

"And if you're longer than that?" She couldn't help but think about his cautions back in Caracas.

She didn't need to elaborate. He understood, perfectly. "Same thing I said before still stands."

They were staying in a room that had been bugged, presumably by the owner himself. Yet he nevertheless believed the man would get her and the children back to the States, just because "Simon" had asked him to.

"I think there's an interesting story in there somewhere," she murmured.

"Not one worth the effort of retelling." He headed for the door, stopped short and backtracked, surprising her right out of her sanity again when he pressed a hard, fast kiss to her mouth.

She swayed unsteadily when he straightened and stepped away from her. His sharp eyes, of course, noticed her swaying around like a tree in a hurricane, and he gave a little nod. "Good," he murmured. "Glad I'm not the only one thrown for a loop." Then he strode to the door, flipped open the multiple locks and peered out.

Evidently, *some* things didn't change, just because they were currently ensconced in considerably nicer—albeit possibly surveilled—digs. "Lock these after me."

She was already heading for the door to do so.

A moment later, he was gone.

She slid the substantial locks into place and turned back to face the lovely suite. She suddenly felt cold, and it wasn't only the reminder that their purpose there at all wasn't a lighthearted one.

Hewitt and Sophia Stanley were still out there somewhere, being held against their will, and their children *were* in danger, as well.

What also had Angeline shivering, though, was the realization that for the first time in her life, she could put a face on the man who sat on the other side of the dinner table from her, with their children scattered along in between in that lovely image of the future.

Brody's face.

Yet he was the man who had—within the last forty-eight hours, no less—admitted that he had no yearning desire to stay in any one place for any particular length of time.

He was the least likely person she knew who'd ever even want that dinnertime ritual with the family, who'd want to see the sun rise and set day after day over the same horizon, much less the same home.

So what was she doing?

Was she keeping the man at arm's length, never taking his flirtations seriously, never letting herself get swept into the wake of his appeal?

No.

She was throwing herself right into his arms, and no amount of reminding herself all the reasons why doing so again would be a monumental mistake seemed to be enough to keep her from taking that flight again. Because, right or wrong, Angeline finally faced the truth.

She was in love with Brody Paine.

Chapter 11

Considerably more than an "hour or two" had passed before Brody returned later that day.

As Angeline had predicted, the kids had been ravenous when they'd awakened. Very aware of the bugs that Brody might not have discovered, she decided it was better to take Eva and Davey down to the restaurant.

She'd been afraid that the kids might slip—call her by her name or something, but they never did. Not even when Roger, insisting on meeting their every culinary desire—right up to and including Davey's requested deep-fried macaroni and cheese—had sat down at the table with them had they given anything away.

If anything, she was as wary of something coming out of *her* mouth. Squelching her curiosity over just how Brody and Roger were connected was nigh impossible, though she managed.

Just.

While Roger, on the other hand, seemed to feel free in asking plenty of his own questions about her relationship with Simon.

She tap danced her way around giving the man direct answers as much as she could, but feared she wasn't really fooling anyone.

Then, when Roger had turned his focus on the children, and asked how they thought their stepfather rated, she sat forward, giving Eva and Davey steady looks in return to the startled ones they gave her.

"They think he's wonderful, obviously," she assured Roger on their behalf. "Of course they love their father, as they should. But Simon has been good to all of us." She turned and smiled, full wattage, into his face, knowing perfectly well the effect that usually had on most members of the male species. "And what about you, Roger? Any woman and child keeping your home fire burning?"

His speculative smile turned regretful. "If there were a beautiful woman such as you who wished to burn any fires with me, I'd certainly consider setting several."

"Stop flattering my wife, old man," Brody said, appearing almost out of nowhere beside their table. He slid his hand, deliberately proprietary, over Angeline's shoulder, and left it there. "Just because you haven't found a woman of your own is no reason to go poaching in my territory."

"What is this accusation of flattery about?" Roger pressed his hand across his heart. "I speak only the truth."

Angeline just laughed lightly, and pushed her chair back, rising from the table. "My head spins," she assured. "But you'll have to excuse us. The children get restless if they sit too long at the dinner table." It was a blatant exaggeration and one that she felt slightly guilty for offering.

But only slightly.

Eva, Angeline noticed as the girl tucked her napkin under the edge of her half-empty plate, was looking a little flushed again. "The meal was very good," she said politely. "Thank you." She elbowed Davey.

"Thank you," he echoed, rubbing his side and giving her an aggrieved look.

"I'll join you in a few, love," Simon-Brody told her. "Roger and I have some catching up to do."

"Of course." She sent a smile Roger's way again, and ushered the children away from the table. She couldn't help wondering if the "catching up" had to do with the matter of getting the four of them back to the States.

"Can we swim?" Davey asked as they left the restaurant. They could see the pool through the gleaming windows overlooking the courtyard area of the hotel.

Angeline resisted the urge to look back at Brody. "Do you know how to swim?"

"My dad taught us," Davey said.

"We're s'posed to wait an hour after eating before swimming," Eva said, giving him a severe look.

"I think that's an old wives' tale," Angeline murmured.

"And besides, we don't have our swimsuits with us," the girl reminded.

They left the lobby behind and headed across the courtyard. "You've got a T-shirt and shorts," Angeline said. "You could wear that. In fact, let's just stop at the swimming pool, right now. You can roll up your jeans and dangle your legs over the side, at the very least."

"Yippee." Davey grabbed Angeline around the thighs and hugged her. He darted toward the pool.

Muffling an oath, Angeline nudged Eva ahead of her, hurrying after his precipitous race for the pool. In contrast to Davey's energy, Eva, however, was showing very little.

Angeline slipped her hand along Eva's ponytail. "Everything is going to be all right," she told her softly.

"I'm not a baby. You don't have to say things that might not be true." Eva sounded fierce, but Angeline still recognized the need beneath that begged for reassurance.

Her heart squeezed. She stopped there in the middle of the narrow sidewalk, facing Eva. Amidst the profusion of lovely flowering shrubs, it seemed hard to believe that anything terrible could touch them.

But Angeline had seen too much in her work to let herself believe that "prettiness" provided any sort of substantial barrier against disaster.

"I don't think you're a baby, Eva," she said with perfect truthfulness. "And I'm not lying because I think you can't handle the truth. I truly believe that this all will turn out fine in the end."

"Because of, um, Simon."

Angeline smiled faintly. She smoothed her hand along Eva's ponytail again. "Between him and the three of us, I think we've made a pretty good team."

She slipped her hand beneath Eva's small, pointed chin. "Keep your faith strong, sweetheart. Amazing things can result."

Her eyes shimmered. "My mom says stuff like that," she whispered.

Angeline let out a long sigh, and leaned down, hugging the girl's narrow shoulders. She knew she'd made the right move when Eva hugged her back. Tightly.

Her throat closed a little. What brave children the Stanleys were. "And I can't wait to meet her and tell both her and your dad what a fabulous pair of kids they've got," she said just as softly.

"I just wish I could talk to them." Eva's fists pounded against Angeline's shoulders in frustration.

"I know, honey. I know."

From his vantage point in Roger's second-floor office, Brody had a clear view of the courtyard and the pool. He saw Davey yanking off his tennis shoes and rolling up his pants. Saw Angeline stop and talk with solemn-faced Eva, then after a while, not looking quite so serious, they joined Davey poolside.

Soon all three of them were sitting on the edge of the pool, their pants up around their knees, as they kicked and splashed each other.

"You haven't told her, have you." Roger sat at his desk, where he'd just finished making the arrangements to help get them out of the country.

Brody leaned his shoulder against the tall window, taking his gaze off Angeline and the kids only long enough to scan the courtyard. Seeing nothing unusual among the lush landscape, he looked back at his *family*. "No point."

"You and I go back a long way, Simon."

"Too long," Brody drawled.

"We would have made a great team," Roger continued, ignoring the interruption. "If you hadn't bailed on me."

"I didn't bail."

"We didn't exactly hang out our shingle, either, my friend." Roger's voice never lost the gait of his native Jamaica, but now it sounded pretty dry. "Sterling and Brody," he reminded. "Attorneys at Law."

"Brody and Sterling," he corrected blandly. "And just because I didn't keep with the plan didn't mean *you* had to ditch it for all this." He gestured out the window. "You were never with Hollins as long as I was, anyway."

"True." Brody heard, rather than saw the fatalistic shrug his one-time partner gave. "I was recruited out of university, while you—"

"I was recruited out of grade school," Brody muttered, exaggerating only slightly. He'd been fifteen when his family was killed, and fifteen when he'd been taken under the wing of Hollins-Winword's main man, the infamous Coleman Black.

Warm and fuzzy, though, it had not been.

"I never did understand why you stay with the agency when you hate them as much as you do."

"The agency makes freaks out of us all," Brody murmured. Not even Roger knew just how "close" a relationship Brody'd had with Cole. "That's not hate.

That's plain fact. Look at the way you decorate your suites around this place." He shot Roger a dry look.

"You don't have to worry about your privacy," Roger added, drolly. "I only monitor the room when I have something to gain from it."

"Sounding like your pirate roots are showing, there, Rog."

Roger's teeth flashed, but his expression stayed sober. "If you didn't like what the agency was making of us, then you shouldn't have gone back in. You left it, Simon. You were free of it all. So was I."

Yet Brody had walked away from the legal practice they'd planned. He'd had a taste of what life—normal life—could be like, and he'd bolted just when he'd been on the verge of feasting on all that normalcy. He'd gone right back to the agency that had failed in keeping his family safe.

He was well aware of the twisted reasoning and wasn't sure if it was better or worse than the other reason he'd gone back.

Because Cole had asked him to.

"You should tell her."

Trust Roger not to let an issue drop. He'd obviously never lost his liking for tenacity. "Why didn't *you* stick with the legal career? Why go into the hotel business? *Here?*" Brody and Sterling, Attorneys at Law, was supposed to have been located in Connecticut, not coincidentally very far from the factory that fronted Hollins-Winword's center of operations.

"We all have our paths to walk, my friend. My path brought me back here."

"The woman you loved died here," Brody said. He

knew that Brigitte's death during her and Roger's last year of college had been the incident that propelled him into the cold bosom of Hollins-Winword. They'd wanted to close the human trafficking ring in which Roger's girlfriend had unknowingly strayed during a spring break vacation with two of her friends.

All three young women had disappeared, their bodies never recovered.

"The last place Brigitte was seen was in the hellhole of a place right on this very location," Roger agreed evenly. "So when it came up for sale eight years ago, I tore it down and built paradise for her, instead. That's my path. Tell Angie who you are, Simon. I recognize that ring she's wearing."

He wished he'd been more sparing with the details of their situation. He'd known Roger would help, he just hadn't wanted to have to ask for it. But the situation was definitely turning for the worse. The sooner Brody got them all back in the U.S. where he could squirrel them away in a location that he *could* trust, the better.

"Every *case* matters to me," he countered flatly. "And who I *am* is Brody Paine. Simon Brody should have died a long time ago."

"Just because your family did, doesn't mean *you* should have, as well."

He didn't bother answering. The argument was old and hadn't been worth fighting even when it was new. "When's the pilot going to be ready to leave?"

"As soon as the ink is dry on the passports." Roger may have left the agency behind, but he hadn't lost some of his more creative talents. "You'll be welcomed back into the States with opened arms and nary a question," he assured. "If Santina's guy is on your trail, he's not going to follow it beyond here."

"The agency could still use you."

Roger just shook his head. "I've made my place, here. And my peace. I am content. You should try it."

"Not cut out for it, I'm afraid." Brody finally turned away from the bird's-eye-view window. "I appreciate the assistance."

"What are old partners for?"

Roger's voice rang in Brody's ears as he headed down to join Angeline by the pool. To hear Roger talk, one would think they'd been partners for decades rather than just two years.

But, he was also the only regular partner that Brody had ever been assigned.

Look how well *that* had turned out.

They'd both decided to leave the agency and open a law practice. Some stupid-ass dream of following in their fathers' footsteps.

Funny how it had turned out. Or not so funny, really, since it turned out that Brody pretty much *was* following in his father's footsteps.

Just not the man that, for the first fifteen years of his life, he'd thought had been his father.

He pushed away the memories at the same time he pushed through the glass doors and entered the courtyard. The sky was still heavy and thick with clouds, but the afternoon air felt warm and sultry.

And when Angeline lifted her head, watching his approach with a faint smile on her face, it wasn't only the air that felt warm.

Tell her, Roger had said.

But what would be the point? He didn't talk about his past with anyone. Roger only knew part of it because Brody had clued him in one drunken night. Roger had told Brody about Brigitte's death. And Brody had told Rog about his parents, the barrister and the surgeon.

Angeline had drawn her legs out of the water, and she pushed to her bare feet, watching him with those dark, melted-chocolate eyes. "You're looking very serious," she murmured when his steps carried him to her side. "Did you reach your friend?"

Translate that to handler, he knew.

Admitting that he hadn't would only emphasize to her what a deep kettle of stinking fish they'd landed in. But he was coming to realize that voicing the lies he was used to wasn't as easy when he was looking square into her lovely oval face.

It was almost laughable, really, when Brody's entire existence for nearly as long as she'd been alive had been a string of lies, one right after another.

The only truth had been the agency—and the man who ran it—who held in its grip the end of all of those strings. Like some damn collection of balloons.

Only if there had ever been any cheery balloons being held aloft on the end of all those strings, they'd long ago popped, leaving nothing but tatters in their place.

"No," he said, opting for truth in at least this one thing.

She drew her brows together. Her concern evident, she touched his arm, only to press her lips together and pull away again. She crossed her arms and the ring on her finger glinted softly. "You think something's gone wrong."

There were two reasons why a handler would maintain silence like this. Because their security was broken, in which case the agent was on his own, or because the agency found itself in the rare position of needing deniability. In which case, the agent was on his own.

Either way, the agent was on his own.

Even Brody wasn't protected from that protocol.

He pushed his fingers through his hair. There were a few scenarios he could think of that would prompt either option, and none of them were pretty.

"Simon?" She was still waiting.

"The last woman to call me Simon was my mother," he murmured.

Her eyes went wide. "I—" She shook her head a little, as if to dislodge whatever words were stuck in that long throat of hers that just begged for him to taste.

"Come on." Proving that he was still a coward when it came to dealing with anything really personal, he turned toward the kids who were splashing at the edge of the pool. "Move it out," he told them. "We've got a plane to catch."

He looked back at Angeline.

She was still staring at him as if she'd never seen him before. "Where are we flying to?" Her voice was faint.

"The one place that I actually trust we'll all be safe," he said quietly. "Wyoming."

Chapter 12

Angeline had expected that they would be flying on another small, private plane.

Brody… Simon…what*ever* his name really was, was full of his usual surprises though. After she'd gathered the children from the pool and they'd cleaned up once more, Roger had driven them to the airport himself. Before he'd dropped them off, though, he'd handed Brody a manila envelope.

The false passports that Brody produced for the four of them from that envelope didn't garner so much as a second glance from airport security. With a few minutes to spare, Simon and Angie Black, along with their two children Eva and Davey, were boarding the jet bound for home.

Roger had even managed first-class seats.

The day seemed as if it had been going on forever, but when they landed in Miami, the sun was still hanging over the horizon, though barely. Brody bought them all pizza in one of the airport food courts. His cash reserve, she suspected, had to be nearly depleted, just from the cost of getting them out of Caracas. How he'd purchased the four first-class tickets back to Florida was a mystery.

Maybe he'd borrowed from Roger.

Her curiosity had to go unanswered, however, as they barely had time to finish eating before they were boarding another flight.

This time bound for Seattle.

As a route to Wyoming, it was definitely going around the long way.

What followed was the most exhausting, circuitous route that Angeline could never have imagined even in her worst nightmares. More than thirty-six hours had passed since they'd left Miami when Brody finally, finally picked up the duffel bag from the baggage claim and headed, not to another airline ticket counter, but to the exit.

Davey was fitfully asleep, hanging over Brody's shoulder like a limp sack of potatoes. Eva looked flushed and glassy-eyed, as she dragged herself along beside Angeline, who *felt* flushed and glassy eyed.

She honestly didn't feel like she could even string two coherent thoughts together, as she—keeping an instinctive grip on Eva's hand—blindly followed Brody onto a small shuttle van outside the airport. Even though the van was empty and they could each have had their own long seat, they sat three abreast, with Davey still on Brody's lap.

Angeline thought it was morning, but she couldn't be certain. Her eyes felt like there were glass shards in them from lack of sleep. She couldn't even be sure where they were.

"Almost there," Brody murmured beside her.

She jerked a little, realizing her head had been sinking down onto his shoulder in the same way that Eva's head had found her lap.

The shuttle driver—a middle-aged man wearing a John Deere ball cap and a grin—looked over his shoulder at them. "You folks look like you've had a long trip. This the front end of your trip or the back?"

"Back," Brody said, his drawl an exact imitation of the driver's. "Took the family to Hawaii." He shook his head, sounding rueful. "Damn glad to be back on my own turf, if you know what I mean."

The driver chuckled. "Yessir, I do." He turned into a long-term parking lot.

Angeline would have smiled at the irony, too, if she'd had the energy. Seemed as if Hawaii was one of the very few States in which they hadn't managed to cross over or land.

The shuttle stopped and let them off, and Angeline braced herself against the weight as Brody transferred Davey to her arms. "Wait here," he said.

Angeline wouldn't have had the gumption to *not* wait. She braced her feet apart, holding the boy in her arms while Eva leaned heavily against her side and watched Brody disappear down a row of parked cars. Within minutes, a dark-colored SUV stopped beside them.

Brody came around and lifted Davey out of her

arms again and strapped him into one of the rear seats. Angeline helped Eva in after her brother before taking the front seat beside Brody. She fumbled with the seat belt and he pushed her fingers away, clicking it into place himself.

"Don't worry," he murmured. "I *own* this one."

She blinked, trying to find the sense in his words. "Really?"

"Would I lie?" His hand brushed down her cheek and she felt herself pressing into his warm palm.

"Yes."

He made a soft sound. "Hang in there, toots. We'll be home soon."

"I don't even know where we are."

"Billings."

"I thought we were heading to Wyoming."

"We are."

"Then why'd we land in Montana?"

His hand finally left her cheek. "Because that's where this was." He patted the steering wheel.

"You always keep a truck parked in the long-term lot in Billings?"

"Pretty much." He sounded remarkably cheerful considering that he had to be just as tired as she was.

"It'll take us hours to get to Weaver from here."

"I never said we were going to Weaver."

She forced her eyes wider at that. They had already left the airport behind. "When you said Wyoming, I assumed—"

"Wrong."

Her lips compressed. She couldn't believe the wave of disappointment that seemed to engulf her. She'd wanted to go back to Weaver. Far more than she'd re-alized until knowing that it wasn't, in fact, where they were heading at all. "I should have known enough by now to ask you exactly what your intentions were."

"My intentions are always honorable," he assured, looking amused.

She closed her eyes and turned her head, resting it against the seat.

"I have a place near Sheridan," he said.

That brought her eyes right open again. She looked at him, lost for words.

"Nobody knows about it. I mean nobody who can connect it to me and what I do. We'll be safe there until I can figure out...everything."

"Oh," she managed faintly. "Is it really yours?"

"The truck or the place?"

"Both."

"Yeah. They're both really mine."

She swallowed. Moistened her lips. "So what, um, what name does it say on the ownership papers?"

"Does it matter?"

Did it? She felt oddly close to tears and blamed it on exhaustion. "No," she lied. "As long as there is an immoveable horizontal surface to sleep on, I don't much care."

"What if I told you there was no furniture?"

"Is there a floor?"

He laughed softly. "Yes."

"Then we're good to go," she murmured and closed her eyes again. Keeping them open simply took too much effort.

She didn't open them again until the shuddering of the SUV jarred her awake.

They weren't still pelting down the mountain after St. Agnes. They weren't still racing toward Venezuela. She wasn't still inhaling Brody's entire being in that heavenly hotel suite that had been overrun with bugs of an electronic variety.

"Honey, we're home." Brody singsonged in his low, deep voice. He turned off the engine and they sat there for a moment, the utter silence broken only by Davey's soft, snuffling snores.

Angeline's curiosity would kick in before long, she knew. But just then all she felt was utter relief at the sight of a long stone-fronted ranch house that sat in the crook of a small hill, with nothing but open field currently covered in undulating waves of green lying around it for nearly as far as the eye could see.

"You planning to sit here for the rest of the day?"

She realized that Brody was watching her curiously. He'd unhooked his seat belt and his door was open. Fresh air was pouring into the SUV. "No." She unsnapped her safety belt and climbed out of the truck, stretching hugely.

There was an entrance to the house on this side. Just a plain door painted a warm ivory to match the other painted portions of the structure. Those were minimal at best; most of the house was faced in rustic stone.

Brody hadn't needed to wake Davey. The boy was already climbing the concrete steps that led up to that side door. He tried the latch, and looked back at the truck. "It's locked, Mr. Dad."

"Yup." Brody took the steps in a couple bounds. He

didn't pull out a key, though, she noticed. Instead, he flipped up an invisible panel near the door, punched in something, and then closed the panel up once again. "Try it now."

Davey turned the knob. The door swung open without a sound. "Cool," he breathed, and without a second's hesitation, headed inside.

"Should you let him go on ahead like that?"

"This is about the only place that I feel confident to let him explore. He's a kid." Brody shrugged. "Let him go adventuring when he can."

Something soft and sweet curled inside of her. "You'd make a good father," she murmured.

His eyebrows shot up into the brown hair that tumbled, unkempt, across his forehead. "Perish the thought." He practically shuddered as he followed the boy inside.

Soft and sweet turned crisp and dry.

She reached behind her and joggled Eva's knee. "Hey there, sweetie. Rise and shine."

Eva slowly peeled open one weary eye, and the girl fairly tumbled out of the truck. Angeline caught her arm, and together they made their way up the steps and inside.

Not knowing what to expect about the interior—maybe all he really did have were bare floors and unfurnished rooms, after all—the sight that greeted them came as a welcome surprise.

The door they'd come in through opened onto a tidy, slightly austere laundry room. On one side was another door, open to reveal a half bath, and on the other was a kitchen that could have popped from the pages of a

decorating magazine. Lots of gleaming granite countertop and stainless steel appliances built into warm
wood cabinets.

Off to one side, surrounded by a bay of windows
that overlooked the—her tired mind tried to orient
herself—the rear of the property, she decided, sat a
large square walnut table, surrounded by four chairs.
It even held a wooden bowl of fruit in the center of it.

From overhead, she could hear the faint thump of
rapid footsteps. Undoubtedly Davey's as he continued his intrepid exploration. She followed Eva from
the kitchen into a hallway that wasn't really a hall at
all but more of an open circle. The staircase—pretty
much a masterpiece of carved wood—curved up the
wall to the second floor. There were a few closed doors
and the other side of the round area opened into a giant
great room.

The house *definitely* didn't look so large from the
outside.

Davey popped his head over the landing above
them. "Eva, come *see*. There's a room for you and a
room for me."

Showing a little more life, Eva went up the stairs
to join her brother.

Angeline crossed the great room, drawn by the view
from the windows on the far wall of the not-so-dis-
tant mountains. Something about that view had everything inside her seeming to sigh in relief and missing
Weaver.

"Come on."

She looked over her shoulder. Standing amid the
collection of leather couches and nubby upholstered

chairs, Brody looked surprisingly "in" place. Which made her realize that she'd never let herself think about whether or not the man even *had* a home. He'd always been just "Brody"—an entire entity, complete and intact all on his own—as if he had no need or desire for the usual things that most people wanted in their lives.

"Where?"

"You wanted a horizontal surface, didn't you?"

The thought that swept into her mind had absolutely nothing to do with the act of sleeping upon one. She tucked her tongue behind her teeth and nodded. "Sleep." The word sounded forced.

And if the way Brody's lips twitched was any indication, he was well aware of the direction of her unruly thoughts. He turned, but instead of heading toward the staircase, he opened one of the doors in that circular nonhallway, and waited, clearly expecting Angeline to precede him.

She passed through the doorway and went a little limp inside at the perfection of the master suite that waited on the other side. At least she assumed it was the master suite. As a guest bedroom, it would definitely border on overkill.

The bed was massive, owing a good portion of that impression to the rich, deep gleam of the wooden bed frame. The mattress was even covered with a thoroughly un-bachelor-like comforter. All golds and reds and browns that were complemented by coordinating pillows—again oversized and beautiful without managing to be frilly or fussy. The tall narrow windows that flanked the bed were dressed with wooden shutters, currently open, and cornices over the top finished with fabric that matched the bedding. There were two chairs sitting alongside each other in another corner with a table tucked between. The perfect spot for coffee in the morning. Aside from them, there was no other freestanding furniture in the room at all. Everything else—shelves and drawers—was constructed of wood that looked similar to the bed and was built into the wall facing it. And in the center of all that detailed woodwork was a fireplace. One of the most perfectly beautiful fireplaces she'd ever seen.

"Who, um, who did the decorating for you?"

He looked wounded. "What? You think I couldn't have done it?"

She walked to the fireplace and reached up to pluck a fat, squat red candle off the mantel. She sniffed it. "You picked out bayberry candles?"

His dimple flashed. "Okay. I hired an outfit to take care of things for me. They *did* follow my instructions," he added defensively. "Do you think I have no taste whatsoever?"

She sat on the edge of the bed and the mattress was so high that her toes actually cleared the floor. "I think," she said slowly, "that I don't really know you at all. I thought I did, but..." She shook her head, her voice trailing away.

He stood with his back to the fireplace. Above the mantel with its artful collection of candles and an engraved wooden box, a large oil painting of a handsome couple posed with two small children was propped against the stone chimney. "But now you don't? What is it you want to know?"

What *did* she want to know? Besides everything?

She looked from Brody's face to the family portrait. There wasn't really a resemblance that she could spot between the faces there and his, but what other purpose would he have for displaying it in his private bedroom if they were strangers?

She realized she was pressing her thumb against the wedding ring that she still hadn't taken off her finger, turning it in a slow circle. "How long have you lived here?" It wasn't at all the deep, meaningful questions that plagued her where he was concerned.

"I had this house built nearly five years ago."

More surprises. For some reason she'd had the sense he'd acquired it more recently. "Built," she said slowly. "But how *long* have you lived here?"

He smiled faintly. "About six months, give or take. I…made more permanent arrangements to be here when I was pulling the gig in Weaver last November."

He meant when he was protecting little Megan.

"Why then?"

He lifted a shoulder. "I was in the vicinity. Easier to take care of the details."

"No. I mean *why* then? If you hadn't really lived here in all the time since you built it, what prompted you to do something about it in November?"

His lashes narrowed. His blue eyes were bloodshot and his jaw was shaded with whiskers. His jeans seemed to hang a little loosely on his tight hips and the blue shirt was definitely looking travel weary.

She could only imagine what state his bandage was in.

He looked, frankly, like hell, yet he was still the most beautiful man she'd ever seen.

"That's not really a question you want to be asking right now," he said.

She shifted, pressing her palms flat on the mattress beside her hips. "Why?" Her voice turned wry. "Don't I have a high enough security clearance to hear the details?"

"No. Because everything I've ever done about this place has been prompted by you."

Chapter 13

Brody's words swirled inside Angeline's head, making her dizzy. Or maybe it was her heart, shuddering around inside without an even beat to save its soul, that was causing her curious light-headededness.

How could *she* have ever influenced something in Brody's personal life?

They'd barely known one another.

That didn't stop you from falling for him.

She ignored the voice inside her head. Moistened her lips and swallowed against the sudden constriction there. "I don't understand."

He rubbed his chin, looking oddly uneasy. And when, less than a moment later, Davey bolted into the room, he looked happy for the interruption.

He leaned over and scooped the boy up by the waist, leaving his arms and legs dangling.

Davey gave a squeal of laughter and squirmed.

Angeline's heart lurched all over again. She looked from Brody and the boy to the portrait once more.

"Where's your sister?" Brody was asking the giggling boy.

"In the bathroom," Davey managed to impart between laughs. *"Again."* He tried to reach Brody's torso with his little fingers, intent on tickling, but couldn't. "Are we gonna stay here until my mom and dad come to get us?"

"That's the plan. Which means we've got to get some food into this place so we don't starve." Brody swung the boy from one side to the other.

Davey went into peals of laughter again.

Clearly, *he* wasn't upset by the latest turn of events.

Angeline pushed herself off the bed, ignoring the weak feeling that still plagued her knees, and started for the doorway.

"Where you going?"

"To figure out what you need in your kitchen."

He shook his head, waving away the idea. "No need. I'll just call up Mrs. Bedford."

"Who's that?" Davey asked curiously, beating Angeline to the punch.

"She," Brody swung the kid upright finally, and brought their noses close, "is my housekeeper," he told him. "And she'll have us set up with plenty of food in just two shakes."

"Two shakes of what?"

"Of you." Brody jiggled the boy again, sending him into another spasm of laughter.

Angeline smiled faintly, as entranced by the unguarded grin on Brody's face as she was by the idea that Brody had something as unlikely as a house-keeper. "I'll just make sure the kids get settled in, then," she said.

"Take a nap," Brody told her, nodding toward the bed. His bed. "I can handle them on my own for a bit."

She pressed her lips together. The truth was, after the last few days she believed that Brody was capable of handling them for a lot more than a "bit." He wasn't just good at protecting children. No matter how much he shuddered over the idea of having his own, he was good *with* children.

It shamed her that she was so surprised by the fact. As if she'd given him short shrift when she—coming from the family that she did—should know just exactly how multifaceted a caring man could be.

"Maybe I should use one of the other rooms," she suggested.

Davey had looped his arm around Brody's shoulder. "But then I'd gotta share with Eva. And I *al-ays* gotta share with her."

Brody's gaze slanted toward Angeline, full of sudden devilry. "Think of his sacrifice, babe. We can't have that."

She swallowed. *That* was the Brody she knew and loved.

Unfortunately, she was well aware that thought had become less a turn of phrase than reality with every passing hour they'd spent together.

"Fine." She headed back toward the bed, watching Brody from the corner of her eyes as she slowly reached for one of the large, decorative pillows at the head of it. She pushed it aside, and turned back the comforter, revealing the smooth chocolate-brown sheets beneath.

He suddenly looked less goading and more…disconcerted. "All right then. Let's leave her to it, Dave, my man." He tossed the boy over his shoulder, setting off more giggles, and headed to the door. When Angeline caught him looking back at her, she deliberately drew back the top sheet and sat down on the bed. She leaned back and slowly toed off one boot. Then the other.

Brody shook his head. "You're dangerous," he muttered, and closed the door on her, leaving her alone in the room.

She flopped back on the bed, her palm pressed to her thundering heart. What was dangerous was thinking that she could ever play with the fire that was Brody Paine and come out unscorched.

She rolled over, tucking the down bed pillow that had been hidden behind the sham beneath her cheek, and wondered how many nights—and with how many women—Brody had spent in the wide, comfortable bed.

Her gaze slid to the portrait yet again.

Whatever had come before didn't necessarily matter, she knew. Because she was only there as a result of the Stanley situation.

She'd do well to remember that particular fact.

Then she deliberately closed her eyes. If she didn't sleep, she'd at least pretend to.

But it wasn't long before pretense became reality.

When next Angeline opened her eyes, there was nothing but moonlight shining through the opened shutters.

The fat pillows had all been removed from the bed
and were sitting, stacked haphazardly on the two chairs
by the other windows. The comforter had been pulled
back across the bed, as if it had been shoved aside by
a tall, warm body.

The evidence that Brody, too, must have slept at
some point right there beside her made something inside her heat. And it wasn't at all the uneasy kind of
feeling she'd had when they'd shared that narrow mattress at St. Agnes.

Now, though, there as no sign of him.

She rolled onto her back, stretching luxuriously.
She felt quite refreshed, even given the fact that she'd
been sleeping fully dressed. She pushed off the bed
and padded across the thick rug that covered much
of the hardwood floors and went into the adjoining
bathroom.

As appealing as soaking herself in hot bubbling
water sounded, she contented herself with a shower instead, dragging the opaque burgundy and gold striped
curtain around the circular rod that hung over the tub.
The water was hot and plentiful and was almost as welcoming as Brody's bed had been. She used his soap,
which smelled like some sort of spicy forest, and his
shampoo, which smelled like babies and made her
want to giggle.

Brody Paine used baby shampoo on that thick sandy
hair of his.

Finally, feeling squeaky clean for the first time in

days, she turned off the water and yanked back the curtain.

Brody was sitting there on the closed commode facing the tub.

She yelped and grabbed the edge of the curtain, dragging it across her torso. Her face felt flushed, and her body felt even hotter. "What on earth are you doing?" He'd obviously showered, too, because his hair was still damp and he'd exchanged his blue jeans and blue T-shirt for clean ones, this time both in black.

"Hey," he defended. "I'm covering my eyes."

He was. With one hand that she didn't trust in the least spread across the upper portion of his face.

She slowly let the curtain drop, almost but not quite revealing her nipples that had gone appallingly tight at the unexpected sight of him, and twisted her lips when the coffee cup he was holding nearly spilled right onto his lap. "As I suspected," she said, managing a tart tone only through sheer effort.

He dropped the hand and extended the coffee toward her. "I was just thinking of you," he drawled.

She shoved the edge of the curtain beneath her arms holding it tight there, and reached for the white mug. Less than a week ago, she would have dismissed his words as pure blarney.

Now, after all the things he'd done, said, she was no longer sure about anything.

She sipped at the coffee, hot, fragrant and strong just how she liked it, and eyed him. His feet were bare and that, more than anything—even her barely protected nudity—made her feel shaky inside.

They were so intimate, she realized. Those bare

feet of his. Lightly dusted with dark hair. High arches. Long, vaguely knobby toes. She pressed her lips together for a moment. "Did you keep your bandage dry when you showered?" The words sort of blurted out of her.

His lips tilted. "I put a brand new one on, ma'am."

She could only imagine the results of that, given the first bandage she'd witnessed. "Where are the children?"

"Snug as bugs in their beds."

"What about supper? Did they eat? I should probably check—"

He lifted his head, cutting off her litany. "I fixed them mac and cheese. Evidently not some fried variety that Davey thinks is the bomb, but it filled their stomachs. At least his. Eva did more picking than anything. They had baths, a few minutes of television and then they had bed. Only thing they didn't have was a story read to them by yours truly," he added drily. "Satisfied?"

She narrowed her eyes at him. "What time is it now?"

"Almost eight. And no, that isn't decaf in case you're about ready to ask that, too."

"I wasn't. I would never make the mistake of thinking you might let a little thing like caffeine stop you, even at eight o'clock at night. Um," she gestured with the mug toward the towels hanging on the wall opposite him. "Mind handing me a towel?"

He hooked a long toffee-colored towel off the rod and held it out to her. She exchanged the mug for the towel, careful to remain behind the protection of the curtain as she dashed it over her wet limbs before wrapping it sarongwise around her, tucking the ends in above her breasts. "Any luck reaching your handler?"

"Not exactly."

She peeked out from the curtain again. "What does that mean?"

"I reached someone," he said. "The situation hasn't changed."

Which could mean anything, she supposed, but since he wasn't looking like they needed to bug out, she'd follow his lead. "It's, um, it's pretty rude of you to just bust in like this, you know. Didn't your parents teach you some manners?"

"My parents were British. They were *all* about manners," he assured. His gaze drifted downward, from her wet hair to her hands clutching the shielding curtain. "Why are you still a virgin?"

She stared at him. The porcelain of the tub was losing its heat without the water pounding on it, and her toes curled against the slick surface. "I thought we agreed that was none of your business."

"It wasn't." He leaned forward, his hands folded loosely between his knees, looking thoroughly casual. As if he held conversations like this in his bathroom most every day. "Now it is."

"*Now?* Why now?"

His casual mien abruptly slipped and her mouth dried at the hunger darkening his eyes. "Because the plan to keep my hands off you isn't going to work much longer."

No amount of effort seemed enough to propel a single word past her lips.

He pushed to his feet. "Do you really think I make a habit of busting in, uninvited, on women in the shower? That I don't know how the bloody hell to wait for an invite?"

She swallowed. "Brody," she whispered.

"So you'd better tell me *why,* love, and make it a good one while you're at it." He stopped when his legs encountered the side of the tub. "One that even my damned conscience can manage to heed."

She sucked in a breath. Moistened her lips. And still nothing emerged but his name. Husky. Soft.

His eyes darkened even more, the blue looking nearly as black as the shirt stretched across his wide shoulders. "That's not helping me any here, Angeline. Are you waiting for marriage? For—" his mobile lips twisted slightly "—hell, I don't know. True love?"

She lifted her chin. "Something wrong with that?"

He muttered an oath. "I should have known."

She slicked her hand over her hair, pushing the tangles behind her ear. "I just never...trusted anyone enough to believe they cared all that much about me. About what was behind," she waved her hand, feeling herself flush. "You know. Behind the genetics. The looks. The, um, the—"

"Body?"

She nodded, feeling foolish.

"I'm sorry to break it to you, babe, but you've got more than your share of both going on," he murmured.

She pressed her lips together. "So men have been telling me since I was barely a teenager. All I ever heard were catcalls and wolf whistles by the idiots. The nice guys, well, they didn't ever call because they figured I was already out living it up, or they didn't want to get turned down. Leaving Weaver didn't help. If anything, it got worse."

She flinched a little when Brody's hand came up and touched her shoulder.

The hunger was still in his eyes, but it was the gentleness in his touch that stole her breath all over again. "And I behaved the same way."

She sank her teeth into her lip. "S-sometimes."

"It was the only way I knew how to keep you at arm's length," he murmured. "You think I didn't know that flirting with you was the quickest road to keeping things simple where you were concerned? That I didn't recognize the stop signs that always came up in those brown eyes of yours?" His thumb traced a slow circle around her shoulder. "I needed those signs, Angeline."

The edge of the curtain wrinkled even more in her tight grip. "Why?"

His thumb slowly, so slowly, dragged down her arm toward her elbow. "Because being with you made me want things I gave up wanting a long time ago." He reached her wrist and stopped, resting over the vein that pulsed there. "You remember when we first met?"

"I could hardly forget."

"You told me about Wyoming. And everything about you—inside here—" he let go of her wrist long enough to tap the center of her forehead "—and here," he drew his finger in a short, burning line from the base of her throat to her cleavage that wasn't exactly hidden by the thick folds of towel tucked there, "shined out like a homing beacon."

He looked up at the curtain hanging from the rod,

and seemed to study it for a moment. "I always thought it was interesting that you'd chosen to go to Atlanta considering the way you always talked about Wyoming. For a long time, I figured that it must have had something to do with a man."

She shook her head. "I was just sticking close to my sister. We missed each other."

"I know how that feels." His gaze slowly dropped again, still studying the curtain, only this time where she held it gripped in her fist. "I bought this land shortly after you and I met and had the house built within less than a year. And I've already told you I started actually living here late last year." He breathed out a half laugh. "Not because I ever expected us to be standing here like this someday, that's for certain."

She waited for his low voice to continue, barely daring to breathe. "Then why?"

"Because I wanted to feel what you felt that first day we met. I wanted to see if I *could.* If it was still in me, or if it had been burned out of me when I was still a kid."

Her eyes went damp. "What happened, Brody? Or is it really Simon after all?"

"It used to be," he murmured. "But it doesn't matter anymore."

The curtain slipped in her loosened grip. "Of course it matters. It's your past." The portrait over his fireplace hung in her mind's eye. "You had a sister. What was her name?"

"Penelope. Penny."

"What happened to her?"

He shook his head. "This isn't about my past. This is about why you've chosen to remain a virgin."

"I think," she began softly, cautiously, "that this is about both." She let the curtain fall away between them. "You want me to give you an inviolate reason why I've never slept with a man. One that will convince you once and for all that I'm off-limits. Not because you're worried that I might be compromising some deeply held belief about sex before marriage or any of that. But because you're afraid that it wouldn't *be* just sex. Because it might open that door on emotions that you like to keep closed because if you don't," her voice was strained, "everything that you've been able to pretend no longer affected you will come tumbling down on you. Like one of those closets that people keep shoving stuff into, again and again and again only to find, one day, they forget themselves and open the door and—" she waved her hand "—whoosh. There are all our issues piled up, nice and unresolved, around our ears."

"Maybe," he countered, "I just like a woman with more experience."

She shook her head and slowly stepped out of the tub. "Are you expecting that to hurt?" Level on the floor with him, she had to tilt her head back to keep her eyes on his. "To push me away? It might work if I believed you. Maybe," she lifted her hands and settled them softly on his chest, "you just feel safer with a woman who doesn't make you feel anything."

His eyes narrowed. He caught her wrists in his hands as if to pull them away from him. "Brave words," he cautioned.

She didn't feel particularly brave. She felt out on a limb in every possible way. "Prove me wrong, then," she whispered.

His jaw seemed to tighten as she twisted her wrists out of his light hold. She reached for the towel and flipped the knot loose.

The towel dropped to her bare feet.

He exhaled roughly. "Thought you were all about playing by the rules."

She stepped out from the folds of terry, closing the last few inches remaining between them, almost but not quite smiling when the man actually took a step back.

"And you're the one who thinks rules were just made to be broken." She inched forward again, until her bare toes touched his, and her breasts brushed the soft fabric of his T-shirt.

"I don't want the thing that gets broken to be you."

There were already too many emotions swirling inside her to examine the way his rough admission made her want to cry, as much for him as for her. "I'm a big girl," she assured softly. She slid her hand behind his neck, tugging his head toward hers. "All grown up."

"I didn't have any doubts about that." His assurance murmured against her lips and his hands finally came around her back, pressing warm and hot against her spine.

She still shivered, but not with cold.

Not when his body felt like a furnace burning through his clothes to her flesh. Not when her blood seemed to expand inside her veins and her nerve endings set off sparks wherever he touched.

"You deserve a bed," he muttered, his mouth dragging down the column of her throat. "Some romance or something. Not tedious flights and questionable hotels."

"This isn't a hotel." She sucked in a harsh breath when his hands dragged over her hips, his fingers kneading. "I'll reserve judgment on the questionable part for now, if you don't mind."

He laughed softly and pulled her right off her feet, until her mouth met his. His hands slid down her thighs, pulling them around his waist, and he carried her out of the bathroom into the bedroom.

She swung her legs down when he stopped next to the bed. He pressed his forehead to hers for a long moment, then shook his head a little, straightening. His fingers threaded through the wet skeins of her hair, spreading it out past her shoulders. "I can't not tell you that you're beautiful," he murmured. "Because you are."

She swallowed. His hands drifted from her shoulders, skimmed over the full jut of her breasts only to stop and torment the hard crests into even tighter points, while need shot through her veins, all collecting in the center of her until she felt weak from it.

Her fingers flexed, desperate for something more substantial to grab on to than air. She satisfied them with handfuls of his shirt that she dragged loose from the waist of his jeans. "What did you do with Delilah?"

He snorted. "You want to know that *now?* God, I am getting old."

She finally got her hands beneath his shirt, and ran them up his long spine, swept out over his wide back. "I've wondered ever since we left San Juan," she murmured.

"I left her with Roger. Compensation for the bugs of his I drowned." He caught her waist again and covered her mouth, kissing any more silly questions she might have uttered into nonexistence.

She pulled in gulps of air when he finally lifted his head.

"Anything else you want to discuss?"

She pushed his shirt higher and he finally yanked it off over his head. As she'd suspected, the bandage he'd covered himself with was almost as much a disaster as the first one had been.

She vowed to change it for him. Later.

She slid her fingers through his, pulling his hands boldly back to her breasts. "Does this feel as good to you as it does to me?"

"That'll take further examination." He dragged his thumbs over and around, again and again as he backed her inexorably against the side of the bed until, off balanced, she tumbled backward.

He must have turned on the lamp near the chairs while she'd been in the shower, because it hadn't been burning when she'd wakened. Now, she was glad for its soft glow as he stood there above her, his eyes dark and full of intent. He undid his jeans and pushed them off, and Angeline let her eyes take their glorious fill.

"*I* can't not tell you you're beautiful," she whispered huskily and slowly lifted her hand toward him.

The mattress dipped when he bent his knee against it. He took her hand, pressed his mouth to the palm of it. Her other hand found his hip, drifted over the unbelievably hard glute that flexed in answer to her touch.

He suddenly grabbed that exploratory hand and pressed it, along with the other above her head.

Her breath came faster, so much emotion rocketing around inside her that she thought she might burst. "What about your chest? I don't want you to undo whatever healing has already occurred."

"If my heart can withstand this, I think that damn knife wound can," he muttered, and pressed his mouth to the pulse beating wildly at the base of her throat. "I could spend a lifetime exploring you."

"I don't want to wait that long," she assured, twining her legs impatiently around his, trying to pull him down to her. She knew he wanted her. There was no hiding that particularly evident, impressive, fact.

"For a virgin, you're quite the demanding little thing, aren't you?" He dropped his mouth even farther, exploring the rise of her breasts.

"Brody—" She pressed her head back in the soft bedding, writhing against his tormenting tongue.

"That's my name," he whispered, as he continued southward. "Feel free to wear it out." And when his mouth reached her *there,* and everything inside her splintered outward, she was afraid she well might, as she cried out his name. Again. And again.

Tears streaked from her eyes when he finally worked his way back up her trembling body. "Now," he said, his body settling in the cradle of her thighs. "Are you sure?"

She arched against him, winding herself around

him and answered the question once and for all as she took him into her body. "God," he gritted, "Angeline."

"That's my name," she returned breathlessly, full of wonder. Full of him. "Feel free to—"

He pulled her more tightly beneath him, and the words died in her throat as heat and pleasure and everything that was right and beautiful in the world came screaming together in the collision of their bodies. And when that pleasure was more than she could bear yet again and she exploded apart in his arms, he groaned her name, following her headlong into the fire.

Eventually, when their hearts finally stopped pounding against each other, he lifted his head.

He looked just as undone as she felt and she sighed softly. Contentedly. "You were worth the wait," she whispered.

His eyes darkened. He slowly kissed her lips.

Then he looked over at the portrait across from the bed that they'd nearly destroyed. "I was born in London. They named me Simon Brody," he murmured. "After him. Until I was fifteen and I learned otherwise, I thought he was my father. Only it turns out that my mother didn't meet Simon until Penny was two and my mother was pregnant with me. They married right after I was born."

She curled her arms around him and his head lowered to her breast. "How did you find out?"

"I found my birth certificate. I was grounded for smoking and bored, so I was snooping. I never expected to find *that*."

"I learned a long time ago that it doesn't take blood for a man to be a father. Did you love him?"

He was silent for so long that she wasn't sure he'd answer. She sifted her fingers slowly through his hair and finally, he did. "Yes."

"Then that's all that matters, Brody. Love is always the thing that matters most."

His hand slid down and caught hers. She knew he felt the wedding ring that she still hadn't bothered to remove. And when he folded her fingers in his, and kissed them, she couldn't stop herself from wishing— just for a moment—that the ring was real.

Chapter 14

"Mr. Dad. Angeline."

The voice was faint, but Angeline sat bolt upright and nearly screamed when she heard a crash from some distant part of the house.

"Stay here." Beside her, Brody was already pushing back the covers. He stopped only long enough to hitch his jeans over his hips and pull something from a hidden panel in the wall as he left the room.

Angeline scrambled out of bed, nearly tripping over the tangle of bedding they'd made. She fumbled her way into the scrubs that were the first thing her hands encountered in the duffel she'd yet to unpack. Her heart was in her throat, waiting for God knew what.

Another cry from Davey?

Another crash?

A gunshot?

Heedless of Brody's instruction, she headed out of the room, stopping short at the panel that was still open. With only the lamp on the far side of the room as her guide, she peered into the wall safe. Stuck her hand in, sweeping it around the walls inside.

Even in the dark hole of the safe, she recognized what her fingers found. Guns. And plenty of them.

She closed her palm around one grip and pulled it off the bracket holding it in place and stuck her head out the bedroom door that Brody had left ajar.

All she heard was the banging of her heartbeat inside her head.

Could Santina's thug have found them even after all their precautions?

She quietly padded across the floor toward the base of the staircase.

"Angeline."

She nearly jumped out of her skin at the sound of Brody calling her name. Loudly.

"What is it? What's wrong?" She started up the stairs.

"Eva's sick. She's burning up." He met her in the hallway and muttered an oath when he saw the gun she held. "Give me that."

He plucked it out of her unresisting hand and Angeline dashed into the room. Davey was huddled at the foot of the bed, looking scared. Eva was curled up in a fetal position, and was definitely fevered. The heat practically rolled off her in waves.

Angeline sat down beside her. "Honey, how long have you felt like this?" She surreptitiously found Eva's wrist and felt her pulse.

"I dunno." The girl shifted away, as if she couldn't bear the touch. "My stomach hurts," she added hoarsely, and promptly threw up across Angeline's lap.

Davey jumped back. "Eeuuww." But he sounded more tearful than anything.

"Run in the bathroom across the hall and grab the towels," Brody told Davey.

The boy dashed out of the room.

"She needs the hospital," Angeline said, looking up at Brody. Everything inside her felt seized up by guilt as she cradled the girl against her. She'd slept the day away after they'd arrived, and after that, she and Brody had—

She shied away from thinking about the hours spent in his arms.

"This could be anything from a bug she's picked up to appendicitis," she told him.

"Here." Davey returned with the towels tumbling out of his arms.

Brody took one and gave it back to him. "Go get this one really wet." Again the boy dashed out and Brody, without turning a single hair, began mopping up the mess.

"I'm sorry," Eva cried.

Angeline lifted the girl's dark hair out of the way for Brody. "Nothing for you to be sorry about, sweetie." She, on the other hand, had plenty. If she'd been paying more attention to the children and less to Brody—

"I want my mom."

Angeline's eyes burned. "I know you do, Eva. She'd be here too, if she could." She took the soaked towel that Davey came back with and smoothed the corner of it over Eva's flushed face. "I want to get you out of these pj's, okay?" The pajamas in question were comprised of the same scrub shirt that Eva had worn in Caracas and Angeline drew it over the girl's head.

Brody added it to the soiled sheets that he'd managed to slide out from beneath Angeline and Eva.

One portion of Angeline's mind wondered how many times he'd had to deal with vomiting children because he was more than a little adept at it.

"All she's got left that are clean are jeans." He was staring into the top drawer of the bureau. "No way are you getting those on her. I'll grab a shirt of mine." He headed out of the room, though she could easily hear his voice as he went. "Come on, Davey. You better get your shoes on so we can take your sister to the doctor."

"Is she gonna be okay?"

"Heck, yeah. You think Angeline and I would let anything happen to either one of you?"

She bit her lip. She wished she felt that sort of confidence. That she *deserved* that sort of confidence. "I'm going to have Brody carry you down to the car when he gets back, okay?"

Eva nodded slightly. "What if I throw up again?"

"Then you do." Angeline pressed her lips to the girl's sweaty forehead. "It's not the end of the world." Brody came back into the room a few minutes later. Not only did he bring a T-shirt for Eva, but one for Angeline, as well as her jeans and boots.

While he helped Eva maneuver into the shirt, Angeline hurriedly exchanged her ruined scrubs for the clean clothes.

"You finish dressing. I'm going to take her down to

the truck." Brody gingerly lifted the girl into his arms and headed out of the bedroom.

Angeline fumbled with the boots, only to realize he'd tucked socks inside them.

And he'd accused *her* of getting caught up in details.

She pulled them on, shoved her feet into the boots and hurriedly caught up to them on the staircase where Davey was already waiting, clinging to the banister. Angeline took his hand and within minutes they were in the SUV, racing away from the house.

Fortunately, when they reached the town, traffic at that hour was nil and they arrived at the hospital in short order. Brody pulled right up in the emergency entrance by the door and carried Eva inside. Angeline barely managed to pull the keys from the ignition before she and Davey followed.

The waiting room was empty and with one look at Eva's condition, the nurse standing by the reception desk waved Brody through a set of double doors behind her.

"Use the passport," Brody told Angeline before the doors closed between them.

She blinked.

"Ma'am? I'll need you to complete just a few things and you can go back with your husband and daughter."

She focused in on the receptionist who was holding a pen and clipboard out toward her. "Right." As a paramedic, she ought to have been intimately familiar with the process of checking in a patient through the E.R., yet she really wasn't. Their end of the paperwork was considerably different than the patient's end.

So she scribbled one of her names of the day—Angie Black—where the receptionist pointed, and filled in the only address that her frantic mind could remember—the one she'd grown up with in Weaver. "We, um, we just moved here," she told the receptionist, as if that would explain her complete and utter inadequacy when it came to answering the simple questions.

Beside her, Davey was standing on his tiptoes, trying to see over the desk. "Where'd Mr. Dad and my sister go?"

The reception smiled at the term. Angeline supposed she must have heard just about anything and everything in her position. "They went back to have the doctor look at your sister and see what he can do to make her feel better." The woman produced a plastic-wrapped sucker and handed it over. "It's sugar free," she assured Angeline.

Davey didn't let that bother him as he whipped off the plastic and started sucking on it.

Then Brody stuck his head through the double doors. "Angeline." His head disappeared again.

She started to call Davey, but the receptionist shook her head. "Let him stay out with me," she advised. "It's a slow night. I don't mind."

Torn, Angeline looked at the boy. What was the likelihood of any harm coming to him there? "Davey, you stay right here with—" she looked toward the receptionist.

"Bonny."

"—Bonny," she repeated to Davey. "No going off and exploring, okay?"

He shrugged and sat down on one of the chairs near the television set. "Can I watch cartoons?"

"We'll find some for you," Bonny assured. "We'll pop in a videotape if need be."

Angeline hurried through the swinging doors.

There was no question where Eva had been taken because she could see Brody standing not far down the hall.

Eva was already on a hospital gurney. One nurse was drawing blood. Another was attaching an IV. And the doctor, a young man who looked old enough to be a grade schooler, introduced himself as Dr. Thomas.

He pulled the curtain shielding the bed closed somewhat and stepped out with them on the other side. "The blood test will confirm it, but I believe your daughter's appendix has decided to create a fuss. The surgeon on duty tonight is Dr. Campbell. He's already scrubbing in. We don't want to waste any time and chance it rupturing. We'll need you to sign the consent papers as soon as they're ready."

Angeline looked at Brody, lost for words. Of course she'd known it could come to this; she wasn't a fool. But knowing and doing were two very different things.

"I'll sign whatever you need," Brody said evenly. His hand closed around Angeline's shoulder. "Just make sure she's all right."

Dr. Thomas smiled reassuringly. "Better that you brought her now, than a few hours from now." He tugged back the curtain again. "Eva, the nurse is going to give you something that's going to make you really sleepy, and then we're going to get rid of that nasty pain in your tummy. Okay?"

Eva's dark eyes were tightly shut. "I wanna go home."

Angeline went to her side, closing that small fist in her hands. She pressed her lips to the girl's temple. "We all want that," she assured her. "You're going to be all right, though. A little while from now you're going to be feeling a whole lot better."

"We need to move her," one of the nurses said in a kind voice.

Angeline nodded and stepped back from the gurney. "We'll be right here waiting for you, Eva."

The dark head managed a small nod of acknowledgment.

Then the nurses were rolling the gurney quickly along the hall.

"She'll be fine," Dr. Thomas assured. "All her symptoms say there's been no rupture yet." He pushed open the doors back out to the waiting area. "Once you finish with the forms, Bonny can tell you how to get to the waiting area outside surgery. It'll be a little more comfortable for you there."

"Thanks," Brody said, turning toward Bonny and the waiting forms. He picked up the pen and with an efficiency that Angeline envied, completed the form. Then he pulled out a cell phone that he must have brought from the house, because she'd certainly never seen it before, and punched in a few numbers. "Mrs. Bedford? Simon Black here, again. I have a bit of an emergency."

Angeline started. She'd thought he'd just made up the name of Black for the purpose of the passports that Roger had produced for them. But obviously, if his housekeeper knew him by that name, he was used to using that particular alias.

"Ma'am?" Bonny drew her attention away from Brody, who was asking Mrs. Bedford if she'd mind coming to pick up Davey from the hospital. "I need your signature, as well." She held out the pen that Brody had used.

Angeline slowly took it and wrote in her name next to his. Only after she'd finished did she realize she'd not used the diminutive of Angie, but Angeline.

She eyed the names, side by side, feeling distinctly off balanced. Simon and Angeline Black.

"Okay." Brody had pocketed his phone. "Mrs. Bedford will be here shortly. Timing couldn't be better, actually. When she dropped off the groceries earlier today—all of you were snoozing like Rip Van Winkle—she had her grandson with her. Cute kid. Davey will like him."

"I can direct you to the other waiting room now if you'd like," Bonny suggested.

A short while later, they found themselves seats in the much smaller, but much more comfortable waiting room. Angeline couldn't make herself sit in one of the upholstered chairs, though, and paced slowly around the room, conscientiously giving the other couple who was also in the waiting room their space and privacy, as well.

Davey sat on Brody's lap, his blond head resting against that chest that Angeline knew from experience was wide and comforting.

Her pacing feet took her back to them. "You should get a tetanus shot while we're here," she told him.

"What's tet-nus?"

"Like a vaccine," Brody told Davey. "I had one a year ago."

"Still." Angeline paced away again. Every time she looked at the clock on the wall, she expected hours to have passed, but instead, it was only minutes.

Before too long, a woman in her fifties, Angeline guessed, arrived. "Angeline, this is Mrs. Bedford," Brody introduced them. "She's the one who keeps the house looking like the Pope himself will be dropping by any minute."

Mrs. Bedford's cheeks flushed with pleasure. "Oh, you and your teasing." She turned her bright gaze on Angeline. "We'd have met earlier but I know you were all just tuckered right out. I'm so glad I'm able to help now, though. How's the girl?"

"She's in surgery."

"Oh, my. Bless her heart. What a miracle that you were here when it happened." Mrs. Bedford sighed a little but then patted Angeline's shoulder as if she'd known her since she was a tot. "Don't you worry, though. The doctors here are just fine. Kept my Joe going when he had a heart attack a few years ago, that's for sure."

Angeline managed a smile. If she'd held any suspicion that the housekeeper might really be associated with Hollins-Winword, they pretty much dissolved in the face of her kindly ordinariness.

The woman was holding out her hand for Davey. "You can call me Mrs. B.," she told him. "How'd you like to go to my house and have some ice cream with me? My husband and my grandson, Tyson, are there, too."

Evidently, the notion of ice cream at midnight was enough to overcome whatever reservations Davey might have. He took the woman's hand and waved as he left with her.

Angeline rubbed her hands up and down her arms. "You're not worried about…you know?"

Brody shook his head. "She's more capable than you give her credit for."

Which just had Angeline wondering all over again.

She began pacing once more, only sitting next to Brody when a surgeon came in to speak to the other couple.

Judging by their devastated expressions, the news was not good.

She looked away. Brody reached over and closed his hand around hers and the urge to pace finally died.

The waiting room was empty except for them when a middle-aged man wearing a white coat over green scrubs entered and looked around. "Mr. and Mrs. Black?"

Angeline and Brody rose from their chairs. She swallowed, and felt Brody's hand slide around her shoulders. "That's us," he said.

Angeline tried and failed to decipher the man's expression as he crossed the waiting room toward them. Her stomach felt tight, her nerves shredded.

"I'm Dr. Campbell," he introduced himself without preamble. "Eva's surgery went very well. She's doing fine."

The relief was nearly overwhelming. Angeline's

knees started to shake. Brody held her even tighter, as if he were trying to lend some strength to her.

"We got the appendix before it ruptured," Dr. Campbell was saying, "which is a very good thing. Her recovery time should be minimal."

"When can we see her?"

"She'll be moved from the recovery room to her own room within the next hour or so. Go get yourselves some coffee. Something to eat. Stretch your legs. That'll help take up the time," he advised, "until she's settled in her room. Unless you have any questions?" He lifted his eyebrows.

Angeline had a million of them, but couldn't seem to marshal her thoughts enough to voice a single one.

And Brody was decidedly silent, as well.

The surgeon didn't seem to notice anything amiss in their reactions, though. As if he were used to it. "I'll be along to check on her again in a few hours. We can talk then, too. And of course you can call at any time. Just ask one of the nurses."

"Thank you."

Brody stuck out his hand, shaking the surgeon's before the man walked back out of the waiting room.

Angeline sank down onto the edge of the chair, pressing her fingertips to her forehead. "This is all my fault." If she'd paid more attention to Eva she might have realized that the girl was suffering from more than just worry over her parents. "She's probably been working on this for days."

"Whether she was or not, it's hardly your *fault*." Brody pulled her hands, tugging her up from the seat.

"People get sick, babe. It happens. The doc's right. Let's get some air."

"I should wait here," she resisted.

"For what?" Brody's voice was soft. Reasonable. His head dropped closer to hers. "Even if Hewitt and Sophia were here, they'd need to eat. They'd have to wait until the doctor cleared Eva for seeing them."

He was right. Knowing it did little to make up for the guilt that swamped her.

"I can't do this," she whispered hoarsely. "I just can't."

She had only a glimpse of Brody's narrowed eyes as she tugged her hands free of his, and slid past him, intent on escaping the waiting room.

She made it out into the corridor before he closed his hands over her shoulders, halting her from behind. Her throat ached and her eyes burned deep down inside her head. "Let me go."

He made a sound she couldn't interpret, and pulled her back into the waiting room, pushing closed the door that had been standing open.

"What's this really about?"

She hugged her arms around herself, feeling chilled. "I'm just tired. And relieved."

His lips twisted. "In the past week, I've seen you in pretty much every state a person can achieve. *Every* state."

She flushed miserably. "This isn't the time to joke."

"Who's joking?" His serious expression told her that he certainly wasn't. "I'm tired and relieved, too, and whatever is nagging at you is more than that."

"Brody—"

"Just spit it out, Angeline."

"I just… I just can't bear to make another wrong decision. The last time I did—" She broke off, shaking her head. "The last time," she tried again, "a boy died."

Brody sighed. He ran his hands down her arms, circling her wrists, lifting her palms until he could slide his fingers between hers. "You're a paramedic, love. Not even you can save everyone."

"I know. But this time, I should have. Just like now. With Eva. I should have recognized earlier that she was really ill! Instead, I was…you and I were…" She slid her hands free of his and raked back her hair. "We're supposed to be *protecting* Eva and Davey." She wasn't supposed to be falling in love with a completely unsuitable man.

"You think Eva's appendix would have been just dandy if she'd been with her parents, or with another bodyguard? Dream on, Angeline. Sometimes the best-laid plans get shot to hell, particularly when there are kids involved. But even if she were nineteen instead of nine, she could have gotten sick like this. There's no telling, and there's sure in hell no blaming."

"*You* would have noticed," she said thickly.

His eyebrows shot up. "Did you see me yanking her to a doctor any more quickly than we did?" He lowered his voice. "Tell me what happened with the boy."

"There's nothing to tell." She felt brittle. "He was only a kid. A gang member, they told me. And there was a shooting. I thought I could reach him from the rear side where the culvert wasn't so narrow." She swallowed. "I was wrong. By the time my partner and

I reached him from the front side, the side *I* should have used in the first place, he'd bled out."

"And now you don't like going through tunnels," he murmured.

"I've *never* liked tunnels," she corrected. "Caves. None of that kind of thing."

"Caves." He let out a sigh. "I read in your file that you were hidden in one when Santo Marguerite was attacked."

She pressed her lips together, disconcerted that she had a file, much less one that he'd read. "The cave wasn't much for size. I was always told to stay out of it. But then someone—a cousin, maybe, because I don't remember my mother doing it—pushed me down into it." Not quickly enough for her to miss the attack on the village, though. "Davey's four," she murmured. "The same age I was when it happened. You suppose he's going to remember the madness we've put those children through these past few days?"

"If he does, his parents will help him deal with it, just like Maggie and Daniel helped *you*."

"That boy still died, Brody. Because I hesitated. Because I knew if I went in that culvert, I'd freeze up."

"But you *did* go in the culvert."

"Too late."

"What about your partner?"

"He was a rookie. He was following my lead."

"So you were human and something went wrong. Are you going to keep beating yourself with it or are you going to pull it together and keep on keeping on? Angeline, I swear I have yet to see you hesitate even when I think you should. You see something that needs doing, and God. You do it. If you'd gotten to the kid any faster than you had would he have lived?"

She swallowed. Pressed her palms together. Shook her head. "Probably not." That's what her supervisor had said. That's what the emergency room doctors had said. "That's the only reason I have a job to go back to when my vacation is up." She waited a long beat, and finally admitted the truth. "If I go back at all. I just... I want to come back to Wyoming. I just don't want to come back feeling like I failed."

"You can't stop helping people, Angeline. You're a natural at it. So who the hell cares if you're doing it in Atlanta or in Weaver. Or Venezuela, or Sheridan for that matter?"

She jerked a little at that. "I put my fear ahead of my job, Brody, and that kid never had a chance. Today, with Eva, I put my...my need ahead of her." She waved her hand, encompassing the hospital waiting room around them. "And look where we are!"

"You made me feel human again," he said quietly. "You knew Eva and Davey were fed and bedded because *I* told you they were. So if you want to blame anyone, babe, it had better be me. Not yourself. You're a paramedic, for God's sake. Not a doctor. You're trained to respond to emergencies, which you've done pretty damn well as far as I'm concerned."

Her throat tightened. "But if I don't go back to Atlanta—"

"—then you don't go back," he said simply. He slid his hand through her hair. "The world's not gonna stop spinning, love, if you change courses. But that guilt?" He looked regretful. "Even when it's deserved, it doesn't do anything but dry a person up from the inside out. Let it go, Angeline."

"What do *you* know about guilt? You've probably never made a misstep in your entire life."

He slowly picked up her hand. The one with Sophia's wedding band. "I know that if I had kept quiet when I learned that Simon Brody wasn't my real father, he and my mother and Penny would all probably still be alive. Instead," he broke off and looked grim. "Instead, word got out to the wrong person that the man who *was* my real father had two kids and an ex-wife whose existence he'd managed to keep hidden for fifteen years. My mother broke the silence between them because of *me*. Because I wanted to know the man who'd really fathered me and Penny. And just like Santina would use Davey and Eva to manipulate their parents if they could, Sandoval tried using my family to manipulate *him*."

Shock swirled through her, thick and engulfing. "Oh, Brody. No. I'm so sorry. Sandoval? The same monster who destroyed Santo Marguerite? London's a far cry from Central and South America. Those were his stomping grounds, I thought. Why would he have reason to go after *your* family?"

"London had nothing to do with anything except that's where we lived. On the other hand, my father, the one who contributed his genes to me that is, was the one person who kept thwarting Sandoval's actions *wherever* they occurred," he said flatly. "And that's why my parents and sister died in a car bombing one fine spring afternoon. It was a total fluke that I wasn't with them."

Her stomach dropped. She stared at Brody's lips, waiting for him to continue.

But the door to the waiting room burst open and a tall, silver-haired man stood there, looking almost as surprised at the sight of *them*. But it wasn't surprise in his deep voice, when he spoke. It was annoyance. Pure and simple. "*There* you are. Bloody hell, Simon. You don't make it easy to find you, do you."

Brody's expression had grown, if anything, even more grim. His lips twisted. "I don't believe you've ever officially met," he told her, startling her out of her surprised stupor. "So let me have the honors. Angeline," he angled his head toward the older man, "meet Coleman Black."

Her stomach dropped to her toes, knowing what was coming even before Brody finished speaking.

"My father."

Chapter 15

Brody watched the color drain from Angeline's face as she looked from him to Cole and back again. Her lips moved, as if she were struggling to find something appropriate to say, which only made Brody feel more like the slug he was for tossing her without preparation into the sordidness that was his life.

Cole gave him an annoyed look and crossed the room, his hand outstretched toward Angeline. "Simon isn't *quite* correct," he said smoothly. "We have met. But you were so small you wouldn't remember." He caught her hand in his, raising it to his lips. "You're as lovely as I would have expected, my dear."

Angeline looked disarmed, color coming back into her cheeks. Cole might be finally pushing retirement but that didn't mean the old man didn't have his charms.

As a father, however, he'd been pretty damn miserable.

"You saw me when I was a child?"

"All long hair and enormous brown eyes with barely a word of English to your name," he assured. "And now, you and my son here have been leading us all around in a merry chase. Needless to say, it was quite a surprise to actually have him call me for assistance." His gaze cut from Angeline to Brody, and there was no charm in the look for him.

It was pure steel.

Of course, the old man wouldn't be pleased that Brody had contacted him. It was entirely outside of protocol.

Brody deliberately smiled. He might be closing the gap to forty by leaps and bounds, but he still knew how to goad the guy, just as he had when he wasn't yet sixteen and Cole had pretty much dragged him, kicking and sullen, from London and taken him back with him to Connecticut.

He'd never sent out announcements that his son had come to live with him, that's for damn sure. Not hard when Brody hadn't actually lived *with* Cole. He'd been in a well-secured house, tended by well-trained agents, none of whom knew the entire story.

Nobody, not a single soul inside or outside of Hollins-Winword knew that Brody Paine was anything other than one more survivor taken under the protective wing of the agency until the suspected terrorist who'd targeted his family could be caught.

Which they never were, since Sandoval was still out there.

To this day, he didn't know if Cole had ever grieved over the loss of the woman he'd been married to for so brief a time. Or his daughter.

He'd never said.

And Brody sure in hell had never asked.

What they did do was exist in a sort of vacuum where Brody did his job and Cole did his, and rarely the twain ever met.

"Brody called you?" Angeline was looking at him with surprise. "He didn't tell me that."

"I told you I reached someone," he defended.

Her lips compressed.

"If you'd shown a lot less stubbornness and more sense," Cole told him, "you would have contacted me the first time you couldn't reach Persia, protocol be damned."

"Persia!" Angeline gave them both a horrified look. "That...that, *girl* who replaced me at the All-Med site is your handler?"

"Was," Cole said. "She's been...replaced."

"But why?"

"Don't bother asking, babe. He doesn't answer questions like that."

"Miguel Chavez discovered she was playing both ends from the middle when she made a few unwise calls while returning that Hummer to St. Agnes. Hewitt was the one who donated that to the nuns, by the way."

Brody felt sure that Cole wouldn't have provided the information about Persia if not for the pleasure of proving him wrong. And he didn't much like that the old man had shown the same curiosity he'd felt about the presence of that expensive truck at the convent in the first place.

"Miguel." Angeline looked dazed. She sat down on the nearest chair. "*He* is involved with Hollins, too?"

"On occasion," Cole said briefly. "As he got to know you through your volunteer work with All-Med he thought you might be a good asset, and that's when I sent Brody to meet you there five years ago."

She shook her head. "Most people would just pick up the phone and set a meeting," she murmured.

Cole laughed.

"Sweet as this reunion is," Brody drawled, "why didn't someone replace Persia sooner?"

His father's laughter died. He looked irritated all over again. "We didn't know where the hell you were. The only trace we found of either of you was an All-Med T-shirt covered in blood on the floor of a cab that was riddled with your fingerprints in Caracas. That's when we were positive it was the two of you, and not Santina's man, who managed to get the Stanley children out of St. Agnes. Until then, we had no confirmation either way. You can imagine the difficulties that has presented."

"Good grief," Angeline hopped back to her feet. "My family doesn't know about the shirt, do they?"

"Unfortunately, yes. The media down there got wind of an aid volunteer seeming to disappear off the planet, with nothing left behind but her bloody shirt. Damn reporters. Always messing things around when they shouldn't. If you'd ever turn on a television and watch the international news, Simon, you might know these things."

Angeline groaned. Any television viewing for them of late had been geared toward Davey's four-year-old tastes.

"But I've let your folks know that you're safe," Cole assured. "I notified them earlier as soon as I heard from Simon."

She pressed her hand to her forehead. "They must have been going mad." She eyed them both. "This is *exactly* why I didn't want them knowing I was involved with Hollins. We're all worried enough about my cousin who's still missing!"

Cole stayed silent on that and Brody wanted to kick him. But the fact was, Ryan Clay *was* missing. Not even the agency had been able to unearth him, and they'd been quietly trying for months. That news wasn't likely to make any one of them feel better.

"Your parents will see for themselves soon enough that you're safe and well," Cole warned. "Daniel told me he and Maggie would be here by morning."

Angeline's hands flopped down to her sides. "Well, great. I never mind seeing my parents. I, um, I have to go check on Eva. I don't suppose in all these revelations you can tell me that her parents are free?"

"I wish I could," Cole told her. "We're working on it," he added. "We know where they're being held in Rio, and that they're very much alive. Getting them out, however, has been proving problematic."

From experience, Brody knew that term could mean just about anything.

"I'll go with you to see Eva," he told her and ignored the eyebrow his father lifted in surprise.

Angeline nodded, moistened her lips and turned toward Cole. "It's been an…eventful night, I must say." She leaned up and pressed a kiss to his cheek. "Thank you. For everything that you've done for me. For my family. It's nice to have an opportunity to tell you that, in person, after all these years."

He smiled faintly. "I like to see a happy ending as much as anyone. That's what keeps me in this business. Sadly, the people closest to me weren't able to find that." His gaze cut to Brody's, and for once, he let his regret show. "But now I have hope again."

Brody didn't even want to know what that was supposed to mean.

He closed his hand around Angeline's elbow and drew her toward the door. Eva would surely be settled in her room by now.

"Simon. A word, please."

He should have known. Cole always had liked to have the last word.

"Stay," Angeline murmured. "Talk with him. Come to Eva's room when you're finished." She looked around him. "Mr. Black, I hope we see one another again."

"Coleman. Or Cole, if you choose." He looked slightly amused. "And I feel certain that we will."

Brody waited until she'd disappeared down the hall and around the corner before he looked back at his father. *"What?"*

"Are you willing to stay on the Stanley children until that situation is resolved? I've already arranged for a team to keep watch over the hospital, either way."

Brody's lips thinned. When had he ever let go of an op before it was completed? "Do you need to ask?"

"I suppose not. You're good at what you do, Simon. Too good when it comes down to it."

"Is there a point in there somewhere? Because I'd kind of like to see how Eva's doing after they've cut her open."

Cole's lips compressed. "Touché," he said evenly. "I was never there when you were in the hospital being patched up from your various escapades. Of which there were *many*. So maybe my point is moot, after all."

He didn't want to care what the man had to say. But he did. For the same reasons that he'd gone back to the agency even after he'd planned to hang out his shingle with Roger.

He *was* like Cole.

Dammit all to hell.

So he stood there. Waiting. "Well?"

"Don't turn into me," Cole said simply. "If Angeline matters to you, and it seems that she does, change your ways and make a life with her. Hang out that law degree you worked so hard to get. Do anything but this. You can't combine being a field agent with a family."

"Tristan Clay did." Hell, Angeline's uncle was pretty high up the Hollins food chain of command.

Cole's expression didn't change. "I could easily name fifty other agents who have not. So what odds would you lay your money on? Whether you want to admit it or not, Simon, you're too much like me. I'm just suggesting you not make the same choices that I did. The cost is too high. You're old enough to recognize what matters in life, and young enough still to do something about it."

"Don't pretend that you know me all that well, Cole. We both know otherwise."

The other man pulled out a pipe, looked around the waiting room that was clearly marked "no smoking" and tucked it away again. "I know enough to recognize the ring that Angeline is wearing."

"It was my mother's first wedding ring from Simon," Brody said tightly. Before she'd been buried, he'd taken it from her favorite jewelry box, the one where she'd kept her dearest possessions. "It has nothing to do with you."

"Did she tell you that?"

"Yes." He bit out the word.

Cole smiled, but there was no happiness in it. Only years of weariness and a sadness that seemed to go a mile deep. "Actually," he said quietly, "it was the ring that *I* gave her."

Then he turned and walked out of the waiting room.

When Angeline found the room the nurse directed her to, Eva was sound asleep.

She sat down beside the bed and rested her hands lightly on the mattress.

The ring on her finger winked up at her.

She toyed with it. Slipped it off easily, for it *was* loose. Yet, in all the madness of the past several days, she'd managed to keep it in place.

"You kept wearing it."

She looked up to see Brody standing in the doorway. "You kept telling people we were married," she pointed out truthfully enough.

His gaze slanted toward the bed, as if he'd already lost interest in the subject. "How's she doing?"

"Sound asleep, as you can see." She curled her fingers, wanting to hide the ring from his too-seeing eyes. "How are *you* doing?"

He exhaled. "Does it matter?"

She pushed back the chair and rose. "Of course it matters, Brody."

"How much?"

She wavered. "What do you want me to say? I don't know what you're asking."

His eyes were nearly black. "I think you know."

Her spine stiffened. Did he want her to lay her soul bare merely for pure entertainment value? "Just what did you and your father talk about?"

"How much like him I am."

"Don't make that sound like such a death sentence," she chided softly. "I know you have your reasons for feeling differently, *good* reasons, but if it weren't for him…" She lifted her shoulders. What more could she say?

"Santo Marguerite might still be standing if Hollins-Winword hadn't tried to intervene."

"You mean if your father hadn't tried." She sighed. "Sandoval is the monster in this story, Brody. Not your— not Coleman Black."

She could see the resistance in his eyes and stepped closer, folding her hands around his. "It wasn't anyone but Sandoval who wanted the land around my family's village. The likelihood that he'd have done something terrible regardless of your father's presence there— of any kind of Hollins-Winword involvement for that matter—is extremely high. If it didn't happen when I was four, it could have happened before I was born, or twenty years after. Am I right? *Am I?*"

"He's still active, obviously," he allowed grimly.

"Exactly. And Sandoval still controls that land, even to this day. My father told me long ago that there's no reasoning with a man like him. My surviving what happened there makes no more sense than you not being in the car that day with your family. We survived. They didn't. That's reality and you and I get to live with it. And maybe," she swallowed, "maybe it's time we stop questioning why, and just accept the blessing for what it is. Your father—I'm sorry—*Coleman* helped me to a new life as a Clay. And I'm assuming he played some role in your life after your parents and sister died?"

"Only enough to make sure nobody else got wind of who I really was. He put a roof over my head in Connecticut and guards on my tail and the only thing we ever talked about was the agency."

"Why would he do that? Because you think he didn't care? Don't you think it might be because he didn't want to lose you, too? It's your past, Brody. You know it better than I, obviously. But regardless of how or why anything happened with your childhood or with mine, here we are. Survivors." She looked over at the bed. "Did he say anything more about them?"

"Just made sure I wasn't going to bail on the situation."

"He wouldn't think that."

He snorted softly. "Like you said once. We're going to have to agree to disagree where Coleman Black is concerned. You don't have to worry about any Santina folks showing up here, though. He told me there's a team watching the hospital now."

"If *he* and all of Hollins-Winword that he has at his command weren't able to track us here until you contacted him, I don't think Santina would be able to find us, either. But now that everything's out in the open, more or less, I guess there's no more need for me to be here. Or, like you said, for this." She slipped off the ring and held it out to him, wanting with everything she possessed for him to tell her that she was wrong.

To tell her that *she* mattered.

That he wanted her to stay for reasons that had nothing to do with Eva or Davey or anything but what had gone between them.

He slowly lifted his palm.

It was not the answer she wanted.

She sucked down the pain inside her, and prayed that it didn't show on her face.

No woman wanted to face the fact that the man she'd fallen in love with didn't return the feeling.

Without touching him, she dropped the ring into his palm.

His fingers slowly curled around it. "The ring wasn't what I thought it was," he murmured.

"It wasn't what I thought, either." Despite herself, the words emerged. She pressed her lips together, keeping her composure together with an effort.

She turned to the bed, wrapping her hands around the iron rail at the foot of it. "So, um, what now? I still h-have a week of vacation left. I'd like to spend it with, um, with Davey and Eva. If you don't mind." Her eyes burned and she blinked furiously, determined not to cry in front of him.

"And after your week is up?"

"Then I'll go back h-home." In all of the time they'd spent together, he'd never before been cruel like this.

"In Atlanta?"

"What do you want from me, Brody? Maybe I'll stay in Atlanta. Maybe I'll go back to Weaver. *I don't know.*"

"Is there anything that you *do* know?"

Stung, she slapped her hands on the rail. Eva didn't so much as stir. "I know I must have been a fool to let myself love you," she snapped. "So if you want to know how much you matter, *now* you do. Are you quite satisfied?"

"I don't know. I haven't been loved in a long time." His voice sounded rusty. "I'm out of practice."

And just that simply, her anger eased out of her, leaving nothing but her heart that ached for him.

"I think you've been loved all along, you just haven't wanted to face it."

"I don't want to talk about Cole."

She angled her chin, looking up at him. "Then who do you want to talk about?"

"You. Me." His blue eyes were steady on her face. "It's been a crazy week."

"It hasn't even been a week," she whispered, feeling choked.

"But it's been years of foreplay."

She flushed and opened her mouth. Caught the faint smile playing around his lips and closed it again.

"I love you, Angeline Reyes Clay. I know that

seems fast, but it's been a long time in the making. And maybe I'm not so far gone that I can't heed good advice when I hear it even if I don't care much for the person delivering it. Maybe I'm just tired of making my way alone. Or maybe the fact that we both survived, like you said, meant we were supposed to find our way here to each other. But what I do know is that I don't want you to walk away from me when your vacation is done. Fact is, I don't want you to walk away from me ever."

A tear slid down her cheek. "Brody."

"I don't want you to go back to Atlanta unless that's really where you want to be. And then, hell, I don't know. I guess I'd follow you there. But then I'd have to drag you back here, because, *babe.* A city? When we've got all of Wyoming at our disposal? If you don't like the house I built, I'll build you another. A dozen if I have to. One thing I can say about Hollins is that it does pay well. I could even start a law practice. But if I didn't, I can still support you. And, you know. Kids. If you wanted."

She laughed, the tears coming faster. "You'd want kids? *You?* Not long ago you shuddered at the idea!"

"I'm a guy," he dismissed. "Don't you think I'd be good at it?"

She tilted her head, tsking. "Brody."

"So?" He looked oddly unsure of himself.

"You're really serious," she breathed, hardly daring to believe that he didn't want just the here and now. He wanted…more.

"I'm a serious man," he said gruffly, pulling her into his arms. "In the serious business of loving you."

He held up his hand and she saw the ring tucked on the end of his index finger. "This was my mother's," he said. "I thought it was the ring my dad—Simon— gave her. She treasured it," he murmured. "But it was from Cole."

"Why didn't you say something before? I thought you'd gotten it from the Stanleys' apartment."

"It was easier to let you think that than let you know that, even then, you mattered to me." His hand shook a little as he drew it down her cheek, and she leaned into his touch, the tears sliding down her cheek.

"I love you, Brody. And I don't want to go anywhere that you're not."

"I'll get you your own ring," he said huskily.

She pressed her lips to his for a long, long moment. Then she drew his hand with the ring to her, clasping it against her heart. "Do you think that Coleman didn't love your mother when he gave this to her?"

A shadow came and went in his eyes. "I don't know anymore."

"I think he did," she whispered. "And you know she treasured it, because you said so. So maybe this *is* the ring I'm meant to have, Brody. Maybe we're all just finally coming full circle. Like the ring itself. No beginning. No end."

"If you want this ring, just say so, Angeline." But the sudden sheen in his eyes gave lie to his wry words, and her heart slipped open even more to him.

This utterly *good* man in his heart, who was a positive whirlwind. Who shocked her and delighted her, who challenged her and had faith in her, even when she didn't have it in herself.

"I want your ring, Brody Paine," she whispered surely. "And even if there were no ring at all, I'd still want you. I'd still love you."

"You think this has been a crazy few days? Be sure, Angeline. Because I won't let you go."

She slid her hand up his chest, over the bunch of bandage she could feel beneath, until she found his heartbeat, pulsing against her palm. "What's a few crazy days when we've got a lifetime of them yet to live?"

His head came down to hers. "Together." The word whispered over her lips.

She closed the distance, her heart as full as it could possibly ever be. "Together."

Epilogue

"Where are the boutonnieres?" Casey Clay sauntered into the room where the groom's half of the wedding party was assembling before the wedding.

"Davey's guarding them on the counter there." Brody pointed to the boy, who wore a miniature black suit like his. Davey, looking important, handed over the sprig when Casey went to him.

Stephanotis or some such thing, Brody knew. He'd been hearing about flowers for the past month. Ever since his and Angeline's plans for a simple elopement flew right out the window.

She hadn't wanted to disappoint her family, she'd told him. And he'd caved rather than see any disappointment darken her eyes. He figured she deserved the wedding of her dreams. It was the least he could do to make up for proposing in a damn hospital room after five of the most insane days of their lives.

Now, he stared at himself in the mirror, trying to get the knot in his damned tie straight. Thank God he had insisted on no bow ties.

As it was, the wedding that he'd figured he could slide Angeline quickly through had turned into a regular circus. They couldn't hold it at the house in Sheridan, because the entire family was in Weaver. Angeline had been raised in the church there, so of course she ought to be married there.

On and on and on.

"How're you holding up?" Max Scalise held out a tall glass of champagne. Brody took it, though he'd have preferred a beer.

"Fine, if I could get this bloody tie straight."

"Just think about the honeymoon," Max advised, thoroughly amused. He reached over and yanked the long silver tie front and center. "You look real pretty."

"Don't make me regret asking you to be my best man," he muttered, polishing off the champagne all too quickly. Roger had sent his regrets that he couldn't make the wedding, so the position had needed filling. And now that Max was the sheriff and married to Sarah, he evidently no longer had reason to loathe the ground that Brody walked. Brody had even begun to actually like the other guy. He was a good cop.

"Don't make me regret agreeing," the other man returned. "What're you so grouchy about? You've got a beautiful woman, and I mean *seriously* beautiful, ready to commit the rest of her life to you. Most folks would just think she needed committing."

"Hilarious."

"This is just a day, Brody. It's the marriage that counts."

"I know. Believe me. I know. It's just all this…" he waved his hand at the flowers, the champagne. "Never in my life did I figure I'd ever be doing this."

"Did you ever figure you'd have someone like Angeline in your life?"

"No." He turned back to the mirror. Started to reach for the tie only to decide it looked fine the way it was. "She's been staying in Weaver for the past week," he finally said under his breath. While he'd been in Sheridan with Davey and Eva and Mrs. B. making plans to open that law practice. Finally. "We're going bloody insane without her. What's it going to be like ten years down the road and she wants to go away for a week or something?"

"God. You do have it bad." Max clapped him over the shoulder. "Suck it up," he advised, obviously amused. "Be a man."

From the sanctuary, Brody heard the organ music begin playing.

"Here." Casey held out the boutonniere. He, like Evan Taggart and young Davey, was serving as Brody's groomsmen. "Don't want to forget your posies."

Brody managed to pin the thing into place without stabbing himself to death and then, just as they'd rehearsed the evening before, they filed into the church.

His eyes drifted over the guests. No "his" and "her" sides, Angeline had said. Because everything from here on out was an "our" situation.

Mostly, he figured, she knew his side would be

pretty damn empty otherwise, and soft heart that she had, she thought that would bother him.

He watched Casey escort his mother, Maggie, up the aisle where orchids dripped from the sides of each pew. Her blond hair was twisted in a sleek knot, her slender figure accentuated by the dark blue dress she wore. Next to her hulking son Casey—who'd definitely inherited the tall-blond-Clay thing—she looked even more petite.

Her eyes met Brody's and she smiled as she took her seat in the front pew. Once she'd taken him to task for dragging his daughter around the world and scaring the life out of them the way he had, she'd welcomed him with more generosity than he deserved.

Clearly, Angeline took after her.

Sitting behind Maggie were Angeline's grandparents, Squire and Gloria. And behind *them,* the rows on both sides of the church were jammed with more relatives. Angeline had counted them off for him one day and the number had been staggering, particularly for a guy who had only his quasi father to claim.

He was sitting in the front row on Brody's nonside.

Again, Angeline's doing. She'd insisted he invite Cole. Brody hadn't believed the man would even show up, but there he was. Just another surprise in his life since Angeline.

The organ music changed suddenly and everyone turned expectantly toward the rear of the church.

Brody realized he was holding his breath.

Sarah came first, and beside him, he heard Max sigh a little at the sight of his wife, who was noticeably pregnant in her long blue dress. And Max had said that

Brody had it bad? He shot his best man a look. Max just shrugged. He was thoroughly besotted and didn't care who knew it.

Close on Sarah's heels was Leandra. As small as Sarah was tall, she came up the aisle, not seeming to look at anyone but her husband, Evan.

"She's pregnant," Max murmured to Brody. "Just told him before they got to the church."

Which would explain the vaguely dazed look on the vet's face, Brody suspected, and felt a definite envy. He'd told Angeline just a week ago that he wasn't getting any younger; they needed to get cracking.

Of course, at the time, he'd mostly just wanted to get her into bed, but she'd blushed and looked so suddenly shy that he hadn't been able to get the hope out of his head.

Davey and Eva headed up the aisle. The boy held a pillow with the rings tied to it in ribbon, and it was a good thing because he kept tipping the pillow back and forth as he grinned widely, happy to be the center of attention. And Eva—fully recuperated in the past six weeks since her appendectomy—looked pretty as a picture with her hair up in curls, wearing the same blue as the women. She had a smile on her face, too, and Brody was glad to see it, since Hewitt and Sophia's absence had been hitting her harder than Davey.

He gave Eva a subtle wink and she wrinkled her nose, smiling wider. Lord, but he was going to miss them. He, the guy who had always preached never getting too attached.

J.D. was sauntering up the aisle, and Brody's mouth dried a little, because he knew Angeline came after her. As if she could read his mind, J.D.'s green gaze was full of laughter as she passed him, and took her place in line. She gave him an audacious wink. Since she'd given Brody the third degree at the rehearsal the night before, evidently she'd decided she could be sparing with her good humor now.

He grinned back at her. Yeah, he liked J.D. She was a good kid.

And then he saw her. The only woman he'd ever loved.

Angeline.

Standing in the rear of the church looking so beautiful he thought his heart might lurch out of his throat.

The afternoon sun slanted through the high windows above their heads, as the organ swelled and she slowly started forward, her hand on her father's arm. She'd told him she wasn't going to wear white, but the long dress she wore looked pretty white to him. The soft-looking lace clung to her figure, looking innocent and sexy all at once.

Her long dark hair was pulled back from her face, only a single, exotic flower tucked in the gleaming waves, and when she finally reached him, she angled a look up at him. She slowly, softly smiled. "You ready for a wedding, Brody Paine?"

As long as she kept smiling at him, there was nothing in life that he couldn't face, he thought. Even a wedding in Wyoming.

"Only with you," he promised and knew he'd do the whole thing a dozen times over, just to see the shining in her eyes.

She tucked her hand surely in his, and handed off

her bouquet of orchids to J.D., and the two of them stepped up into the chancel with the minister, who beamed a smile over all of them and opened his bible.

"Dearly beloved," he began, only to be interrupted when Davey suddenly bolted for the rear of the church.

"Mom! Dad!" His voice filled the rafters. Eva suddenly dropped her bouquet and pelted after him.

Angeline's startled eyes met Brody's and they all turned.

Sophia and Hewitt Stanley were rushing up the aisle, grabbing their kids up and swinging them around.

Angeline bit her lip. She looked up at Brody, who didn't look as surprised as everyone else. Nor did Coleman, when she gave him an inquiring look.

He smiled. Lifted his hands.

In their pew, Angeline's parents were holding hands and looking amused. After all, twenty-five years earlier, Angeline's arrival had very nearly interrupted *their* nuptials.

"I suppose you knew they were coming," Angeline whispered to Brody.

"I wasn't sure when they would get here. They were extracted two days ago," he told her. "There was a lot of debriefing. At least a few of the Santina group are going to be out of commission for a long while."

"And Sandoval?"

He shook his head. "Not everything can be solved, sometimes."

Davey was dragging his parents by their hands toward them. "Mr. Dad, this is my *real* dad."

Both Hewitt and his wife were pale from their ordeal, but the hand he extended was steady. "Thank you," he said simply.

Sophia's eyes were wet. She held Eva tight against her.

Angeline crouched down and touched the girl's cheek. "I told you faith could do amazing things." She felt Brody's hand squeeze her shoulder.

Eva's face was wet with tears as she twisted an arm around Angeline's neck, too. "I love you, Angeline."

"I love you, too, sweetie. And I'm going to miss you, but we'll see each other again." Her eyes blurred with the promise as she rose and faced Sophia. "I feel like I know you."

"And I feel like we will never have truer friends," Sophia returned, looking just as tearful as her daughter. She hugged Angeline tightly. "But we are interrupting. We would have waited outside if we'd realized the ceremony had already begun. But there was a message from a Mrs. Bedford that the children were *here*."

"Of course you had to come. Right away," Angeline assured. She brushed her hand down her antique gown. "So now you'll stay...find a seat," she suggested, laughing.

Coleman gestured, and the four of them joined him in that front pew. He rescued the pillow with the rings that Davey had dropped on the floor. His gaze hesitated for a moment on the smaller of the two bands. Then he handed it to Brody. "You'll be happy," he told him gruffly.

"I know," Brody replied simply. He took the pillow and handed it off to Max. Then he turned to Angeline. "Shall we try this again?"

She dashed her fingers over her cheeks and nodded. She folded her hand through his arm again, and they stepped up into the chancel where the minister was looking slightly bewildered. He opened his bible once again.

"House is going to feel empty without them," Brody murmured before the man could begin speaking.

Angeline huffed out a puff of air. "You know, don't you. Are you going to *ever* let me surprise you?"

He gave a bark of laughter and caught her around her waist, lifting her right off her toes. "Brody," she gasped, but she was smiling and looped her arms around his shoulders.

"Every day with you is a surprise, Angeline," he told her and kissed her deeply. The guests were laughing. Some cheering. She barely heard any of it.

Oh, she loved this man who loved her.

The minister cleared his throat. Loudly. "If we could have a little order, here?"

Brody set Angeline on her feet again. He reached out and opened the bible for the minister, pointing at the pages. "Right there," he said.

The minister's lips thinned. But there was a definite twinkle in his eyes that even *he* couldn't hide. "Never a dull moment when there's a Clay around," he murmured. "All right then." He lifted the bible higher. Looked at Angeline and Brody, then at the congregation behind them. "Dearly beloved…"

* * * * *

Lynnette Kent lives on a farm in southeastern North Carolina with her six horses and six dogs. When she isn't busy riding, driving or feeding animals, she loves to tend her gardens and read and write books.

Books by Lynnette Kent

Harlequin American Romance

Smoky Mountain Reunion
Smoky Mountain Home
A Holiday to Remember
Jesse: Merry Christmas, Cowboy
A Convenient Proposal

The Marshall Brothers

A Wife in Wyoming
A Husband in Wyoming
A Marriage in Wyoming

Harlequin Superromance

The Last Honest Man
The Fake Husband
Single with Kids
Abby's Christmas
The Prodigal Texan

Visit the Author Profile page at
Harlequin.com for more titles.

A HUSBAND IN WYOMING

Lynnette Kent

Chapter 1

June

Here comes trouble.

Standing outside the barn, Dylan Marshall watched as dust billowed up behind the vehicle approaching in the distance. He swallowed against the dread squeezing his throat. If he could have avoided this encounter by any reasonable means, he would have. The next four days were going to be absolute hell.

At last the Jeep came into full view, its dark blue paint now mottled with dirt. Going too fast, the car barreled up the last hill and hurtled along the road toward the ranch house, where it screeched to a stop with a spray of gravel.

Dylan shook his head. *Somebody needs to slow down.* His boots felt as if they had lead in them, but he managed to move his feet and descend the hill toward the house. After a long day driving cattle, all he wanted was a shower. Dirt had settled in the bends of his elbows and the creases of his jeans, the cuffs of his gloves and at the base of his throat. He could taste it on his tongue.

He also wanted some dinner and a chance to sit down on a chair instead of a saddle. But most of all, he wanted to get clean.

He did not want to meet the press.

The door on the Jeep opened and a pair of high-heeled boots hit the ground. Standing up, the driver saw him coming, shut the car door and walked forward. Like two gunfighters, they moved slowly, warily toward each other, hands at their sides as if poised to draw a pistol and fire.

Dylan stopped with about ten feet between them. "Jess Granger?"

She was tall and slim, with long, shapely legs showcased by skinny jeans and those fashionable boots. Shiny brown hair whipped around her head, blown by the never-ending Wyoming wind.

Pulling the long strands out of the way, she nodded. "From *Renown Magazine*. You're Dylan Marshall?"

Her face could make Da Vinci weep—big eyes, the cheekbones of a goddess and a wide red mouth that stirred a man's blood to the boil.

He tipped his hat and then closed the distance between them, removing his gloves so he could shake her hand. "Welcome to the Circle M Ranch." A warm, slender palm returned his grasp. Dylan let go slowly, smiling in pure appreciation of her beauty.

Spreading her arms wide, she took a deep breath and blew it out. "There's a lot of space out here. Such a big sky."

"Are you a New York native?"

"I've lived there for half my life, so it feels like it. I've done my share of traveling, but this is my first time in Wyoming. I'm ready for a Western adventure."

"We'll do our best." A drop of sweat rolled down the nape of his neck. "Let me get your luggage." Stuffing his gloves into a back pocket, he crossed to the car and opened the rear hatch.

She whirled to follow him. "That's okay. I can—"

He pulled out her two bags before she could finish. "Got it. Come into the house." Leading the way onto the porch, he set down the big red suitcase and opened the screen door, nodding her through. "Be our guest."

He was determined to be polite. The only way to survive this interview was to keep control of the conversation, making sure Jess Granger learned only what he wanted her to. Reporters could be ruthless, but his job for the next four days was to give this New York journalist a peek at his life and his sculpture without actually revealing anything important. The gallery where he'd be showing his work had insisted on a big publicity push. Their bottom line: no article, no exhibit. After the way he'd sabotaged his career two years ago, Dylan knew he was lucky to get this chance for a significant show. If he wanted his work to be seen, he had to cooperate with the gallery—and with Jess Granger.

But he didn't want his emotional guts dissected in a fancy magazine for strangers to read. His three brothers deserved their privacy, as did the kids staying with them for the summer. Fortunately, Dylan considered himself an expert in the art of shooting the bull. Try as she might, he'd make sure Ms. Granger discovered only the most harmless details.

He set her bags by the hallway door while she sashayed inside and circled the living room. "Nice," she said, with a surprised expression. "Quite upscale for a bachelor pad."

"We try to stay civilized."

"So I notice." She homed in on the one sculpture in the room, a bear figure he'd made while still in high school. "Is this yours?"

And so it started. "Yep. An early piece."

"It's…clever. Obviously talented." Her words echoed the art critics he remembered from his time in that world—conceited and condescending. "But not at all similar to the work you were doing when you came out of college."

Hands in his front pockets, Dylan tried to stay relaxed. "I took a different direction for a while there, exploring new materials, new techniques. I tried to give people what they appreciated. What they wanted to see."

Jess Granger nodded, setting the bear in its place. "You certainly did that. For five years, you were the darling of the international art scene, the name everybody talked about. You had sculptures in the major art fairs and showed up at all the right parties.

"Then—" she turned around and snapped her fingers "—you disappeared. Just gone, without an explanation or a goodbye. There hasn't been a hint of news about you in more than two years. My editor was surprised to hear that you have a new show opening, and downright shocked that Trevor Galleries would sponsor this article."

Arms crossed, eyes narrowed, the reporter stared at him. "They sent me to get the story, Dylan. They want to read all about this comeback of yours. What does it mean, personally and artistically? What are your plans? Will you be returning to New York, or Miami? Or working in Europe? And, the most important detail… Why in the world did you drop out in the first place?"

Dylan cleared his throat. "You dive right in, don't you?" he asked. "Would you like something to drink or eat, first? A chance to get settled?"

"No. Thanks," she said, after a beat. "You had scholarships to European art schools. Blue ribbons at juried shows around the country. The critics all raved. You were a sensation before your twenty-fifth birthday. Why would you give that up?"

"Inspiration comes and goes," he said. "You can't always predict where it'll lead."

Jess Granger shook her head. "Artists don't just abandon their careers. What have you been doing in the two years since?"

"Working."

"On what?"

He shrugged a shoulder. "It's a ranch—there's a lot to do. In fact," he added, "I won't be able to sit around talking for four days. We've got a full schedule here in the summer, from sunup to sundown. Not including studio time."

"I'm not here to disrupt your life." Her hands went up in a gesture of surrender. "This article is supposed to provide positive press for you and your show. I intend to convey how you blend your art with your lifestyle."

"Sure. 'A Day on the Ranch' is all you want."

"I can't force you to confess." She actually pouted at him, making the most of that beautiful mouth.

Dylan only grinned at her. "With your looks, I suspect you can persuade a man to confide all his most dastardly secrets."

Her face eased into a sassy smile. "I promise not to reveal where you hid the bodies, anyway."

"I don't worry about that." Flirting was much more fun than dueling over the truth. "This is the Wild, Wild West, after all. It's the superhero tights in my dresser drawer I'm concerned about. We artists are a weird bunch, you know."

Jess Granger laughed out loud. "What a story angle!"

He enjoyed the sound of that laugh. "Anything to draw readers, right?"

"I do try to stay on the right side of the truth." Her sudden frown said he'd hit a sore spot. "So you'll have to show me the tights before I commit to print."

Dylan chuckled. "Once you're in my bedroom," he promised, "we'll see about that."

Jess winked at him. "An interesting prospect." Maybe flirting was the way to get Dylan Marshall loosened up and talking. Otherwise, he'd stonewalled her so far.

And she certainly had no objection to trading banter with such a gorgeous specimen. He'd always been handsome, thanks to those long-lashed, dark chocolate eyes and a sensitive mouth framed by a square jaw and determined chin. Three years ago, though, he'd seemed too young to take seriously, wearing designer suits and an edgy haircut, dating top models and rich socialites. Observing from a distance, she'd considered him a brat. Talented, but spoiled.

Today, Jess had to admit that his exile had caused a huge change in Dylan Marshall, on the outside at least. There was a maturity in his face she found immensely appealing. With his narrow hips, long legs encased in snug jeans and broad shoulders under a blue-checked shirt, he could certainly lay claim to the legendary cowboy assets. He even wore a white hat, to finish off the hero image.

But her assignment was to get behind that image and discover the truth. Judging from his evasions so far, an aggressive approach did not bode well for the interview. She would have to handle him carefully, or she wouldn't get the details her editor demanded.

Before she could renew her offensive, a husky blonde dog padded into the room from the rear of the house followed by a big man with light brown hair and dark eyes like Dylan's.

"Welcome to the Circle M," the man said in a bass voice. "I'm Wyatt." He wore jeans and boots but had a back brace fitted over his chambray work shirt. "Make yourself at home."

Jess shook his hand, noticing calluses indicative of

physical labor. "That seems pretty easy to do. I appreciate your hospitality."

"No trouble." He glanced at the canine standing beside him wagging her tail. "This is Honey. She runs the place."

"She's beautiful. Can I pet her?"

"She'll be insulted if you don't."

Bending over, Jess carefully stroked the tawny head. "Nice to meet you, Honey. You're a good dog, aren't you?" She didn't have much contact with animals, so she was never quite sure what to do with them. But Honey's brown eyes seemed friendly. Her tail wagged and she licked at Jess's wrist with her long red tongue.

"Wyatt's on restricted duty," Dylan explained as she straightened up. "He took a fall and broke a couple of bones in his spine. We're attempting to fill the gap he's left, but that's about as easy as trying to drive a truck with the engine missing."

"An exaggeration," Wyatt said, giving her a slow smile. "I understand you're from New York. Have you traveled much in the Western states, Jess?"

"I've visited Colorado and New Mexico for interviews, and I've skiied in the Rockies. But I've never had the chance to experience authentic ranch life."

"You're in the right place," Dylan said. "We're about as authentic as it gets when it comes to cowboys." He paused. "Well, unless you consider that Ford's a lawyer and Garrett's a preacher. They're a little out of the ordinary. Wyatt's the genuine article, though. A rancher through and through." He obviously admired his brothers and wasn't afraid to say so.

Footsteps sounded on the porch outside. "Hey, Dylan, get your butt out here. You're supposed to be—" Another cowboy in a white hat stomped into the house, but stopped short when he caught sight of Jess. "Oh…sorry. I didn't realize we had company."

"This is Jess Granger," Dylan said. "The reporter I mentioned would be here. Jess, meet my forgetful brother Garrett."

Garrett Marshall took off his hat and smiled as they shook hands. "I wasn't expecting you to arrive today. There's been a lot going on." As handsome as his brothers, he shared the same strong face and athletic build, but his eyes were blue, and his build was somewhere in between Wyatt's and Dylan's. He wore his light brown hair in a conservative cut and the uniform that ranch life apparently called for: jeans, boots and shirt. "I guess this means you won't be supervising the dinner detail," he told his younger brother.

"We've got seven teenagers staying on the ranch," Dylan explained when Jess glanced at him in question. "A sort of summer camp for some of the troubled kids in the area. My sister-in-law-to-be talked us into helping her out. So there's a bigger crowd than usual on the premises."

"That's quite a project." She didn't expect to be impressed with their efforts. In her experience, damaged kids couldn't be changed with a few weeks of attention, no matter how well-intentioned. "Sounds like a lot to fit in around ranch work *and* getting ready for an art show. When do you sleep?"

"Whenever he sits down," Wyatt said.

"Or stops moving," Garrett added.

Dylan rolled his eyes. "Thanks, guys. Just label me lazy in front of a reporter for a national magazine. No problem."

"We'll keep it off the record," she promised him. "What do the kids get to do while they're here?"

"Come observe for yourself," Garrett said. "They're not quite finished for the afternoon."

A distraction might ease Dylan's resistance. "Can I take pictures?"

"Sure, why not?"

"Let me get my camera."

"And a hat. That creamy New York complexion will burn in the Wyoming sunshine," Dylan said as he placed her bags in a cool, shadowed room off the hallway in the back of the house. "I hope you'll be comfortable in here."

The room had been furnished with rustic simplicity, soothing and peaceful, and the connecting bathroom was clean and bright. "I'm sure I will." She pulled her camera out of her shoulder bag. "But I didn't consider bringing a hat."

He nodded. "I figured you probably hadn't. Wait here just a second." The thud of boot heels retreated down the hall and then returned. Dylan appeared in the doorway with a white Western-style hat in his hands. "This should do it." Standing in front of her, he placed the hat on her head. Then he spun her around to face the mirror above the dresser. "There you go. Looks great—you're already a bona fide cowgirl."

Jess gazed at their reflection, feeling the warmth of his body behind hers, the weight of his palms, his breath stirring her hair. Awareness dawned inside her. She had to think about taking a breath.

"It's a new approach," she said, and was appalled at the quavery sound of her voice. "Thanks."

"Uh...you're welcome." Dylan sounded a little stunned, as well. He cleared his throat and stepped away. "You might want your hair in a ponytail—it's always windy on the ranch. I'll wait for you outside." In an instant, he was gone.

Releasing a big breath, Jess took off the hat and went to her suitcase for a brush and an elastic band. She took extra moments to thoroughly smooth and braid her hair, recovering her equilibrium in the process.

This new Dylan Marshall—the grown-up version—wasn't what she'd expected. She'd come prepared for a sulky, reclusive artist, someone hiding away from the world he'd once conquered.

The rumor at the time was, of course, that a love affair gone wrong had sent young Dylan into exile. No woman ever claimed to be the cause of his disappearance, though, and the attention of the art scene quickly shifted to a new talent.

The man she'd just met didn't appear to be pining away. He seemed comfortable, satisfied...solid. His sexy grin, the confident and flirtatious attitude, the broad shoulders and narrow hips—all combined into one seriously hot package. And there was chemistry between them. Those moments in front of the mirror had affected them both.

But she was flying back to New York on Sunday, giving her only four days to get what she needed for the article. With his three brothers as well as seven teenagers on the premises, there wouldn't an opportunity for her to get beyond a professional acquaintance with Dylan Marshall. Which was too bad, because she was tempted to want more. Very tempted.

But even if she had been staying longer, she'd reached the point in her life where a simple fling just wasn't enough. A few days...weeks...even months of good times and good sex didn't compensate for the emotional quagmire she went through when the relationship ended.

And it always ended.

Besides, her life was in New York. Her apartment and her job, her favorite coffee shop and the laundry that folded her shirts just right—all were in New York. Fun and games with the world's handsomest cowboy wasn't enough to make her give up her laundry service.

So she would keep her dealings with Dylan Marshall strictly business, and she'd leave with a well-written article and no regrets.

Above all, no regrets.

Dylan found himself out on the front porch without realizing quite how he got there. His brain had switched off, and all he could do was feel. Those seconds with Jess Granger's slender shoulders under his palms, her scent surrounding him and her eyes gazing through the mirror into his, had been...well, cataclysmic. He'd walked away a little disoriented.

Women didn't usually befuddle him like this, even beautiful ones. Ever since he'd discovered the difference between boys and girls, he'd made a point of getting to know as many of the opposite sex as possible—as friends, as lovers, as human beings. He considered women to be a separate species and thoroughly enjoyed all their unique, feminine attributes.

Somehow, he would have to maintain his usual detachment when it came to Jess Granger. He had to keep their relationship under control, avoid letting her get too close. She was, after all, a journalist. She'd come specifically to delve into his life and, more important, to reveal to the public as many of his secrets as she could discover.

Because of the person she expected him to be. The person he'd once been.

At eighteen, he'd left home determined to "make it big." He'd had talent but he'd also gotten lucky and done some sculpting that the "right" people thought they understood. They'd invited him to their playgrounds and he'd gone along because he was young and stupid and flattered by the attention. To a kid from tiny Bisons Creek, Wyoming, attending art parties in Paris, France, appeared to be the pinnacle of success.

He knew better now. His life in that world had come to a screeching halt one chilly afternoon during a conversation that lasted maybe five minutes. Later, standing in a Paris sculpture garden, he'd surveyed his own work and felt completely detached from its purpose, its meaning, its origin.

All he'd wanted at that moment was to go home. To be with his brothers, inside the family the four of them had built together. After years away, he'd craved the life he'd once worked so hard to escape.

He'd been on a plane less than twelve hours later.

And once he got to Wyoming, he hadn't left in more than two years. He certainly hadn't courted the attention of anyone in the art world. But then Patricia Trevor called him, having seen a piece he'd donated to a Denver hospital charity auction. She suggested a gallery exhibit of his recent projects, and he was vain enough to say yes. He wanted exposure for his ideas as much as ever. If he didn't have something to say, he wouldn't spend time or effort on the process.

But he didn't expect his former fans to understand or appreciate this current approach. Jess Granger's article supposedly launching the show would probably bring down a hailstorm of derision on his head. That was the way the art world worked—you gave them what they wanted or they cut you off at the knees. In spite of her beauty—or maybe precisely because she was so beautiful—he expected the same treatment from her.

The screen door to the house opened and the lady herself stepped onto the porch, a high-tech camera hanging around her neck. "There you are." She squinted against the sun. "It is bright out here. Thanks for the hat."

"You're welcome." A compliment on how she looked in the hat came to mind, but he ignored the impulse. "Let's go watch the kids."

Walking side by side up the hill, Dylan found himself searching for something to say. "We took them to a rodeo and most of them decided they wanted to compete."

"Sounds dangerous."

"Not so far." They crested the hill and approached

the group of kids gathered on the other side of the barn. "They're still at the learning stage." In the natural way of things, he would have put a hand on her shoulder to bring her closer to the action.

"Come watch," he said, keeping his hands at his sides and feeling as awkward as he probably sounded. "You can meet everybody. They're practicing on the bucking barrel."

The bucking barrel was a fifty-gallon drum suspended sideways by metal springs from four sturdy posts. With a rider sitting on the barrel, the contraption tended to bounce around, mimicking the motion of a bucking horse or bull. Ropes could be attached at various points, allowing spectators to increase the range of motion and the unpredictability of the ride.

"That's Thomas Gray Cloud." Dylan pointed to the boy currently riding the barrel. His dirty T-shirt testified to a fall or two already.

"All he holds on to is that one rope?" Jess shook her head. "I can't imagine. At least he wears a helmet."

"Ford, the legal eagle, made sure of that. But the secret is balance. You try to stay flexible and move with the animal, keeping your butt in place and using your arms and legs independently."

She looked over at him, her golden gaze intent on his. "Is this the voice of experience?"

He nodded. "I rode saddle broncs. The horses wear a special saddle—with stirrups—and you hold on to a rope attached to the horse's halter. It's slower than bareback riding, but style counts a lot more."

Her attention shifted to Thomas. "I think you're all crazy."

As they reached the group around the barrel, Thomas lost his balance and fell off to the side. He pounded a fist on the ground, but rolled over and got to his feet right away.

"My turn." A bulkier boy stepped up to the barrel. Thomas gave him a dirty look but backed out of the way, dusting his hands off on the seat of his jeans.

"Marcos Oxendine," Dylan told Jess. "One of our more challenging kids."

But today Marcos seemed to be on his best behavior. Grinning, he climbed onto the barrel, wrapped the rope around his gloved hand and yelled, "Let's go! Aiyee!"

The kids on the four corners began pulling their ropes, causing the barrel to tilt and sway in all different directions. Their encouraging shouts rang out in the afternoon air, recalling the roar of the grandstand crowd at a real rodeo. Marcos stayed on for nearly eight seconds, using his upper body to counter the motion of the drum he rode. When he finally did come off, he sat up laughing, while the spectators around him applauded.

"Again!" he demanded. "I'm doin' it again!"

Dylan glanced at the reporter beside him to gauge her reaction. What he noticed was that she stood with her hands in the back pockets of her jeans, and the stance did great things for her figure. He shifted his weight, cleared his throat and refocused his attention on the kids.

Marcos's second ride didn't last as long, but he moved away agreeably enough when Lena Smith marched up and announced that she wanted to go next.

Jess turned to Dylan with a shocked expression. "These events allow women to compete?"

"Yes, and there are a couple of women out there today riding against men. Lena is interested, so we wanted to give her a chance. And she's actually pretty good."

The girl proved his words, staying on for a full eight seconds, though Dylan suspected the rope pullers were going a little easy on her.

Still, she grinned when she got down. "That is so cool."

Beside Dylan, Jess Granger shook her head. "This was not what I pictured when you said you were conducting a summer camp. I thought, you know, arts and crafts—collages made with pinecones and sticks they pick up on a hike."

"Nope. We've been working on their riding skills—none of them could sit on a horse when they showed up here. On Friday we're taking them on their first cattle drive. You'll have to come along and observe."

"Um… I'm another one who's never been on a horse before I got here."

He gave her a wink. "We might have to work on that."

"By Friday?"

"There's a full moon tonight."

"That sounds like a threat."

"Could be. In the meantime, come meet my brother Ford and his fiancée."

Introductions took place as the kids dispersed, the boys heading to their bunkhouse and the three girls to the cabin they shared with Caroline. "They get an hour or so to reconnect with their phones," Caroline explained to Jess. "We wouldn't want anybody going into withdrawal."

"I certainly would, without mine. Dylan said that these are some of the troubled kids in your area."

"That's right. Most of them have had some kind of run-in with the legal system."

"They seem pretty cooperative, overall. Not as resistant as I would expect."

"Today's a successful day," Ford said. Caroline nodded. "And we've been together for a few weeks, developed some relationships. Do you have experience working with teenagers?"

"No, not really. But I have known some kids with problems." Jess Granger gave a short laugh. "In fact, I guess you could say I was one. I grew up bouncing in and out of the foster care system. At about the same rate my parents jumped in and out of jail."

Dylan swallowed hard, unsure of what to say. The Marshall brothers had lost both their parents before Wyatt turned sixteen, but they'd always had each other to depend on. He didn't want to consider how hard life might be without some kind of family you could trust to take care of you.

After a few seconds of silence, Ford found the right words. "You've obviously not only survived that experience, but thrived."

Caroline put a hand on the journalist's arm. "I would love to have you talk to our kids, especially the girls. You're such a great example of what responsibility and persistence can accomplish. Please say you'll spend some time with them while you're here."

Jess Granger looked surprised. "If you think it will help, I'd be glad to."

"You have to be careful around Caroline." Ford put his arm around his fiancée and squeezed her shoulders. "If she can find a way to use you in one of her causes, she will. That's how the Circle M ended up hosting this camp in the first place."

"The world needs people who push for ways to help others," Jess said. "They're the ones who make a difference." She turned to Dylan, still speechless beside her. "Would this be a good opportunity for the two of us to talk? I was hoping to see your studio, get some insight into your new work process."

He had plenty of reservations about that plan, but no valid reason to refuse. "Sure." To Caroline and Ford, he said, "We'll catch up with you two at dinner."

Then, with a sense of dread, he headed toward the studio, leading the enemy directly into the heart of his most personal territory.

Jess caught up with Dylan as he angled away from the ranch house, across a downhill stretch of grass toward what seemed to be another barn, though this building was gray, not red like the one at the top. "You haven't said anything."

His handsome face was hard to read. "I admire your achievements, against such odds. Were you close to your foster family?"

"Which one?" She wanted to push his buttons, shake his self-control. "I lived with five different couples. Ten brothers and sisters. Not all at once, of course."

"That sounds pretty tough." They reached the corner of the building but he continued past it, toward a stand of trees where the land flattened out. The grass was longer here and greener than on the hill, bending and swaying in the ever-present wind.

Jess stopped to take some pictures, and had to catch up with him again. "Where are we going?"

"To the creek."

"Why?"

"You wanted to understand my process."

They stepped under the shade of the trees and the temperature dropped about ten degrees. Jess removed her hat to let the breeze cool her head. "That feels so good."

Dylan nodded. "Part of the process."

He'd taken his hat off, too, letting the wind blow his wavy hair back from his face. There was a straight line across his forehead where the dirt from his morning's work had streaked his skin below his hat. It looked funny, yet also appealing, since it spoke of the physical effort he'd made. Jess was suddenly aware of his bare forearms, his flat stomach and tight rear end. Taking a deep breath, she pivoted away to study the scenery.

Trees and shrubs grew right up to the edge of the water. Along the edge of the stream, the trees were interspersed with rocks and boulders, some as big as cars. The creek bed itself was covered with smaller rocks and stones, which created a sparkling music as the water flowed over them.

"Beautiful," she said, snapping more photographs, moving around to get different angles and light levels. "Like visiting a national park somewhere, but it's all yours. No noisy, nosy tourists traipsing around to spoil it." She grinned at Dylan. "Unless you count me."

"You're definitely nosy. Not too noisy, so far." He gestured to the big, level rock he stood beside. "Come sit down."

"Okay." She sat on the rock and he joined her, leaving a space between them. Shadows from the leaves above danced across them, a flicker of gold and gray on their faces. "Now what?"

"Be still for a few minutes. Listen."

Being still wasn't Jess's habit. Most of the time when she was sitting down, her fingers were flying over the keyboard, typing an article or doing research on the internet. Now, with nothing to do, she had to grip her hands together to keep them off her camera— there were several terrific shots she could get from this position, including some close-ups of Dylan himself. Profiled against the trees, he radiated a calm control that was the essence of the cowboy ideal.

An essence very different from the frenetic artist he'd appeared to be three years ago. What had changed him? Or perhaps the question was, what had driven him in the first place? How did a boy who'd grown up in this setting, with the kind of values his brothers clearly considered important, end up in the limelight of the contemporary art scene? How would his work be different now? Was he ready to step back onto the international stage? Or did he have a different plan?

Would he answer her questions honestly, or leave her to draw her own conclusions? How well could she get to know him before she had to leave?

Dylan turned his head to look at her. "What do you think?"

"I think I'm dying to see your studio."

He glared at her with narrowed eyes. "Are you ever distracted?"

"Not if I want to keep my job."

"Does your job depend on my article?"

Jess shrugged. "I'm as useful to the magazine as my latest work. And there are lots of hungry writers out there hoping for a break. I'm the only support I've got, so staying employed is kind of a high priority."

After a long moment of stillness, Dylan sighed and got to his feet. "Well, then, Ms. Granger, I guess we'd better get down to business."

Chapter 2

The door to the barn was blue, in contrast to the weathered gray boards of the exterior, with a full panel of glass panes. Dylan walked inside, then faced Jess and held out an arm. "Be my guest."

Cool air greeted her as she stepped over the threshold. "Air-conditioning?"

"Wood stays more stable at a constant temperature."

The scent hit her all at once, a combination of varnish and glue and trees that cleared her sinuses. "It must make you drunk to spend time in here. That's a powerful room deodorizer."

He grinned. "I guess that's why the hours go by so fast when I'm working. I'm always a little high."

"So this used to be a regular barn?" The space was huge, open from wall to wall and clear to the ceiling, except for the supporting posts. A staircase in the corner led up to a railed loft stretching halfway across, where she could see a bed and a couple of chairs. "You sleep here, too?"

Dylan shrugged. "I remodeled over the years after we moved out here—with help from my brothers, of course. It's convenient not to walk out into a snowstorm in the middle of the night when I'm falling asleep." Then he hunched his shoulders again, and grimaced. "You know, I really would like to take a shower. Why don't you look around the place while I do that? Then we can talk some before dinner."

"Great." Jess watched him jog up the steps, then turned to survey the workshop around her. Tables of various sizes, most hand-built of unfinished boards, filled the space. Dylan's work area appeared to occupy the center of the room, where hand tools lay neatly arranged by size and use—saws, chisels, screwdrivers and other arcane devices she'd didn't recognize. Several surfaces held pieces of wood, also organized by size, from the smallest chips to branches four feet long. Some tables held sticks and limbs that had been sanded, stained and finished to a smooth shine. They were beautiful elements, but not the kind of material Dylan Marshall had utilized in his popular, critically approved sculptures.

What had he been up to?

For an answer, she moved to the tables lining the walls of the barn, which held figures of varying sizes—from a slender, twelve-inch form to a massive piece at least four feet square.

"Oh, my God," she said, in shock. "What in the world has he done?"

She recognized the animal she was staring at as a buffalo, about two feet long and not quite as tall. A collection of sticks and branches had been fitted together to create the figure, each curve and hollow of the body being defined by a curve or hollow in the wood. Every piece had been separately finished and polished to a deep sheen, allowing all the natural variations in color and grain to contribute to the texture of the image as a whole.

"Amazing."

She moved to the next sculpture, a fish twisting up out of a river. The scales of the fish's skin, the lines of the body and the base of splashing water had all been created with the same technique, fitting hundreds of tiny sticks together to produce a unified whole.

Jess ran a finger along the fish's spine. "Incredible detail."

On the next table there was a stalking wolf, almost half life-size, and a rabbit stretched out at a run, both executed with enormous visual talent and technical precision. Walking around the room, she appreciated the many hours Dylan had poured into these sculptures. That bear she'd seen in the living room at the house had been an early prediction of this full-blown talent. No doubt there would be many buyers for these beautiful works of art.

But… She covered her eyes with her shaking fingers.

The response of the art world Dylan had once conquered would be scathing. Cruel. Because of who he'd been and what he'd done, when the critics evaluated these pieces, they would laugh. Then attack.

And her article, the one Trevor Galleries had sponsored as a comeback announcement, would be the call to arms.

Jess dropped her hands to her sides and shook her head. "Artistic suicide."

Why would Patricia Trevor, the owner of the gallery, choose this kind of work to exhibit? Her showrooms were known for presenting avant-garde, cutting-edge art. Surely Dylan was aware of that. Why would he expose himself to ridicule this way?

From the loft above, she heard the shower cut off. He would be coming down soon, wanting to get her reaction to his pieces. Expecting her to appreciate his output of the past two years.

She needed some time to frame a response. Panicked, Jess ducked under the loft and headed for the shadows along the rear wall of the barn. One of the tables she passed held small clay figures, probably models he'd made as he planned the larger wooden pieces. The entire surface of another table was stacked high with books—anatomy manuals, collections of wildlife photographs, volumes on working with wood, finishes and stains.

The table in the corner under the stairs was illuminated by a large hanging light and covered with sheets of paper. These were his sketches, Jess realized as she came closer, three-dimensional drawings of animals in different poses, from different angles. Some of the studies she recognized from the sculptures she'd already viewed, but not all. He clearly had ideas for more work.

Footsteps sounded on the floor above her. "Be down

in a couple of minutes," Dylan called. "Just making myself presentable."

"No problem," Jess said loudly. "Take your time." She'd inadvertently glanced up as she spoke, but as she brought her gaze down again, a picture on the wall behind the drawing table caught her attention. She hadn't noticed any other hanging art in the studio, so this one must be important.

The drawing was deceptively simple—a woman with a baby in her lap. Looking from behind the woman, over her shoulder, the viewer could see the very young child with its feet tucked against the mother's belly, its head resting on her knees and its tiny hands curled around her two middle fingers.

It's a boy, Jess decided. Something about the baby's face convinced her of that fact. The delicate lines and shadings were so persuasive, so filled with emotion, she felt as if she was indeed standing in that room, visiting with mother and child. She could almost hear the woman's voice, singing a nonsense song, and her son's infant gurgle in response.

Suddenly, Dylan spoke from right behind her. "What in the world are you doing back here?"

Jess Granger whirled to face him, her mouth and eyes wide with surprise. "I didn't hear you come down."

He hadn't expected her to get this far into the studio. No one but him came into this space. "I can be sneaky. There's nothing important here in the dark under the stairs."

"Except for this wonderful sketch." She nodded toward the frame on the wall. "Is it yours?"

"No." Dylan pulled together a bunch of the papers spread over his drawing table and started to straighten them. He shouldn't be such a slob, especially with nosy reporters showing up to investigate.

She wouldn't let the subject drop. "It's not signed. Did you know the artist? Have they done other work?"

How was he going to get out of this? "We're here to talk about sculpture, right?"

"Right, but—" She gasped and then leaned over to pick up one of the papers on the table. "What's this?"

He saw the sketch and swore silently. "Not much. Just an...idea I was playing with."

When he reached for the sheet, she held it away from him. "This is your brother. Wyatt, right?"

"At least you recognize him." He wasn't sure how to get the drawing away from her, short of wrestling her to the floor.

And now she was in full journalist mode. "Are you working on this as a sculpture?"

"Just considering it."

"You haven't started. Why not?"

"What did you think of the stuff that's done?" Dylan said desperately. "Isn't that what you're here to write about?"

"It is." She blew out a breath and put the sketch on the table. "But you won't want to talk about that, either." Stepping around him, she went toward the main part of the studio. Dylan followed, as prepared as he could be for what lay head.

"These are fantastic sculptures," she said, walking along the line of display tables to survey the various pieces. "Lovely representations of the wildlife you obviously value."

"But?"

"But, Dylan, this is nothing like the abstract work you were doing in college and afterward—the cerebral, confrontational pieces that got you noticed. You know as well as I do, the art that gets talked about isn't a reproduction of reality. Nobody on the international art scene will be interested in a statue of a buffalo."

Truth, with a vengeance. He shrugged. "That's not my problem. This is what I came home to do. I won't apologize for it."

"I wouldn't expect you to. The question is, what am *I* doing here? Any article I write about your new style is going to bring down catastrophe on your head." She paused for a moment. "And mine, for that matter. My editor will not appreciate a neat-and-tidy piece about a wildlife artist. It's just not what *Renown* readers expect."

"I can understand that." He stroked a hand over the head of a fox on the table near him. "So cancel the article." That would mean she had no reason to stay, of course. He didn't acknowledge the sense of loss that realization stirred inside him.

But Jess was shaking her head. "Magazine issues are planned long in advance. I've got a certain amount of space in this issue. I have to write an article. And after my last assignment…well, I need to turn in good copy."

"What happened?"

She gave a dismissive wave. "I showed up to interview the next country music legend and found him having an alcohol-fueled meltdown. Smashing guitars, punching walls, throwing furniture. I waited two days for him to sober up. But then all he wanted to do was get me into bed. My editor was not happy. I need to revive my career with this piece."

"No pressure there." Now he felt responsible to help her keep her job.

"Exactly. Anyway, Trevor Galleries paid for ad space because we were doing an article on you. It's a complicated relationship, advertising and content." She continued walking, examining his work.

"No," she said, finally, "you won't be coming back to the contemporary art scene. Not with these sculptures. I'm going to have to find some way to slant this, make it work for my editor. I'll have to find another hook." She stared at him with a worried frown. "Any ideas?"

From being the subject—victim—he'd become a co-conspirator. "All I can do is talk about what I know." He couldn't believe he was giving her a reason to stay, offering to expose himself like this. "Try to explain the changes I've made, the reasons I focus on wildlife now." Not everything, of course. Some secrets weren't meant to be revealed. Ever.

She didn't seem to be convinced. "That might work. The 'soul of an artist' kind of thing. But you have to be honest and open with me. I can't turn in a bunch of clichés. Not if I plan to keep my job."

"Got it." He would be spilling his guts so Jess Granger could remain employed. That was not at all what he'd planned to do with this interview. There would have to be some kind of payback. "But I want something in exchange."

"And what would that be?"

"The same access. To you."

Her hazel gaze went wary. "You're not writing an article."

"If I have to drop my defenses, you should, too."

"I don't have any defenses."

"Right. No problems at all with the foster care issue." Her cheeks flushed. He stared at her until she looked away. "Deal?"

A long silence stretched between them. "Okay. Deal." She pulled in a deep breath. "So tell me something I can use. Something about your abstract work. What were you thinking when you created those pieces?"

Dylan propped his hip on the corner of the table under the fox and drew a deep breath of his own. "Okay. My second semester in college, I took a sculpture class with Mark Thibault. You know him?"

"Sure. He's a well-respected critic in contemporary art. He introduced you to the scene. 'The biggest talent I've come across' was the quote, I believe."

"Yeah, well. Mark exaggerates. Anyway, he challenged me to explore abstraction. No figures, no representative stuff. If I submitted that kind of project, he promised to fail me for the semester."

"You cared about grades? Artists are usually rebels in that respect."

He chuckled. "I had three older brothers who were paying, in one way or another, for that class. I owed them good grades. So I worked my butt off for Mark, but he was never satisfied. He kept criticizing, rejecting, pushing me harder and harder. The deadline was approaching for the final project, and I still didn't have a passing grade."

Her hands went into her back pockets. "What happened?"

Dylan gazed up at the ceiling he and his brothers had insulated and paneled with finished boards. "I was sitting in the dorm with some friends, drinking beer out of cans. As guys do, we'd squash the cans when we emptied them and pile them on the table." He cleared his throat. "In my intoxicated state, I started studying the cans, the shapes of them after they'd been deformed. I chose three that seemed interesting and worked on sketches, playing with their relationships to each other. When I sobered up, I figured out how to make forms using rusted oil drums and a hammer, filled them with concrete and then ripped parts of the drums off."

Jess was grinning. "And Mark loved it."

"Oh, yeah. I did, too—it was great to work on a larger scale, to physically manipulate such harsh materials. I felt like I'd opened a door and found a wild new world."

"Did Mark learn the source of your inspiration?"

"After that sculpture won a blue ribbon, I confessed. He just said, 'Whatever works, son. Whatever works for you.'"

She gave another of those rich, deep laughs of hers. "And an art prodigy is born."

"There you go." He glanced at the window and saw with surprise how long the shadows from the trees had grown. "We're going to miss dinner if we don't head for the house."

"Dinner sounds terrific." She brought her hands out of her pockets, relaxing the pose that distracted him. "Something about all this fresh air makes me hungrier than usual."

"Wyoming affects people that way." He opened the door for her to walk through. "But afterward," he warned her as they walked up the hill, "it will be your turn to bare your soul."

When she and Dylan entered the house, Jess saw all the Marshall brothers in the same room for the first time. Four handsome cowboys, cleaned up and smiling at her, was enough to set her heart to pounding.

She fanned her hot face with her hand. "Taken together, you guys are a little overwhelming." Dylan looked especially fine, something she'd been trying to ignore ever since he'd surprised her in the studio.

Cheeks flushed, every one of the brothers hooked his thumbs in his front pockets and gazed down at the floor. Jess chuckled. "There's definitely a family resemblance."

An expression of horror crossed Dylan's face. "Say it ain't so!"

Garrett snorted. "You should be so lucky."

"Caroline's supervising cleanup in the bunkhouse," Ford said, ignoring his brothers. "She'll be over when the kids are done."

A voice spoke up behind Jess. "Dinner's ready. You all should come sit down."

Hearing the unexpected voice, she pivoted to find a

blonde woman standing in the doorway to the dining room. A curly-headed little girl peeked around her hip.

"Susannah and Amber Bradley are staying with us for a while," Dylan explained as they moved toward their seats. "And Susannah's making sure we're all going to have to buy a larger size in jeans."

Jess couldn't believe the table full of food, all for an ordinary evening meal. A steaming bowl of stew occupied the center of the feast, surrounded by dishes of mashed potatoes, rolls, green beans and a tossed salad. "I can see why. I'm sure it's all delicious."

Before she could pull out her chair, Dylan had done it for her. Garrett did the same for Susannah, after she'd gotten the little girl settled in a booster seat. Opening doors, pulling out chairs—compared with everyday manners in New York, all this chivalry would take some getting used to.

A sense of unreality stayed with Jess as she ate. When had she last sat at a family table? For Thanksgiving or Christmas, maybe, at the last foster home she'd lived in. Not in the middle of the week, though. And that foster mother hadn't been very skilled in the kitchen.

"I was right. This food is amazing," she said, taking another helping of stew. "It's a lucky thing I'll only be here a few days." She met Susannah's gaze across the table. "You're a wonderful cook. Or maybe I should say chef."

Susannah laughed. "Cook, definitely." Her crisp accent hinted at an East Coast upbringing. She wore her fair hair in a knot at the crown of her head, with wisps escaping to frame her face—a beautiful woman in a household of handsome single men. The possibilities for romance were certainly plentiful, but she must already be married.

"Does your husband work on the Circle M?" Jess asked, following that train of thought.

Susannah winced. An uncomfortable silence fell over the room, till Dylan stirred in his chair. "Susannah's husband is…trouble. She and her kids are here to stay safe."

She felt her cheeks heat up. "I'm so sorry. Being nosy is a job qualification. But I didn't mean to touch on a sore subject."

"Of course not." The other woman had recovered her control. "You couldn't possibly have known. Don't worry about it." She glanced around the table. "Can I get anyone more to drink? Do we need more food?"

Groans answered her and for a few minutes they all concentrated on their meals, which Jess figured was a polite way to allow her to save face. She was quite sure she'd never met a family so mannerly.

But then, the families she'd grown up with weren't always the most respectable members of society. Some of them had tried. Some…had not.

"Jess, you're from New York, is that right?" Garrett sat directly across from her. "You'll find it a lot less crowded out here."

She nodded. "Wyoming has the smallest population per square mile of any state, doesn't it? I'm not used to walking around without dodging other people."

"When the teenagers congregate, you can find yourself doing some dodging." Ford winked at her. His dark gold hair glinted under the light of the chandelier. "They take up a lot more room than you might expect. Especially now that they're more comfortable with the place."

"How long has your program been operating?" Surely that would be a safe topic, after the disaster she'd created with Susannah.

"This is the first year," he said. "And we're in week three. The first days were pretty rough—"

"Try 'impossible,'" Dylan said in a low voice.

Garrett glared at him. "We got through them. And things get better every day."

"Till the next disaster," Dylan nodded, as if he agreed. "You can bet there will be one."

Garrett started to respond, but Wyatt spoke first. "What about this cattle drive you're planning to take the kids on?" His deep voice broke up the tension. "Where do you intend to go?"

Jess couldn't follow the references to different fields and pastures and fence lines and gates, but the brothers evidently reached a consensus about the route they'd be following with kids and cows. Susannah and Amber would be driving to meet them on the way with lunch.

"Wyatt can ride with you to give you directions," Ford said. "Think that'll work, Boss?"

"Sure." His glance across the table seemed almost shy. "If Susannah doesn't mind."

She gave him a soft smile. "Of course not."

Jess raised her hand. "Can I ride in the truck, too? I'd hate to miss the excitement."

Dylan frowned at her. "Now, I was planning to teach you to ride directly after dinner. You should be ready to join us on horseback by Friday."

Ford grinned. "In case that doesn't work out, you're certainly welcome to a seat in the truck."

"Thank goodness," Jess said with relief, and earned a general laugh.

Susannah stirred in her chair. "I'm amazed at how well you all understand the land and its character. What a privilege, to take care of your own piece of the earth." She pushed her chair back and stood up. "I'll clear the dishes. Garrett, the ingredients for ice cream are ready."

Jess started to rise. "Let me help."

But Dylan put his fingers over hers on the table. "Not a chance. You relax." The skin-to-skin contact shocked them both, and they jerked their hands apart again. He cleared his throat and reached for her plate. "We've got minions to spare."

"Everybody should have minions," she said, and he smiled without meeting her eyes. Jess realized she was holding the hand he'd touched in her other palm, and quickly laced her fingers together, setting both hands on the table.

Caroline appeared in the doorway of the dining room. "The kids are ready for ice cream," she said. "More than ready." To Jess, she said, "Come outside and meet everybody. They're pretty mellow after dinner."

Outside, a group of boys was playing catch in the open space in front of the ranch house. Three girls sat on the floor of the front porch staring at their phones. "Lizzie Hanson, Becky Rush and Lena Smith," Caroline said, indicating which name belonged to whom.

"Girls, this is Jess Granger. She's a journalist who's come to write an article about Mr. Dylan."

Lizzie, a slender blonde wearing far more makeup than necessary, looked up from her phone. "A journalist? You mean, a writer?"

Jess nodded. "Yes. I write articles for a magazine."

"Did you have to go to school for a long time to do that?"

"Four years of college."

The girl heaved a sigh. "That's a lot."

Redheaded Becky nudged Lizzie with an elbow. "You could do it. You like to write."

"Do you?" Jess sat in the nearby rocking chair. "What do you write?"

Lizzie shrugged one shoulder. "Just stuff. Things I make up."

"Well, that's the way to start. The more you write, the better you get at it." She caught Lena's gaze. "You were riding the bucking barrel this afternoon, weren't you? That's pretty impressive."

The girl shrugged. "It's fun. Women can do the same things men do."

"Absolutely." Jess grinned at Caroline when Lena's attention returned to her typing. "Are the teenagers churning the ice cream?"

"That's the plan."

"I've seen pictures," Jess confessed. "But I've never actually eaten homemade ice cream."

"That's okay," Becky told her, with a grin. "I never had any till I came here, either. But it's awesome."

"Thanks." Jess grinned back at the friendly girl. She really didn't seem to be the troublesome type.

Garrett had carried the ice-cream maker out to the area in front of the porch and was adding ice and salt to the bucket. "Okay, guys," he called. "I need some strong arms over here."

The boys sauntered toward the porch. "Not exactly a stampede," Jess commented. "Typical adolescents."

"They wouldn't want you to believe they were enthusiastic." Caroline smiled while shaking her head. "Cooperation is not cool."

"How well I remember." Jess caught Caroline's quick glance in her direction, but she didn't say anything else. She didn't want her memories to disrupt the peaceful evening.

Thomas, one of the boys she'd watched this afternoon, took the first shift on the ice-cream crank. Caroline introduced another boy, Justino, who gave her a solemn "Hi," before sitting down next to Lena. They immediately became completely absorbed in each other, locking gazes and murmuring a conversation for their ears alone.

Jess looked at Caroline with a raised eyebrow.

"They kept it a secret," Caroline said quietly, "until after they got here. Ford and I have been standing guard duty to be sure they stay where they're supposed to be after lights-out." She gave a mischievous grin. "That has its pluses and minuses."

Ford opened the screen door at that moment and came to stand beside Caroline. Although they didn't touch, the meeting of their gazes was as warm as a hug.

With an uncomfortable fluttering in her chest, Jess shifted her attention to the ice-cream process.

"It's getting hard," Marcos said.

"Let me," Thomas ordered. "You been doing it forever."

Marcos shook his head. "You started. I'm still doin' okay."

The other boy pushed at his shoulder. "Give somebody else a chance."

Marcos rounded on him, fists clenched.

Seeming to come from out of nowhere, Dylan stepped between them. "It's my turn, guys. Stand aside."

Both boys retreated as Dylan bent over the ice-cream churn. He grabbed the handle but groaned as he cranked it. "This *is* hard. Can't be too much longer till it's done."

Jess couldn't decide if he was faking it to make the boys feel better. He did continue to rotate the handle for a while. But he'd averted a fight. She had to admire his presence of mind.

Once the churn was open, he came across the porch to hand her one of the two bowls he carried. "Enjoy."

"Thanks." She sampled cautiously, discovering a rich, smooth treat that rivaled any vanilla ice cream she'd ever tasted. "Wow. You must have the magic touch."

"A great recipe helps." Dylan settled into the rocker beside hers. "Lots of eggs and sugar and cream. Susannah makes a mean custard."

"Mmm." Jess didn't want to confess she didn't understand what he meant.

"What's your favorite flavor?" he asked.

"At home by myself with a movie? Mint chocolate

chip. For my birthday, I go to a shop in Brooklyn and order Earl Grey tea ice cream. How about you?"

"As far as I'm concerned, the more chocolate, the better. Dark chocolate with dark chocolate chunks and dark chocolate syrup. On a dark chocolate brownie."

Jess found herself watching as he licked his spoon clean. Swallowing hard, she shifted her gaze to the darkness beyond the reach of the porch light. "I believe I get the idea."

Most of the kids had settled down separately to eat their dessert, except for Justino and Lena, who sat hip to hip. Susannah Bradley had brought Amber outside to sit on the other side of the porch, where they were joined by a boy Jess hadn't seen this afternoon.

"That's her son, Nate," Dylan said, when she asked. "He's a natural horseman—has taken to riding like he was born in the saddle. Speaking of which..." He grinned at her. "Are you ready for your riding lesson? The moon's rising."

She decided to call his bluff. Standing up, she said, "Sure. Let's go."

"Great." If he was surprised, it didn't show. "I'll take our dishes inside."

In a moment, he reappeared. "Right this way, ma'am."

As they walked away from the house, she frowned at him. "Do I remind you of your mother?"

"I don't remember much about my mother. She died when I was six." His solemn expression revealed more than he probably realized. "Why?"

"You called me 'ma'am.'" Now she felt foolish. "I'm not that old."

"Sorry. It's just a habit—we tend to say it to women of any age out here." He sent her a smile. "I'll try to remember you're sensitive about that."

"I'm not sensitive."

Dylan gave a snort.

"Just accurate," she insisted. "I'm only thirty-five." Eight years older than he was, in fact, which was another reason to keep their relationship strictly platonic. Except her reactions to him weren't following that rule.

Jess decided to change the subject. This was supposed to be an interview, after all. "I understand both your parents passed away when you were all quite young."

He nodded without turning his head. "Wyatt was sixteen and I was eight when our dad died."

"You didn't have family to take you in?"

"Not that we knew of." He shrugged one shoulder. "We did okay by ourselves."

"Have you always lived on the Circle M?"

"Not in the beginning. Wyatt got a job with the owner, Henry MacPherson. We all eventually came here to live and work."

They reached the top of the hill and headed toward the barn. Dylan strode ahead to reach inside the big, open door, and light poured out into the evening.

Jess stepped through and then stopped in surprise. "I've never been in a working barn before. In fact, this is only the second barn I've ever entered in my life." A high-ceilinged aisle stretched along the side of the building, its beams and paneling aged to a rich, deep brown. She took a deep breath. "What is that sweet smell? Kind of grassy, only…more, somehow."

"Hay." Dylan pointed up to a loft filled with stacks of rectangular bundles. "About five hundred bales of grass hay."

"Ah. Bales. No wonder horses enjoy eating it. Must be delicious." Walking forward, she started down a cross-aisle with partially enclosed rooms on each side. The lower halves of the walls were built of boards, but the upper halves consisted of iron bars. The entrance to each room was a sliding door. "These are stalls where the horses stay?"

Dylan had followed her. "Yes, they're stalls, though we don't usually keep the horses in here unless they're hurt or sick. They prefer being out to roam around."

Along the rear of the barn were compartments with full walls and regular doors. "Feed room," her guide explained, showing her a space that resembled a kitchen, minus the oven and dishwasher. He opened another door. "Tack room—for saddles and bridles, horse equipment in general."

"Oh, wow." Rows of saddles lined one wall, with racks for bridles on another. Jess took a deep breath. "I love the scent of leather. Mixed with hay, it's a very evocative aroma." Sensuous, even. But she kept that impression to herself.

"The essence of a barn, as far as I'm concerned."

When they walked around the corner, they arrived at the other end of the aisle from where they'd started. A double half door looked out into a large dirt area ringed by a wooden fence. "That's the corral," Dylan said. "The site of your riding lesson."

Jess leaned her arms on the top of the door, relaxing into the warm, breezy night. "Where's my horse?"

He joined her to gaze out into the darkness. "On the other side of the fence, in the pasture."

"And this full moon you talked about?" The indigo sky was dotted with more stars than she'd ever witnessed. "I'm not finding it."

Leaning over the top of the door, he pretended to search. "Yeah. That's a problem."

"I guess I'll settle for a barn tour instead of a riding lesson by moonlight." Facing into the barn again, she leaned against the door and surveyed the interior of the building. "It's beautiful. And so neat. No dust or dirt anywhere."

"Old Henry MacPherson was a bear about keeping the place tidy. Now it's second nature to all of us."

"He didn't have a family?"

"No kids, and his wife died in her fifties. We're lucky he took us on after our dad died."

"That must have been especially tough, since you'd already lost your mom."

"Wyatt kept us together. He's one determined cowboy." Dylan leaned sideways against the door, arms crossed over his chest, his gaze intent on her face. "But it sounds as if you were on your own. No brothers or sisters?"

Her whole body tensed. "Is this my interrogation?"

He frowned at her. "I was thinking of it as getting to know you."

Jess blew out a short breath. "No siblings by birth. Some of the families I stayed with had more than one kid."

"I guess it would be hard to get close to anyone if you weren't sure how long you'd be staying."

This was not something she *ever* talked about. "Yes."

"Was this in New York?"

"I grew up in Connecticut. Different towns, depending on who I was living with."

"Do you still enjoy snow?"

She couldn't help laughing at the question. "I do, as a matter of fact. It makes the world all fresh and clean, at least for a little while."

"Me, too." He was quiet for a moment. "So you went to college, got your degree and now you're a staff reporter for a glossy, upscale magazine."

Jess let herself relax again. "Pretty much, I suppose. If you skip all the unsuccessful rags I wrote for during the first eight years or so."

Dylan's brown gaze focused intently on her face. "Where did you get your drive to succeed? We had Wyatt—he was just born responsible, I guess, and he made sure the rest of us grew up that way. Now we're trying to give these camp kids a chance to understand how they can succeed in life. Who did that for you?"

"Nobody did that for me." The confession broke some kind of dam inside her. She gripped her hands together, trying for control. "Sometimes they made the effort, but I wasn't ready. Or I'd get kicked back to my mother, have to start taking care of her again. One couple didn't have time—six kids in a two-bedroom house make for a lot of work. One couple was only in it for the check. And I was never in the same school long enough to get a teacher on my side."

When Dylan started to speak, she held up a hand. "I raised myself, reading stories that showed me how kids are supposed to grow up. Judy Blume, Beverly

Cleary, Ann Martin and Madeleine L'Engle—I guess you could say they raised me. I grew up to be a writer because they showed me how to live. Libraries were my true home."

Pushing away from the door, she stalked down the aisle toward the front of the barn.

"Jess, wait."

She stopped halfway but didn't turn around. "I never saw ice cream made at home. Till tonight." Shaking her head, she waved him away and stepped out into the night.

Chapter 3

Dylan let her get about halfway down the hill before he went after her. "Jess, hold up."

She didn't stop until he grasped her upper arm. By then they'd reached the front porch. Fortunately, the crowd had dispersed and there was no one to watch.

"Haven't you heard enough?" Her hoarse voice held tears. "What else do you want?"

"Just to make sure you're okay."

Her shoulders lifted on a deep breath. "Of course. More courtly manners from the Marshall brothers. 'Chivalry 'R Us.'"

"That's right." Under his palm, her arm was slender, but the muscle was strong. "Why don't we sit down for a few minutes?"

Without answering, she stepped up onto the porch. Dylan let her go, though he wasn't sure she would sit down until she actually did so. He dropped into the chair next to her and set his elbows on the arms. "You owe me one."

She sent him a sideways glance. "One what?"

"One probing question requiring a self-immolating answer."

That got a ghost of a laugh. "Oh, good. I'll give it some serious consideration."

"It's a golden opportunity."

"I'm sure. You were never very open with interviewers back then. Always the same flip answers."

"They didn't want to hear the truth."

"I would have."

"Maybe. And then you could have torpedoed my brilliant career."

"Instead, you did it yourself." The ensuing silence was filled with expectation.

Dylan understood he had only himself to blame for the direction the conversation had taken. But no matter how beautiful Jess Granger might be—and she was damn beautiful, with light from the house windows glinting on her hair and shining in her eyes—he wasn't about to tell her *everything*.

"Artists change direction all the time. I'd said all I wanted to with that approach."

She raised one eyebrow. "After five years? When you were only twenty-five?"

"I have a short attention span."

"Which is why you now build sculptural mosaics with small pieces of polished wood."

"There's this medicine…"

Jess slapped her hands on her knees and stood up.

"I get it. You're not going to give me the truth about what happened to drive you away from abstract art." She walked to the front door. "Then I'll say goodnight. It's been a long day."

Dylan joined her at the door, putting his hand on the frame. "I bet it has. You've come two thousand miles from your world to mine." Through the screen, he saw that the living room was empty. "And I should do some work."

She gazed up at him, though not very far, because she was tall. "That would be interesting to watch." Then she put her hand up to hide a yawn. "But I was up at four. I'd probably fall asleep with my head on a table."

"You can save that for another night." That full, rosy mouth tempted him mightily. Was it as soft, as sweet, as responsive as he imagined? It would take just a light taste to find out.

Jess's hand landed flat against his chest. "You're not doing that, either. Good night."

Before he could react, she opened the screen door and walked inside, then disappeared into the shadows of the hallway. He heard a door shut firmly.

"Guess she told you."

Dylan jumped at the sound of Wyatt's voice. "What are you doing sneaking around?"

"Taking a walk. How's the interview going?"

"Rough. She wants more than I'm willing to say."

The Boss stepped onto the porch. "What have you got to hide?"

His brother was another person who didn't have to know everything. "I don't want you and Garrett and

Ford pestered with the kind of attention an article in this magazine can generate."

"What kind is that?"

"Condescending, disparaging, disrespectful. Or, worse, you could start getting calls from women who want to hook up with a single cowboy who owns his own place. They might even arrive unannounced."

Wyatt grinned. "Could be a way for Garrett to find a wife."

"You, too, for that matter." An instantaneous frown greeted that suggestion. "Even more important, these kids shouldn't be advertised across the country as problems. That label would stick with them for the rest of their lives."

"Excellent point. So how are you planning to handle this situation?"

"We're working on an angle, Jess and I." Though he had a feeling that she hadn't given up her basic agenda any more than he had.

"What the hell does that mean?"

"I'm not sure." Dylan raked his fingers through his hair. "The work I've been doing the last two years is... different from what she expected, which is another problem. I guess it's up to me to figure out an explanation she can use that doesn't drag my guts out in the open for everyone to study."

"I can see how she'd be surprised—that oversize concrete-and-metal style you worked with in college doesn't mesh with the figures you're making now." The Boss tilted his head. "For the record, I like the new stuff better."

"I'm sure you do." Dylan put a hand on his brother's shoulder. "The *Renown* readers won't, but they'll recover. Meanwhile, if I'm going to make some progress tonight, I'd better begin."

Wyatt closed the screen door between them. "Hope you get some sleep."

"Me, too."

Once in the studio, though, he couldn't settle down. The latest piece waited—a mare and newborn foal he'd started building only a few days ago. He'd meant to avoid cuteness, intended to convey the perilous nature of birth in the wild—of life in general. A happy ending wasn't guaranteed. For animals or humans.

Dylan paced between the tables as his thoughts ricocheted around his skull, which was not at all conducive to creativity. On this kind of night, he often went down to the creek for a little while and let the water's silvery chuckle soothe his mind.

Or would he just spend those minutes mooning over Jess Granger?

"Damn it." He stalked to the rear of the studio, under the loft, and went to the drafting table. She would be in here sometime in the next day or two, so he might as well get this mess straightened up. No one was allowed to view his sketches. They were for his use alone.

But as he organized the papers—a stack for the ones he had sculpted, a stack for the ones he might get to, the trash can for failures—he came across the drawing of Wyatt that Jess had found. In a moment, another human figure surfaced from the pile—a woman with a baby in her lap. Dylan sat down in the chair and laid the two sheets on the surface in front of him. He should throw these away, too.

But if he did, he would only draw them again, as he had so often over the years, always determined that *this time* he would take the project all the way. *This time* he would create the sculptures that lived in his brain.

He never had. And he wasn't sure why...except that when he tried, he came up against a mental brick wall that stretched higher, wider and deeper than he could reach. What he wanted to create stood on the other side. And he couldn't get through.

With a sigh, Dylan stacked the two pages, folded them in half and dropped them in the trash. There was no point in beating himself up over what he couldn't produce. He had plenty to do over the next couple of months to get ready for the gallery show, and he was comfortable with the work that had to be done. Letting go of those images would free up more energy for the tasks at hand. Artistic and otherwise.

With the remaining sketches neatly slotted inside a file folder, Dylan made his way to the mare and foal and sat down, forcing himself for the first few minutes until the process started to flow—

A knock on the door jerked him around and he swore as he dropped the piece of wood he'd just glued. What had happened now? His brothers rarely bothered him at night except for an emergency.

Through the glass, though, he could see this was not a brother. He opened the door. "Jess? What are you doing here?"

Her hair was loose again, rippling around her shoulders and lifting with the wind. She wore a bulky blue sweater over a T-shirt and what appeared to be plaid flannel boxer shorts, with sneakers on her feet. Her legs, minus jeans and tall boots, were shapely and smooth. Gorgeous.

"I couldn't sleep." She'd taken off her makeup, revealing light freckles over her nose and cheeks. "I thought I would come watch you."

"Oh." He cleared his throat. "Okay. Come in." The last thing he needed when he was having trouble working was an audience. Especially *this* audience. "I was about to make some coffee. Join me?"

"Yes, please." She drifted along the display tables while he brewed two cups. "Heavy cream and two sugars, please."

"I like mine sweet, too." He brought her a mug. "Is your room not comfortable?"

"Oh, no, it's great. Flying just disrupts my internal clock."

"I remember. Eventually you stop being able to tell what time it should be." They were standing by a big-horn ram he'd finished a few months ago. "I haven't missed that, the last couple of years."

"You don't enjoy traveling?"

"I enjoy visiting new places. My preference would be staying somewhere for a month—or six—and really getting to know the people and the environment. I'm not into 'if it's Tuesday this must be Rome.'"

Jess eyed him over the rim of her cup. "Not just four days?"

"You won't know everything about this place in four days or four months or years." He didn't mean it as a challenge.

But she heard one. "I think you'll be surprised."

So they were adversaries again. Dylan didn't intend to argue with her about who would win. "Anyway, make yourself comfortable—not that there are many decent chairs to sit in around here. I'm going to get to work."

"Thanks. Just pretend I'm not here. I don't want to disturb your process."

Yeah, right. Dylan lost count of how many mistakes he made in the next hour as he tried to concentrate with Jess Granger in the room. She'd rolled his desk chair out from behind the staircase and over to where he was working. He couldn't argue that she'd picked the most comfortable seat available. The problem was the way she curled her body into its leather embrace, knees drawn up and ankles crossed, looking all warm and cozy. That blue sweater didn't reach much below the hem of the boxer shorts, so there was a long length of leg left to view, if he happened to glance over.

Which he did, too often. And each time he found Jess's gaze intent on his hands. She didn't say anything, but he was constantly aware of her presence.

Eventually, though, the spirit of the piece drew him in. Dylan found his focus, fingering through the collection of wood on the table for the next element, making adjustments, setting the fragment just right. He worked until his neck began to ache, until his back stiffened and his fingers fumbled, until his eyes burned.

"Enough," he said, capping the glue and pushing away from the table. "I give in."

A single glance at Jess revealed she'd surrendered

before him. Arms folded, eyes closed, she'd slipped down in the chair to rest her cheek on the padded arm. She was deeply asleep.

In his studio. At 3:45 a.m. What was he supposed to do about it?

He *should* wake her, walk her to the house and send her to bed in the guest room while he returned here. And how painful would that be, for both of them? There was a reason he'd built the bedroom loft. All he wanted at this moment was to drop onto the bed and pass out.

He *could* leave her in the chair to sleep, even if she might not be able to straighten up for the next three days. That would teach her a lesson, though he was too tired to figure out about what.

Or...there was a king-size bed upstairs, a place to get some real rest without taking a predawn walk through damp grass.

Dylan rubbed his eyes and then put a hand on Jess's shoulder. "Hey, you. Bedtime."

Her eyes slowly opened to show him the bleary, confused expression of the very tired. "Huh?"

"Let's go." He took her hand and pulled.

She sat up with the coordination of a rag doll. "I don't understand." Her eyelids drooped.

"I'm tired. We're going to bed."

He'd carried her halfway up the steps before his last statement fully penetrated. Jess came awake, twisting in his arms. "No. We can't."

"Yes. We can." He took a tighter grip under her soft, bare knees and her arms, driving himself to the top of the staircase. Keeping hold, he walked over to the side of the bed and set her on her feet. "Crawl in."

"No." This protest was weaker. When he pulled down the covers, she gazed at the pillow with longing.

Dylan was about to collapse himself. Palms on her shoulders, he sat her down, slipped her sneakers off and tucked her feet under the sheet before pushing her backward. "Sleep."

Before he made it around to the other side, she had rolled onto her stomach and burrowed into the pillow.

He scowled at all those curls flowing across his dark blue sheets. "Make yourself at home."

Then he grabbed the blanket folded at the bottom of the mattress and flung it over himself as he sat down in the recliner by the window. He'd spent many a night snoring at the television from this spot, and it was usually only a matter of minutes until he called the day done.

This was, however, the first time he'd ever done so with a woman in his bed.

Somehow, his favorite chair just didn't feel so comfortable tonight.

OH. MY. GOD.

Jess didn't even have to sit up to realize where she was. From where she lay on her side, she could see the railing of the loft in Dylan's studio, as well as the top of the staircase. In such a comfortable position, she could be only one place.

His bed.

She couldn't recall how she got here. Her memory pretty much blanked out around two thirty, when she'd checked her watch while Dylan pursued his meticulous work at the table. Another cup of coffee had kept her awake for a little while but not, apparently, long enough.

Not remembering how she got up here meant she didn't remember what had happened *after* she got here. She seemed to have her clothes on, which was reassuring, if not conclusive. No one's arms were wrapped around her. Or hers around them. Also comforting.

If she turned over, would she be staring into his face? Gazing into those dark chocolate eyes with their teasing glint? Was he under the same sheet—was the warmth she savored the result of sharing a small, dark, intimate space with him?

Jess didn't consider herself a coward. She'd lived in bad neighborhoods, attended schools where violence was a daily event, bruised her knuckles on other girls' jawbones. But the possibility of confronting Dylan Marshall on the other side of the bed seemed only slightly less risky than leaping over the loft rail to the floor below.

Then she realized she could swing her legs out of bed, stand up and at least be on her feet when she confronted him. Big improvement.

When she spun around, though, she found the worst of her fears unfounded. The other side of the giant bed lay undisturbed, the covers still pulled over most of the pillow. She'd slept alone.

Blowing out a relieved breath, she ignored the regret lurking in her mind. She reminded herself that spending the night—actually having sex—with the subject of her interview violated her standards of professional behavior. Of course, she'd never been tempted before, but that didn't matter. Rules were rules.

All she could see of Dylan, in fact, was a single sock-covered foot sticking out from underneath a blanket draped over what appeared to be a recliner facing the television. Talk about standards—he'd let her have the bed all by herself, even though there was plenty of room for two people to lie down and never touch. She didn't know many guys with that kind of personal code—these days, everyone seemed to be looking out for their own good at the expense of everyone else.

And why not? Who takes care of you if you don't?

Dylan would, the treacherous part of her whispered. She ignored it. She had to.

Carrying her shoes, Jess hurried quietly down the stairs, resisting the impulse to stop and make a cup of coffee. She glanced at her watch as she pulled on her sneakers and slipped out the blue door. Five fifteen. The sun had yet to rise into the sky, but there was plenty of light, a sort of golden glow that promised a beautiful day. Soft breezes rustled the tree leaves, and she could hear birds. Real birds, not just pigeons clucking on the sidewalk. Her sneakers and her ankles got damp as she brushed through the grass—when had she last experienced dew? How long since she'd walked on anything but a sidewalk?

Only when she stepped onto the porch of the house did she consider that the door might be locked. Then she'd be trapped outside, sitting in a rocking chair in her pajamas, until somebody inside woke up and emerged from the house—which was just one of the more embarrassing situations she could imagine. Especially if that person was Wyatt Marshall, the most intimidating of the four. She had a feeling he disapproved of her enough already.

But the knob turned easily in her hand. This wasn't Manhattan, after all. Who needed to lock up in the middle of nowhere?

Slipping into the living room, Jess gently closed the front door. There was a little squeak, but surely not enough to wake anyone. Most people slept with their bedroom door shut, right?

As she crossed to the hallway, the aroma of coffee permeated the air. The Marshalls must have their pot on a timer, so the brew would be prepared when they got up. She had one on her coffeemaker at home. Of course, she usually got up about eight...

"Good morning." Through the opening to the kitchen, she saw Garrett Marshall leaning against the counter. He gave her one of his handsome smiles and lifted his mug. "Coffee?"

"Um...thanks." Pulling her sweater around her, Jess sat on a stool at the breakfast bar. Now she regretted not having put clothes on before going to the studio last night.

"It's a glorious day." He brought milk and sugar to the bar. "Been out for a walk?"

She wanted to lie. Or just run away. "Not exactly." A sip of coffee fortified her resolve. "I couldn't sleep last night, so I went over to watch Dylan work."

Garrett paused in the act of drinking. He didn't move, his face didn't change—he just stared at her.

"I fell asleep in the chair. And didn't wake up until a few minutes ago."

"In the chair?"

"Um…no."

He nodded. "I'm guessing Dylan slept in his recliner."

"What makes you so sure?"

"He prefers his women conscious."

Jess sputtered her coffee through a laugh. "And you know this because…?"

"Because Dylan doesn't take advantage of people. Well…" Garrett chuckled. "He might be a little lazy when it comes to chores. You won't catch him making a meal. But he isn't deceptive. What he says or does is the truth."

"The whole truth?"

"Ah. That's different."

Might as well do some work, since the opportunity had presented itself. "Did you and your brothers follow his career, before he returned home?"

Forearms on the counter, Garrett palmed his coffee mug back and forth. "For the record? I did. Ford was in San Francisco building his law practice, so I'm not sure if he realized what was going on. Wyatt uses computers because they're fast at calculations, but anything he reads on the internet probably contains the word *cattle*."

"What did you think of Dylan's work? His life?"

"His abstract work wasn't anything I'd ever have associated with my little brother. And as far as I could tell, his life was pretty much what you'd expect from a kid given too much attention and not enough responsibility."

"Why did he come home?"

"Because he missed us?" He shook his head and

took a sip of coffee. "Although that was part of it, something else happened. Something that shook him to the very foundation of his soul."

"But he hasn't shared what it was?"

"No. And I wouldn't get my hopes up, if I were you." His stern blue gaze focused on her face. "Dylan keeps his secrets. He seems easygoing, accessible. But underneath, he's got some solid shields. Nobody gets all the way inside."

She could see how much that bothered him. As a minister, he might wish his brother would confide in him on difficult issues.

But to her chagrin, before she could say anything, Jess was ambushed by a huge yawn. She had to cover her mouth with both hands to hide it.

Grinning, Garrett straightened up. "The kids are usually ready to start their riding about nine o'clock, after breakfast and cleanup. It's not six yet. You could probably grab at least a couple hours' sleep before then. Susannah will be glad to make you something to eat when you're ready."

"That sounds wonderful." Her eyes watered with weariness. "I appreciate the coffee."

"I'm up early every morning. Join me whenever you like."

Jess shuffled to her room, closed the door and fell facedown on the bed with her feet hanging off the edge because she still had her sneakers on.

The next thing she heard was a knock on the door. "Still alive in there?"

Dylan's voice.

"Sure," Jess mumbled, and could barely hear herself. She cleared her throat and tried again. "Sure. I'll be out in a few."

"Great. There's a pair of boots in the kitchen with your name on it."

A fast shower got her blood moving and within fifteen minutes she had dressed and braided her hair. Makeup posed a dilemma—sunscreen moisturizer, of course, but did she require the full work-up for a day on the ranch? Or should she keep in mind that this was a professional assignment and prepare accordingly?

She settled for mascara and lipstick, though the face in the mirror seemed unfamiliar. "Nobody will notice," she assured herself. "This isn't Manhattan."

In the kitchen, Susannah slid a plate in front of her as she sipped her second cup of coffee at the bar. "There's more if you want it." Her smile was as sunny as the morning pouring through the big windows. "Enjoy." She looked over at Amber, sitting next to Jess. "Finish your cereal, sweetie. Then we'll go outside."

The atmosphere in the kitchen was cozy as Jess attacked a cheese omelet with crispy bacon and the best biscuits she'd ever eaten anywhere. Susannah seemed constantly busy—cleaning counters, putting away some dishes, taking out others. Jess felt as if she'd stepped into a TV show, one of those family sitcoms from the sixties where the mother stayed home and took care of the kids while the dad went off to work and made lots of money to keep them all comfortable. Where everybody loved everybody else and disagreements were settled with words, not fists.

A world she'd never lived in and wasn't sure really existed...until now.

Pushing her empty plate away, Jess groaned. "I'll be going home ten pounds heavier on Sunday. The plane will probably crash from my weight."

Susannah laughed. "You'd be surprised how much you work off just walking around. And Dylan said you've got a riding lesson, so that's even more calories. Your boots are over by the door." She turned to her daughter. "Are you finished, Amber? Ready to go outside?"

"Yes! Yes!" The little girl started scrambling off the chair before her mother could get there. In her hurry, she unbalanced the high stool. "Mama!"

On reflex, Jess reached out to scoop Amber up before she hit the floor. "Phew," she said, cradling the warm body against hers. She'd never held a young child this close in her life. "Gotta be careful," she said, a little breathless.

Amber wriggled hard. "Down. Let me down."

Jess put her feet on the floor, making sure she was steady. "There you go."

"Good catch. Thanks." Susannah took her daughter's hand. "Outside for you. Gotta run off some energy."

Watching them walk hand in hand across the sun-streaked wooden floor, Jess was struck again by the sensation that she'd stumbled into a strange, incomprehensible new world. "*Alice in Wonderland*," she muttered, shaking her head. "I've fallen down the rabbit hole."

"What's that?" Dylan stood leaning against the frame of the dining room door. "Susannah said you were here."

He was so damn appealing, with that engaging grin and the twinkle in those dark eyes. He'd already been working this morning, and his sleeves had been rolled up to his elbows, revealing forearms tanned by the sun and sculpted by hard work. The open throat of his plaid shirt, his broad shoulders under slightly damp cloth, the slim jeans riding low on his narrow hips...

A bolt of lust drove straight through Jess's body. She squeezed her eyes shut for a second, clenching her fists against the force of it.

"You okay?" Dylan said, straightening up. "Maybe you need some more rest." He started toward her.

She held up a hand to ward him off. "I'm great. So what's up with these boots?"

"This is Cash." Dylan led Jess to the horse standing by the corral fence. "As in, Johnny Cash."

She didn't stand too close. "A black horse. Naturally."

"Come stroke his neck. He's as quiet as can be." He saw her swallow hard before she took the step that would let her reach Cash's side. "You haven't been around animals much, I guess."

"No. Pets and foster kids don't always mix well." She ran her palm along Cash's sleek throat. "He's smooth. Warm." Her nose wrinkled. "And he smells funny."

"Horses have their own scent. It's not Chanel, but it's one of my favorites." Dylan leaned close to Cash's face and took a deep breath. "Mmm." The horse blinked but didn't move. "See—he's really calm." He took a brush from the bucket he held and handed it to Jess. "Why don't you give him a brushing?"

Raising a skeptical eyebrow, she gazed at the brush. "How is that done, exactly?"

She got the hang of the process quickly enough, once he showed her the short, outward flicks that worked best for getting rid of dirt. "I've cleaned his feet already, so you won't have to do that," Dylan told her.

Her big eyes widened. "You clean their feet?"

"Even with shoes, their soles are softer than you might think. We make sure there are no rocks stuck in there to bruise them, no sores or other injuries. Now we can go get the tack."

In the tack room, he pointed out Cash's gear. "I'll bring the bridle and blanket. You can carry the saddle," he said, teasing her a little bit.

"Right." Jess walked gamely to the rack he'd indicated, grabbed the horn and the back rim of the seat and pulled.

Luckily, he was standing right behind her when she staggered under twenty-five-plus pounds of leather. Her body pressed against his, and Dylan pulled in a deep breath even as he clamped his hands on her waist to keep her steady. "Whoa, there. I thought you'd tell me what I could do with that saddle."

She blew an irritated breath off her lower lip. "I should have. But it's your equipment I dropped. I guess you can deal with it." Stepping over the saddle, she walked to the door before looking back. "I'll be outside with Cash."

When he followed her into the corral—carrying the saddle under one arm, the bridle over his shoulder and the blanket in his other hand—she stood near the horse's head, touching his nose with her fingertips.

She glanced up as he arrived beside her. "So soft. And he doesn't bite." Her smile, when her gaze returned to Cash's face, was sweet and young. Without makeup, she seemed more approachable, easier to accept.

Like someone he might have gone to school with. Dated. Even married.

"He's a good boy." Dylan slung the saddle blanket onto the horse one-handed, straightened it out and then placed the saddle. "Cash turned twenty this spring."

"Is that old for a horse? They race three-year-olds in the Kentucky Derby, right?"

"Right." He bent to tighten the cinch. "I wouldn't race him across the ranch, though he'd probably go for me if I asked. But walking you around, he'll be great."

In another minute, he'd fastened the bridle straps and put the reins over the horse's neck. "Now, I can give you a leg up or you can pull yourself into the saddle. Which do you prefer?"

She glared at him. "After that trick in the tack room, I'll do it myself, thanks very much."

He stood at Cash's head, just in case. "Left foot in the left stirrup. We always mount from this side. One hand on the horn, one on the back edge. That's called the cantle."

"Right." Jess stood for a moment, considering, and then put her hands where he'd instructed. From past experience, Dylan expected a groan and a fumble as she tried to get her foot high enough to climb into the stirrup.

So his lower jaw dropped when she lifted her knee practically to her shoulder, easily slid her foot onto the tread and lightly pulled herself to stand on the left leg before swinging her right over and sitting down on the saddle.

"Like that?" She grinned down at him, obviously pleased with herself.

His turn to scowl. "You lied. You've done this before."

"No, I swear. But you didn't ask me about what other sports I might practice."

"Such as…"

"Karate."

"Ah. That makes you a dangerous person to know." No surprise there. Dylan pulled his hat a little lower. "Time to ride. Take up the reins. Squeeze your heels against his sides."

By the end of thirty minutes, Jess looked at home in the saddle, as if she'd been riding for years. Before an hour had passed, she and Cash were jogging both ways around the corral. In her white hat, long braided hair and skinny jeans, she definitely took the prize for the prettiest, not to mention sexiest, cowgirl he'd ever seen.

But she's not a cowgirl. She's a reporter. He was having trouble remembering that fact, and even more trouble not taking this morning at face value, as an experience shared between friends.

He shook his head. *Friends. Yeah, right.*

"Good job," he said as she finally came to a stop in front of him. "The kids will be jealous of your skill. Except for Nate. He's as talented as you are."

She stroked the side of Cash's neck. "Where are the kids? I forgot to ask."

"Trail riding, as a last prep before the cattle drive." To his own ears, he sounded terse. "You should get off now. Even if you're in great shape, you might be a little sore tomorrow. Come out of the stirrups on both sides. Then bend forward, bring your right leg over and slide to the ground."

She vaulted off with the grace of a gymnast. "That's pretty easy."

"You make it look that way." Dylan led Cash to the fence and exchanged his bridle for a halter before removing the saddle and blanket. "If you want to brush out the sweat where the blanket has been, I'll put this stuff away." He headed toward the barn without waiting for her agreement. His shoulder blades itched as if she was staring at him while he walked away.

When he got back, Cash gleamed like a fancy black car. "Nice." They walked the horse to the far end of the corral, where Dylan took off the halter and let him into the pasture. Right away, Cash kicked up his heels and raced across the field at full speed, tail flying high.

Dylan snorted a laugh as he closed the gate. "A two-year-old colt with a twenty-year-old's knees."

Jess stood beside him. "I'm glad you didn't show me that version of him before I rode. 'Cause I can assure you, it wouldn't have happened."

He didn't answer. Couldn't figure out what to say. His brain warred with his gut, churning him up inside. Smart and stupid, safe and crazy, were all mixed up.

"Oh, the hell with it," he growled. "Let's get this over with." He turned to face Jess Granger, cupped her face in his hands and tilted her chin up with his thumbs. Then he kissed her.

Chapter 4

As far as Jess could tell, this would not be over with anytime soon.

His mouth was firm against hers, but not harsh. Just...inexorable. She might have predicted this moment when she first saw him yesterday. And she agreed—they should satisfy their curiosity and then move on.

But there seemed to be no end to the ways their lips fit together, or to the variations of sensation they could create for each other. She circled her arms around his neck, and the closeness changed their contact, melding them more deeply. Their tongues touched, tangled, and they both gasped. His scent reached her—the tang of lemon, a trace of pine and an edge of spice, blended with the sweet musk of his sweat. The way her head spun, Jess could have been totally intoxicated at eleven o'clock in the morning.

Perhaps that was why she was so swept away, so overwhelmed and enthralled. Dylan's kisses confirmed a link between them, a spiritual connection she'd never thought she'd have. His solace and support, his concern and confidence, blanketed all the cold places inside her. She'd waited her whole life to get warm.

At the sound of a distant shout, though, Dylan raised his head. "Damn." His mouth looked as swollen, as ravaged, as hers felt. Staring into his face, she imagined his lashes might be wet.

"What's wrong?" She grabbed his biceps to keep herself upright. Her knees were too shaky to depend on.

"They're coming this way."

Jess followed his line of sight and saw a string of riders cresting the top of a distant hill. They hadn't reached the far pasture fence, but it wouldn't be too long.

His fingers untangled from her hair. He took a deep breath and stepped away, dropping his hands. "I've made a mess…there's a bathroom in the barn, with a mirror. You should go."

"Sure. Okay." She made her fingers loosen on his arms. "Yes."

"I believe the kids are expecting you for lunch," he said. "A picnic at the creek. But I've got some…chores to do, so I might not get there in time." After a pause, he added, "See you later."

Before she could say anything, he climbed the gate and dropped over to the other side. He walked to a beautiful white horse with brown spots all over its coat. They greeted each other with what Jess considered a hug—the animal folded its long head over Dylan's shoulder while his arms went around its neck.

The horse raised its head and in the next instant Dylan somehow threw himself up and onto its bare back, a maneuver that made mounting with a stirrup from the ground seem clumsy and silly. Without saddle or bridle, they started to move at a walk and then a jog, as she had with Cash, and then into a smooth motion that reminded her of a sailboat on a rolling sea. Although the kids on their horses were getting closer, Dylan rode off in a different direction, and then down a hill until he was lost from her sight.

Quite an exit.

Once within the cool shadows of the barn, Jess found the bathroom and locked herself inside. She sat on the small bench against the wall and pressed a wet towel over her face, striving for composure that was a long while coming.

They were just kisses. You're thirty-five years old. Not fifteen.

But no one had ever kissed her like that. No man had ever offered her such a spectrum of experiences— mental, physical, emotional—and touched only her face. Sex was sex and she'd had her share, most of it good, some of it terrific. None of it could compare with what had just taken place.

Or maybe that was simply what she wanted to feel, what she wanted to believe had happened. Dylan Marshall had gotten to her, somehow. For whatever reason, she needed this to be something special.

Which was ridiculous. She wasn't here for a relationship. She didn't want a relationship. What she needed and wanted was a story.

But how could she pursue the article, after this episode? Her objectivity about him had been completely destroyed. Anything she wrote would be biased by the emotional reaction he'd incited. And by his reaction to her.

Wait a minute.

Was that the point? Had those kisses been calculated to produce exactly that response? Could Dylan Marshall be devious enough to seduce her as a way of slanting her work? Did he believe she could be manipulated?

Jess pressed the wet towel harder against her eyes. She didn't want to accept that Dylan could be such a slick operator. He'd flirted with her, she'd flirted with him, and she thought they'd both understood it as a way of finding common ground. Fun, but basically harmless.

Those kisses had not been harmless. Would she ever forget that soaring sense of completion when his mouth softened on hers, the exquisite sense of being understood?

Noises outside the bathroom signaled that the kids had arrived. Wearily, Jess stood up and went to stare at the mirror over the sink. She'd smeared mascara all over her cheeks, and the only soap she had to wash with was a rough green bar. As for her hair...luckily, there was a comb in the medicine cabinet. That damage she could repair.

The damage to her ego, her spirit, her...heart? She wasn't so sure.

* * *

Dylan slowed Leo to a jog when they got close to the creek, and then finally to a walk. When they moved under the trees, the horse put his head down and began to graze. Sliding off to the side, Dylan walked to his favorite boulder and sat. A minute later, he stretched all the way out and put his hat over his face. With luck, he'd fall asleep and not have to think. Surrounded by water and grass, Leo wouldn't wander off.

Unfortunately, Dylan's mind wouldn't wander, either, but returned with excruciating accuracy to his most recent mistake. A mistake he would live with for a long time to come.

Just a kiss, he'd decided. *Her lips, my lips, nothing special, let it go.*

Not in the least. First, there was the smoothness of her cheeks against his palms. Cool, too, even after an hour of riding. And those big hazel eyes, deep-set and intense. Registering surprise and then, in the next instant, desire.

Which was a big part of the problem. Her mouth had been warm, soft and ready. He'd lost his head with the first taste. After that, the only consideration had been making her feel good, letting her do the same for him. Pure pleasure in the giving and the taking. His body stirred just remembering it.

She wasn't supposed to turn him on. He didn't want to want her. Hell, he *couldn't* want her—what would be the point? Come Sunday, she'd be flying off to New York and he would stay in Wyoming. End of story.

Besides, she came from a world he'd deliberately rejected. The women he'd met in the contemporary art world were beautiful, like Jess. Many of them were smart, like her. Would he bring them home to meet Wyatt?

Not only no, but hell, no.

Jemima, Constance, Amabel, Olivia…lovely ladies, all of them, busy enjoying their wealthy, privileged lives. Dylan had enjoyed their privileged lives, too— his sculptures had given him access to their parties, their adventures, their friendship. More than friendship, in fact. Just casual connections, though, which none of them had taken seriously. He hadn't, either.

Underneath his hat, he blew out a long breath. This line of thought was one he avoided if at all possible— another reason to keep his distance from Jess Granger. She wanted to take him back to that point in time, to probe the mystery he'd deliberately created. She wanted to know about Noelle.

Swearing, Dylan sat up and jammed his hat on his head. Leo glanced over and gave a snort.

"My sentiments exactly," he told the Appaloosa. "I won't go there." Elbows on his knees, head down, he pulled at a tall blade of grass. "I can't."

Kissing Jess had been amazing. Disorienting, confusing and exhilarating. But he was twenty-seven years old. He'd shared kisses with…well, with enough women to understand how the game was played.

Get over it. Move on.

A sudden chill poured through him, from brain to belly. Maybe he didn't understand the game so well, after all. What if…what if Jess Granger had used those kisses to pursue her agenda? Sure, he'd started it, but her response could have been calculated to…*stimulate*, for want of a better word, his cooperation. Maybe she planned to seduce him into telling her the whole truth.

"Not gonna happen." He stood up and walked over to his horse, swung up onto Leo's back and urged him away from the creek. He did have chores to do, and brothers who would pester him until he'd finished.

Not to mention a reporter to deal with who ranked up there with Mata Hari in terms of technique. But now that he realized her intentions, he could counter her maneuvers with a few of his own.

They called it fighting fire with fire. And Dylan couldn't wait to feed the flames.

The kids' picnic took place beside the creek, but farther away than the place Dylan had shown her yesterday. Jess was given a basket of paper plates and napkins to carry as she walked along with the crowd, going downhill from the red barn and away from the house. In the distance, the rolling plains of grass that created the ranch were framed by the blue-and-purple peaks of the Big Horn Mountains. Above all of it stretched the clearest sky she'd ever seen.

Caroline stepped up beside her. "How was your riding lesson?"

"Enjoyable, as far as I'm concerned." Till the end. Or, maybe, especially the end. "Cash made it easy for me."

"He's a great old pony. Ford told me that Cash is the first horse Wyatt trained when he came to work on the ranch."

"He must be very talented with this cowboy stuff."

"They all are. Dylan started at the youngest age,

and he's by far the best rider. Did you watch him go off on Leo this morning? I grew up with horses, and I'm not nearly so comfortable riding bareback. And without a bridle, forget it."

"Are you from this area? One of the neighboring ranches?" Talking about Caroline would be a way to avoid talking—or thinking—about Dylan.

Of course, talking about Dylan was her job. The reason she'd come and the reason she wished she could leave.

Caroline nodded in answer to her question. "But my dad and I aren't on speaking terms—he doesn't approve my line of work. Though I'm still close with my mom, the Marshalls are my family now."

Jess stared at her with raised brows. "Is this the Circle M Home for the Discarded and Difficult? That would include me, of course."

To her relief, Caroline laughed. "Could be. In fact, I was wondering if you would be able to talk with the kids after lunch, since we'll all be together and they should be reasonably settled. Not a huge formal speech or anything, just a conversation about how you set goals and achieved them, even with a challenging background."

"I'll be glad to." They arrived at the bottom of the hill, to find that Susannah had spread a checkered tablecloth over the wooden table where the kids were placing the various items they'd carried to the site—plates of sandwiches, bags of chips, a big bowl of fruit and another of salad. Thomas and Marcos had managed to cooperate long enough to transport a yellow cooler of water for drinking.

"This looks wonderful." Jess handed Susannah the paper products she'd carried. "What a great place for a picnic."

"Isn't it?" Susannah glanced around, finding Amber at the edge of the water with her brother, Nate, standing right beside her. "The more I see of the ranch, the more I love it. Wyatt is so lucky to live here. All of them are," she added, with a flush rising in her cheeks.

"Does the creek have a name?" Though shaded by tall trees, the banks of the creek itself were covered with rocks and boulders, which made perfect lunch sites for the kids.

Garrett stepped up to the table. "It's a branch of Crazy Woman Creek."

Jess pretended to think hard. "Let me guess— named after a legend about a Native American woman whose tribe was killed by soldiers."

"Or a woman settler whose family was killed by warriors." Ford joined them and began to fill a plate. "Take your pick."

"How about…" Jess grinned. "How about an independent woman who bought her own land, built the house by herself and ran the ranch her way?"

Leaning against a nearby tree, sandwich in hand, Wyatt chuckled. "In the old days, they would have thought that was the craziest story of all."

"Of course," Caroline said. "They all knew a woman couldn't get along in this world without a man to take care of her." Smiling, she elbowed Ford in the ribs. He nudged her right back.

"It's the other way around," Wyatt said. "A man needs a woman to take care of him." When they all looked at him in surprise, his cheeks reddened. "Seems to me."

"Then it's a good thing you and I have Susannah," Garrett told him. "At least for now."

Wyatt's face went blank. "Guess so."

Jess noticed that Susannah was sitting with her kids on a nearby rock—close enough to hear the comments and have her cheeks turn bright red.

The easy conversation left Jess with a smile on her face as the kids gathered to clean up the table. She surveyed the area, trying to choose a suitable amphitheater to gather them for her "talk." Taking her place on a nearby rock, she nodded at Caroline to indicate she was ready to begin. In another minute, an audience of teenagers had circled in front of her.

Starting out, she met each one's gaze directly. "Good lunch, right?"

The kids responded with nods and a "yeah" or two, but the standard adolescent apathy was on display.

When she said, "Especially the brownies," more enthusiasm surfaced.

Jess would work with what she had. "So, the point of this meeting is for me to admit to you that I spent a lot of my life in the foster care system. I was five years old the first time I went into a foster home, and I left the last one when I graduated from high school."

Thomas stared up at her from under his brows. "How come?"

She took a deep breath. "My mom did drugs, but not much of anything else. We didn't always have a place to stay or food to eat. My dad sold drugs, but he disappeared a lot. They spent time in jail, and I would be placed with people who would take care of me. Then my parents would be released and regain custody. We seesawed like that till I was old enough to leave."

Lizzie raised her hand. "Doesn't it bother you to talk about it?"

"Should it?"

"Well...aren't you...doesn't it embarrass you when your parents are...?"

"Criminals? Yes. But it wasn't my fault." She gave them all another straight look. "That's one thing you must understand. Parents screw up. You can love them, but that won't make them suitable role models. You have to separate who you are from who they are."

Marcos was drawing pictures in the dirt. "Did you get hurt?"

"I was never abused. The people I stayed with weren't always lovey-dovey. But I got food and clothes and medicine when I was sick."

Thomas threw a small rock toward the creek. "So what's the big deal? Why should we bother listening to you? Doesn't sound so bad—you got places to go where nobody beat you up. They weren't drunk every night and making you do bad stuff." He jumped to his feet. "Why are you wasting our time?"

"Because you've all made some bad choices in your lives. And I've been in situations where those same options were offered to me."

"But you didn't make mistakes 'cause you're just too cool, huh?" Justino shrugged. "Too bad we can't all be cool like you."

Jess nodded. "I know. I'm sorry for you."

There was a shocked silence, before the rest of the

kids—and the adults—saw her grin and realized she was joking. Laughter broke up the tension and Thomas, looking flushed and uncomfortable, sat down.

"I'm not too cool to make mistakes," Jess told them. "I smoked—cigarettes and weed. I've tried pills, booze and coke. I cheated on tests, stole from grocery stores and had fistfights with other girls. And one boy. I won."

The kids were staring at her with wide eyes. She didn't dare glance at the adults. "I did everything any of you has done." She noticed Lizzie's self-conscious flush.

"But guess what? I didn't continue that behavior. I didn't get hooked on drugs or alcohol—I'd spent my whole life watching my mom craving her next fix and doing whatever it took to pay for it. I watched one of my foster dads die from lung cancer. I got caught stealing and spent a night in jail with women just like my mom, and I knew I never wanted to do that again."

Another deep breath. "In my first foster home, I made a friend. Trini was two years older than me, but she was really nice to a scared little girl. We got to stay together for almost two years till my mom came to get me. But Trini and I swore to stay friends. BFFs, you call them today.

"And we did, till Trini turned sixteen. After that, I would call, but she never seemed to be around. And when we did talk, she was…different. Impatient. Then insulting. When she left her foster home, she didn't leave me a way to get in touch with her. I found out, when I went back to my mom, that she was a gang member's girlfriend. He beat her up whenever he felt like it. One day he hit her too hard and she died."

After a pause, she said, "That's why you're listening to me. Because I've already made the mistakes and I know what happens when you do. Because the nice people over there who started this camp really want each and every one of you to have a life— a whole entire eighty-years-long life, with someone to love you forever and kids and grandkids and a home you share with them all, a job you're proud of, a sense of self-worth and confidence and peace that comes with making good choices. All of that is possible for each one of you."

Thomas raised his hand. "Do you have all that?"

Jess met his gaze and uttered her only lie. "I do."

Why don't I believe her?

Standing behind the other adults, Dylan had arrived in time to hear most of Jess's talk to the kids. Her frankness didn't surprise him—she seemed pretty comfortable with herself and what she'd been through.

"Not the kids and grandkids part," she said, grinning at the teens. "But I have a great job and a great life in New York."

He noticed that she didn't mention a husband or significant other…or even casual friends to share her days and nights. Maybe that's what made him doubt she was as successful in her personal life as she claimed— from the very first he'd had the impression of her as solitary. Jess struck him as a person who preferred to remain unattached. Self-sufficient.

But she didn't want the kids to know that.

Lizzie put up her hand. "If you did all those bad things, what made you change? Why didn't it get worse?"

Jess nodded. "Terrific question. One answer—books."

Marcos rolled his eyes. "You read books on making mistakes?"

"You can do that," she told him. Then she shrugged. "But who wants to?" That got her a laugh. "No, I read stories about other kids. Novels about girls who had really awesome lives, and whose biggest problems were the mean children they had to babysit. Or getting a boy to like them."

Justino sneered. "Talk about lame." Lena punched him in the arm.

"I read about boys who traveled through time and space to save the world. Girls can do that, too, though there weren't as many of those stories when I was a teenager as there are now. I read about growing up in the middle of a place like this." She stretched her arms wide. "But without running water or electricity, when you plowed the ground with horses or oxen to plant your crops and you drove to town in a wagon."

"I hate reading," Thomas said. "It's boring."

"I bet I could find you a book that's not boring. The thing is, books show you what's possible, from stories about what has truly happened to stories about something so crazy you can't begin to believe in the truth of it. Books distract you when you're bored. They comfort you when you're sad." Jess swallowed hard. "Losing Trini was hard. She was my only long-time friend, and I didn't know what to do without her in my life. The only way I could get through the hours without screaming was to read. Fortunately, I found a series of books about magic, strange creatures and fantasy countries. I buried myself in that world when I couldn't face the one I lived in. Otherwise… I might have started making some really bad choices of my own."

She let the silence lengthen while the kids considered. "That series inspired me to start writing on my own. First I continued those books—wrote about what happened after 'the end.' Then I created new characters and put them in the world that author created. I became immersed in my own writing, and that gave me a way out of the pain and anger I experienced over Trini." Once again, she locked gazes with each and every kid. "You guys could do the same thing."

That suggestion earned a loud chorus of denial, though Dylan noticed that Nate and Lizzie remained quiet.

"It's true," Jess insisted. "Every single one of you could write a readable story."

"Why bother?" Justino asked. "Somebody gonna pay me to waste my time?"

Jess held out her hands. "They pay me."

"You're ol…you're a grown-up."

"I got my first check for writing a magazine article when I was seventeen."

"What did you write about?" Lizzie, again.

"Trini. A national magazine held a contest to get published and I won."

"Was there a prize?" Marcos wanted to know.

"Five thousand dollars."

They all stared at her with their mouths open.

"Wow," Becky said at last. "That would be so cool."

Dylan managed to keep his jaw in place, but he was impressed. Jess was, apparently, a star in her own world.

Thomas recovered his control. "Yeah, right. I ain't got a computer to write stuff on. Even if I wanted to, and I don't."

"Pencil and paper work just fine. In fact..." Jess glanced at the adults. "We could probably find some paper on this great big ranch. A few pencils. You guys can try writing a story."

Marcos fell back onto the ground and covered his face with his arms. "No way."

"Think about this." She leaned forward, her face lit with enthusiasm. "You can travel anywhere in the universe. Not just this world, but any planet, star, moon, galaxy. What kind of place would you go to? That's all you have to do—describe where you would go and one thing you would do when you got there."

Still lying down, Marcos groaned. "Sooooo stupid."

"Reading and then writing were my way out," Jess told them. "Trini's story drew the attention of colleges, and a college degree gave me what I needed to make a career. I'm not saying that all of you will become professional writers because you started reading. What I am saying is that books contain ideas. And ideas can take you anywhere you want to go."

"I'm not doin' it," Thomas declared. He started to stand up, but a glance at the adults behind him quashed the idea.

"Who's going to read it?" Lizzie looked almost as excited as Jess.

Jess got to her feet. "That would be your choice. You can share what you write, or not. I happen to believe it's worth the effort just to sit down and try."

Caroline walked around to stand beside her. "I agree. It's pretty warm out, so we'll spend a cool hour at the bunkhouse, imagining where we'd go and what we'd do. Then you all can get some rodeo practice before dinner."

"I'd rather eat dirt," Justino muttered.

"That could be arranged," Dylan responded under his breath. Wyatt, standing beside him, heard and frowned.

"Don't forget to take something up the hill with you," Caroline called as the kids began to disperse. "We can empty the water into the creek."

"I'll get that." Dylan picked up the canister and climbed over the rocks with it. When he turned around, the group had already crested the hill and was headed toward the barn.

All except Jess.

"Some resistance is to be expected," she said with a wry smile. "But this might not be my most brilliant idea ever."

He dropped down off the last boulder, near where she stood. "The point of our camp, as I understand it, is asking them to do what they've never done before and to consider what they want from the rest of their lives. It seems to me you covered both those objectives."

"Maybe. Or maybe I just gave them something to complain about."

"Something different to complain about, you mean. Thomas and Marcos are always whining about this or that."

"From the things they said, though, I gather they don't have easy lives. One story can't change everything. But it's a start." She joined him as he walked away from the creek. "It would really be great if we had books they could keep."

"The Marshall brothers did some reading as kids. We probably have books stashed in boxes in the attic."

"You might not want to give those away. And these kids would probably really appreciate *new* ones. How many of them have ever had a new book of their own? The first novel I ever bought is still sitting on my shelf." Jess blew a frustrated breath. "I could order titles online, but they wouldn't get here until at least Monday. And I'll be gone by then. Which is okay, because you've got plenty of help. But…" She shrugged. "It would be fun to watch them discover stories. The way I did."

"Then I guess this is your lucky day."

She gave him a sideways look. "Because you kissed me?"

He'd said it without recalling that part of the morning. "Of course." He flashed her a grin and winked. "But also because I happen to know someone who owns a bookstore."

She pretended to be surprised. "There's a bookstore in Wyoming?"

Dylan scowled at her. "Spoken like a true New Yorker. Not only is there a bookstore in Wyoming, there's one in Bisons Creek."

"Never heard of that place."

"It's the town closest to us—you didn't pass through on the way in, but it's about a five-minute drive from here."

"Well, then, I can go right now, and bring back the books before dinner." She gave him a big smile. "That's terrific."

They reached the barn and saw Caroline heading from the ranch house to the bunkhouse with a ream of paper in her arms and a bundle of pencils in her fist.

"Writing stories," she called. "What a great idea!"

"Is she always so cheerful?" Jess asked. "And so busy?"

"Definitely busy," Dylan confirmed. "Though when we thought Ford was returning to San Francisco to work, 'cheerful' did not apply to Caroline. But since he's come home and they got engaged, she's all smiles. Ford, too, which is kind of weird. He's always been the serious one."

A wistful expression drifted through Jess's hazel eyes. "Lucky for them." Then she shook her head. "How do I get to the bookstore?"

He cleared his throat. "One thing about this particular shop—it's not always open. The owner is a friend of mine, Kip Glazier. He rode bulls until an injury took him out of the sport. Now he has a tidy little horse ranch to take care of, but he decided the area needed a bookstore, so he set one up. Let's go down to the studio and I'll call him to ask if he can meet us there."

Jess frowned when Kip said he couldn't arrive till four. "So I guess the books have to wait till after dinner."

"The kids will be mellower then," he suggested, and she laughed at him.

"Sure."

"We will, too. After dinner," he said, in answer to her questioning stare. "Why don't we get cleaned up, meet Kip and then have supper in town? We have an excellent bookstore *and* a diner in Bisons Creek."

"A booming metropolis. But that sounds good. We can work on the article while we eat."

"Right." He hadn't thought that far ahead—hadn't thought at all, in fact, beyond the idea that as long as they were in town, they could have a meal that didn't include teenagers or his brothers. Thinking ahead did not appear to be one of his skills today.

Bringing her to the studio again, for instance. Jess was prowling the room, examining the sculptures. "The whole is definitely greater than the sum of the parts," she said, staring at the eagle.

Dylan went over to make coffee. "I'll take that as a compliment."

"Be my guest. But the same was true of your abstract work. The figures you produced came in groups, and it was the relationship between the members of the group that gave the whole ensemble meaning." She accepted the mug he offered. "So why did you stop? Why is this—" she used her arm to indicate the entire studio "—more valuable to you?"

Dylan retreated as far as the table behind him would allow. Taking a sip of coffee, he tried to construct a reason that would make sense and convince her to leave him alone.

"I don't know how you'll package this for your audience," he said. "You must be an excellent writer, though, to have won that prize when you were seventeen."

"I am good. But a talent for writing isn't all the business requires anymore."

"Beauty and talent ought to be enough."

"What is it I'm supposed to package?"

He gulped down more brew. "First, there were the materials. Concrete, plastic, iron, aluminum—hard, usually. Unyielding. From there, it's a step to uncomfortable. Then there's the size—I was working with forklifts to move the sculptures. The cost of transport could eat up most of a commission fee, if there was one. How about the environmental factors? When the world decides abstract art has gone out of fashion, what happens to those pieces? A landfill, where they never degrade? Or a jetty on the ocean, maybe, with other big lumps of concrete. Trash. I was basically creating pieces of trash, which people decided they liked until they changed their minds."

She tilted her head toward the eagle. "How is this different?"

"If we threw all of these sculptures out onto the prairie, they would eventually become part of the prairie again. The glues would dissolve, the finishes would degrade, the wood would fall prey to insects and weather and degenerate. Inside, they will last decades. Outside, these all revert to their original components."

Jess nodded. "The materials speak for themselves— wood you pick up off the ground, natural glues, stains and finishes. And the size, of course, is manageable."

"These sculptures can be moved by hand. They're scaled to be appreciated as parts of our lives, not to overwhelm with brute force. When I was twenty, brute force appealed to me. Then I grew up and realized I couldn't impose myself on others, on nature. That wasn't how I wanted to connect with the world."

He closed his eyes for a moment, trying to create a whole from these different parts. "I guess all this boils down to the idea that I don't want to create sculpture in opposition to the natural world. I want my work to be an extension of the world I live in. Make sense?"

"Sure." Passing in front of him, she walked her mug over to the coffeemaker and headed for the door. "I'll be at the house when you're ready to go to the bookstore. That gives you a couple of hours."

With the door open, she looked over her shoulder to meet his eyes. "Maybe by then you'll have figured out what would be so damn terrible about simply telling me the truth."

Chapter 5

At four fifteen, Jess was sitting in the living room, chatting with Susannah and watching Amber play with her baby doll—carefully wrapping and unwrapping the blanket and pretending to rock her to sleep. The little girl lifted her head when the door opened. "Dylan!"

The doll dropped to the floor as she jumped up and ran to hug his knees. Grinning, Dylan picked her up and tossed her toward the ceiling. "How are you this afternoon, Miss Amber?"

"Fine." Caught securely by his steady hands, she settled in the crook of his arm. "Did you come to play with me?"

"I can play with you for a minute." He wore a maroon-checked shirt with the sleeves rolled up at the cuffs, black jeans and boots. His damp hair waved back from his face, exposing his striking bone structure. At that moment, he looked more artist than cowboy. "What shall we play?"

"Horsey!"

"We can do that." He carried her with him and sat down in one of the recliners by the fireplace. The little girl slid down to sit on the points of his knees. Holding her hands and bouncing his knees, he said, "Ride a little horsey into town, uphill, downhill and all around." On the last word he straightened his legs and she fell backward, hanging upside down from his grip.

"Again!"

Watching the two of them, Jess couldn't help smiling. Amber's giggles made her think of a bubble bath with froth you could hear. A glance at Susannah revealed a mother's love and pride, along with affection for the man entertaining her daughter. As for Dylan, he was enjoying himself, too. He would be a terrific dad one day, when he had kids of his own.

Jess sobered at the image that idea conjured up, though Dylan's future children had nothing to do with her.

Amber took four more rides before Dylan stood up and set the little girl on her feet. "That's your ride for the day, Sunshine. Ms. Jess and I have to drive into town." He looked at Susannah. "And we'll get dinner while we're there, so don't worry about us for tonight."

"Have fun," Susannah said as Jess stood.

Jess smiled at her, and walked through the screen door as Dylan held it open. By the time she stepped off the front porch, she allowed the smile to fade. She'd been angry when she left the studio two hours ago, and her mood hadn't changed.

Dylan came up beside her, his expression as stern as she'd seen it since her arrival. "This is my truck." He opened the passenger door of one of the big pickups parked near the house and shut it once she was seated. Climbing in on the driver's side, he started the engine, reversed the truck and then headed down the long drive she'd traveled yesterday, all without saying a word.

Jess had been driving yesterday, focused on her destination and not the scenery. Today she took a chance to enjoy the landscape—rolling green fields stretched to the horizon in every direction, with a backdrop of blue-green mountains and that incredibly blue sky arching overhead.

"This place is so beautiful," she said sincerely. "I love the flowers mingling with the grass." Blossoms in pink, yellow, blue and white popped up everywhere.

Without glancing her way, Dylan nodded. "Now you know my answer to at least one of your questions—who would want to work anywhere else?"

"I concede your point."

The remainder of the ride to town passed without conversation. Dylan didn't speak and Jess was certainly not going to venture another question for him to dance around.

Part of what he'd said to her this afternoon was probably true—environmental issues, the difficulties in creating gigantic art installations and the question of material use were debated in art circles year in and year out.

But she didn't believe those were his main reasons for deserting a promising career. Those were the kinds of concerns artists incorporated into their work, refining and evolving their style. No one vanished from view because he thought concrete was heavy and bad for the planet.

Dylan didn't *want* to tell her the truth. Pretty soon, she'd begin to suspect he'd murdered someone and run away so he wouldn't get caught. If she could discover anyone who'd gone missing besides Dylan Marshall, she might actually start looking for proof.

The little town of Bisons Creek fit into the cleft of two swells in the prairie, with a wide Main Street but no traffic light. Brick buildings lined the thoroughfare, their design more utilitarian than decorative, and the houses along the road tended to be practical instead of pretty. There were lots of trees, though, which surprised Jess. And many of the businesses had placed planters beside their front doors and filled them with brightly colored flowers.

"Is there a creek in Bisons Creek?" she asked. Watching, she saw the corner of Dylan's mouth twitch in what might have almost been a smile.

"Not anymore." He turned onto one of the streets that crossed the main road. "There was, when the place was settled in the 1890s. But highway construction diverted the water, so the town is now high and dry."

"Is that good or bad? I know there are lots of water issues in the West these days."

"In this case, it's a good thing. The creek ran along the east side of town. Old photographs show a muddy mess on Main Street when the banks overflowed. People are probably just as happy to live without that hassle."

Dylan stopped the truck in front of a small house with clapboard siding and a sign on the front porch rail that announced The Necessary Book.

"Cute name," she said as they followed the sidewalk to the house. "I hope he stocks at least seven readable books for teenagers."

"More like a hundred," Kip told her, when they got inside. He was shorter than Dylan and whip thin, with dark hair and sparkling blue eyes. "Teenagers are my target audience—they're the ones we need to get hooked on reading and to continue. Come this way."

He led them into what would once have been a bedroom, but was now painted black with fluorescent designs scrawled on the walls in chalk. "Kinda crazy, but I get decorating advice from my teenaged nieces." Beanbag chairs in neon colors sat in the center of the room, with bookcases of various sizes and colors lining the walls. "I'm sure we can find what you're searching for in here."

"Pretty terrific, if you ask me." Dylan bent to examine the selection on one shelf. "If this store had existed when I was younger, I'd have been in here whenever we came to town."

Jess knelt by a different assortment to run a finger along the titles on the spines. "We need this one." She pulled it out. "And this, and this." Grinning, she looked up at Kip. "You're a treasure chest hidden in the middle of the desert. I may have to write an article about The Necessary Book."

Dylan gave a long whistle. "Better watch out, Kip. Give her an interview and she'll want to pry out your deepest, darkest secrets. Being a rodeo star, I expect you've got quite a few."

Laughing, Kip held up his hands. "Not me. Pure as the driven snow. I showed up, got on my bull, got off and moved on."

His friend stared at him, one eye squinted. "I seem to remember quite a few buckle bunnies clustered around that old jalopy of yours. Let's see, there was a Gretchen, and a Marla. Bobbie Jean and Terri…"

Walking on her knees, Jess moved to the next bookcase. "Not all secrets have to do with…um…romance." But it was interesting to note that his mind had jumped in that direction. Maybe those rumors about his disappearance being linked to a woman were truer than she'd realized. She would have to review her research and pull up the few facts she'd found. Having met the man, she might better understand what she'd learned.

"The best ones do," Dylan assured her, further piquing her interest.

At the end of an hour, the three of them had selected four times as many books as she'd intended to buy. "This way, they have choices," she said, handing Kip her credit card. "I can't begin to guess what each of them might select to read."

Dylan leaned an elbow on the counter. "I just hope they appreciate your effort. Your feelings won't be hurt if the reaction isn't exactly…enthusiastic, will they?"

Kip shook his head. "You are not the biggest fan of humanity, that's for sure. Our friend here used to be an optimist," he said to Jess, "always seeing the bright side. But since he came back home, he's taken a darker view, especially when it comes to the population of the planet. Some days, he's downright gloomy about it."

A glance at Dylan revealed that he was definitely gloomy about the direction of the conversation. "Reading the news these days is enough to depress Pollyanna. Have you got what you need, Jess? We haven't even checked out the rest of the store."

"I could spend hours just browsing." She picked up the bag of books. "But Kip probably wants to get home to his ranch. Thank you so much for opening up this afternoon." At the door, she looked back. "Can I call you about an interview? I'd like to run the idea of an article by my editor."

He shrugged. "Sure. I can use the publicity. Take it easy, Dylan. You two have a nice evening."

Jess frowned as she crossed the porch. Kip sounded as if she and Dylan were on a date.

The man in question stood at the bottom of the steps, hands held out. "Let me carry that for you."

"It's not heavy. They're all paperbacks." She stepped around him on the sidewalk and headed toward the truck. She couldn't decide what bothered her more—that this wasn't a date or that Kip had assumed it was one.

"Okay." Dylan got to the truck ahead of her and opened the door. "Let me hold the bag while you get in."

She glared at him. "Are women in Wyoming so helpless that their men have to do everything for them in case they hurt themselves?" She regretted the words as soon as she said them—there was no call for bad

manners, even if she was irritated with…with somebody. About something.

But he took her seriously. "As a matter of fact, Wyoming women are strong, independent, capable and
intelligent. And to show them how much we appreciate all they can do, we like to offer them special
courtesies."

Jess expected him to turn around and leave her to
shut her own door.

Instead, he simply took the bag away from her. "So
if you'll climb in, I'll shut your door and then stow
these books. Do you have a problem with that plan?"

What could she say? "No."

To his credit, he didn't slam the panel, but closed it
gently. He did the same when he put the books in the
back. By the time he'd seated himself and started the
engine, Jess was feeling thoroughly ashamed of her
temper tantrum.

"I apologize for being ungrateful," she said, staring
straight ahead. "All this gallantry makes me nervous.
I'm not used to it."

"I find it hard to believe that the men you go out
with in New York don't use good manners."

"They aren't louts. They chew with their mouths
closed." Not that she'd dated much in the past few
years. Before she'd reached thirty, the Manhattan sin-
gles scene had lost its appeal. "Some of them open
doors."

"Glad to hear it." He aimed the truck into the parking lot beside a building with a sign for Kate's Diner.
"This is the best food in the county, except for Susannah's. Also the only restaurant in Bisons Creek." His

grin emerged. "Shall I wait for you to come around and open my door? Would that restore your independence?"

"But then we might have to deal with your wounded masculine pride—a dangerous prospect. I'll let you get out on your own, thanks."

"You're sure?"

Jess scowled at him. "I'm hungry. Let's go find some food."

And some answers to her questions. She didn't want to provoke him in public, but an entire day had passed without any concrete progress on the interview. At this rate, she'd be making up the article as if it were a fiction short story.

As little as he wanted to cooperate, Dylan might prefer that solution, anyway.

Dylan wasn't surprised to find the diner full of customers, practically all of whom he knew. He nodded and smiled at them as he guided Jess to the one open table along the wall.

"I'm going to pull out your chair," he said into her ear. A whiff of her cologne teased his senses. "But only because everybody is watching. Don't take it personally."

When he sat down across from her, she was smiling. "There does seem to be a lot of attention directed this way."

"That's a small town for you."

The smile faded. "I remember."

Before he could probe that reaction, their waitress

arrived. "Hey, Dylan. Haven't seen you in quite a while. Guess you all are busy up there with those kids?"

"Hello, Ms. Caitlin. We are pretty busy this summer, with one job or another. This is Jess Granger, a magazine journalist. Jess, Caitlin's on the rodeo team at her college, planning to turn pro."

The pretty blonde nodded. "Barrel racing is my life. Are you writing about rodeo? I'd be glad to talk to you."

"Actually, I'm writing about Dylan, here. But I'm learning about rodeo, and I might be able to make an article on that subject work."

"You're writing about Dylan? That's cool. He was awesome with saddle broncs. I remember when I was a little girl watching him ride."

Dylan put his head in his hand. "Now I feel old. Just get us some drinks, Caitlin. Take your young self away."

"So old. You're all of twenty-seven." Jess was laughing at him. She looked so gorgeous, laughing… but then she sobered suddenly. "I've got as many years on you as you have on her. Now I'm depressed."

"Caitlin will be lucky if she's half as beautiful when she's your age."

Her eyes narrowed. "That doesn't help, thanks all the same."

He decided to challenge her. "Why not? You said this afternoon that you have a great life with all you could want. You wouldn't be able to say that if you were nineteen and just starting out."

"True. At nineteen I was working three jobs to pay for college, and sleeping four hours a night."

"What kind of jobs?"

"Waitress. Laundromat attendant—that's when I got my schoolwork done. Research assistant, where I learned how to mine the library and computers for information."

Caitlin brought their drinks—Dylan's usual iced tea and a diet soda for Jess. "The special tonight is fried chicken and gravy with potato salad, green beans and Kate's homemade rolls. Or I can bring you a menu."

"Do you have a big salad?" Jess asked. "Lots of vegetables? And vinaigrette dressing?"

"Sure. Do you want cheese or cold cuts on it?"

"No, thanks. But I would enjoy one of those rolls."

Dylan ordered the special and sent the waitress on her way. "You're the smart one, given how much Susannah is feeding us. But I can never resist Kate's chicken."

"Ah, but I noticed all those pies in the cabinet behind the counter. I'm imagining the day will end well with a piece of coconut cream pie." She folded her arms on the table, elbows in her hands. "So let's get down to business here. Where do you envision your career going in the future? What is your long-range plan?"

At that moment, a hand landed on his shoulder. "Hi there, son. How are you doing?"

Dylan got to his feet to shake the portly man's hand. "Good, Mr. Harris. I hope you're well." He leaned down to kiss the cheek of the tiny woman just behind him. "Mrs. Harris, you look so pretty this evening. Did you get your hair fixed?"

She giggled. "You always notice, Dylan, dear. Wish

somebody else would." Her gaze went to Jess. "It's so nice to see you out with a young lady for a change. I swear you live like a monk most of the time."

"The nicest girl in town is already taken," he said, but he felt his cheeks heat up. "This is Jess Granger. She's writing a magazine article."

"About Dylan? Well, that's very nice. Is this a magazine we can get here in town? We'll all be glad to read about our hometown boy."

"Um…" Jess obviously didn't know how to explain.

Dylan stepped in. "I'll make sure Kip orders a bunch of copies for his bookstore."

Mr. Harris saw Caitlin hovering at the end of the aisle with their plates. "We'd best let them eat, Merle," he told his wife. "Though this young lady could use more than just a salad, pretty as she is. Have a good night," he said, shaking Dylan's hand. "Don't do anything I wouldn't do."

"Which gives us a lot of leeway," Dylan said as he sat down. "I hear he was a wild one as a teenager. And if his grandsons are anything to go by, the stories are true."

"Oh, they're true." Caitlin set Jess's salad in front of her, and then gave Dylan a huge plate of chicken. "My granddad was one of his pals, and he tells some crazy tales." Hands on her hips, she surveyed the table. "Anything else I can get you right now?"

"A longer belt," Dylan suggested. "But we're fine, thanks." When Caitlin was gone, he looked across at Jess. "As we were saying before, I probably do know everyone in town. You said you understand what that's like."

"Did I?" She speared some lettuce and a cucumber slices with her fork.

"You mentioned growing up in small towns in Connecticut."

"I talk too much. But, yes, I grew up where people tend to know what you've been doing, where you're living, and can list the mistakes you've made. They remember you're a foster kid and they disparage you for that fact."

"Is that why you're living in New York City? You prefer the anonymity?"

"I went to NYU for college. And stayed for the jobs."

"You must have friends from school you still see."

"A few. But this is supposed to be my interview. Do you take your dates to other towns, so people here don't bother you?"

He sipped his tea. "They don't bother me. I'm always proud to be out with a beautiful woman for dinner."

Her exasperation was obvious. "This isn't a date."

"Is there a reason it couldn't be?"

"I'm here for an interview."

"Is there someone in New York who would mind that you'd gone out with me?"

"No!" She stared at him in frustration. "You're incorrigible."

"Just trying to get the facts." So she didn't have a lover or husband. At least he'd gotten one piece of information out of her.

"Without answering *my* questions."

"You're more interesting."

"*You* are the subject of the interview, damn it."

The entire restaurant heard her, and a short silence fell. Then conversation and clatter picked up again. Jess sat across from him, still glaring, her cheeks flushed red.

"Everything okay back here?" Kate herself stepped up to the table. A tall, well-built woman, she'd run the restaurant since the husband who'd named it for her had died ten years ago.

Dylan introduced her to Jess. "She's frustrated with me."

Kate nodded. "That's a pretty standard condition for most of us at one time or another. Dylan has his own ways of meeting expectations."

Jess nodded. "So I gather. I'm considering thumb-screws. Or the rack."

"His brothers probably have a few torture devices they'd allow you to use."

"I am not a problem," Dylan protested. "Ask me anything you want." He was taking a risk, but he figured he could handle the worst.

The reporter didn't say anything for a few moments, but eyed him with speculation in her golden gaze. "Why did you choose sculpture as your means of artistic expression?"

"I like being able to consider an object from all different angles. A subject changes, depending on your perspective."

"Slippery as an eel," Kate said, and returned to her kitchen.

But Jess seemed satisfied. "How do you decide what subject you want to work on?"

"As you saw, I make sketches of what I observe as I'm out working on the ranch. When I'm ready to start something new, I'll be drawn to one of those when I look them over. Or I'll witness a scene that stirs me, and go with that. It's kind of a random process."

"Do you build more than one sculpture at once?"

As long as she asked such specific, process-oriented questions, Dylan didn't mind answering. They talked until their plates were empty, until they'd each polished off a slice of coconut cream pie and a cup of coffee. The shadows outside had lengthened by the time Jess relaxed against the back of her chair.

"I'm impressed," she said, pulling her hair behind her shoulders. "No evasion or equivocation."

"You were throwing softballs," he told her. "Not even fast-pitch."

Her grin acknowledged that fact. "I wondered if Kate was going to have to play umpire."

"She would, if necessary. And she'd be good at it. Shall we head home to the Circle M?"

Jess nodded and picked up her purse. Dylan meant to pull out her chair as she stood, if only to annoy her, but Cindi and Dan Bowman passed their table just then, requiring an introduction and some chitchat.

Once the couple moved on, Jess got to her feet. "Beat you to it," she said as she walked by. Then she waved the check Caitlin had written up in front of him. "And I'm paying."

Short of wrestling over the piece of paper—which had its own appeal—there wasn't much he could do about the situation. "Apparently I'm not the only one who's sneaky," he said, holding the door for her to leave the diner.

"A job qualification for journalists," she told him as they walked to the truck. "You find out what you need to know by whatever means necessary."

"Is that a threat?"

"More of a promise. Or you could just tell me the truth and get the process over with. Like pulling a tooth—one quick jerk and it's done."

Dylan grinned at her as he started the engine. "Ah, but sometimes it's more fun to extend the process, make it last as long as possible."

She frowned and shook her head at him. "Incorrigible."

The sun hovered above the Big Horns as they drove to the ranch. Dylan rubbed his burning eyes a couple of times during the trip. The long stretch of working late was catching up with him, and he was going to have to get a good night's sleep pretty soon to keep him going. With luck and lots of coffee, he could hold out till Sunday, when Jess would leave.

For some reason, that prospect didn't appeal to him tonight the way it had yesterday. He wasn't so anxious anymore for the nosy reporter to take off again, even if that meant continuing to dodge the questions he didn't want to answer.

Of course, that was a dangerous state of mind. And due, no doubt, to those kisses at high noon. He found himself reliving those moments more often than he wanted to admit, and, even worse, anticipating a repeat experience.

Fortunately, when they drove up to the house, all the

kids were outside after dinner. They'd set up a badminton net and were batting shuttlecocks back and forth. Even Justino and Lena had joined in the fun. Ford and Caroline were playing. Amber swooshed her racket around without actually hitting anything.

"I have to wait my turn," Garrett said as Dylan stepped onto the porch behind Jess. He nodded at the bag she carried. "What did you two buy?"

"Books," Jess announced with a grin. "Lots of books for teenagers. They can trade them around for a few weeks. There should be something for everybody to enjoy."

"That's a terrific idea." Garrett got to his feet and put his arms around her. "And a very generous donation on your part. Thanks so much."

She emerged from his hug with a blush in her cheeks. "Just creating my future audience, you know. Where should I put these out so the kids can sort through them?"

Garrett bore Jess off to the bunkhouse to set the books out on the tables there. Dylan sank down into one of the rockers on the porch, suddenly too tired to do much more than watch other people having fun. When was the last full night's sleep he'd had?

"Hey, you." A hand shook his shoulder. "Wake up."

He opened his eyes. "I'm awake."

Wyatt snorted. "Sure. You were snoring."

"I never snore."

"You have three brothers who beg to differ."

Dylan knuckled his eyes. "They all snore."

"Maybe you ought to get some rest."

"I'm fine." He shook his head hard, trying for full consciousness. "All good."

Ford came to the edge of the porch. "I'm with the Boss. Get some sleep. We've got things covered till morning. Tomorrow we'll need you fully functional on the cattle drive."

"Jess—"

"Will manage the rest of the evening without your attention. She's over there with the kids, talking about books. We'll tell her you're working. Go to bed."

"Okay, okay. I give up." He almost tripped down the steps to the ground. "Shut up," he said, before anyone could remark on his lack of coordination. "I'll be up early tomorrow. Night."

At the studio, he considered lying down on an empty table rather than climbing up the stairs, but convinced himself to make the effort. Fortunately, he had an effective jack to help get his boots off. A second later, he put his head down on the pillow.

And smiled. The world's most famous scent still lingered from the morning when Jess had lain there.

Chanel. A sure ticket to sweet dreams.

Jess expected some of the grudging reactions from the kids with regard to the books. The usual suspects complained loud and long about first having to write something and now being expected to read. In contrast, though, Nate asked if he could take three books, Lizzie and Becky took two each, and Justino and Lena cooperated without comment.

What thrilled her, though, were the seven pieces of writing she received—one for every camper and all of them at least half a page. Each of them had made an effort. She couldn't wait to read what they'd come up with.

So she said good-night to the adults early and went to her room at the house, settled into the armchair with a cup of tea and began to read.

"I wud go to New York," wrote Marcos, "and ern mony to by stuf, like fast cars and tikets to ball games. I wud be real rich and not take crap from nobudy. I wud by my mom a house and she cud have people clene it for her all the time. And bring her tee to drink and make her food wen she wanted it and wash her dishs."

Blinking away tears, she pulled out Lena's page. "I would go to LA with Justino and we would become movie stars and wear butiful clothes and have a shofer to drive us from our butiful house in Beverly Hills to go shopping on Rodeo Drive. And my brothers would come live with us and go to privet schools and grow up to be smart so they could get good jobs in an office and wear sutes and not have to dig in the dirt to make money. I would send money to my dad so he could keep his tractor fixed and hire men to help him on the farm because my brothers are gone. And maybe he could find somebody to marry who would cook for him and take care of his house, like Mama did. And Justino and I would get to make movies all over the world and everybody would go see them because we are so butiful."

Jess pulled in a deep, shaking breath and thumbed through for Lizzie's paper. Since the girl had some writing experience, perhaps her piece would be more imaginative and not quite so wrenching.

Ten minutes later, Jess was striding through the quiet house and down the hill toward Dylan's studio. Even though he would be working, she couldn't wait to share Lizzie's composition with him. He would be as startled and as pleased as Jess was herself.

She reached the blue door and knocked briskly on one of the glass panes. "Dylan? Dylan, it's Jess."

When he didn't answer, she peered inside, but couldn't see him at the table where he'd worked last night, or at any of the others. He might be under the stairs, sketching. But surely, he would have heard her...

She rapped on the glass again. "Dylan!"

Then she saw him, barefoot and rumpled, coming down the stairs from the loft. He hadn't been working. He'd been sound asleep.

"I'm so sorry," she said, when he opened the door. "I thought—"

"What's wrong?" He rubbed a hand over his hair. "Somebody hurt?"

"No, no. I—"

"Glad to hear it." He nodded, a sexy, sleepy smile curving his mouth. "Then I'll just go back to that terrific dream I was having."

Before she could react, he pulled her into his arms. And then he covered her lips with his own.

Chapter 6

All the different sensations struck him at the same instant. Her hair tumbled over his forearms and the backs of his fingers like a waterfall, wild and untamed. That scent she wore surrounded him—floral with hints of citrus and spice but as cool as a blossom under snow. She felt small in his arms, thinner than she appeared and delicate, though he believed she possessed the strength to subdue a man.

Her mouth alone, full and sweet and agile, might very well be his undoing. He couldn't seem to get close enough, draw deep enough from the swell of emotion her lips evoked. The curve of her waist under his palm, the roundness of her bottom and the point of her shoulder blade offered pleasures he'd never understood until this night, this moment. Holding him tight around his waist, she pressed her body against his, and Dylan groaned low in his throat. A nip of her teeth, a buff of her tongue, and his knees dissolved.

This—*this*—was all he'd ever wanted, all he needed, this sense of belonging and rightness and *possibility* that they could find together. Just kissing, for God's sake. And when he had her naked, underneath him, sex with Jess was going to be the most incredible, consuming, inspiring...

Oh, jeez. What was he thinking?

Dylan stilled his hands and his mouth, and turned his head away from hers. He couldn't do anything about his fast breathing, or the pounding of his heart against her breasts.

"It was a great dream," he said, finally.

Jess hadn't moved. "I believe you."

He dropped his arms and retreated, feeling her hands slide over his belly as he moved away. "This seems to be my day for jumping your bones. I—"

She held up a hand. "No. Don't say you're sorry. I'm not."

He managed a smile. "That's nice to hear. What brought you over here?"

"I dropped it." She scanned the floor around them and picked up a piece of paper she found lying under the table. "I wanted you to read Lizzie's composition from this afternoon."

"Have a seat," he told her, taking the page she held. "Want some coffee?"

Jess shook her head. "No, thanks. I plan to sleep tonight. Maybe you should skip the caffeine, too. You look like you could use more rest."

"Caffeine doesn't keep me up." Which was a lie,

or why else would he drink it? "Give me a minute to go through this."

Lizzie had written a poem.

In dreams I fly between the clouds and watch from seagull's view
The rolling waves, loitering shells and roughly sculpted sand.
Umbrellas, boldly striped, hide the day.
Bare bodies, oiled, catch the rays.
A wooden pier points out to sea, drawing fishes to their doom,
But offering trinkets bright and sweet to lure a human hand.
The scent of salt blooms on the wind.
I wake and mourn to be a girl again.

When he finished, he gazed at the woman in the chair next to him. "Wow. Is it my imagination, or is she really good?"

"I think she's exceptional for someone her age. I can't believe her teachers would ignore this kind of talent." She frowned. "Maybe, since Bisons Creek is such a small town, the schools don't offer programs to address gifted students."

"Caroline might be more of an expert on those issues. My guess would be Lizzie doesn't share with very many people. But she knew you would read this and she wanted you to be impressed." He handed the page to Jess. "We've got the cattle drive tomorrow, but maybe on Saturday you and she can do some serious talking. I'm sure your encouragement will mean a lot to her."

"A couple of hours doesn't constitute much of an effort." She frowned at the paper. "She needs consistent support and feedback. I can imagine how much that would have meant to me when I was her age."

"Maybe you and Caroline can talk to her together? Then Caroline can stick with it after you've left."

"Yeah…" Jess left her chair and paced between the tables, her gaze sliding across his sculptures as if they weren't there. "There should be more I can do, though."

Dylan wasn't sure what else to say. The limitations to what she could accomplish in the time available were pretty obvious. She'd be gone by Sunday afternoon, which accounted for his current state of frustration, as well as hers.

At the far end of the room, Jess turned, and then stopped. She stood motionless, staring at nothing while Dylan took the chance to appreciate her beauty, as he had once appreciated the Venus de Milo. Jess Granger was even more glorious, however, for being alive.

"I want to stay," she said.

He sat up straight. "What?"

"I want to stay on the Circle M. Would that be possible?"

Dylan rubbed his eyes with the fingers of both hands. "I don't see why not. For Lizzie's sake?"

"For all the kids." She came returned sit beside him. "All of them could use help with their reading and writing. The rest of you are as busy as you can handle with the other projects you have going on and the ranch chores. My shifts with the kids would give you a break to get other work done, including your sculpture, so maybe you could get more sleep at night. It's the perfect answer."

"I hesitate to bring this up," Dylan said. "But don't you have a job? And what about the damn article? Wasn't there a deadline of some sort?"

"I can write the article here and email it to my editor. That's no problem. I probably would have been working on it at home, anyway. As for the job, well, I do have vacation. I think I could get the okay to use it now."

He stared at her. "That's not an offer I would have expected from someone in your position. I'm not even sure I'd have suggested it myself. I voted against the summer camp idea when Caroline proposed it."

"You had other priorities. And you have to admit that working with the kids takes your attention away from sculpture." Jess shrugged. "That's a hard choice to make."

Maybe. But right now, he was glad he'd lost that particular vote. "In any case, you are welcome to stay as long as you'd like, of course. I'm sure Caroline, Ford and Garrett will be glad to employ your energies in every way possible."

"I'm so excited." Her smile could have lit the room if he hadn't already switched on the lights. "This will be a lot of fun."

"I hope you say the same a week from now. First, though, you've got to get through the cattle drive. Are you riding Cash tomorrow?"

"I'm riding in the truck with Susannah and Wyatt. One lesson doesn't qualify me as a working cowgirl."

"You'd do fine." A huge yawn spoiled the effect of his compliment.

"You have seven kids to look after. That's enough for the four of you." She got to her feet. "And you ought to get some sleep. I'm sorry I woke you up."

"No problem. Just let me get my boots on and I'll walk you to the house." He headed for the stairs, and was surprised to find that Jess arrived at the bottom step with him.

She put a hand on his arm. "No. This is one of those moments when I'm asserting my independence. This isn't Central Park. I can walk myself to the house. You should go upstairs and climb into bed."

He discarded the first idea that occurred to him, an image of the two of them in bed together. "I can stay awake long enough—"

"No," she said again. "Go to bed. Alone," she continued, in answer to the lift of his eyebrow. "Sleep."

"All right. Can I walk you to the door?"

"I suppose." When they reached the designated area, she flipped the lights off. They stood in the dark, barely able to see each other. "Good night, Dylan." To his surprise, she reached up and kissed him lightly. "Sleep well."

Just that gentle touch set his body humming. "Sure. We'll be up and out early. Don't forget your hat."

"I wouldn't dare." She slipped out the door and closed it behind her, waved and then headed up the hill toward the house.

Dylan waited in the dark until he was more than

sure Jess would have reached the house and gone inside. Then he flipped on the lights. He might be yawning, but his body remained full of tension, unable to relax. His brain buzzed between past and present, what had been and what could be. What *could* be, but…

Jess Granger was a self-sufficient woman who lived and worked in Manhattan, loved the big city and didn't like small towns. She shared the values of that world—values Dylan had deliberately forsaken when he came back home. A serious relationship between them could never succeed when their core beliefs were so starkly different.

And if he'd learned anything at all during his stint on the abstract art scene, surely he had learned the value of commitment and fidelity in relationships. Casual sex led to catastrophe, as far as Dylan was concerned. He wouldn't go down that road again.

Not even for someone as special as Jess.

Thanks to the time difference, Jess was able to catch her editor at work before Susannah and Wyatt were ready to leave and follow the cattle drive in the truck.

"Are you surviving out there in the hinterlands?" Sophia Accardi asked. "Has the wind whipped your skin raw?"

"Moisturizer is definitely a girl's best friend in Wyoming. But I'm near a town with a diner and a bookstore. Plus more handsome cowboys than I can count. What else do I need?"

"Do they chew tobacco?"

"No, Sophia. They don't smoke it, either, like some people." She'd nagged the other woman for years but had yet to convince her editor to drop the cigarette habit.

"Never mind that. All done? Ready to come home?"

Jess swallowed. "Um…getting there."

"I don't like the sound of 'getting there.' What's the problem? Have you or have you not discovered the answer to the question of what happened to Dylan Marshall?"

"I've discovered some of the answer."

"'Some' sounds evasive. Trevor Galleries wants this article to make a big splash, Jess. They've paid big-splash money. You have to deliver big-splash content."

"I know."

"Otherwise, I'll find a writer who can. This is a business. I have to look at the bottom line."

"I understand." Jess took a deep breath. "While we're talking, can you okay a few days off for me? I need to stay…for the story."

"Your copy is due—"

"Yes, but Dylan Marshall is slow coming around. Give me the week. I'll come back with the truth." She was becoming pretty convincing at this lying thing.

"You'd better. We've had some good years together, sweetie. I'd hate to see it end."

The line went dead. Jess stared at her phone. "You're all heart."

Susannah came to her bedroom doorway carrying a basket of food, with Amber skipping along behind her. "We're ready if you are," she said.

"All set." Jess put her phone on the dresser and picked up her camera, smiling at the thought of leaving Sophia and *Renown Magazine* behind as she went out to enjoy the rest of her day.

An hour of travel along a web of gravel-and-dirt roads brought them to their rendezvous point with the cattle drive.

"The good thing about today's route," Wyatt said from the backseat as Susannah stopped the truck, "is that we can park here on the bluff overlooking the valley and watch them gather the cattle up along the river and push them on. We'll get kind of a wide-scale view of the process."

"Sounds like the perfect photo op. And I brought my zoom lens," Jess said, opening her door. "I can get close-ups as well as distance shots. How long will it be before we see them?"

"They'll come from the south end almost any moment now." Wyatt pointed to the left. "And exit to the right. We'll meet them for lunch just on the other side of those trees. It's a small pasture, ideal for holding this herd together while we eat."

"Do the kids understand what to do?" Susannah was keeping an eye on Amber, busy with her coloring book in the backseat of the truck. "There must be some skill involved in herding cows."

Wyatt got out and leaned against the grille of the truck. "The trick is to have a leader moving forward, and then using your wranglers to apply pressure from the sides to keep the animals moving. The cattle at the end of the line will want to keep up with the others that way. Ford will be at the head, with the kids on the sides. Garrett and Caroline can supervise, while

Dylan will be riding at the rear in case of stragglers."
He blew out a deep breath.

Jess noticed the sigh. "Would you be the leader if
you were out there?"

"I usually bring up the tail. Dylan's a good man
in front."

"When will you be able to get back to work?"

"On a horse, maybe Christmas." He winked at
her. "Or when I get sick of sitting around. Whichever
comes first."

She considered the implications. "So you'll be
shorthanded through the summer and fall. That's a
long time."

He nodded. "You're not kidding. Caroline's been
taking up some of the slack while she's here for the
camp, but she's supposed to be in her office, not herding cattle."

"That's right, Dylan mentioned she works for the
Department of Family Services."

"And she has lots of clients to cover. Ford's still
winding up his work for the law firm he left in San
Francisco, plus handling legal cases in town, too. And
Garrett's church requires his attention, of course. No-
body's covering just one job here right now, except me.
And Dylan, I guess."

Jess looked at him hard. "You don't consider
Dylan's art a job?"

Wyatt shrugged one shoulder. "I'd call it more of a
hobby. A sideline."

"He made some pretty impressive money with that
sideline." She tried to swallow her indignation. "Some
of his art pieces sold for six figures."

"Money doesn't define what's important in life."

"Getting paid for work is generally the definition of a job. He'll be selling the work he's doing now, as well. Trevor Galleries is very eager to publicize this upcoming show."

"Which is why you're here. But what's your point, Ms. Granger? I'm pretty sure you've got one."

She pulled in a deep breath. "I'm surprised you treat something that means so much to your brother as a hobby."

His blue eyes were stern. "Dylan's a cowboy first and foremost. He'd tell you that himself."

"But is that the way he wants to live his life? Maybe he'd like to be an artist who does ranch work as a hobby."

"That's not an option this summer." He glanced to the left. "There they come."

The noise struck her first—a hundred different versions of "moo," all sounding at once, and repeated time and time again. In protest? Or did cows just need to talk while they moved?

Then she could hear the other voices, as kids shouted "Hey!" and "Git" and "Yah." There were whistles in the mix, sharp and clear. Jess thought she could detect Caroline's voice among the other sounds, though she couldn't be sure.

Finally, she could distinguish Ford's light blue shirt at the front of…well, it looked like a big black cloud rolling along at his heels. A very noisy black cloud. As she watched, the cloud resolved into individual animals, black cows ambling forward, jostling and bumping each other, crowding together and shouldering their way through as they followed Ford on his bright gold horse. The horse's name was Nugget, he'd said, and the color was called palomino. Caroline's horse, Allie, was also palomino, but a darker shade. Jess could just make out Allie now, on the far side of the river of cattle. There were three other horses with her, but she couldn't tell the riders apart in their helmets.

On the near side, she found Garrett in his red shirt and four teenagers riding with him, doing pretty well at keeping the procession going forward.

"I can't figure out which one is Nate." Susannah had come to stand beside Jess, holding Amber in her arms. "Watch the cows, sweetie. Isn't that amazing, how they're all staying together? Nate's down there helping."

"Can I wave to him?"

Susannah laughed. "I don't think he'll see you. But you can try. We'll both wave."

Jess glanced at Wyatt, to share the humor of the moment with him, but found an expression of pain on his face, instead. Not physical pain, she thought, but emotional. As soon as he realized she was watching, however, his expression went blank.

He gave a brisk nod. "They're doing a good job."

Turning back to the scene, she lifted her camera and began taking pictures, trying to capture the action as faithfully as she could. With the telephoto lens, she found Becky on Caroline's side of the herd with Nate, both of the kids doing their best to keep the cows together. Lizzie, on her pony, Major, was farther away. The girl was making no effort to work with the others, which left Caroline shorthanded. Lena and Justino rode with Garrett, Thomas and Marcos.

Jess set her sight on Ford at the moment when he turned Nugget directly toward the river. "They're going across?" she asked, without losing her shot. "Is that dangerous?"

"Have the kids been through water before?" Susannah wanted to know.

"They're fine," Wyatt said, his voice calm and quiet. "The kids and the cows have been through water plenty of times. Don't worry."

The cows didn't seem quite as comfortable as he'd predicted. There were calves among the adults, and the little ones tended to balk. Or run away, which required a rider on a horse to bring them back. Caroline demonstrated how it was done as she sent Allie after an escaping calf and blocked its way until it rejoined the herd. Garrett took one on his side, and his black horse gleamed in the sunlight as he shifted in one direction and then another, convincing the calf to go with the flow.

Ford continued to ride forward, and most of the cows seemed to be following him and Nugget. The water in the creek was only up to the horses' knees, and once the cattle realized this, most seemed to understand the best way to go was through the middle. With the exception of Lizzie, the kids on each side kept the pressure on, and with Garrett and Caroline chasing strays, the process seemed to be a success.

Jess finally located Dylan at the tail end of the drive. Working actively to keep the stragglers on both sides from wandering off, his pony moved like a dancer, swaying and jumping as necessary to do the job. Sitting straight and tall, Dylan appeared to be in complete control, always a step ahead of the cattle he tended.

But then Wyatt straightened up. "Damn."

"What's wrong?" Jess and Susannah asked at the same time.

"They're falling out on Caroline's side. Not enough pressure."

As if a pipe had sprung a leak, the remaining cows on the far side of the creek were refusing to go into the water, and instead started trotting beside the stream. In an instant, the cows on Ford's side had started running, as well. Dust roiled in the air, and the only sound was the thunder of hundreds of hooves. All the horses were now speeding up, while two black torrents of cows stampeded toward the north end of the valley and a four-board fence in front of a wall of trees.

The only thing in their way was Nugget, with Ford on his back.

Galloping just ahead of the cows on his tail, Ford sent Nugget into the creek again, directly across the path of the original runaways. As if bent by his will, the flow of animals curved just shy of the fence, turning in upon itself to become a slowly milling congregation of unhappy, but uninjured, cattle.

Wyatt took off his hat and wiped his forehead with his shirtsleeve. "The boy is good. I'll give him that."

Watching through her lens, Jess said, "Wait. Somebody's on the ground."

Susannah stood at her shoulder. "Can you tell who?"

"I can't find the horse. It went into the trees on the hill." She brought the camera up and focused the lens, scanning until she found Dylan kneeling on the ground beside a prone figure.

"Lizzie," she said, feeling hollow inside. "Lizzie fell off."

Dylan saw the moment when the drive started to go wrong, but there wasn't much he could do to stop a train from behind. He figured Ford would turn them in on themselves and end the run. His big brother was talented that way.

The problem was seven kids in the middle of a cattle stampede. Horses tended to bolt when the cows did—they were all herd animals and reacted instinctively. Most of the teenagers could probably handle the situation and would sit back, relax and keep their heels down. They'd stay in the saddle okay.

But Lizzie was a nervous rider at best. As long as Major, her pony, did exactly what she expected, she was happy. If he made any sudden move, she panicked.

And so Dylan was watching when Major took off, just like the rest of the horses. Lizzie did all the wrong things—hunched her shoulders and jerked on the reins, giving Major something to pull against and a reason to keep running. Her hands came up and she wobbled in the saddle. Then, with a scream you could hear above the cow noise, she went down.

He threw himself off Leo and landed beside her on his knees, panting. "Lizzie? Lizzie, can you hear me? Are you okay?" He put a hand on her shoulder, brushing her blond hair away from her face. "Say something, sweetie."

"It hurts."

"What hurts? Your arm? Your leg?" She lay on her side, and he wasn't sure he should move her.

"Everything." She sniffed. "I want to go home."

"We need to make sure you're all right, first. Can you wiggle your fingers and toes?"

Eyes closed, she wiggled her fingers. The toes of her boots moved. "Yeah."

"How about your hands and feet? Your arms and legs? Do those move?"

He checked her over and couldn't see any obvious bone breaks. "Let me help you sit up, sweetie."

"It'll hurt."

That was probably true. "But you don't want to lie here in the grass. We want to get you someplace more comfortable."

With a lot of coaxing, he got her on her feet. He thought she might have twisted her wrist. "How about getting up on Major again? Miss Caroline found him and brought him back. He's sorry he ran off. The cows spooked him."

"No!" She jerked away from Dylan's hold, which indicated an overall lack of injuries on Lizzie's part. "I never want to be on a horse again. I want to go home."

Caroline rode up, holding Major's reins. "You can't walk, Lizzie. It's too far."

"I can go in the truck. It's right up there."

"Are you going to climb the cliff? They can't drive down here."

The girl put her face in her hands and started to cry. Dylan stared at Caroline and shrugged. "She could get on behind you."

They finally convinced Lizzie to ride Allie with

Caroline, but only to the site where they would eat lunch. *Then* she would never get on a horse again.

Dylan signaled to Wyatt to move the truck to meet up with Caroline and Lizzie. Ponying Major alongside Leo, he helped Ford and Garrett get the cattle drive to move forward again. He'd stayed up until after three sanding wood last night, but at least with all the action going on, he wouldn't risk falling asleep in the saddle.

The cows didn't like going through the creek any better the second time, but the wranglers' tempers had gotten shorter with the setbacks and their voices firmer, so the whole herd made it across without losing any more calves or personnel. Ford led them through the gate in the fence, the boys and Becky and Lena kept a strong presence along the sides of the string, and Dylan pushed the very last of those dogies straight through into the lunch pasture.

"And all we have to do after this is repeat the process," he told Jess as he sat down beside her on the log she'd chosen. "Minus the creek. We don't have to cross water again today."

"You look tired." She frowned at him. "Something tells me you didn't go back to bed last night."

He grinned at her. "That would be the problem. One way or another."

She frowned harder. "I would punch you but I have a sandwich in one hand and a drink in the other."

"I'll consider it done. Did you get some good pictures?"

"Loads of great shots, till the drama took over. Do you think Lizzie really wants to go home?"

"At this moment, she does. The shock of hitting the

ground is a jolt to your emotions as well as your body. She's been so careful, she hasn't come off before this. Maybe when she realizes she's not hurt, she'll calm down."

"The rest of the kids managed pretty well."

"Most of them have fallen at least once. Even Nate. Sometimes being too careful works against you. Taking a fall can boost your confidence."

Jess turned her head and their eyes met. Dylan heard the echo of what he'd just said, saw the same recognition go through her mind. The moment went still—no wind, no chattering kids, no bawling cattle, just the two of them alone, acknowledging a new understanding.

Ford produced one of his piercing whistles, and the silence broke. "Time to get lunch cleaned up so we can move on," he announced. "Make sure all your trash gets to the truck."

Dylan shook his head, put his hands on his knees and pushed himself upright. "What the trail boss says is law. I'll take your trash."

But, as usual, she had to be independent about the issue. "I can manage." She walked with him to the truck. "You're going to be short a helper—"

"Wrangler, we call them."

"Short a wrangler. And there's an extra horse. Will that be a problem on the rest of the trip?"

"It's definitely less than ideal. We could move these cows with three or four experienced people, but keeping an eye on the kids and the cattle complicates the process. I do have an idea about how to solve one problem, though. If you're willing."

"Me?"

"You could ride Major. The pony Lizzie was on."

She laughed. "You want to put me on a horse somebody else fell off of? The prospect doesn't thrill me."

"Lizzie fell off because she panicked. You won't do that. Will you?"

Again, their gazes held. "No, I don't think I would. He's a good horse?"

"The best. And you'd be a big help. It's more fun than riding in the truck, too."

"Now, that's a solid argument. Okay, I'm game. Do I have to wear a helmet?"

"Yes. Wouldn't want to damage that high-powered brain of yours."

"You said I wouldn't fall off."

"Does your magazine have a lawyer on staff?"

"Yes."

"You're definitely wearing a helmet."

Once she'd climbed into Major's saddle, Dylan realized he'd have to lengthen the stirrups. "You're quite a bit taller than Lizzie. We'll have to make some adjustments." He put a hand on her knee. "Bring your leg forward so I can get to the straps."

So there he was, with Jess's slender, shapely thighs right at face level, trying to keep his mind on buckles and straps. "Can you bring your foot down so I can see how long…that's right." He cleared his throat. "Now stand up in the stirrups, and forgive the intrusion, but—" There was no way to tell how far off the seat she was except by touch, so he slipped his hand between her legs. It had to be his most awkward moment with a woman. Ever.

Dylan stepped back quickly. "Okay, you're set. Just keep your heels down and your chin up. You'll do great." Jess's cheeks looked as red as his felt. To avoid her gaze, he turned to Leo and swung himself into the saddle. "As they used to say on TV—head 'em up and move 'em out!"

Garrett took over the tail end of the drive. Marcos moved over to work with Nate and Becky, while Justino, Lena and Thomas stayed with Dylan and Jess. Ford threaded the leaders through the gate and the procession restarted, with the uphill portion of the trip ahead of them.

Despite his confident talk, Dylan worried that a cattle drive wasn't the optimal setting for Jess's second experience on horseback, but she proved him wrong. She took a few minutes to get used to Major's gait, which was shorter and faster than Cash's, but once settled she became a working part of the team. She kept Major close to the herd, applying the pressure they needed to move the cattle forward. And she did it with a smile, clearly enjoying the adventure. Her cheerful attitude infected Thomas, who'd done his work with a scowl most of the morning, as well as Lena's and Justino's outlooks. The afternoon became the fun experience they'd hoped it would be for the kids, at least on his side. All thanks to a snobby journalist from New York.

They reached their destination at about three in the afternoon. Ford opened the gate to the pasture but then circled around behind to help push the cows through rather than lead them. Recognizing the cool green grass they'd been craving all day long, the calves and their mamas trotted straight across the field for as long as they could stand before coming to a dead stop and starting to graze. After all the effort, the day turned peaceful as the humans sat on their horses and simply watched the result of their labors.

"So how do we get back?" Thomas asked. "Is somebody coming to pick us up?"

Dylan looked at him. "You're sitting on your transportation."

Marcos groaned. "Man, my butt is tired," he whined. "I gotta get off."

Lena didn't say anything, just took her feet out of the stirrups and slid down from her horse. "I have to walk around. My legs are all cramped."

"We can break for a few minutes," Ford conceded. "Caroline's got candy bars in her saddle bag and Garrett carried water. We'll all feel better with a snack."

And they did, for a while. But at the end of the day, when five adults and six teenagers rode their horses up the hill and stopped outside the barn, determining who was the most exhausted would have been a challenge. Dylan had found himself falling asleep in the saddle more than once on the way back, to the point that Jess had reached over and pushed him up straight, afraid he was going to fall off the horse. Fortunately, they were almost home at that point. He contemplated skipping dinner and going straight to bed. Then his stomach growled, reminding him that he should eat, too.

They all led their horses into the corral and were parked around the fence, slowly removing saddles, bridles and blankets, when Wyatt emerged from the barn. Dylan was bringing Jess's saddle to the tack room, and so was within earshot when his oldest brother spoke with Ford and Caroline.

"Lizzie called home and no one answered. She reached her dad on his cell phone. Her parents are in Las Vegas."

Caroline gasped. "They didn't inform me they would be leaving town. When are they coming back?"

"That's just it," Wyatt said. "She told them she wants to leave the ranch. Today."

Ford lifted an eyebrow. "And they said…"

"They have a room reserved for three weeks. They'll be home 'sometime' after that."

Garrett had heard, too. "Who's listed on her paperwork to call in case of emergency?"

"Her aunt." Wyatt cleared his throat. "She and her husband are in Vegas, too. There's nobody left in Bisons Creek to take Lizzie in."

Dylan filled in the blanks. "Except, of course, for us."

Chapter 7

"Not bad for an older woman."

Jess glanced over as Dylan put his dinner plate on the table and sat down next to her. "Thanks. I think."

"You are thirty-five, after all. Who knew you still had it in you to wrangle cattle?"

To celebrate their cattle drive accomplishments, the teenagers had been given the night off from cooking. Ford had grilled steaks and ears of corn while Susannah had baked potatoes and thrown together a big salad. Dessert would be the chocolate cake she and Lizzie had spent the afternoon baking. Now everyone had settled at the long table in the bunkhouse to enjoy the meal.

Jess gave Dylan a dirty look. "You're asking for trouble, cowboy. I have that article to write up, remember. Insult me, and I'll get even."

He sighed and rested his head on his hand, poking at his steak with his fork. "Yeah, we still have that to deal with, don't we? Couldn't you just write about the camp instead?"

"Not unless you want to explain to Trevor Galleries why they're not getting the punch for their advertising dollars."

"The one time I spoke with Patricia Trevor, she struck me as a person who keeps a close watch on her bank balance. In fact…" Sitting up straight, he cut a piece of meat, but didn't eat it. "In fact, I wondered why she called me in the first place. She doesn't usually feature Western art. She's more interested in glitz and glamour, from what I've seen of her ads. But she said my reputation alone would bring in business. I guess that's where you come in with this blasted article."

"Since the new gallery she's opening is in Denver, maybe she expects Western themes to be more popular here."

"Could be. Of course, Denver considers itself pretty sophisticated."

Jess eyed his plate. "Why aren't you eating?" When had she started worrying about him? And why? He had three brothers to do that.

"I'm too damn tired. And too damn hungry not to."

As a distraction, she glanced at the girl huddled over her plate at the end of the table, also not eating. "I wish I could say I'm surprised that Lizzie's parents would leave without telling anyone." With a sigh, Jess forked up a mouthful of potato and butter. "But I've seen much worse."

"Not lived it, I hope."

She glanced around to gauge who might be listening. Not that she had secrets, after yesterday afternoon's confession. "I was usually safe. But then, Lizzie is safe. I bet she feels abandoned, though. And that's cruel."

"But the other girls will help her out. Caroline is here. And you're staying, which will give her something else to focus on. Maybe she can consider this her own private writing retreat."

"Anything I can do." She smiled, but then remembered she hadn't yet canceled her return reservation to New York. "By the way, you haven't noticed my phone lying on a table somewhere in the house, have you?"

"No, but I can check more closely. It's not in the kitchen or living room?"

"Not that I saw. I talked to my editor this morning before we left and got the okay to stay out here for a week, as long as the article came in on deadline. I remember putting the phone down on the dresser in my room, but it's not there. I figured I wouldn't need it on the cattle drive."

"Service out there isn't reliable, anyway. And the cows drown out most other sounds."

"I noticed." She also noticed that he'd pushed his plate away with only half his dinner finished.

He noticed her noticing. "After all the calories Susannah has been feeding us, I don't expect to be wasting away anytime soon."

"I'm sure I won't." Her cheeks heated up at being caught watching out for him. "My jeans will all be too tight when I get back to New York."

"I doubt the guys there will complain."

Rolling her eyes, she stood up from her chair. "I'll take your plate if you're finished. Do you want cake?"

"Is that a rhetorical question? It's chocolate."

"Right."

Friday night, Jess had learned, was movie night, when the kids were allowed to watch television from dinner until bedtime. Tonight's movies were science fiction, which landed at the bottom of her preference list. She was prepared to be polite, but as she dried dishes while Dylan watched, she discovered she didn't have to.

"I'm not a sci-fi fan," he confessed, handing her a salad bowl. "Ugly monsters bursting out of people's chests? No, thanks."

"What would you rather watch?"

"Cowboy movies, which they're not making too often these days. Or anything historical—pirates, gladiators, even World War II. The more accurate, the better."

Jess dried the bowl without responding. How could something as simple as a movie preference set her pulse racing? So they shared a taste in films. Big deal. Anyway, movies based on Jane Austen books probably did not fall under Dylan's "historical" category.

He passed her the serving platter. "I even enjoyed the films they made from Jane Austen's books. Not much action, but there's something so beautiful about England. And, of course, there are the horses. I'm a sucker for a movie with horses."

Jess dropped the platter, which shattered on the concrete floor. "Oh, damn! I'm so sorry!" She hunkered down to pick up the pieces.

"Stop, we'll get a broom." He put a hand on her shoulder. "Really, Jess, you're going to get—"

As he said it, she hissed at the sudden slice of glass across her palm. "You're right. I am."

Caroline came up with a broom. "You two move out of the way so I can sweep this up." She saw Jess holding a paper towel to her hand. "You got cut? Poor thing. There's a big first aid kit at the house. Can you make it there with the paper towel? Just go on, now. I've got this."

Dylan went with her, keeping his arm around her waist as if she might faint. "It's not that bad," she assured him. "Just a shallow cut."

He shuddered. "That sounds terrible. I'm not so good with blood."

She laughed at him. "Then why did you come?"

"Moral support."

But in fact, when they got to the ranch house kitchen, he pulled out the first aid kit and took over the bandaging process. "This is deeper than you said."

"It's practically stopped bleeding already." His fingertips were warm on her skin.

"Do you see your phone, while you're sitting there doing nothing?"

"No. I can use my computer for now. But I do need my phone."

Dylan smoothed the tape over her palm. "I guess you won't be riding for a few days. It's lucky we had our cattle drive today, since we needed your help." He was still holding her hand in both of his, rubbing his thumb lightly over the back of her wrist.

She was starting to get chills from the contact. Pulling away, she said, "Let me go check the living room. Maybe I just don't remember what I did with the phone."

"I'll check the studio," Dylan said, after they'd searched underneath all the cushions and pillows. Honey followed them around the room, as if maybe she could sniff out what they couldn't find otherwise. "It could be there and I just didn't notice it. I don't keep track of my phone most of the time."

When Jess sat down on the rocker, the dog planted herself at her knee, clearly expecting to be petted. "I'm beginning to understand why people have animals. It's very soothing to stroke their heads, have them lean against you."

Dylan sat forward with his elbows on his knees and his hands clasped. "You could have a dog of your own, couldn't you? Or a cat. They're more self-sufficient. Like you."

"Are there cats on the Circle M? I haven't seen one."

"We have barn cats. They keep the mice away. But they tend to be pretty shy."

Shaking her head, Jess relaxed into the chair. "I doubt I'm home enough to keep an animal. I go out of town for several days at least every six weeks on interviews. What would the poor dog or cat do then?"

"One of your friends would stop by and keep them company," Dylan said. "It would be good for both of them."

"I'm not sure there's anybody who would do that for

me. I suppose there are services you can hire. But then you've got a stranger coming into your house when you're not there. It sounds too complicated to me."

"Your life sounds too solitary to me."

She sat up straight and stared at him. "I'm here to talk about your life, not mine."

"You can't have one without the other."

"That's ridiculous. Of course I can. I'm a journalist."

"Not with me."

"I'm not a journalist with you? What does that mean?"

"In my opinion, we've progressed to being friends. Even more than friends."

"Dylan—" The problem was, she couldn't deny the truth. How had this gone so wrong?

"And that gives me the right to be concerned. You don't seem to have a man in your life, and you don't have friends who would come over to take care of a pet. You don't have a family to depend on. Is there anybody in your life you care about? Anybody to care about you?"

"I have friends."

"Have you called them, since you've been here? Have they called to make sure you arrived?"

"We get together when I'm in town."

"Who do you call to bring you medicine when you're sick?"

"I have a pharmacy that delivers."

"Well, that's great." He slapped his hands on his thighs and stood up. "Do they deliver chicken soup, too?"

"That's the Chinese place down the block." Jess

smiled at him as she left the rocking chair. "It's nice of you to worry about me. But I've lived on my own for more than fifteen years. I'm an expert."

"You shouldn't have to be." He came to stand in front of her, putting his hands on her shoulders. "Everybody needs someone to take care of them."

"And what happens when that *someone* leaves? Or changes their mind? Or dies? Relationships always end, Dylan. What are you supposed to do then?"

"Not always. But if they do, you keep going. You find somebody else."

She shook her head. "Thanks, but I'm satisfied depending on the one person I'm certain will always stick around—myself." Stepping away from his hands, she walked to the door of the hallway. "I'm going to get my plane ticket changed, and then turn in early. I'm pretty tired after that ride this afternoon."

"I'll bring your phone over if I find it," he promised, his handsome face solemn, his dark eyes sad. "See you in the morning."

Jess didn't wait to watch him leave, but walked down the hallway to her room and closed the door firmly behind her. All these people with their smiles and good intentions had diminished her detachment. A few hours of solitude would restore her objectivity and balance. She hoped.

Crossing the room, she reached for her leather tote bag, which carried her computer as well as every other possession she might conceivably need if the airline lost her suitcase. When she picked it up, the unexpected lightness caught her attention and she stood it up on the bed, spreading the handles to peer inside.

The computer was missing, along with its power cord. And the remaining contents of the bag were wrecked. Makeup had been pulled out of the toiletries bag and left lying open, with eye shadow, mascara and face powder now streaking the silk lining of the tote. The papers in her wallet and the notebook she always carried had been pulled out and scattered through the bag. The wallet itself was missing.

Swearing softly, Jess fetched a towel from the bathroom and spread it over the bed, then upended the tote over it and shook hard. The disturbed contents tumbled onto the towel, along with a dribble of pink moisturizer and the bottle, from which the cap had been removed.

"It's ruined," she muttered. "Totally destroyed."

Feeling sick to her stomach, she sorted through the articles on the towel, making a pile for the trash, one for makeup she could still use and another for the items that were supposed to be in her wallet.

"I've been robbed," Jess said aloud. "Vandalized and robbed."

The kitchen was crowded when Dylan strode into the house on Saturday morning. "Call the sheriff," he said loudly. "My studio has been vandalized."

They all straightened up, and Jess gasped. "Dylan, no!"

"Pieces knocked over and thrown around, tools bent, mangled, scattered. He set a fire on the floor, for God's sake. All my sketches, burnt to a crisp. I didn't switch on the light last night so I didn't see it. Not till this morning." He was breathing hard. "The wooden pieces didn't burn well, so I guess he gave up.

Or didn't have time. I can't believe this. Who would do such a thing?"

"He was here, too," Wyatt said. "Jess has been robbed."

Dylan stared at her. "Your phone?"

"My wallet, cash and credit cards," she said. "The computer and the phone."

"Damn, I'm sorry. That's a hell of a thing to happen. Though not," he said, turning back to Ford, "entirely unexpected. Have you talked to the kids?"

"Not yet. There's nothing to indicate one of the teenagers knows anything about this."

Coffee splashed out of several mugs when Dylan pounded his fist on the counter. "Who else?"

"All of us—including the kids—were away from the ranch yesterday. Someone could easily have come in and taken whatever they wanted."

"For the first time in twenty years? Come on, Ford, isn't that a little naive?"

Carolyn stepped forward. "Let's take a wider view, Dylan. Just because something hasn't happened in the past doesn't mean it didn't happen yesterday."

He met her bright green gaze. "I hate that one of the kids might have betrayed our trust. But it seems the most likely answer. They could have told someone we'd be gone—the perfect setup." Shaking his head, he finished wiping up the spilled coffee. "So I take it we won't be going to the rodeo this afternoon."

Garrett poured himself another mug. "Why not? We aren't going to spend the day interrogating the kids with thumbscrews and branding irons."

"You have to talk to them, at least."

"We'll talk to each one individually," Ford said. "But before you even ask, I don't intend to search everyone's bags."

Jess said, "I agree. These aren't hardened criminals. They won't be able to lie convincingly."

Dylan started to say something smart, but stopped himself. They'd come to this conclusion without him, so there was no point in protesting. "What about your files, Jess? Are they backed up?"

She nodded. "I save everything online, so I can retrieve my work."

"That's smart of you." He looked at Wyatt. "Is anything else missing?"

His brother nodded. "Beer from the fridge. My phone and my computer, which I'd left on my dresser. Garrett's computer is at the church and Ford had locked his in his truck. We didn't have money lying around, besides Jess's. Most of the electronics are too big to carry easily or hide."

"How about the tack room? We've got silver spurs in there, silver conchas decorating a couple of saddles…"

"Everything's where it should be." Ford's hand came down on his shoulder. "Just try to calm down. It's especially terrible that this happened to a guest in the house. We'll be replacing the cash and the phone—"

"No, you won't," Jess said.

"Yes, we will," the lawyer insisted. "And maybe we'll figure out who did this and get it all back. But until then, we carry on with the day as planned. We'll just be sure the house is locked tight this afternoon while we're gone."

"I'm staying," Wyatt said. "I've been to my share of rodeos."

"Even better," Ford said. "Now, Dylan, let's go check out your studio before we have to get the kids working on breakfast."

As his brothers and Caroline walked ahead, Dylan kept pace with Jess. "I can't believe we're still going to the rodeo. The least we could do is stay home until the sheriff has come out."

She held her hands out in a helpless gesture. "What can they do? The stuff has been gone since yesterday afternoon."

"Something, at least—we could examine tire tracks, take casts of footprints. I have some plaster in the studio."

"Right, Sherlock. I think locking the door when you leave is the best strategy I've heard all morning."

"We've never had to do that before." He hesitated at the entrance to the studio. "Do you suppose it's just coincidence that this happens during the same summer we have seven adolescent troublemakers staying with us?"

Jess didn't say anything, but he could read her face.

Dylan nodded. "Yeah, me, neither."

Ford and Garrett and Caroline condemned the damage in his workshop. "This is terrible," Ford said. "I hate seeing your sculpture attacked like this."

"That's three pieces I have to replace in the inventory for the showing in November," Dylan told him. "I'm supposed to produce twenty-five individual sculptures, and I was going to have to push to get the last two done. I don't know how I can possibly work up three replacements." He pushed his hair back from his face. "If I don't have enough to show they might cancel the whole event."

Jess gazed at him, speechless with distress. But the worst part for Dylan was that he couldn't move anything, couldn't pick up his sculptures and see how bad the damage was, until after a deputy had examined the scene. Witnessing his studio as a crime scene made him sick to his stomach.

With seven kids to take care of, though, the morning soon resumed its standard routine—breakfast in the bunkhouse followed by general house cleanup for both the boys and the girls. Complaints were lodged, as usual, but somehow the necessary tasks got done, even though the kids disappeared one after the other to talk with Ford, Caroline and Jess.

And the results, as Dylan had predicted, weren't useful. "They lie better than you expected them to," he said, when the adults reassembled in the kitchen at noon. "Should have used the thumbscrews."

"Or else they didn't do it," Garrett pointed out, frowning. He seemed to be frowning a lot lately. "Innocent until proven guilty?"

"We called the sheriff's office," Ford said. "Wade Daughtry said he'd investigate who from the outside might have done this."

Dylan rubbed the nape of his neck, where a headache had started. "And you still plan to go to the show this afternoon?"

"Maybe it's for the best." When he sent her an incredulous look, Jess said, "Why sit here stewing about it, waiting for the deputy? We can all use a diversion.

It'll be my first and probably only rodeo." Then it was her turn to frown. "But somebody will have to pay my way."

Dylan put an arm around her waist and squeezed. "I'll be honored to take you as my date."

"This isn't a date. I'll repay you." She glared at him. "And we can talk about your rodeo days for the article."

As they gathered to load up for the trip to Buffalo, however, Caroline walked down from the girls' cabin with a harried expression on her face. "Lizzie is refusing to go."

"She enjoyed it the last time," Dylan said. "What's different?"

"A fall," Garrett told him. "And her whole attitude."

"I can stay home with her," Caroline said. "Maybe we can talk and I can persuade her to stay in the program." Her glance at Ford was loaded with regret.

"Or I could," Jess said. "I wanted to meet with her about her writing, anyway."

"You'd miss the rodeo," Dylan protested. "Our date."

"It was not a date," Jess insisted. "This is more important."

"I'd hate to have you pass up the show," Caroline said. "I wonder if Lizzie would go if she could ride in the car with you and talk about writing."

Jess nodded. "I'll ask."

While she was gone, the boys and Lena climbed into the van they were using to transport the kids. Dylan remained outside with Ford and Garrett.

"This is a hell of a thing to have happen," he told

them. "I knew there would be trouble when we brought those kids to the ranch."

"If you say that a little louder they'll be sure to hear you," Garrett snapped. "The theft is not related to the kids."

"Neither of you is sure of your facts," Ford said in a taut voice. "And having you argue about this doesn't help. Dylan, why don't you ride with Caroline and Jess? You'll agitate the situation if you ride with us and the guys."

"Not a problem for me." Dylan walked to his truck, where Caroline and Becky were waiting. "Where's Susannah?"

"She decided to stay home. Amber wasn't too happy about going to a rodeo. I think she has some bad memories from when her dad would act out after he lost." Nate's dad was a cowboy and perennial loser at bull riding.

"Poor little girl." He glanced at the girls' cabin and saw Jess and Lizzie coming down the hill. "We've got Lizzie on board, anyway. Let's climb in. The show starts in just under an hour."

With Caroline riding shotgun and Jess, Lizzie and Becky in the backseat, Dylan followed the van off the ranch. The rearview mirror showed the blonde girl huddled in on herself in the middle, with her friend staring out the window on one side and the journalist on the other. Jess caught him watching and gave a tiny shrug. He nodded in encouragement, and made a thumbs-up sign for good measure.

"So, Lizzie," she started, "I really liked the poem you wrote on Thursday. Do you write poems often?"

Shrug.

"You painted a lovely picture of a day at the beach. Have you been to the beach?"

Head shake. And then, when an answer seemed unlikely, "I want to go."

"I went once," Becky said. "In California. The water was cold."

"Did Lizzie show you her poem?"

"Yeah. But my favorite is the one about horses."

"Did you write about the horses when you came to camp?"

Nod.

"I'd be glad to read that one. This is my first experience with horses, too."

"I ripped it up."

Caroline gasped, and Becky made a sound of protest. Dylan tightened his grip on the steering wheel.

Jess stayed calm. "Yeah, sometimes when you're angry it feels good to tear up something you wrote about. Kind of like revenge."

"Yeah."

"Did it make you happy?"

"Not really."

"When I rip up my work, I end up feeling as if I punished myself. Usually, no one else finds out. And wouldn't care if they did."

Lizzie sighed. "Horses are stupid."

Dylan couldn't stay quiet. "In some ways, they are, but not always. Can you imagine what would happen if a horse—especially a short one like Major—stood still while the herd ran toward him?"

This pause lasted so long he was sure he'd made a huge mistake.

Finally, though, she answered. "He'd get run over."

"He would. You would, too, if you were in the saddle."

Another extended silence. "So he was protecting me."

"He was staying safe the only way he knew how. We depend on horses to do that and try to anticipate danger. You just weren't quite ready for his reaction. He didn't mean to dump you. Believe me, I've ridden horses that tried, and they're very good at it."

"In the rodeo?"

"And at the ranch. You can get a horse with a bad attitude. But Major is not one of those horses." He waited a moment. "I think you know that."

"Yeah."

He looked into the mirror and nodded to Jess. *Back to you.*

"What else have you written about?" Jess asked. "Do you write stories? Make up characters and follow them through their adventures?"

"She writes about a girl wizard," Becky said. "Her hair changes color when she does magic."

"Shut up," Lizzie told her. "She'll think it's silly."

"If you enjoy it, it isn't silly," Jess promised her. "Tell me more about this wizard."

Lizzie wouldn't, but Becky had obviously enjoyed the story and shared the details as they finished the drive to Buffalo. If there was a resemblance to certain wildly popular books already in print, Dylan decided there were enough differences to make the story impressive.

"When you're a published author, you'll have to come to Bisons Creek and do book signings," he said to Lizzie as they got out of the truck. "We'll all be proud to say we knew you when."

She gave him a shy smile. "I will."

"But for now, we have to help Ms. Jess enjoy the rodeo. This is a youth event," he explained to the woman in question. "For kids eighteen and under. Not quite as dangerous as the grown-up version, and sometimes a lot funnier." Because it was the Fourth of July, the arena was decorated with red, white and blue bunting. American flags fluttered wherever you looked, and patriotic balloons had been tied to every available post. The music blaring over the loudspeaker was dedicated to home and country.

Jess surveyed the holiday crowd. "So this is the kind of rodeo the campers might want to enter?"

Ford and Garrett joined them, with the boys trailing along behind. "Our hope is to sponsor a local youth rodeo at the end of the summer," Ford said, "giving everybody a chance to compete."

Dylan stared at him. "I hadn't heard about that. When did you come up with this idea?"

Caroline put a hand on his arm. "It's still just an idea, Dylan. We haven't made any definite arrangements."

"You didn't think I might want to be included in the discussion?" His brothers and Caroline exchanged guilty looks. "What did Wyatt say?"

"He's supportive…" Garrett's voice trailed off.

"But you assumed I wouldn't be. Hmm, wonder why?" He shook his head. "This is turning out to be a very interesting day." Gazing around a bit blindly, he found Jess standing beside him and grabbed her hand. "We'd better get to the stands. Lamb-bustin' is about to start."

"Lamb-bustin'?" she echoed. "What in the world is that?"

"Junior league bull riding. Young kids start out riding lambs. They don't buck much and they're close to the ground."

"Do the sheep mind?"

"No animal enjoys having someone on its back— that's basically like being prey. But they don't get hurt. And sheep aren't all that smart, so I doubt the trauma lasts."

"What a crazy world this is."

The boys headed up to the top of the stands to find a place to sit. With Jess's hand still in his, Dylan followed them and took seats as far away from the rest of his family as he could manage. Lizzie and Becky sat on Jess's other side.

"Are you throwing a tantrum?" Jess asked him. "Will it make a difference?"

"Yes. And probably not." Dylan shrugged. "They mean well."

"They don't seem to take your sculpture very seriously. They regard it as something to be done after every other chore has been taken care of."

"That worked okay when we didn't have seven kids on the premises. Now that we do, something has to give."

"Actually, I argued with Wyatt about this yesterday, before lunch."

"You did? Why?"

"I told him I'm surprised that he takes your dedication to your sculpture so lightly. He described it as a hobby, or a sideline."

"Ouch." Not that he was surprised. "A man of the land, our Wyatt is."

"But you stay here. You could go to a place where your art was taken seriously."

"This is my home. They're my family."

The first event in the arena was, of course, the flag ceremony, with a pretty blonde girl in red, white and blue riding her Appaloosa horse around the ring, carrying a big American flag. As "The Star-Spangled Banner" blared from the announcer's booth, the crowd stood and joined in on the words. A glance at the kids beside him showed Dylan that most of them were mumbling along, though Thomas and Marcos, of course, remained scornfully quiet.

"Now for the action," Dylan said when the crowd sat down again.

A little girl riding on the back of a sheared lamb started out across the arena, only to slip off about halfway. Laughing, Dylan squeezed Jess's hand without letting go. "Who would want to miss this?"

She grinned. "It is pretty funny."

But her eyes were worried.

As soon as the lamb-busting ended, the teenaged boys started clamoring for something to eat and drink. With a glance at Jess, Dylan volunteered the two of them to supervise the process. They followed the kids down to the food aisle, where they all scattered to different stands in search of their favorite treats.

"What would you like?" he asked Jess. "Fried cookies or pickles? Pigs feet on a bun?"

"How about some ice cream?"

"Perfect."

As they stood at the corner of the bleachers, licking chocolate-covered cones and waiting for the crew of teens to return from their forays, Jess suddenly sent him a piercing look.

"What?" he said. "Do I have chocolate on my chin?"

"Yes, as a matter of fact." She reached up with a napkin and wiped his face. "But I was wondering if you remember that you owe me."

"What do I owe you?"

"The answer to one probing, self-immolating question."

"Oh, that."

"Yes, damn it. That."

He took a deep breath and blew it out. "Okay. Go for it."

She hesitated, staring at him, her brows lowered in concentration.

"My ice cream is melting," he reminded her.

"Right." Now *she* took a deep breath. "Suppose you had to choose between your family and your art. Which one would you keep?"

Chapter 8

Jess had no idea how Dylan would answer her question.

Evidently, neither did he. She waited, chasing drips on her ice-cream cone, while he finished his, wiped his face and hands and threw the napkin in the trash. He didn't say a word.

Becky and Lizzie reappeared with drinks and giant pretzels in their hands. Thomas and Marcos came up with roasted turkey legs while Nate brought a flavored ice cone that was half blue, half red. Justino and Lena each carried a foot-long sub sandwich and a giant drink. Jess wondered if Lena would consume the whole thing, and how she stayed so thin if she could.

Walking back to their seats, Dylan kept an eye on the kids but didn't volunteer any of his usual quips and comments. Even after they sat down, she could tell his attention was not focused on the ribbon pull, a timed event where kids had to run out and pull the ribbon off a goat's tail to stop the clock.

She'd given him a problem to solve. He remained preoccupied, and spent most of the afternoon with his elbows on his knees and his hands gripped together, staring across the landscape into the distance. Jess noticed the worried glances from his brothers, but didn't spend much sympathy on them. The whole family had been taking Dylan for granted. Someone ought to wake them all up.

She did, however, miss his hand holding hers.

When the saddle bronc event started, his awareness returned to the arena. He looked at her and smiled. "Hi."

"Welcome back."

"Thanks. Now you'll get to watch some serious riding—these high school kids have been practicing for years."

She accepted that he wasn't ready to talk. "Why don't they just go pro?"

"There are rules to protect them. The animals they'll be riding here aren't as big as the ones on the pro circuit, and not as skilled. There's a score for the rider, but also a score for the animal in these events. And sometimes the animal gets hooked on adrenaline just like the human does, and tries its best to get rid of the pesky critter between its shoulder blades."

"Imagine that."

He talked her through the rough stock events, as he called them—saddle bronc, bareback and bull riding. Despite the fact that these animals were smaller and less aggressive, Jess thought the sport seemed too dangerous.

"I can't imagine sitting here and watching my child or my husband get thrown around," she told him as they walked to the barbecue tent for dinner. "Would you let your child compete in a rodeo at those upper levels? As you did?"

Dylan grinned. "Hey, that's another question. I'm not sure I owe you that one." He sobered quickly. "Look, we're helping these kids learn to ride a bucking animal. The chances that any of them will go on to compete are slim—it's more about the fun and the riding skills at this point. Ford rode bulls in college, Garrett did bareback and I was on saddle broncs. Wyatt's such a big guy, he was into calf roping, and he was a master at it."

"None of which answers the question. Would you let your son or daughter ride a bull?"

When he met her gaze, the pain in his eyes seemed out of proportion to the subject. "If I had a son or a daughter, I would do everything in my power to protect them from ever getting hurt, including rodeo rides." He tried to brighten up. "But then, I've got that artistic taint, you know. You ought to survey the rest of the family, see what they think."

"I might just do that."

After dinner, Jess discovered, there was a rodeo dance. The teenagers from the Circle M were anxious to stay, and once Caroline had reminded them of the rules—no going outside, no going to the bathroom alone, no leaving with anyone whether known or unknown—they were given permission to enjoy themselves. Ford and Caroline joined the dancing right away, and were a pleasure to watch.

"That's called a two-step," Dylan said in her ear. "Want to learn?"

"I'm not much of a dancer..."

"Yet," he said, and grabbed her hands. "Slow, slow, fast-fast." He demonstrated, moving his feet side to side. "That's all there is to it. Slow, slow, fast-fast."

"Slow, slow, fast-fast. That doesn't seem too hard."

They joined the crowd and shuffled around in a circle, saying the words to each other. Occasionally she got confused, and Dylan smiled. For longer and longer stretches, though, she kept going and he grinned. That grin made her feel happier than she could remember ever being before.

Which was a scary experience. But not scary enough to make her stop.

"Okay," he said after their second circle, "we're going to try something new. Just relax, keep doing what you're doing. I'm going to pull a little on this hand and let this one go—keep dancing..."

The next thing she knew, Jess had turned in a circle. "It's a spin! I did a spin!"

"Yep. Do it again."

By the end of the song, she'd also learned to go under his arm and come out again, and they were beginning to look as natural as the other couples.

"This is so much fun," she told him as they walked off the floor holding hands. "I could dance all night."

"Sounds like a song I heard once."

Garrett straightened up from the wall. "You two picked that up fast."

"Jess is a lethal weapon," Dylan explained. "She takes karate. You want to watch that you don't make her mad."

The other Marshall held his hands up. "I'm a man of peace myself. But can I have the next two-step?"

"Of course." Only after she said it did Jess notice the frown on Dylan's face. Maybe she should have asked him. But really, what harm could a dance do?

Garrett led her to a place on the floor with the next appropriate tune. She was still saying "Slow, slow, fast-fast" to herself, but things seemed to be going pretty well.

Then he said, "Dylan mentioned you'll be staying past Sunday to work with the kids on reading and writing."

Jess nodded. "I'm really excited to have this opportunity. I didn't realize how much I would enjoy spending time with teenagers."

"And Dylan, too, I guess."

She lost her place in the pattern and stumbled. "I'm not sure what you mean."

"You two are…involved?"

"Why would you ask? And why would I tell you either way?" And that was assuming she knew the answer, which she did not.

"You will be leaving eventually, right?"

"I have a life in New York." Sort of. "What's your point, Garrett?"

"I'd hate to see my brother hurt because he fell too hard and then had to let go. It might be best to put some distance between the two of you—"

A hand clamped on Garrett's shoulder and jerked

him around to face a furious Dylan. "Being a minister—hell, being my brother—does not give you the right to interfere in my life. Back off. Now."

To his credit, Garrett did not seem flustered. "Just looking out for you, Dylan. You're not the best at protecting yourself." He considered Jess as the other couples danced around them. "I didn't mean to insult you. You're a beautiful, intelligent, fascinating woman. But he's my little brother." In the next moment, he was gone.

"Let's dance." Dylan took her in his arms and they moved into the now-familiar rhythm. "I'm going to punch him one day."

"You haven't yet?" Jess was pretty irritated by the encounter herself. In her opinion, the older Marshall brothers needed some guidance when it came to living with their younger brother.

"Not since I was thirteen. But I think the time might have come around again."

They danced till the music changed, then went to stand against a different wall from the one Garrett was leaning on. Dylan pressed his fingertips against his eyes. "I think the time has also come for this day to be over."

Jess glanced around the dance hall. "Maybe Caroline does, too. Looks like she's rounding up the teenagers. Will there be fireworks before we go? I love fireworks."

Dylan grinned. "Me, too. But the animals don't. No sense causing a panic in the pens."

She hadn't thought of that, of course. "Got it."

The drive home was quiet. Becky and Lizzie both

dozed off almost as soon as the truck left the rodeo arena. Even Caroline nodded sleepily in the front passenger seat. Becky leaned against the window glass, snoring slightly. But Lizzie stayed sitting up straight, until Dylan turned a corner and her head fell against Jess's shoulder. The girl didn't wake up, but continued to sleep.

Jess smiled—she'd never had a child sleep on her shoulder before. Or anyone else, that she could remember. Her love affairs, such as they were, hadn't included falling asleep sitting on the couch.

After a long silence, she was surprised when Dylan spoke out of the darkness. "I didn't answer your question."

She kept her voice low. "I didn't know if you'd decided."

"It took a long time, especially after Garrett staged his intervention at the dance. I was ready to hop on a plane to New York right about then."

"He cares about you. They all do."

"Yeah." He sighed. "And I care about them. Which, when I get down to it, is the answer. I was gone for five years. I came home on purpose and I don't plan to leave again. Ever. If that meant giving up sculpting... I would."

"I hope your brothers realize how much you're prepared to sacrifice for them."

"The Marshall brothers stick together. Ford came back from San Francisco. I'll be here, on the ranch. It's what we do."

Jess pondered his choice for the remainder of the drive. She admired Dylan's dedication to family—

what a gift, to have such a fine man so committed to you and your welfare. At the same time, she regretted the artistic talent that would never be given full expression. As long as he remained part of the workforce on the Circle M Ranch, and as long as his brothers continued to take advantage of his willingness to help out whenever he was needed, Dylan wouldn't be free to stretch himself to his full potential. He would only continue the work that fit into his lifestyle, without considering how much more he could accomplish. She would love to see what he could do with those two sketches, the one of Wyatt and the mother and child. But she felt sure he would never push himself on those pieces as long as so much of his energy went to ranch work.

He simply couldn't afford the emotional and physical drain. He was running close to empty as it was.

Wyatt, Susannah and Amber were on the front porch of the house when the truck and the van pulled up. The drowsy teenagers straggled to the bunkhouse and the cabin, except for Nate, who sat down on the porch floor with his little sister in his lap. Wyatt came over to Dylan's truck and opened the door for Caroline, then Jess.

"I wanted to talk to you for a minute," he said. "The sheriff's deputy was out this afternoon. His opinion echoed yours, Dylan. Having the teenagers here practically guaranteed this kind of incident, as far as he was concerned."

Caroline made a growling noise. "Yes, law enforcement is quick to suspect kids, whether or not there's evidence." She glared at Wyatt. "I am willing to bet all

the money Jess lost that this was not one of our kids."
Then she turned on her heel and walked toward the
cabin without waiting for a response.

"I didn't say I agreed with the man." Wyatt heaved
a sigh. "I'm tired and I'm going to bed. Good night."
His boot heels sounded on the porch as he went inside. Susannah, Amber and Nate had already vanished.

Ford watched his fiancée stalking up the hill. "I
think I'll go smooth ruffled feathers. Night."

"I'll check on the boys," Garrett said. He looked at
Dylan, and then Jess. With a nod to each of them, he
headed toward the bunkhouse.

"Well, that party ended fast." Dylan dropped his
head back to gaze at the sky. "Want to go for a walk?"

"In the dark?" But his hand had already found hers.
She followed willingly.

When he turned off the path to the red barn, she
realized where they were going, and let him lead her
down the hill to the creek. Without a mishap or a stum-
ble, Dylan took her straight to the stone they'd sat on
before. By that time her eyes had adjusted to the dark
and she could detect the silhouettes of the trees, black
smudges against the night, and the lighter surfaces of
the rocks, the froth of foam in the creek.

They sat side by side, still holding hands. The boulder beneath them radiated the day's warmth. "I hate to
go in there," he said, nodding toward the studio. "Not
without making things right."

"You could sleep at the house, wait till the morning."

"Yeah. I might do that. That couch is pretty comfortable."

The darkness around them was far from silent—over the rushing water she could hear chirps and burps in every direction. "What makes all the noise?" she asked Dylan.

"Crickets and frogs, cicadas. The usual outdoor chorus."

Jess picked her feet up. "Do they bite?"

"No, silly. Haven't you sat and listened to bugs at night?"

"I've been an urban dweller my entire life. I didn't play outside much."

She drew a quick breath as the pad of his thumb stroked along her jawline. "No wonder your skin is so fine. You haven't let the sun get to it." He stroked again. "You don't even need makeup. Those freckles across your nose are lovely."

"People expect the mask." His fingers curved around the nape of her neck and lifted her hair up off her shoulders. "That feels wonderful. It gets heavy sometimes."

"I bet." His fingers threaded through the length. "You could keep it shorter. You'd still be gorgeous."

"Then I'd have to change my profile picture. And longer hair makes you look younger, if you keep it styled."

"So many rules in your business." Strong fingers massaged her left shoulder, and then her right. "You must stay tense."

Jess shivered. "You're taking care of it."

"Glad I can help." She relaxed as his arm circled her back, with his hand resting at her waist. "See how I did that? Pretty smooth, hmm?" His lips touched her temple. "I love your perfume. Thank God for Coco Chanel."

She actually giggled. "You've got a pretty sexy scent, yourself."

His other hand came up to her cheek and turned her face toward him. "At least I don't smell like a horse tonight."

Before she could laugh, he bent his head and swept her into a kiss. She wasn't surprised, but she gave a small gasp, because his mouth felt so wonderful joined with hers.

Dylan chuckled. "It's amazing," he said, his breath whispering over her lips, "how good we are together."

"Dylan…" She tried to be sane. "This isn't a smart idea…"

"You're my diversion," he murmured. "Keeping my mind off my troubles."

Jess understood that reasoning all too well. The night had turned fluid, a swirling darkness where the anchor was his shoulder under her palm and their mouths locked together, moving, sliding, clinging as they created an intensity of pleasure she'd never known. Her hand on the back of his neck discovered the smoothness of his skin and the crisp waves of his hair. She explored further and found the sleek muscles of his upper arm under the crisp cotton shirt, the light dusting of hair on his bare forearm.

"It's not fair," she told him as he skimmed his mouth over her chin and along the curve of her throat.

"What's that?"

"You've got two arms around me, but I can only use one."

"Simple to solve." In the next moment, he eased her down, until they were lying side by side on the boulder. "Better?"

She circled both her arms around his shoulders. "Much."

He groaned as she ran her hands up and down his back. "Oh, yes."

For all Jess noticed, the stone beneath them might have been a feather bed. She was consumed in Dylan, stroking her hands over the long lines of his body, the firm muscles and smooth skin under his shirt. He kept an arm under her head, but his other hand managed to be everywhere—her breasts, her thighs, her belly and, tenderly, her face.

"Beautiful," he said, pressing his kisses against her breastbone. "You are so beautiful." He raised his head to meet her eyes, a glint of laughter in his own. "Your soul is beautiful, too. I wouldn't want you to think I'm a superficial guy."

"Superficial has its useful moments." She skimmed her hands along his ribs. "Carry on."

Dylan fingered the neck of her T-shirt, and Jess gasped when he slipped his hand inside to graze his knuckles against the tops of her breasts. "I would undress you right here under the stars, but with our luck, a teenager would come wandering down the hill for the first time since they've been here. That's the kind of day it's been."

He helped her sit up again, then got to his feet and held out a hand. "We can go to the studio. Or..." She heard his deep breath. "I can walk you to the house. Your choice."

The moon hadn't risen, so he was a form in the dark, a cowboy-shaped shadow. And she wanted him.

The rules she'd set for herself raced through her mind.

Taking his hand, Jess stood up beside him. Then she turned and led him across the grass toward the blue door.

Dylan opened the studio door but didn't turn on the overhead lights, leading Jess around the tables using only the glow from a single lamp by the bed in the loft. Atmosphere mattered to women. After starting this seduction on a rock, he figured he could make at least a little more effort.

And he refused to think about the catastrophe in his studio.

"Would you like some wine?" he asked as they climbed the steps still hand in hand. "Or a drink? I have whiskey, coffee and iced tea. Take your pick."

"You," she said at the top. When he turned to look at her, she pushed at his chest, walking him backward until the bed hit his calves. "Just you."

Grinning, he allowed her to push him until he fell onto the mattress. Jess came down on top of him, with her knees on either side of his hips.

"Just." She kissed him, and then started on the buttons of his shirt. "You."

The night went wild. By the time she got his shirt unbuttoned, he had pulled her T-shirt over her head and thrown it away.

Then he groaned. "I'm glad I didn't know what you wore underneath that black shirt. It would have made me crazy all day." She was sexy as hell in a red, low-cut bra. "Does the bottom match?"

She gave him a wicked smile. "Maybe."

Dylan groaned again. "I'm dying, here." He went for the buckle on her belt and then the snap on her jeans. Just a short slide of the zipper proved the truth.

Velvet skin and red silk lingerie sent him over the edge. He wanted to touch, to taste every inch of her, and he made the supreme effort. She countered him with moves of her own, kisses and nips in unexpected places, her palms sliding intimately across his flesh, her wicked whispers making him that much hotter. He didn't believe he could last a second longer, and yet he held back, not wanting the most incredible experience of his life to end. Sex had never been this good before. Would never be this good again with anyone but Jess.

Suddenly she was underneath him in the way he'd fantasized, naked and eager, her big golden eyes pleading with him to give them both the climax they craved. With their bodies joined, Dylan began to move, slowly, carefully at first, but then faster and stronger until he lost control and the two of them reached the firmament together.

Afterward, he managed not to fall on top of Jess, but to the side. It took a while for him to catch enough breath to speak. "You okay?"

"I'm wonderful." Head on his shoulder, she curled against his side like a contented cat. "You?"

"Perfect." He kissed her forehead. "Or as close as I'll ever get."

A laugh shook her. Then, between one breath and the next, Jess Granger fell asleep.

Dylan chuckled. Without disturbing her, he reached down to the foot of the bed and grabbed the blanket, covered both of them with it, and then he let his eyes close, too.

He woke her sometime in the night to make love again, more slowly but with even more intensity. The next time he opened his eyes, dawn was lighting the windows and Jess was coming up the stairs with two cups of coffee. She wore her black T-shirt, which almost reached to the top of those red panties.

"I'm pretty sure I don't need another stimulant," he said as she handed him a mug. "You're quite enough, thanks." He bent his knees to tent the blanket and conceal his body's predictable response to...well, to everything about Jess Granger.

She toasted him with her cup. "I should probably have sneaked back into the house under cover of darkness. Garrett will be in the kitchen by now."

"Garrett's long gone. It's Sunday, so he goes to the church in town early to review his sermon and make sure everything is ready for services."

"In that case..." She set her cup on the bedside table and threw herself on the bed beside him. "We could get more sleep. Or something."

He put his cup down and let himself fall into her kisses for a few minutes, then pulled back slightly. "I am supposed to be feeding the horses in about twenty minutes."

Jess joined him under the covers and put her warm palms on his bare chest. "That's plenty of time."

Dylan was only a little late to feed the horses, but he found Ford there ahead of him, putting grain in buckets. "Good morning," his brother said evenly, without pausing in his task.

"Yes, it is. I'll take those out to the field." He whistled as he waited.

"You're in a fine mood for so early."

"Sometimes you just wake up that way."

Ford cleared his throat. "Your private life is your business—"

"Thanks, that's all you should say." Dylan stepped over to pick up the stacked buckets.

"But she *will* leave."

"I'll deal with that when it happens."

"We need you functional."

He rolled his eyes. "What am I, fifteen? I've dealt with much worse in life than being dumped. I can handle my own relationships without falling apart. Though God forbid anybody but Wyatt require a respite. The whole place would fall to pieces." He walked across the corral toward the pasture gate, no longer whistling. His mood didn't matter to the horses, who were all stationed at their usual tubs, waiting for breakfast.

His brothers couldn't seem to leave it alone. When he went into the house, Jess was nowhere to be seen but Wyatt was seated at the dining room table with his coffee, obviously waiting. The door to the kitchen was closed.

"Got a minute?" he asked, but his tone didn't invite a refusal.

So Dylan sat down. "Could we skip the lecture? Consider it said?"

"Sure. Can we assume you'll keep your relationship

out of sight so the kids won't get the impression that this is approved behavior?"

"What's not to approve? Wait, I know." He held up a hand. "Only within the bonds of holy matrimony. Could I just point out you don't seem to have a problem with Ford and Caroline spending the night in town together?"

"They're engaged. And they're not on the ranch. Playing games under the teenagers' noses is asking for the same kind of behavior from them."

"Yes, Wyatt, we will be discreet. Yes, Ford," who had just walked into the room, "I'll keep my chores done even when Jess has to return to New York." He hadn't said it aloud before that moment. Maybe he hadn't quite believed it would happen. "And I'll try to be sure my 'hobby' doesn't interfere with anybody else's life." He pushed the chair back and stood. "Anything else?"

At that moment, Susannah pushed the kitchen door open. She carried a plate in one hand and a coffee mug in the other. "Hi, Dylan. I thought you might want to eat in here instead of the kitchen."

He shook his head. "Thanks, but I'm not hungry. I'll be in the studio cleaning up, if somebody needs me." Brushing by Ford, he left the house with a slam of the screen door.

When he reached the bottom of his hill, instead of going into the studio he walked down to the creek and sat on the boulder he thought of as his. Or, now, *theirs*. Memories of the moments they'd lain there seemed to drift over him like falling petals on the morning breeze.

He didn't regret what he'd done. How could anyone regret such a wondrous experience? He'd be content to spend the rest of his life waking up with Jess Granger in his arms.

But, as his brothers had so kindly pointed out, that was the problem. Jess wouldn't stay. He couldn't imagine why she would make that choice, even if she had fallen in love with him in a matter of four days. And that wasn't at all realistic, even if he'd fallen in love with her.

Why else would he make love to her? He hadn't changed his mind about casual sex, or commitment. His brothers thought they were so smart, trying to warn him off from getting too involved—they didn't see that he was already too involved, had been since Thursday afternoon, when he'd listened to her talk about her past and realized what a strong and dependable person she must be. A woman who could build a successful life with absolutely no one's help would be a partner he wanted to make a home and family with. He would trust her with his life. More important, he would trust her with the lives of his children.

But there was no reason to think Jess had fallen in love with him. She didn't want to need people—he understood that. And he had no idea how he could convince her that relationships could be permanent, could last an entire lifetime.

Dylan laughed at himself. He wasn't sure how he knew relationships could last a lifetime. He'd never had a romance last six months.

Except that Wyatt had been there for him every day of his twenty-seven years. Ford and Garrett, too, even if they ticked him off. If he cast his mind further afield, he could think of others who had demonstrated that kind of loyalty to him. Mr. and Mrs. Harris had celebrated their fortieth anniversary last fall. Several couples in Garrett's church had seen their fiftieth. Hell, Kip Glazier had been his friend since fifth grade. Seventeen years was a long time.

But just promising Jess forever would mean nothing. And how would he show her, except day by day? He didn't have much to offer to keep her in Wyoming. Nothing she valued, anyway, such as laundries and Chinese takeout, fancy ice cream, a good job and a place of her own without his brothers watching her every move. And not just because she was such a pleasure to watch when she walked.

He would have to accept the idea that she would go. She hadn't mentioned how much longer she'd stay, but a week would be pushing it. She'd probably need more clothes, if nothing else.

And so he would enjoy this week, treasuring every moment they were together. Even when they weren't alone, he'd value the time he could watch her, talk with her, learn from her. When they were alone, he would make those moments a sensual and satisfying experience. And when the day came when Jess had to leave, he would watch her walk away with his pride intact, if not his heart.

But then, an artist could do great work with a broken heart.

"Here again?"

There she was, looking more gorgeous than ever. "Yeah... I wasn't quite ready to tackle the cleanup."

"I wasn't sure what was going on. You said something about church…"

"We haven't been making the kids go—didn't want to offend anybody's parents. Garrett does a…what's he call it?…a homily, right after lunch. Sunday morning is sleep-in day for the kids."

She sat beside him, but not close enough that they were touching. "Your house isn't well soundproofed."

"I figured you would hear the conversation."

"I could leave—"

He put his hand over hers, clasped in her lap. "No. You wanted to work with the kids this week. You should have that chance. And I want you to stay. If that matters."

"Of course it does. I just hate making trouble with your brothers."

"You won't be the first girl who did."

"Or the last?"

An interesting question, coming from Jess. "I'm getting pretty old. My troublemaking days may be over."

"Ancient," she teased. "I noticed last night how weak you are."

"Yeah, I'm sorry about that."

Jess stood up and drew him with her. "Susannah had me bring your breakfast over here. Come have something to eat. In just four days, I know you're always starving."

"Must be your nose for news."

"A man's appetite isn't news. Just a fact of life."

"Wisdom and beauty, all in one package."

"Are you ever serious? Do you ever give a straight answer?"

Dylan opened the door to the studio. "I'm thinking about it."

Jess had brought the computer Ford had loaned her, but first she helped Dylan put the studio to rights. Of the three pieces set on fire, only one had been seriously burned, the eagle in flight, but the damage was mostly scorching and not actual destruction.

"Kind of interesting," Dylan commented as he examined it. "Like the story of Icarus, who flew too close to the sun with wings made of wax. The eagle flies too close and his wings are scorched."

"Or else it's a comment on the quality of our environment—the lives of eagles are threatened by what's happening with pollution."

He nodded. "That, too. Maybe I should incorporate scorching as a technique. I'm always willing to learn new tricks." Glancing around the studio, his face relaxed from the tension he'd worn for the past twenty-four hours. "This is better. I can handle the rest of the work. You're relieved of cleanup duty."

Relieved that Dylan was feeling in control again, Jess opened the computer and started putting together the article she needed to write. Having the subject right there to verify facts and quotes was a luxury she didn't usually enjoy.

On the other hand, telling this particular story without having all the information proved quite a challenge. She had checked her research of the women he'd dated while in the limelight, but no one stood out as a potential heartbreaker. Noelle Kristenson had been his last girlfriend mentioned in the gossip columns. But she'd remained prominent on the social scene after Dylan left. Jess couldn't establish any kind of connection between his abrupt departure and their relationship.

Unless she asked. "Do you remember Noelle Kristenson?"

"Um…sure. Pretty lady." He didn't look up from his sweeping.

"You dated her."

"I did."

"Right before you came home."

"If you say so."

"Did she have anything to do with why you left?"

He was quiet for a full minute. "Yes."

Finally. "You had a fight?"

"Yes."

"You were so in love with her?"

"No!" He rubbed his hands over his face. "No, I didn't love Noelle. But what she did—I couldn't deal with it."

"What did she do?"

This silence lasted much longer, as he stood motionless with the broom. "Most men probably wouldn't care. It's a choice, right?"

"Dylan, what happened?"

"Noelle got pregnant." He pulled in a deep breath. "She didn't tell me. Until after she'd had an abortion."

Chapter 9

"She wouldn't surrender her lifestyle," he continued. "Not even for nine months. I would have taken the baby to raise, but she didn't give me the chance." Raw pain roughened his voice.

"That's terrible." Jess immediately thought of the drawing of mother and baby he kept above his drawing table. Now she knew who the artist had been. "Children are so important to you."

"They should matter to everyone. And I kept thinking that my parents could have made the same choice. They had three sons and not much money. Mom was already sick. They could have eased the load." He lifted his chin to meet her eyes. "What if your mother had made the same decision? Would you trade your life, hard as it's been, for…nothing?"

"Of course not. Life is always worth living."

Dylan nodded. Then he walked over to a window, standing with his back to her. "The worst part—the despicable, shameful part—is that when she told me, for just a second... I was relieved." After a pause, he said, "I hate myself for that."

"You're human."

His shoulders rose on a deep breath, and he turned to face her. "So there you have it, Ms. Granger. My deep, dark secret. I went to see my piece in the sculpture garden in Paris that afternoon and I didn't recognize anything about it as belonging to me. I couldn't imagine how I'd ever believed that kind of work meant something. And I realized I didn't want to be the person I'd become, who could dispose of a child as easily—more easily!—than a hunk of concrete and iron. So I caught the first flight out and came home." He held his hands out from his sides. "End of story."

Jess watched from across the room as he faced the window again. She had the truth now. With such great material, the article would write itself. Her editor would be thrilled with this kind of sexy, emotional twist. She wouldn't use Noelle's name, of course. Her job would be to protect the woman, while exposing Dylan to public scrutiny.

"Why reveal this to me now?" she asked him. "Why put such a weapon in my hands?" Then she had an insight. "Your brothers don't know what happened, do they?"

"No. I wouldn't give them the pain. I'm telling you because I love you. I want you to have the truth about me."

"Dylan—" Her heart thundered in her chest. "You can't fall in love in four days."

"Maybe *you* can't. But I did." His grin was a ghost of its usual self. "I'm not expecting anything, Jess. I understand you've got a life you intend to return to. I'll enjoy you while you're here, and when you go, I'll have some great memories. Don't worry—I won't be maudlin about it. That's not my style."

"No." She couldn't catch her breath. Her hands were cold and her face blazing hot. Maybe she would pass out. Shock did that to people.

Dylan didn't come across the room and attempt to persuade her. "I'm going to take Leo out for a ride," he said instead. "Give you some breathing room. I'll be gone a couple of hours." He picked up his hat from the table and waved briefly before letting himself out the blue door.

Jess put her head down on her arms. This was worse than waking up in his bed that first morning. Today she'd woken up to find herself in his heart.

And it would be so terribly easy to stay there. So comfortable to let herself love him in return.

In fact, despite what she'd told him, she already did. She'd loved him under the stars by the creek, and all during the passionate storm they'd raised in each other throughout the night. She'd loved him on his knees in the dust beside a fallen Lizzie, and riding off across the field on Leo's bare back. As hard as she'd fought not to, Jess might have loved Dylan Marshall from the moment she saw him, not quite five days ago.

But he could never find out. The worst thing she could do for Dylan would be to confess that she loved him, too. He would want to build a future for the two of them, together.

And Jess was certain that she was the last woman Dylan Marshall should marry.

With her back aching from the uncomfortable chair, she got up and walked around the studio, hardly noticing all the exquisite sculptures she passed. She ended up, as she'd probably subconsciously intended, at the drawing table and the beautiful sketch above it. If she had to bet, she would wager a month's pay that the drawing had been done by Dylan's mother, capturing a moment between them when he was an infant. Something about those wide dark eyes had always reminded her of him.

The vandal had taken some of the drawings from the table and used them to set the fire. But the trash can, pushed inside the kneehole of the desk, had escaped his notice. On a hunch, Jess crouched over the container and fingered through the pages, curious to see what Dylan had thrown away. Most of the sketches were of sculptures he had already shown her.

But he'd thrown away the two drawings of people— his copy of his mother's picture and the bust he'd done of Wyatt. At least he hadn't crumpled them up. Jess pulled them out of the trash still smooth, with only a single crease in the center.

Why would he discard work with such potential? Why wasn't he dying to translate these images into solid form? What kept him blocked?

Taking the sheets to the table where she'd been working, Jess slipped them behind some pages in her notebook. She wasn't sure if she wanted them for

Dylan or for herself. But she couldn't let them disappear.

Then she sat down at the table again and pulled the computer in front of her. She had a challenging task ahead—to salvage Dylan's current career, restore his reputation and somehow convincingly relate his story without ever hinting at the truth.

When Dylan brought Leo back to the barn after their ride, the kids were out and about, hanging around in the general vicinity. As soon as he got off they started gathering around him—they all seemed to love his flashy, spotted horse, and Leo was a sucker for being spoiled, so the combination worked out well. Even Thomas and Marcos liked taking Leo to the wash stall for a rinse, drying him off and combing out his mane and tail. Becky and Nate, the real horse lovers, cleaned the horse's feet and fed him treats while Lena and Justino used the gathering as an excuse to be together. Today, there didn't seem to be as much comfortable chatter as usual, but the past days had been busy with the cattle drive and the rodeo. Everybody might just be tired. Dylan knew he was.

Lizzie, he noted also, didn't participate. She sat on a hay bale at the front of the barn, playing a game on her phone. She'd never been comfortable with any horse except Major, and now that trust had been broken, which set her apart from the rest of the group.

Dylan walked over and leaned on the wall next to her. "Having a nice day?"

She shrugged a thin shoulder. "It's okay."

"I have to say, I'm very impressed that you're a writer."

"I'm not a writer. I just write stuff down that I make up."

"As far as I'm concerned, that qualifies you as an official writer. I write when I have to, but I've never been good at it."

"But you make sculptures. And you can draw. You're an artist."

That wasn't the direction he wanted to take with the conversation. "Yes. We're all born with certain talents, I guess, or maybe certain ways we choose to express ourselves. I couldn't write a poem in a month of Sundays."

"But you can ride a horse."

That was the opening he wanted. "So can you."

"I wasn't born wanting to ride."

"Funny thing, neither was I."

She frowned up at him. "You weren't? I thought all of you started being cowboys when you were little."

"Nope. Wyatt was sixteen when he rode his first horse. I was eleven. We lived in town and never even saw horses, except from a distance, until then."

"Did you fall off?"

"I've probably fallen off a hundred times, and that doesn't even include when I was learning to ride bucking broncs. We all fall off. The trick is to get back on."

Lizzie shook her head. "I was so scared those cows would run right over me."

"That didn't happen, did it? Major kept you out of the way." He crouched down in front of her to look into her face. "I have a trick we could work on, just you and me. I think it would help you stay on. It's the way I learned."

She eyed him with suspicion. "What is it?"

"Can you trust me? We'll go try it out right this minute, while everybody is busy."

"Will I get hurt?"

"Absolutely not."

"Okay." She followed him down the aisle to pick up a halter and a helmet, then across the corral to the pasture fence.

"Major's right there, waiting for us," Dylan pointed out, and went to bring the pony in. "Now we're going over to the mounting block." Once there, he positioned Major beside it. "All I want you to do, Lizzie, is get on."

"There's no saddle!"

"That's right. I want you to get on his bare back."

She retreated almost to the fence. "I can't do that. I'll slide right off."

"No, you won't, because you can hold on…" He grabbed a handful of Major's black mane. "Right here. He's got a nice flat spine and a good solid handle attached to his neck. You won't fall."

Dylan waited through her indecision. He figured she hated being the only one who wouldn't ride. Facing the coming week isolated from her companions couldn't be a pleasant prospect.

Finally, she took a step forward, and another. She got to the mounting block and stood on the top. "Now what? Where do I put my feet?"

"He's going to stand real still. Bend over and grab some of his mane with both hands and hold on tight.

Then just swing your leg over, like you would with a saddle, and sit down."

Lizzie took a deep breath, grabbed Major's mane and then threw her leg about halfway over.

"Keep going," Dylan told her quietly. "That leg's gotta hang off the other side."

With the next try, Lizzie ended sitting on Major's back, hunched over close to the pony's neck.

"Straighten up," he instructed her. "Let your legs stretch all the way to the ground."

"They won't do that."

"Pretend they will. It'll help you keep your balance." She pushed her heels down. "That's exactly right. So now keep those legs stretched and those hands in his mane. We're going to go for a slooooow walk."

She squeaked as Major took his first couple of steps, and she wobbled a little. But the pony did have a flat back and a smooth gait, so in a matter of minutes, the girl started to adjust. Dylan didn't say much, just an encouraging comment here and there as he led Major slowly around the corral, changing directions occasionally, going in straight lines and circles, as Lizzie rode.

When they came to a stop, he grinned at her. "Look at you—a bareback rider! How does it feel?"

Being fourteen and "cool," she couldn't admit how much she'd enjoyed the experience. "Okay, I guess. But how do I get down?"

"Pretty much the same way. Lean forward, bring your right leg over and slide off."

She practically bounced when her feet hit the

ground. "Wow. That was..." She glanced at Dylan and away again. "Pretty good."

"I'm glad you think so. We can do some more work, getting you better balanced and more comfortable out of the saddle. Then getting into the saddle again will be easy." He stepped close and bent to whisper in her ear. "Hey, Lizzie. You got back on the horse. You're a rider."

Despite herself, she grinned. "I am, aren't I?"

Jess stood in the barn, watching as Dylan and Lizzie high-fived each other out in the corral. She'd been planning on talking to one or more of the teenagers about their writing this afternoon, but had found them all occupied with Dylan's horse. And then she'd watched the man himself rehabilitate Lizzie, teaching her to ride without a saddle, of all things.

His brothers didn't even realize what an asset they had in their little brother. Of course, they'd probably take the credit for having been the ones who brought him up. But Jess thought Dylan's best qualities— caring, commitment and honesty—were choices he'd made for himself. He wasn't simply a product of his environment and his family. He'd deliberately decided what kind of man he intended to become and then arranged his life accordingly. She could only admire that determination.

Even if she couldn't share that life.

Lizzie didn't see her in the doorway as she slipped out the side gate of the corral. While watching Dylan lead the pony back to the pasture, Jess became aware that a squabble had broken out between the kids working on Leo. Well, two of the kids, anyway.

"I'm walkin' him out," Marcos said. "It's my turn."

"Who says?" Thomas had a snarl in his voice. "Nate did it last time. I haven't done it. It's my turn."

"Come on, guys." Becky sounded almost like one of the adults. "Do you have to argue about everything?" Justino and Lena sat on a nearby bench, absorbed in one another and their phones.

"When somebody takes advantage," Thomas growled, "then, yeah, you have to argue."

Jess walked through the barn until she found the big concrete-floored stall where they had rinsed the horse. "I'm not an expert, but angry voices don't seem like the right choice when you want the animal you're working with to stay calm. Maybe you guys should chill out."

The two boys glared at each other across Leo's back. Meanwhile, Becky untied the horse and walked it between them. "I'll take him to the pasture. I haven't done it, either." She grinned at Jess as she passed.

The anger level hadn't receded much. Jess thought fast. "Thomas, I wondered if we could talk about your writing and reading this afternoon. I'm really interested to hear how you're enjoying the book you chose. Would now be a good time?"

"Do I have to?"

Jess couldn't say yes, but she stared him down.

"Okay." He headed toward the exit.

"We have to clean the place up," Marcos yelled after him. "I'm not doin' it by myself."

"I'll do it," Nate said quietly, from the rear corner of the stall. "Just go on."

"Hey, man. That's great." In the next instant, Marcos had disappeared.

"Sorry," Jess told the boy. "Do you want some help?"

He smiled, and suddenly he looked like his mother. "I enjoy doing it without them. It's a lot more fun without all the complaining."

She laughed with him, and went to find Thomas, hoping this session wouldn't be the struggle she anticipated. He had waited for her at the dining table in the bunkhouse, as sullen as a student sentenced to stay after school for bad behavior. Jess recognized the demeanor, having often been one of those kids herself.

"Thanks for meeting with me," she said as she sat across the table from him. "I appreciated what you had to say in the paragraph you wrote. And you write very well."

His dark gaze was cool as it met hers. "Just because I'm Indian doesn't mean I can't speak and write the English language."

"That's true. You have a strong sense of the injustice that's been done to Native Americans."

"That happens when you live on the rez. You get to see how far a treaty goes."

"What do you think of *The Last of the Mohicans*?"

"Kinda slow."

"It was written almost two hundred years ago."

"Yeah. But what happens in the story is interesting. A lousy ending, though."

"You've read the entire book?"

He shook his head. "No, but when you put Indians and whites together, the ending is always bad for the red man."

* * *

Peace reigned on the ranch that evening, as kids and adults gathered in the living room. Wyatt had started a nice blaze in the fireplace and Susannah brought out the makings for a treat involving marshmallows, chocolate bars and graham crackers.

"They're called s'mores," Dylan informed Jess when she asked. "You roast the marshmallow, then close it with a chocolate bar between two graham crackers. Here." He gave her a skewer with a marshmallow on it. "Take this to the fire and get it nice and brown."

Before she could decide it was brown enough, though, the marshmallow caught on fire. "Dylan! Help!"

The kids around her were laughing as he came to the rescue. "That's perfect." He blew the fire out. "Get your crackers and chocolate ready. Now…" He laid the marshmallow down on the chocolate bar. "Squeeze them together. That's right." The skewer slid out from the chocolate-marshmallow goo. "You're good to go."

Jess tried a bite, ending up with chocolate dripping down her chin. "That is…oh, gosh…amazing. So delicious." She finished the whole sandwich and licked her fingers. "You people sure know how to eat."

"Yes, we do." All the kids went back for a second treat but Jess shook her head when Dylan offered the ingredients. "My clothes aren't going to fit me to wear them home," she protested. "At this rate, I'll have to borrow a trash bag."

She saw his smile dim at the words and realized she'd hurt him. But he would be better off remembering that she wouldn't be here for long, that their time together was temporary. Surely that would be best for both of them.

Susannah brought out coffee for the adults and hot chocolate for the kids, and then Ford took a guitar out of its case and began to strum.

She'd had no idea the Marshalls boasted musical talent, too. But throughout the evening, she heard Ford play all types of tunes—rock, folk, country and even rap. Dylan and Caroline both had good voices, and they harmonized on many of the songs Ford played.

The kids had their own favorites, from silly camp songs such as "On Top of Spaghetti" and "Row, Row, Row Your Boat"—that one, at least, Jess had heard of—to more popular songs from the pop and rap styles. Becky and Lizzie sang a song together, and Thomas and Marcos mugged their way through several more. Nate sat in the corner with Amber, who soon fell asleep in his lap in the dark. Justino and Lena, of course, were glued side by side with their phones in their hands. But even they swayed to the beat and sang a chorus or two.

For the most part Jess watched, and marveled at the circumstances that had brought all these different souls together. Caroline and Garrett had made the plan, but it would never have become a reality without Wyatt's strong determination to be a force for good in his community. Ford and Dylan might have opposed the idea to begin with, but no one could deny their contributions to the welfare of these kids.

And the kids themselves deserved credit for taking the risk to be here in the first place. Jess wasn't sure she would have accepted such an opportunity—the chances of looking bad in front of her peers would have been far too high. Especially at their age.

But then, she'd never opened herself up to a challenging relationship. Not after Trini. And not after her parents, those never-to-be-depended-upon adults in her life. Jess could recognize that she'd deliberately cut herself off from people who might get too close, ask too much of her without giving anything in return.

So how could she ever expect to fit in here? Caroline was obviously a woman for whom giving came naturally. Susannah, too—her care of her children demonstrated her emotional involvement. Garrett, as a minister, had made giving and caring his life's work. Wyatt had kept his family together and raised three younger brothers on his own. That level of self-sacrifice was beyond anything Jess had experienced.

And Dylan...well, Dylan never seemed to think of himself first, but was always trying to meet the needs and expectations of someone else. He had said to her that he would give up his art career before he would give up his family. That was why he squeezed his sculpture into the time left over at the end of the day, rather than making a perfectly reasonable demand that he be allowed to pursue the career he loved for part of the normal schedule. He ran himself ragged rather than impose his artistic drive on his brothers.

What made his efforts possible were his innate easy-going nature and the abiding love he offered to his family...that he'd offered to her. She'd never met a man so open, so willing to please. None of his brothers could match Dylan for unselfishness—each of them had managed to pursue his own agenda, often at Dylan's expense.

But Jess would admit she was biased. She wanted Dylan to have whatever made him happy. Whatever brought him pleasure, joy, contentment, satisfaction— all the blessings in life—she wanted for Dylan Marshall.

Which was why she had to go. As the kids sang songs around her and the adults smiled at each other and at her, Jess knew she needed to leave the Circle M Ranch as soon as she could. The longer she stayed, the more difficult she would find it to do the right thing.

And doing the right thing was the only way she could help Dylan now.

By the time Ford's voice had gotten hoarse and the kids had eaten all the s'mores they could hold, Jess had gathered her resolve and planned her getaway. She'd even slipped out of the room for a few minutes and made a plane reservation on the computer. Wednesday, she would fly back to New York with a heart full of regrets. But at least spoiling Dylan's life wouldn't be one of them.

Walking to the studio after the kids had gone to bed, she recounted Thomas's comment about white men and red men to Dylan, who laughed loud and long. "A smart kid. He should become a politician— he's already got the sound-bite technique mastered."

"*If* he straightens out his life," Jess said. "He's got quite a temper—one look from Marcos can set him off like a match to dynamite."

"They're friends one minute, enemies the next. We could probably use a counselor out here to work with them. Caroline's trained in direct casework and sociology, not clinical treatment."

"With all the positive intentions you and your brothers have demonstrated, surely these kids have gained a sense that the world can be a better place. I can't help but believe I could have had a much easier adolescence with such decent people on my side."

He took her hand. "You succeeded on your own. That's something to be proud of."

"But—" She wasn't quite sure how to say what she wanted to him to know. "I would be different, I think."

"I don't know of anyone who would want you to be different. Certainly not me." He raised the hand he was holding to kiss the backs of her fingers.

"Oh, no? Wouldn't you want me to be more open, more approachable? Someone friendly and sociable, not wary and reserved?"

He shook his head. "You're not being fair to yourself."

"Someone who likes big parties and big families, who's comfortable in a crowd with lots of kids running around?"

"Jess." He gave her hand a shake. "I love what you are. That's all."

She blinked to clear the tears from her eyes. "You want a family, Dylan. Children love you and you love them in return. You complain about the teenagers, but then you take time to help them with their problems, their fears and concerns. You *need* a family of your own to care for. And I… I couldn't give you that."

"What do you mean?"

"When I was twenty-five, I had to undergo a hysterectomy because of fibroid tumors. They were benign. But... I can't have children."

His face lost its color. "God, Jess. I'm so sorry."

She shrugged. "I didn't expect to have kids. I don't know anything about them, or how to be a parent. I wouldn't let my foster parents close enough. Anyway..." She turned away and stood up out of her chair. "More of me blurting out my history. Sorry about that. I'm going to go up to the house, leave you to get some work done."

Dylan caught her hand again. "Don't go." The tone in his voice conveyed his intentions more clearly than words.

Jess looked back at him. "There's no future for us, Dylan. No sense in getting more involved."

He got to his feet. "I love you. I want as much of your time as I can have, for as long as it lasts."

"You deserve so much more."

Then he kissed her, and put his arms around her. She couldn't think of what was wise or smart or good. Only that she wanted him as much as he wanted her. That she loved him, too, as much and as deeply as she understood the meaning of the word.

But at least she hadn't told him so.

Chapter 10

Dylan awoke on Monday morning to the sound of rain on the tin roof of the studio and a view of dripping eaves through the window. He was sorely tempted to burrow under the covers with Jess and sleep for another couple of hours, wake her up with some slow, easy loving, and then amble over to the house, with his arm around her shoulders, for one of Susannah's gigantic breakfasts.

But there were several aspects of that program his brothers would object to, the first being that the horses hadn't been fed. That whole amble idea, once the kids were awake, wouldn't go over too well, either.

So he pushed himself out of bed, showered and dressed, then left a note for Jess saying he'd meet her for breakfast after his chores were done. She smiled in her sleep when he dropped a kiss on her forehead—the second-best way to start his day.

Between feeding in the rain, setting up the tack room for the kids to use when they cleaned their saddles and bridles, sweeping out the barn and brushing down some cobwebs from the ceiling, he didn't get into the house until close to ten o'clock.

Jess was waiting for him in the living room. "I told Susannah you were coming. She's making your breakfast. But I wanted to talk to you first."

"Sure." He waited till she sat on the couch and took the cushion next to her. "What's going on?"

"I called Patricia Trevor in New York, mentioned I was finishing up the article and just wanted to get her slant on the show and your current approach. I can't believe what she had to say."

"What was it?"

"First, she didn't really remember what kind of work you were doing now and asked me to describe it."

"Well, that's a kick in the ego. I've sold a few pieces here and there, and she said she'd seen one, which was why she called in the first place."

"Then she said that what you were doing sounded rather 'pedestrian,' but that it didn't matter."

"Didn't matter?"

"Because she believes your name alone will draw people to the show. Her main objective is to showcase the Denver gallery itself, and the best way, she decided, was to bring in a crowd. People would meet her, she could make contacts and they'd remember her when they were shopping for real art."

"'Real.' Okay." He blew out a breath. "But why me? I haven't shown in two years."

"She said she wanted to use the notorious—her word—aspect of your reputation. The unsolved mystery of your disappearance. And she figured you and your agent would be desperate and wouldn't ask for as much money as someone who'd exhibited more recently."

"Can't say she's wrong there. My agent was all over this offer." Dylan fell back against the sofa. "Anything else to add to the debacle?"

"As far as the article was concerned, she wanted as much dirt—again, her word—as possible. 'Anything to make noise,' she said. 'The more salacious, the better.'" Jess had tears in her eyes. "I'm sorry, Dylan. I informed her she'd probably be disappointed in the article and hung up before I started swearing at her. I figured you'd want to know."

He linked his fingers with hers and squeezed her hand. "I'm not surprised at Ms. Trevor's attitude, just that she'd be so honest about it. But here's what I think." He stood up and pulled Jess to her feet. "With such low expectations, how can I lose? People will see my work, they'll like it or they won't, they buy or they don't. But I'll have had national exposure in your magazine and a fancy gallery showing. If she can use me, I can use her, too."

"Good point. And you could do some advertising on your own behalf, in magazines aimed at Western art collectors."

"Exactly. You probably have an idea of which ones would be useful. Or can figure it out for me."

"Of course." She threw her arms around his neck for a hug. "You're right—proactive is so much more productive. We could plan an advertising campaign to get the right kind of people into the gallery that night."

Susannah appeared in the doorway to the dining room. "Breakfast is ready. Hope you two are starved. I got a little carried away."

"So are we," Dylan said, grinning. "But isn't it a great feeling?"

Breakfast turned out to be the high point of the day. Jess and Dylan spent a couple of hours researching magazines that would be receptive to advertisements, but when she went to get her camera to take photographs of his work, she realized for the first time that it, too, had been stolen.

"I can't believe I didn't think of it," she said. The memory card with all the shots she'd taken since she'd arrived was in the camera. "I hadn't saved those photos online yet. I've been too busy."

"I'm so sorry." Dylan stood at the door to her room. "It's hard to understand why something can't be done. There aren't too many places in eastern Wyoming to sell stolen goods. Seems like the sheriff's office could have checked those out by now."

"Maybe selling the stuff isn't the point." She was frustrated enough to say exactly what she thought. "Maybe just making us miserable is the goal."

"Which leads us back to the kids."

Jess nodded, but then saw Caroline standing behind Dylan. "I understand why you don't want to believe this is linked to one of the teenagers," she told the other woman. "But they are complicated creatures who don't always return the goodwill they've been offered."

"I know that's true." Caroline slipped past Dylan to enter the room and give Jess a hug. "And if it's one of ours, there will be consequences. Ford called the sheriff's office. Deputy Daughtry will be out tomorrow morning to talk to the kids. We'll try to get some answers as to who's responsible."

"Thanks." Jess tried to let go of her anger, but losing her camera and the photographs was a heavy blow. She sat down to work with Justino and Lena on their writing after lunch, but found herself more quick-tempered than usual.

Justino's paragraph had been the shortest of all the kids' efforts. He'd written it in Spanish. On the same page, Jess wrote a translation.

I'm not in school and I don't have to finish this stupid writing assignment. When I grow up Lena and I will get married and move to Los Angeles. I will become a famous record producer and make lots of money so I can take care of her the way she deserves. The world I imagine is the one where I'm rich and Lena loves only me.

"Did I get it right?" Jess asked him.

His sullen expression answered without a word.

"I think what you imagine is wonderful. Taking care of people you love is an important goal. I just hoped you would give me some idea of how you planned to do that."

He shrugged. "I said I'd produce records. Latino music," he said emphatically, as if to prove a point.

"How do you get to be a producer?"

"You work for a company. Or you start your own."

"Do you need money to start your own label? Where does that come from?"

Justino surged to his feet, and his chair fell over behind him. "Why the hell are you bugging me about this? I wrote your stupid page. Leave me alone!" He stomped across to the boys' bedroom and slammed the door behind him.

Jess looked at Lena. "Why did he become so upset?"

"He doesn't want to think that it will be hard. Justino likes things to be easy."

"If he doesn't stay in school, that's probably not going to be the case."

The girl sighed. "I know. I try to tell him but he wants the respect of the boys he hangs out with."

"Gang members?"

Lena shrugged and avoided Jess's gaze.

The possibilities for tragedy in this scenario piqued her temper. "Remember the story I told you about my friend Trini? That could so easily be you, Lena, if Justino joins a gang. He won't stay the same sweet guy you love now. And you'll find yourself doing things you never believed you would do, just to keep him." She gripped the girl's arm. "Please, make sure he stays away from that life. For both your sakes."

"Ow." The girl pulled away. "That hurt. We'll be fine. We take care of each other." Her phone, lying on the table, vibrated to signal a message. "Can I go now?"

"Sure."

Jess stacked the papers lying on the table. "That went well." Glancing around the room, she saw Marcos over on the couch, playing a game on his phone. She had meant to talk with him today, too, but after fighting with Justino, it didn't seem like such a good idea. Nate appeared to be deep in his book, and she would hate to disturb him.

Finding Becky meant a walk through the rain to the girls' cabin, but at least she'd be more receptive. Jess wiped her sneakers on the mat outside the door and knocked. "Girls? It's Jess. Can I come in?" She opened the door as she spoke and stepped inside…

…to find Lizzie lying on the couch in a suggestive pose, having her photograph taken by Becky.

With Jess's camera.

"That's mine," Jess said.

"I know. I'm sorry." Becky put the camera in the chair next to where Jess stood. "I'm really sorry."

Lizzie scrambled to sit upright. "We only borrowed it. Really."

"You ask when you borrow something. Taking without asking is stealing."

Both girls hung their heads. Lizzie swiped her fingers over her cheeks.

"Do you have everything else? The computers and the phones?"

Becky looked up in panic. "No. Oh, no. We didn't take anything else. Honest."

"How am I supposed to believe you?"

"Check our stuff. Really, that's the only thing we took." Lizzie rushed to the bedroom and brought back a duffel bag. "See? There's nothing but clothes and makeup."

If only to scare them, Jess pawed through the messy bag. Then she went into the bedroom and made a show of examining the remaining duffels, looking under the beds and in all the closets. She checked the bathroom and the kitchen cabinets, though she'd stopped expecting to find anything.

Back in the living room, she picked up her camera. "I have to report this to Ford and Caroline. I don't have a clue about what they'll decide to do."

"You can't send me home," Lizzie said. "There's nobody there."

"True. But we could hand you over to the sheriff. He might put you into a foster home under temporary custody until your parents get back." She pretended to consider the idea. "Or into a juvenile detention center. I'm sure there's one in Wyoming somewhere."

Then her despair got the better of her and she gazed at the two of them, sitting side by side on the couch. "I just don't understand why you would risk what you have here. People who care, who are spending money and time on you...for what? An hour's fun? Just because you can? I guess I should know the answer, because I was a kid who made trouble. But mostly I made trouble for myself. I didn't try to hurt other people. Especially not the ones being nice to me."

Jess turned and opened the door. "I guess I'm not as much like you as I thought." Then she crossed the porch and descended the steps, holding the camera under her jacket against the rain.

She found Dylan in his studio, working on the

mare and foal sculpture. He looked up as she stepped through the door and she pulled the camera out for him to see.

"You found it? Where?"

"Becky and Lizzie had it."

"What?" He got to his feet. "Did they take everything? Did they do—" he gestured to the rest of the room "—this?"

"No. They invited me to search their bags, and I inspected every cabinet in the house. I believe the camera was separate. Stupid, but separate."

He ran his hands through his hair. "These kids— I hate to say it—but I don't understand how they can stay here. The situation gets worse by the day."

Jess put a hand on his arm. "Wait until tomorrow, when the deputy comes. If there's new information, or no information, if the kids don't have anything to say…then you can talk to your family about closing the camp." She gave him a wry smile. "As Lizzie pointed out, you're stuck with her till her family returns. I suggested detention or foster care, but those probably aren't real options."

"Too bad," Dylan said, his expression glum. "Maybe we'll just lock her in a stall until her parents can be bothered to show up."

"I'll volunteer for the first shift of guard duty."

That made him laugh. "You would, too." He pulled her into his arms and set his cheek on her hair. "You're a pleasure to have around, Jess Granger. I'm glad you careened into my life last Wednesday afternoon."

"Is that a comment on my driving?"

An argument, especially a manufactured one, was

a way to keep her emotions under control. Jess wanted to pull away as easily, as slowly as possible, putting distance between them so the break wouldn't be as hard when it came.

"What do you mean by 'careened'?"

The sheriff's car arrived at promptly 10:00 a.m. on Tuesday morning. Wade Daughtry stepped out, and Dylan could tell he'd taken special care with his uniform to look as official and intimidating as possible. He was a big man, anyway, as tall as Wyatt and square with muscle. Dylan felt a little intimidated himself.

"Hey, Wade." They shook hands and then faced the kids, seated in a line on the edge of the porch. The rain had dried away and the day had dawned bright with sunshine. "Any news?"

"Yes, as a matter of fact. Let me break it all at once."

"It's your show."

Wade nodded to the rest of the Marshall clan and Caroline, and Dylan saw his eyes widen when he caught sight of Jess. But then he got right down to business.

"I'm here because there's been theft and vandalism recently on this property. Phones and computers went missing, along with money and credit cards. Property was damaged, and there was an attempt at arson. I want to ask each of you, at this moment, if you have any information related to these crimes or the person who might have committed these crimes."

Wade stared for a minute at each kid. He started with Becky, who flushed bright red, till all her freckles looked dark brown. She gave a tiny shake of her head.

Lizzie, beside her, had gone white. Huddled with her arms wrapped around her waist, she said a silent, "No."

Lena hadn't lost her self-confidence. "Nothing," she said loudly. "I don't know who would do that."

"Turn your phone off," Wade told her, "and put it away till we're done here."

She flashed him a resentful glare, but did as he said.

Justino tried bravado. "You don't have the right to question us," he declared. "We're minors. You need our parents' permission."

"Understand that I'm here for information," Wade said. "If I have to, I'll take you to the office, call your dad and then I'll question you. But you would probably prefer I do it right here." The threat chilled his voice. "Do you know anything about these crimes?"

The boy's "no" sounded small.

Nate didn't have to be asked twice. "I would tell you if I did." But Dylan saw his gaze slide toward Thomas and Marcos, sitting on his other side.

Wade moved to stand directly in front of Thomas and Marcos. "You two have been in trouble before. I'm giving you a chance right now to get out of this before things get rough."

"I don't know nothing," Marcos said.

Thomas snorted. "That's crap. Ask him about his brother Jimmy. Go on, ask him."

Wade looked at Marcos. "Well? Your brother is Jimmy Oxendine. He's got quite a record."

"Maybe, but I didn't have nothing to do with this. Maybe you ought to check *his* friends out." He nodded at Thomas. "Some of them ain't such good guys."

"Don't put this on me." Thomas shoved at Marcos's shoulder. "You're the one who's hanging with a gangsta crew."

The fight exploded in that instant. The boys lunged at each other, all the tensions of the past few days coming to a head. Swearing, punching and kicking, they rolled off the porch and onto the ground as the rest of the kids cleared the area.

Standing closest, Dylan went for Marcos while Wade grappled for a grip on Thomas. Ford and Garrett joined the effort and finally, with one man holding each arm, the four of them pulled the struggling adversaries apart. Bloody noses and swollen eyes testified to the sincerity of their violence.

Before anyone could say a word, a petite dynamo marched into the space between the two. "Enough," Caroline shouted. "That's enough. I'm ashamed of you both." All the fight went out of Thomas and Marcos. They stood slumped and silent.

Dylan did not, however, let go of the arm he held.

"These boys are not going to admit knowing anything," Caroline told Wade. She was as angry with him as with the boys. "If you have news, just tell us. If not, we've got wounds to patch up here."

"We found the phones and computers in a pawn shop down in Cheyenne," Wade said. "And we got a video of the kid who brought them in. Roberto Pena."

Justino jumped to his feet. "I don't believe you. My brother wouldn't do something like this. No way!"

Marcos lifted his head. "I told you I didn't have nothing to do with it."

"So did I." Thomas glared out of a rapidly blackening eye.

"I didn't doubt you," Wade told them. "You're the ones who fought about it."

Now they looked embarrassed as well as battered.

"Why would Roberto come out here to steal?" Justino demanded. "To—to wreck things?"

Ford sent the girls and Nate back to the bunkhouse and the cabin. Now he came to stand beside Justino. "Marcos and Thomas, go to the kitchen with Miss Caroline to get cleaned up and put some ice on those bruises. Justino, we can talk in the living room."

Once they'd settled, Wade explained. "It seems you'd been texting Roberto about this place you were staying and all the nice things just lying around. You know Roberto's been caught stealing before. You know he has a drug habit. Maybe you didn't know how jealous he's been of the deal you've got here."

Justino looked genuinely surprised. "No, I didn't— I wasn't helping him do this. I swear."

Wade glanced at Ford and Wyatt. "I'm leaving that to the Marshalls to decide. But Roberto took advantage of all of you being on the cattle drive, which you told him about, too. And he decided to help himself to some of the property. Then, being the unpredictable sort, he got mad and did some damage. Maybe he thought you'd get blamed, and he'd get even."

Sitting with his head in his hands, Justino started speaking in Spanish. Some of the words even Dylan couldn't translate, but some of them he could. "That's enough."

The boy looked up. "I'll go home. I'm sure you won't want me here anymore. I can only say I'm sorry.

I never meant for him—" He shook his head. "He's so messed up."

"We'll talk about it," Wyatt said. "If we have the computers and phones back undamaged, that's the main thing."

"We'll need to keep them for evidence," Wade said. "But eventually they'll be returned to you."

"How old is Roberto?" Ford asked.

"Eighteen," Justino said.

"He'll be tried as an adult," Wade added.

"I'll talk to him." Ford got to his feet. "We'll find out what can be done."

Dylan followed him into the dining room. "Are you saying you're going to offer to defend Roberto on these charges?"

"I'm saying I'll learn what the situation is. He might be able to reduce the sentence if he pleads guilty and gets into rehab."

"Ford, you saw what he did in my studio. He ruined Jess's bag and stole our property. Why would you defend him?"

"Because the legal system works when even the guilty have representation. I'm not the best criminal attorney in the state. But I may be the only one he has access to."

"We have public defenders in this county."

"Overworked, underpaid public defenders. Let it rest for now, Dylan. We'll have a meeting tonight and talk over the options." He went through the door into the kitchen, effectively ending the conversation.

When Dylan turned, he found Jess standing behind him. "Did you hear? Ford—" He broke off, shaking his head. "I can't believe this. That aspect of the man's mind is beyond my comprehension."

"Dylan?" Wade had stepped into the room. "I'm going to head out, unless there's something else you folks need right now."

"No, we've got the facts, finally, thanks to you. When you arrived, I didn't have a chance to introduce you to Jess Granger. Jess, this is Wade. He was a good friend of Ford's in school."

Wade's grin was shy as the two shook hands. "I'd heard Dylan brought a lovely lady into Kate's the other night, but *beautiful* was obviously a better word choice. It's nice to meet you, Jess. I hope you'll be staying around for a while."

"Thanks, Wade. I wish I could stay, but I'll be flying back to New York this week."

Dylan heard the finality in those words. She'd already booked a reservation. Jess had made definite arrangements to leave.

"Well, that's too bad. Maybe you'll visit again sometime soon? Dylan could bring you into town for dinner again."

"It's possible. I can't say I enjoyed this morning, but I do appreciate what you've done."

It's possible in that tone of voice meant *not likely.* And though Dylan had known the inevitable was coming, he still felt as if his insides were being shredded.

"I'll look forward to that," Wade said. He held a hand out. "Take care. If you want my advice, you'll wind up this camp and return those kids to their families. You've got an explosive situation up here."

"I believe I've mentioned that to the people in

charge. But the kids deserve help and we're doing what we can."

Wade shook his hand. "Good luck. I'll keep in touch."

"Thanks, buddy." He walked Wade to the front door, and saw Justino still sitting on the couch in the living room. The boy usually carried himself with pride, but at this moment he was hunched over his folded arms, defeated.

Despite his reservations, Dylan couldn't leave him there alone. He sat down on the recliner next to the fireplace. "It'll work out, Justino. If you say you didn't intend for your brother to hurt us, then we'll believe you."

"I'm ashamed that he's done this to your family. And I wish I could make it up to you, what he did to your workshop, your sculptures. But I can't."

"No, you can't. Except by making sure you don't follow his example in your own life. Stay away from the kind of influences that led him to do these things. That would be what I would ask as a way to make amends."

Justino nodded. "I understand. Can I be excused now?"

"Yes." Dylan figured the boy would make a beeline for Lena—he hadn't realized she'd been waiting on the front porch until he saw them walking away together, hands tightly clasped.

Jess came into the living room and sat where Justino had been. "You are the most amazing man. What you said to him about making amends was perfect."

"It's the only thing he can do."

"But not everyone would have been able to forgive and forget that way."

Dylan shrugged, feeling his cheeks heat up. "I guess, from what you said to Wade, that you're getting ready to leave. Had enough of the Wild, Wild West this morning? It's been pretty rowdy, I'll say that."

"No. But I have to go back."

"I know." He got to his feet, suddenly very tired. "I just hoped maybe I'd get a chance to change your mind before you left."

Chapter 11

The meeting Ford had promised took place late in the evening, after a morning of rodeo practice and another bareback lesson for Lizzie, plus a long trail ride in the afternoon. The overall mood was tense, given the morning's revelations, but Jess enjoyed her tour through different parts of the ranch. She found herself blinking away tears as she brushed out Cash's coat. He'd been a good friend to her.

Over a chili dinner, Caroline told the teenagers they could watch weeknight television that evening, something they hadn't been allowed to do since coming to the ranch. Jess couldn't help being pleased that most of them kept books in the vicinity as they sat around the bunkhouse—even Marcos had laid his baseball book on the arm of the sofa. He wasn't reading it, but the possibility existed, which she considered a real achievement. Although her time with the kids had been short, she liked the idea that she'd made a difference in someone else's life.

With the kids occupied, the Marshall brothers and Caroline took their coffee and pieces of the apple pie Susannah had made into the living room and settled in the various chairs. Jess stayed with Susannah in the kitchen, but the open doorways made the conversation easy to hear.

"So, we have some issues to deal with," Ford said, his voice calm and cool. Jess smiled as she realized she could recognize each brother's voice, having known the four of them for a only week. "We were aware this project would be a challenge when we took it on. I admit, these are the kinds of problems I foresaw when Caroline proposed the plan. But while I opposed the idea to begin with, I now believe we should do everything we can to keep the camp functioning with all the kids here. The question is…how?"

"I agreed with Ford from the outset." Dylan's tone carried more energy, more urgency. "Because I was thinking about this show I have coming up and the work I wanted to complete. I understand that these teenagers need help, that their lives are at a tipping point, for better or for worse. But we're the ones taking the punishment, here. I suggest we at least rearrange the program, make the schedule less intense. Have them on the ranch a couple of times a week, rather than staying here 24/7. I'll drive around and pick them up myself, on the days they come. It would reduce our risk. There's nothing to guarantee the same kind of crazy situation won't come up again."

"The judge handed Justino, Marcos and Thomas over to my custody," Caroline pointed out. "If they aren't here, they go into a community service program five days a week."

"Then they could come here on the weekends," Dylan replied. "Why wouldn't that work?"

"I'm tied up at church all day Sunday," Garrett said. "I wouldn't be here to help. And I think sending them home for most of the week dumps them into the environment we are trying to neutralize in the first place."

"We can't save the world," Dylan countered.

"We can try." Ford and Caroline said it together and there was laughter—though not, Jess thought, from Dylan.

"Wyatt, what about you?" Ford asked.

"We've had trouble, and I regret that." The oldest Marshall's voice was deep and measured. "But I'm of the same opinion now as at the beginning. We owe Henry MacPherson to help other kids the way he helped us."

"So we just continue on with the same plan?" Dylan's patience had worn thin. "Not protecting ourselves, not making any effort to counteract the violence that shows up on an almost daily basis?"

"That's exaggerating, Dylan." Garrett was irritated. "Come down off your high horse."

Jess caught her breath. "He shouldn't have said that," she whispered. Across the counter, Susannah shook her head, apprehension in her wide eyes.

"My high horse? No, actually, that was not one of the sculptures that got damaged when Justino's brother vandalized my studio. Thanks for your concern."

Garrett tried to retreat. "Look, I didn't mean—"

"And don't worry about the destruction of Jess's property, either. Some makeup, a leather bag—no big deal. She gets her phone and computer back, and we'll cover the cash." The rocking chair creaked, as it did when someone stood up. "Except that a guest in our house can't assume she's safe because we've got criminal elements on the property."

"Dylan, sit down." That was Ford.

"No. Because not only did we have a drug addict running rampant when we were out of the way, but two of the girls felt comfortable enough to walk into Jess's room and take her camera. 'Just borrowing,' they said. Right."

"Becky and Lizzie?" Caroline asked, her voice shaky.

"Of course. Because Lena and her boyfriend are always around some corner, making out." That wasn't precisely true...

...and they let him know it. "They've been cooperative."

"We keep a close eye on those two."

"They understand the rules."

"The real problem—" Dylan's voice cut through the protests "—is that you all are willing to take the risks. First, because you care. And that's admirable. But second, I think you've each got some pride involved here in making this project turn out well. You want to be able to say that you saved these kids from disaster."

Heated denials rang through the house.

Dylan spoke over them again. "And third, because you don't care about the damage. Wyatt hardly uses his cell phone. A computer is easy enough to replace. We pay Jess for hers, and she's taken care of. But nobody else has put hundreds of hours into building statues that can be destroyed in the blink of an eye. Thank God, Roberto is a lousy arsonist, or I might have lost almost every piece of work I've done in the last two years. The entire exhibit for the Denver showing is sitting in my studio. Not to mention that studio is my home.

"But for you guys, my art is a hobby. A sideline. Something I can do to keep me occupied and out of your way. That was the plan when I was a kid, right? 'Here's some paper and crayons, Dylan. Go draw something. We're busy.'"

"You know it's more than that," Wyatt said.

"I do. You don't. You don't understand the *need* I have to create. The burn to shape and mold and carve and bend, to watch meaning come into existence beneath your hands. It's not fun, it's not entertaining or soothing. It's vital."

Jess found herself wiping tears off her cheeks.

"You don't understand that this—making art—is the only connection I have to my past. I can't remember our mother. Not the flicker of an image, not a sound or a smell. I have one sketch from her as my childhood memory. But when I draw, when I build, I am grounded. I'm certain of where I come from.

"Having the kids here threatened me in a way that none of you has experienced. And so you want to go on the same way, with the same possible outcomes. But I can't do it anymore."

His boot heels sounded on the wood floor. Jess headed for the living room.

Caroline and the other Marshall brothers were on their feet. "Where are you going?" Ford asked. "What are you planning to do?"

"Dylan, settle down," Garrett ordered. "We can work this out."

Wyatt cut across them with a single question. "Are you leaving?"

Dylan paused at the door and turned around with a surprised expression on his face. "No, of course not. This is home."

"Then what do you mean when you say you can't do it anymore?"

"The art. I'll stop."

"You can't do that," Jess blurted out. She looked at Wyatt and then Ford. "Don't let him stop."

Dylan's face was surprisingly calm. "It's okay, Jess. I told you—if it came to a choice between family and art, I choose my family."

"But you don't have to choose," she said.

All of the people in the room stared at her. "It's not just about the vandalism," Dylan said. "The time demands, the fragmented attention—I can't keep struggling between the ranch and sculpture."

She stepped next to him and put a hand on his arm. "I know. But what I've come to realize is that the art you make is all about your family. For the last two years, every sculpture you've built has been an aspect of your brothers and the life you share with them. Not just the forms of the creatures you observe here on the ranch, but the spirit you embody as you work, the aspirations you have for the land, the animals and each other.

"Do you think it's a coincidence," she said, gazing straight into his eyes, "that your most recent piece is a mare and foal? That image of nurturing reflects what's going on at the ranch now, as your family works with these kids and strives to help them grow up into strong, healthy adults."

"That makes sense," he said slowly. "What I do in the studio isn't in spite of the family and the ranch. It's my way of expressing what's important to me. Which is the family."

"But you don't have to be a cowboy," Jess said more softly. "The choices you make and the values you cherish join you to this family."

Dylan shook his head. "The ranch is who we are. It's what we do."

"We're brothers, first and always," Wyatt said. "The ranch came after."

"Long after," Ford agreed. "Henry MacPherson saved us by bringing us here, without a doubt. But that doesn't obstruct our personal choices. I'm an attorney, remember?"

"And I serve a church," Garrett added. "We don't take these careers any less seriously because we're also involved on the Circle M. Even this summer, when Wyatt's out of commission, I'm still preaching, still visiting members."

"And I'm meeting with clients," Ford said. "We all work around each other's commitments. You've been here every day. You know how it goes."

"But you left your San Francisco practice," Dylan said. "You gave it up for the ranch."

"I *chose* to rejoin my family. The same way you did, two years ago." Ford put his arm around Caroline and pulled her close against his side. "I love the land, don't get me wrong. But it's the people that matter."

Hands on his hips, Dylan dropped his chin to his chest. "I get consumed by the process. Walking out of the studio just kills me when I'm so deeply involved." He lifted his head. "That's what I mean. This isn't a hobby, something I can do in my off-hours. I need... more time. All the time there is."

"Maybe we haven't paid enough attention to what you need," Garrett said.

"Could be we didn't take your complaints seriously." Wyatt held his youngest brother's gaze. "That can change."

"Nobody will ever replace you around here," Ford said. "But we can hire somebody to handle most of your jobs."

Dylan let his jaw drop. "You're serious? You'd go that far?"

"You deserve the life you want to live," Wyatt said. "If you can be satisfied here with us while you create the art that drives you, then we'll make it happen."

Garrett came over and put a hand on his shoulder. "And we'll talk with the kids about security. Maybe they can try going without their phones for a day. Or a week. Who knows, maybe we can switch over to using phones only on weekends. We have been naive, as you said. We'll beef up security, change locks, whatever we have to do to make the place more secure. Including your workshop."

"Especially my workshop," Dylan said. "But thanks. I appreciate the thought. And will you take over my morning feedings?"

His brother sighed. "You're going all the way with this, aren't you?"

Dylan laughed. "Man, you'd better believe it."

When the meeting finally ended, Dylan took Jess back to the studio. With the lights on, he walked around the place, taking a fresh view of his own work.

"You're right," he told her, still surprised. "I couldn't see the forest for the trees, so to speak. But it's here. All of us, our personalities, we're here. The buffalo—that's Wyatt. The fox is Garrett and Ford is the eagle. I'm the elk. And I don't know if you've noticed this one…" He went to a spot near the end of a table, and picked up a small figure. "These are rock wrens, nesting. Reminds me of Caroline."

"That's very sweet. I hadn't noticed it before." She came to take the statue from him. "You're right—that's Caroline taking care of everybody."

"But I believe I'll have to create a new piece for you. An owl—a western screech owl."

Her frown appeared on the instant. "I don't screech!"

He tilted his head. "Can you say that a little louder?" She pouted at him when he grinned. "But you are wise, like the owl. You've made such a difference in my life." Taking her hands, he pulled her to stand in front of him. "And now you're going away. Is there anything I can say to change your mind?"

From the regret on her face, Dylan guessed the answer. "Then I won't try. We'll just enjoy the rest of our night. Come upstairs with me."

He feared she might say she had to pack, or get some sleep. But Jess simply smiled and led the way. "It will be my pleasure," she said quietly.

When he woke up in the morning, she was gone.

But lying on top of the covers were the two sketches he'd done—the bust of Wyatt and his version of his mother's drawing. Jess must have pulled them out of the trash. She hadn't left a note, but he got the message.

Do these, she might as well have said. *It's time.*

Dylan worked through the rest of the summer, hour upon hour of focused effort he'd never before enjoyed. When he was stuck, he'd take a ride on Leo, or help the kids with their rodeo lessons, but he could walk away now, return to his studio and concentrate anew. He slept at night, his bed comfortable, if lonely. Jess's absence was a constant ache, like a stitch in his side every time he moved. The only solace was his work.

As the fall started, he found himself spending longer hours, staying up later and feeling almost as tired as if he were still doing ranch chores. The kids went back to school and the ranch quieted down. Wyatt began picking up more of the ranch responsibilities— which was a relief to everybody because he'd become increasingly grumpy about "sitting around doing nothing."

October brought the issue of *Renown Magazine* with his article in it. Kip ordered a hundred copies and managed to hang on to two—one for Wyatt, Ford and Garrett and one for Dylan. But he had already received his own copy in the mail from Jess—the first he'd heard from her since the summer. He'd thought about calling, emailing, even writing a letter…but he didn't intend to stalk her. They'd had a summer affair, and now it was over. If he was still in love, that was just too bad for him.

The article was beautifully written, of course, and made him sound downright glamorous.

"Working in a secluded woodland setting, with Crazy Woman Creek running nearby, Dylan Marshall crafts his sculptures one meticulous piece at a time, assembling the whole image with the patience of a Zen master. Having renovated a working barn for his edgy and yet entirely functional studio, Marshall collects his materials from the landscape around him, a new approach to the concept of 'found art.' Although not abstract in the traditional sense, the figures emerge from his construction process in spiritual form, representative of concepts and paradigms only hinted at by his earlier nonfigurative work…"

Dylan laughed as he read the ten-dollar words, so typical of the overblown prose he'd once been used to hearing in the art world. "Doesn't mean a damn thing," he said to himself. "Except that she likes the way it looks." The article skirted the whole issue about why he'd abandoned the art world—"a personal crisis of confidence," Jess had called it, "a reassessment of his work and its place in the world." He wondered if that had been specific enough to save her job.

She'd scrawled across the front cover of the magazine, "You're famous... Again! Love, Jess." He wished she meant that the way he would.

November arrived. He and his brothers spent days building custom crates for each of the sculptures, packing and padding them and moving them into a horse trailer for transportation to the gallery. He made the drive down to Denver by himself the week before, but his family would be arriving on the day of the show, as would Patricia Trevor, the gallery owner. Fortunately, the manager and the security guard at the gallery helped him unload and arrange the exhibit. It wasn't the premium treatment he'd received when the art world thought he was on fire.

But Dylan knew where this work had come from and what it meant, which was what mattered to him now. And the exhibit was beautiful—the gallery provided linen-covered blocks of different heights for the sculptures, with linen screens dividing the large space into more intimate rooms and giving the pieces the right scale. Track lighting on the ceiling ensured that beams of light illuminated the colors and grains of the woods he'd used, making every figure seem to glow on its own. The walls of the gallery itself were plate glass windows looking out on the city, adding a sense of motion and energy. Dylan couldn't have asked for a more perfect setting in which to show off his art.

On the day of the show, he went to his hotel in the late afternoon to shower and change. After so many weeks of hard work, he allowed himself to lie down for just a few minutes to rest his burning eyes and aching back.

The ringing phone woke him up. "Where the hell are you?" Ford said. "The crowd's here and the artist isn't. What's going on?"

"Ten minutes," Dylan yelled into the phone as he dragged off his jeans. "Ten minutes!"

He arrived at his first show in almost three years with his hair still damp and the aroma of shaving cream lingering around his face. Garrett opened the door as he reached it. "Late, as usual," he said, leaning in for a one-armed hug. "Go get 'em."

Dylan could barely make his way across the room for the crowd. Patricia had hoped for an attendance of twenty, but this seemed to be closer to two hundred. He wasn't sure how to find her in the press of people, but then a tiny, white-haired woman with bloodred fingernails latched on to his arm.

"Just like the old days," she said, in the haughty tones he recognized from their two phone conversations. "Always assuming the attention will be there when you deign to appear." Then she raised her voice. "Ladies and gentlemen, please let me introduce you to my newest protégé—renowned artist and sculptor Dylan Marshall."

After that, he couldn't see farther than three feet in front of him because there was always someone standing right there, shaking his hand, admiring his work, offering to pay three or four times whatever he asked for one of his statues. He probably seemed to be the arrogant artiste to them…or else really stupid. He just couldn't think of what to stay, couldn't take everything in. In his wildest dreams, he'd never expected—

Jess.

As one person in front of him moved out of the way, he saw her. She stood all the way on the other side of the room, champagne glass in hand, wearing a short skirt and tall heels. And staring straight at him.

Dylan started walking, brushing past people who spoke to him, sidestepping those who tried to block his progress. Jess moved toward him, and people stepped out of her way, until they were confronting each other across the centerpiece of the show—the mother and child sculpture he'd built through the summer and the fall.

"I didn't realize you were coming," was his brilliant opening line.

"I couldn't stay away." She frowned at him. "You're thin. You haven't been eating."

"I've been working, though."

She nodded. "I can see that. It's...breathtaking. More beautiful than I could possibly have imagined."

"So are you." Dylan glanced around at the crowd, wishing for a moment of privacy. "When did you get into Denver?"

"Later than I intended."

"How long are you staying?"

"As a matter of fact—"

At that moment, Patricia sank her claws into him again. "Come with me. The mayor wants to talk to you about a commission."

"But—" He looked over his shoulder, flung out a hand...

...and felt Jess's palm against his. "I'm here," she said, when he drew her close. "I'll be right here."

With Jess's hand in his, the rest of the evening passed easily. She had her own fans in the crowd, people who had read the *Renown* article on Dylan and had come because of it, as well as people who read the magazine because of Jess Granger's writing.

There were conversations about abstract versus representational art, carving versus mosaic, different woods and glues and stains—Dylan maintained his focus through them all, remembering names and faces, accepting compliments and the occasional criticism with assurance. He didn't require anyone else's good opinion. His brothers were here. Jess stood by his side. His world was complete.

The chaos began to subside about 9:00 p.m. "We have dinner reservations," Garrett said as his brothers prepared to return to their hotel. "We'll wait for you at the restaurant."

"Right..." He'd lost Jess for a moment in the bustle, but then found her in a corner, engaged in serious conversation with a man whose face people across the country had seen many times on their television and theater screens. Waving goodbye to the stragglers just leaving, Dylan made his way over and stood nearby, trying not so subtly to eavesdrop.

But they'd finished their talk. "I'll be in touch," the actor told Jess, and gave her his card. Then he shook Dylan's hand. "Great exhibit. I bought two of the pieces—love that screech owl and the mare and foal. I've got just the places for them in my new house." In an instant, he slipped out the door and into a limousine waiting at the curb.

Dylan looked at Jess. "Was that really—"

She nodded. "He offered me a job. As the editor of a new magazine."

"But…you have a job."

"Um, no. I resigned."

He cleared his throat. "Why?"

"I realized I wanted to do something more than entertain, or even inform. Working with the kids…even for just a few days…that changed me. I want—I *need* to do something that makes a difference in people's lives. Maybe even grumpy teenagers' lives."

"Do you know what that is?"

Jess smiled. "I'm not sure. Teaching, maybe?"

Dylan took her hands in both of his and raised them to his lips. "You would be an amazing teacher."

Around them, the gallery was closing down, the lights shutting off. Having locked the door, the manager began pulling shades over the glass windows. "Gotta go, Dylan," he called. "I want some dinner."

"Right." Looking around, Dylan surveyed the collection of his work, some of which he wouldn't ever see again. "An amazing night," he said. Then he turned to Jess. "Mostly because you were here. Why did you come?"

Without waiting for an answer, he led her through the back room of the gallery and out into the alley, and then around to the sidewalk. Snow had started to fall.

"Perfect," he said, still holding her hand. "We haven't had any snow at home yet." Realizing he was stalling, he faced her. "Now, tell me. Why are you here?"

Snowflakes perched on her long hair and on her eyelashes. "I expected to go back to my life. Write the article and move on. I mean, I knew I wouldn't stop loving you, but I could live with it. I thought."

Dylan blinked at her. "You didn't say you loved me. Before."

"I was trying to do the right thing. Offering you a chance to find somebody who would give you kids. Making it easier by not telling you I love you, too." Her gloved hands covered her face. "I was so stupid."

"Yes."

She let her hands fall away and laughed. "Instead, it's only gotten worse. Like freezing to death—I'm a little colder every day when I'm not with you. Eventually, I'll just fall asleep and die. Emotionally, anyway. And what good will I be to myself or anyone else if I freeze over?"

He took hold of her shoulders. "What do you want, Jess?"

"I want to be alive, Dylan, the way you are. You and your brothers and Caroline and Susannah—you don't just exist, as I've just existed my whole life. You *live*. And I want to live, too. I can't give you your own children. But I'll give you everything I have."

Anger flooded through him. "Do you realize how miserable I've been?"

Jess nodded. "I do. I've been miserable myself."

"You wasted months when we could have been happy together."

"I know. I'm sorry."

"And now you want to just waltz back and take up where we left off? I suppose you want a proposal, too. A wedding and all that goes with it?"

She swallowed hard. "Yes, please."

He glared at her, frozen by wrath…and then in an instant it melted away like spring frost. "Okay. Now come here."

Wrapping her in his arms, he brought their mouths together and erased the past five months with kisses, hot and seeking and wild, completely inappropriate for a city sidewalk and completely necessary as he reclaimed the love he thought he'd never hold again.

"Get a room, why don't you," yelled somebody walking past them.

Dylan drew back. "I have a room. How long do you suppose my brothers are prepared to wait?"

Jess grinned. "Would all night be too long?"

"Not for me," Dylan told her. "Forever isn't long enough for me."

* * * * *

WE HOPE YOU ENJOYED
THIS BOOK FROM

HARLEQUIN
SPECIAL
EDITION

Believe in love. Overcome obstacles. Find happiness.

Relate to finding comfort and strength in the
support of loved ones and enjoy the journey
no matter what life throws your way.

6 NEW BOOKS AVAILABLE EVERY MONTH!

Mikey's fingers contracted. "Suppose I told you that the
hotel I own is actually a casino," he said slowly, "and it's
in Las Vegas?"

Bernie's eyes widened. "You own a casino in Las
Vegas?" she exclaimed. "Wow!"

He laughed, surprised at her easy acceptance. "I run it
legit, too," he added. "No fixes, no hidden switches, no
cheating. Drives the feds nuts, because they can't find
anything to pin on me there."

"The feds?" she asked.

He drew in a breath. "I told you, I'm a bad man." He
felt guilty about it, dirty. His fingers caressed hers as they

neared Graylings, the huge mansion where his cousin lived with the heir to the Grayling racehorse stables.

Her fingers curled trustingly around his. "And I told you that the past doesn't matter," she said stubbornly. Her heart was running wild. "Not at all. I don't care how bad you've been."

His own heart stopped and then ran away. His teeth clenched. "I don't even think you're real, Bernie," he whispered. "I think I dreamed you."

She flushed and smiled. "Thanks."

He glanced in the rearview mirror. "What I'd give for just five minutes alone with you right now," he said tautly. "Fat chance," he added as he noticed the sedan tailing casually behind them.

She felt all aglow inside. She wanted that, too. Maybe they could find a quiet place to be alone, even for just a few minutes. She wanted to kiss him until her mouth hurt.

Don't miss
Texas Proud *by Diana Palmer,*
available October 2020 wherever
Harlequin Special Edition books and ebooks are sold.

Harlequin.com